Those who enjoy history and a good plot are in for a treat as they read this work. The author brings together a variety of interesting characters and situations that will keep the reader page-turning to discover what will happen next. It is a pleasure to recommend this book to readers of historical fiction. I think they will really enjoy it, and in the process learn a lot more about the Reformation and France in this era.

—Joseph Kicklighter, PhD.
Professor Emeritus of History, Auburn University

Twisted Fate

12/20/2019

Twisted Fate

To Mont

Have a Blessed New Year!

Frank Harrelson

Frank Harrelson

MOUNTAIN ARBOR
PRESS
Alpharetta, GA

This is a work of fiction. Names, characters, businesses, places, and events are either the products of the author's imagination or are used in a fictitious manner. All historical persons and events are written in the interpretation and understanding of the author and do not claim to be absolute truth.

Copyright © 2018 by Elephant Mountain Press, LLC

All rights reserved. No part of this book may be reproduced or transmitted in any form or by any means, electronic or mechanical, including photocopying, recording, or any information storage and retrieval system, without permission in writing from the author.

ISBN: 978-1-63183-226-0

Library of Congress Control Number: 2018946832

10 9 8 7 6 5 4 3 2   0 7 1 6 1 8

Printed in the United States of America

♾This paper meets the requirements of ANSI/NISO Z39.48-1992 (Permanence of Paper)

Cover designed by Saul Cathelin, Paris, France: Artistic Painting by J. H. Vernet; Photo © ACTIVE MUSEUM/Alamy Stock Photo: Photo of Author © Frank Harrelson, Elephant Mountain Press, LLC

To Melvin, my French-born grandson

Contents

Preface

Twisted Fate tells the story of the sixteenth- and seventeenth-century Huguenots. They were Frenchmen who, in the 1500s and 1600s, gave up their Catholic beliefs and pursued the teachings of the Protestant Reformation, which began in 1516 in the thirteen cantons of Switzerland. Huldrych Zwingli,[1a] a well-educated Catholic priest, opposed the Catholic Church's participation in the hiring of Swiss army troops for protection.

In 1517, Martin Luther,[2a] a Catholic priest, gave even greater emphasis to the budding Reformation with the posting of his "Ninety-Five Theses"[2b] on the door of a Catholic church in Wittenberg, Germany. Then, in 1518, Zwingli,[1b] from the pulpit of a Catholic cathedral in Zurich, repudiated the papacy and proclaimed the Bible the sole guide of faith and morals.

He also denounced fasting, the veneration of saints, and the celibacy of the clergy.[3] Because of the earlier invention of the Gutenberg press around 1450,[4] people throughout Europe were kept informed of the protests of these two Catholic priests. The Reformation later split from just the people of Switzerland and Germany, and spread throughout Europe. France was no exception. John Calvin[5] (born Jean Cauvin in 1509, in Noyon, Picardy, France) followed the teachings of Martin Luther, as well as the Reformist leaders in Switzerland. Educated in theology and law, Calvin left France in 1534 and moved to Basel, Switzerland, where he authored his book *Institutes of the Christian Religion*. In 1536, John Calvin moved from Basel to Geneva, where his book was published.[6] His Reformist teachings and lectures influenced many Frenchmen, who became the voice of the reformed religion in France.

The actual Wars of Religion in France began about 1562 with civil unrest between the Catholics and the Reformists. In 1598, when King Henri IV of France, a Protestant himself until 1593, was about to assume the throne as king, he issued the Edict of Nantes,[7] which he hoped would end the religious wars. On paper, the edict seemingly granted the Huguenots of France a certain degree of personal, religious, and civic freedoms, which they enjoyed in degrees until the reign of King Louis XIV. Louis was an absolute political and religious monarchist.[8] Believing in One God—One Church, he was under personal moral pressure, as well as considerable pressure from outside forces such as the Catholic Church, to revoke the Edict of Nantes. His action very quickly led to the killing of a multitude of Huguenots in Paris, as well as in Protestant strongholds throughout France. La Rochelle suffered a great loss of life.

Ministers and elders of the Reformed Church, as well as ordinary citizens who practiced Reformist beliefs, were arrested, tortured, and imprisoned. In many cases these persons were executed by a shot to the head, a saber through the heart, hanging, or beheading on the guillotine. After being arrested, prisoners were often exiled to French-controlled islands and territories to work as slaves. Others were imprisoned as slaves on French galleons in the Mediterranean Sea and forced to work beneath the dignity of ordinary crewmen.

One of my distant great-grandfathers[9] was a senior elder in the Reformed Church of Paris. He died a martyr in prison, having never renounced his Protestant beliefs. Two of his sons escaped France to Holland. The brothers later immigrated to England, and then to Charles Towne (present-day Charleston) in the then-English colony of Carolina.

The eldest brother, Daniel, later arrived in 1692 aboard an English privateer sailing from Jamaica.[10]

This book tells the early history and struggles of the Huguenots in France using fictional characters, as well as portraying actual events and real persons of history. This book is also a tribute to my Huguenot ancestry, which was revealed through very long and intensive genealogy research, and to Huguenots throughout the world. In no way do I wish to condemn or demean today's Catholic Church for what happened over half of a millennium ago. But it is very important to note that history cannot be altered. Fact is fact. Monarchical rule, political pressures of the Catholic Church, demands of the nobility, and the desire for religious freedom framed the events of the times; this story needs to be told. History cannot be reinvented. It is tragic that throughout history man has suffered brutal atrocities at the hand of their fellow man, far too much of it done in the name of religion.

A number of people have encouraged me to write this book. They are fascinated with the research findings of my family history. Most notable has been Sandra, my wife of more than fifty years. I thank her for her interest and support in this effort. Without her encouragement and allowing me to write, the project would surely have remained just an idea. I am also very appreciative of the intense editing that she has done on my thoughts and words. It is with great hope that you, the reader, enjoy the book and find new meaning in your life by reading of the struggles of the brave Frenchmen who risked loss of life to have personal and religious freedom. May we never forget!

Frank Harrelson

First Families of South Carolina
Huguenot Society of South Carolina

Acknowledgments

Special thanks to Nicole Dixon, Cheryl Litton, Emily Salisbury, and to my publishing consultant, Yolanda Rowland, for their support and professional advice.

Sincere appreciation and gratitude is expressed to my wife, Sandra, for inspiring me to do research and the time to write this book, and doing a first edit for me.

I am also grateful to Saul Cathelin in Paris, France, for his masterful creation of the cover for the book. Monsieur Cathelin is a talented and creative graphic designer and writer.

Internet-researched information on kings, dress, food and drinks of the sixteenth and seventeenth centuries, armed conflicts, Martin Luther, John Calvin, Huguenots' creeds and beliefs, Catholic beliefs and worship, La Rochelle and other cities of France, Huguenot history, types of ships and design for the period of the book, various edicts of the kings, Siege of La Rochelle 1627–28, and other miscellaneous topics of the time period written about: Creative Commons License Deed; Attribution – ShareAlike 3.0 Unported (CC BY-SA 3.0).

Introduction

The early roots of Christianity were given significant importance by Constantine XI,[11] the last of the Greco-Roman emperors of the Byzantine Empire. He affected the laws of the empire with moral principles, raised his children as Christians, and stopped the persecution of Christians. On his deathbed, Constantine asked to be baptized. Adorned in an innocent white robe of a neophyte, having laid aside the purple robe of a ruler, he was baptized and soon died peacefully.

After Constantine's death in 1453, the Byzantine Empire in Turkey grew in power and influence throughout Europe. Control was centered in the city of Constantinople (present-day Istanbul, Turkey). Defended by the army built under the rule of Constantine, the city was subsequently captured by the Ottoman Empire's army, led by Sultan Mehmed II.[12] Although the loss of Constantinople was a devastating blow to ancient Christendom, it nevertheless ushered in a modern age of Christianity. A counterattack to retake Constantinople, led by the pope himself, failed when he was killed in battle. After capture of the city, the Turks gained a foothold there and used the city as a base to spread their culture and Islamic beliefs into Christian Europe. Although the Greek Orthodox Church remained intact in Constantinople, Hagia Sophia, one of its largest churches, was converted into a mosque by the conqueror Mehmed II.[13] Many Greeks subsequently fled to the Latin West. The Greeks who remained in Constantinople were minimized as citizens, and their religious practices were curtailed. Those who fled to what is now present-day Italy took with them the knowledge and the documents that would prove to give great impetus to the Renaissance movement.

The Byzantine Empire was considered the continuation of the Roman Empire, or otherwise known as the Second Rome. After the fall of Constantinople, there were competing claims to be the Third Rome. Russia's claim to Byzantine heritage clashed with Mehmed's own claim to it. Other claimants, such as the Republic of Venice and the Holy Roman Empire, faded into history, with the Vatican itself remaining the final claimant to the title of Third Rome.

In the latter half of the 1400s and early 1500s, popularity and influence of the Roman Catholic Church spread throughout Europe. France was no exception. By 1517, François I[14] was the King of France, and Catholicism was the country's official religion. In Germany, Martin Luther, a German priest unhappy with the practices of the Catholic Church, gave great emphasis to the Protestant Reformation, which had already begun in Switzerland, by posting his demands on the church. Luther was disgruntled with the Church's practice of selling relics of the Church. He also found issue with the selling of indulgences,[15] a practice in which the Church accepted payment of money in return for the partial or full remission, or forgiveness, of sin, and for the reduction of a given number of days in Purgatory, or to escape Purgatory entirely. In other words, the selling of indulgences supposedly sped up one's entry into Heaven. Another area in which Luther disagreed was the Church's teaching that the pope was chosen by God as His sole representation on earth, and that only he could offer prayers to God. Ordinary humans were not permitted to personally pray to God. Only the pope could speak to God on behalf of people on earth, and again, that required payment of money. Furthermore, the Church believed that the act of doing good deeds while on earth was the pathway to eternal life in Heaven. Luther believed instead that eternal life was a gift given by the grace of God. Luther also opposed the fact that commoners were not allowed to see the priest conduct the Church's Mass. They were kept behind a wall or a tapestry. Only the wealthy and influential supporters of the Church were allowed to sit in sight of the priests, and even they did not witness the transubstantiation of the Communion elements. This ritual was performed by the priest behind closed curtains.

The Church was becoming extremely powerful and quite wealthy; the common man was becoming ever poorer. On October 31, 1517, Luther posted his proclamation on the red door of the All Saints' Church in Wittenberg, Germany.[16] His proclamation gave protest to practices of the Church, particularly baptismal practices and the absolution of sin. Luther believed that salvation was a gift freely given by God, and was to be received by the grace of the Holy Spirit through one's faith and trust in Jesus Christ, the Son of God; salvation was not given only because of good deeds done by man.

Like Huldrych Zwingli, his predecessor in Switzerland, Luther believed the Holy Bible to be the only source of divinely revealed knowledge, and rejected the belief of the Catholic Church that only an ordained priest could offer sacrifices to God on man's behalf for the redemption of sin. Luther's beliefs were radical for the times, and boldly challenged the authority of the Church. Pope Leo X was enraged. Because Luther would not retract his proclamation and abandon his beliefs, he was excommunicated from the Church and declared an outlaw by Charles V, the Holy Roman Emperor. Thus was the setting for the beginning of the Protestant Reformation in Germany, which quickly spread throughout Europe.

Later, Luther's translation of the Wittenberg Bible from Latin to the language of the people made it accessible to common folk. This had an astounding impact on the Church and on the culture of Germany, and later influenced the translation of the King James Bible into English. One of the most important effects was the spread of evangelism among persons who chose to believe in and practice his beliefs.

John Calvin, born Jean Cauvin on July 10, 1509, in Noyon, a town in the Picardy region of France, was a theologian influenced by the writings and teachings of Martin Luther. Calvin was a defining figure during the Protestant Reformation. In 1530, Calvin broke from the Catholic Church, and afterward religious tensions rose against Protestants in France, forcing Calvin to flee. He went to Switzerland, where in 1536 he published his famous theological work, *Institutes of the Christian Religion*, and became the pastor of a church of Frenchmen who had sought religious haven in Switzerland. His brand of Protestantism became known as Calvinism[17]; his teachings attracted a large following of people in France, who left the Catholic Church and joined into a loose confederation of persons with similar beliefs. The early practice of their beliefs was at services held in members' homes, and later in churches known as Reformed churches.

There were certain cities of France that were strongholds of Protestant believers. La Rochelle, a commune on the mid-Atlantic coast of France, was very prominent among these cities. It was the major seaport on the west coast of France, as well as a major boat and shipbuilding city. In fact, most of the cities in France with concentrations of Huguenots were along or near the Atlantic and Normandy coasts. Île-de-France (Paris), the South of France, and the eastern region of France, including Lyon, remained predominantly Catholic with a far fewer number of Huguenots. Throughout the 1500s and the 1600s, La Rochelle would suffer much for its Protestant beliefs. Besides damaging sieges to the city by government and Catholic forces, persons of Reformist beliefs were often threatened with harm, including death, if they did not renounce their Huguenot beliefs and return to the Catholic Church, the alleged church of the true and only faith.

Historical Perspective

La Rochelle

In order to gain an understanding of the events leading up to the beginning of the story, the reader needs to understand La Rochelle's place in the drama of history. In ancient times, the small commune was just a quaint hamlet and the capital of the province of Aunis on the Bay of Biscay, along the Atlantic coast in central France. The city was controlled at different times by both English and French forces. The old province of Aunis, with La Rochelle as its capital, was originally occupied by the Romans; however, it was conquered in AD 507 at the Battle of Vouillé[17] by an army of Franks under King Clovis I. Later, the province came under control of the English royalty when the Plantagenet family acquired it in 1152, as part of the dowry of the French Queen Eleanor of Aquitaine upon her marriage to Henry II of England.

By the twelfth century, the one-time fishing village of La Rochelle had begun to flourish and diversify. In 1130, while La Rochelle was under French control, Guillaume X, the Count of Poitou, made the city a free port.[18] This commune status gave the city significant administrative and judicial freedoms. Later, Eleanor of Aquitaine upheld the freedoms granted by her father. One of the several freedoms enjoyed by the citizens of La Rochelle was the right to mint coins in their own workshops, and the right to own and operate tax-exempt business franchises. Even the poorer citizenry of La Rochelle was positively affected by the freedoms granted. Aunis returned to French control in 1224, under Louis VIII, and remained in French hands until 1360, when it returned to England under terms of the Treaty of Brétigny. France regained final control of Aunis and La Rochelle in 1371 when the French, led by Charles IV, defeated the English.

In August 1572, events connected between the marriage of Marguerite of Valois to the Protestant Prince Henri III of Navarre (later to become King Henri IV of France) led to the attempted assassination of Admiral de Coligny, a popular Protestant leader, and to the Saint Bartholomew's Day Massacre[19] in Paris. The assassination attempt was ordered by Catherine de' Medici, mother of Henri III, out of fear of the influence that Coligny was having and might continue to have on her son, who had always seemed to show interest in Protestant beliefs and creeds. Many Huguenots arriving in Paris for the wedding were of Huguenot nobility, and were strong supporters of Henri III. Catherine's plan was to execute en masse these practitioners of the Reformed faith. It was arranged for the bridal party and royalty to be elsewhere, while nearly all of the visitors were locked in the church; the church was then set on fire. All persons inside perished. The assassination and massacre at the church had the tacit approval of King Charles IX.[20] The ensuing violence ended in 1573 with the Peace of La Rochelle. This treaty restricted the practice of Protestantism to three cities in France: La Rochelle, Nimes, and Montauban.

La Rochelle and the neighboring Île de Ré continued to prosper and grow; with prosperity came greater participation in the practice of Protestant beliefs, and many Protestants from other cities began to move to the west coast of France, particularly to La Rochelle.

In April 1598, King Henri IV himself, a former Huguenot, converted to Catholicism in order to assume the throne in 1589[21] (but who was in many ways perhaps still a Protestant at heart) and issued the Edict of Nantes.[22] This edict was intended to create civil unity and opportunity for all the people of France. However, since France was still largely Catholic, the resulting effect separated civil unity from religious unity. Perhaps, because of King Henri's past religious affiliations, this was done unintentionally. While the intended edict was decreed to treat Huguenots as more than heretics and grant them a degree of religious tolerance, it still affirmed Catholicism as the national religion. Huguenots were expected to observe Catholic holidays, church restrictions on marriage, and were not exempt from paying a tithe to the Catholic Church. Practice of the Protestant faith was specifically limited to certain areas of France.

The edict offered the Huguenots reinstatement of their civil liberties—such as the right to work in their chosen occupation, the right to work in civil service for the government, and to serve in the armed forces of France. Perhaps most importantly, they were given the right to bring grievances directly to the king.

Certain military strongholds, such as La Rochelle, were designated places of safety for the Huguenots. These strongholds were financially supported by the king. In addition, a number of forts intended as places of refuge were allowed, but were to be maintained by the Huguenots. This act of national toleration was uncommon in Europe. As might be expected for that period in history, citizens of all countries were expected to follow the religious practices of their king or ruler. Believing that it went too far in trying to appease the Huguenots, it is needless to say that the Catholic Church and the French Parliament were unhappy with Henri's edict. The Huguenots believed, of course, that it did not go far enough in the treatment they were to receive. Concessions favorable to these parties were sought and obtained. However, the Parliament of Rouen, which was the most resistant to the ideas set forth in the edict, did not approve and failed to register it until 1609. Because an original copy of the edict had been sent for safekeeping to the Protestant Conference in Geneva, Switzerland, it is clearly evident that subsequent concessions were most favorable to the wishes of the Catholic mainstream of France.

However, the edict was registered by the various parliaments of France as irrevocable, with the exception of the certain provisions dealing with the military and pastoral freedoms. These were to be renewed every eight years. They were renewed by Henri IV in 1606, but with a reduction in financial subsidies, and again in 1611 by Marie de' Medici, shortly after the assassination of her husband, King Henri. Hopefully this would mark the end of the religious wars that had wracked France since the latter part of the 1500s.

In the early 1600s, the number of merchants, craftsmen, artists, writers, and professional people had significantly grown the population of La Rochelle. These were the creative middle-class members of French society. La Rochelle had become a major world port and a political force, with a majority of its citizens being a part of this middle class. This prosperity and religious practice of the Protestants later became a great concern to the Catholic Cardinal Richelieu, who had been appointed Chief Minister of France by Louis XIII, now the king of France. It is certain that Richelieu, a powerful force in the Catholic Church, would have liked to have been the king of France, but this was an impossibility since he was not in the royal lineage. Louis was beholden, despite his personal indifference, to Richelieu and the Church to remain in power, so he more or less turned a blind eye to Richelieu's wide-ranging efforts to control and stymie the growing Protestant movement.[23]

Attempts were made to implement wide-ranging regulation of Huguenots' practices and religious freedoms. In 1622, there was a Huguenot rebellion. A fleet of Huguenot ships battled a royal fleet near the Île de Ré, but was defeated. This led to the Peace of Montpellier,[24] which was signed on October 18, 1622. The treaty between King Louis XIII and Henri II, Duke of Rohan, ended the battles between royalists and the Huguenots, confirmed the terms of the Edict of Nantes, and pardoned Henri II. This allowed the Huguenots to maintain their numerous forts and garrisons.

This treaty between the king and the duke seemed to have brought an end to the struggles between the Huguenots and the French royalists. However, the peace was short-lived.

In 1625, Henri II and his brother, Soubise, once again led an uprising against the French government. Although Soubise did capture part of the Atlantic coastline, this revolt led to the recapture of Île de Ré by the royal fleet. The Huguenot fleet of La Rochelle was soundly defeated, as were Soubise and his troops.[25]

After the Huguenot uprisings had been put down, Louis XIII was easily persuaded by Cardinal Richelieu that the answer to preventing future uprisings was to suppress the Huguenots and to make Catholicism the one true faith of France. After this was declared to be the first priority of the French kingdom, the English came to the assistance of La Rochelle by sending an expedition, but their effort ended in failure. The effect was to initiate an Anglo-French War, which lasted from 1627 to 1629. In 1627, cannons in La Rochelle fired on the royal troops. This resulted in Richelieu's decision to use the full force of the French military to decimate La Rochelle. Troops concentrated in the area, fortifications were strengthened, and new ones were built. Finally, in the summer of 1628, Richelieu himself led a final siege on the city until October of that year. The siege lasted a total of four months, resulting in extensive loss. The aftermath of the destruction included many buildings and homes in the city, loss of the city's defenses, and loss of the social and religious privileges which the Huguenots had enjoyed. The results led to the deaths and executions of a large number of the Protestant faithful.

In the years following the Wars of Religion, steps were taken to restore the infrastructure and culture of La Rochelle. There was the fur trade with Canada and the sugar trade with the Antilles Islands, in both the New World and the new colony settlements in America. It was a period of artistic, as well as cultural, achievement for La Rochelle.

Despite the growing prosperity of La Rochelle and France in general, the Huguenots continued to be generally persecuted and harassed by the government and by the Catholics. During the final years of the reign of King Louis XIII and the beginning years of the reign of Louis XIV (the grandson of Henri IV), the terms of the Edict of Nantes changed from time to time and year to year. Implementation changed with new declarations and orders from the king and French council, which would vary according to domestic politics and France's relations at the time with foreign powers.

Finally, in October 1685, in an effort to stabilize his power and control over the country, King Louis XIV decided that the country, in the interest of national and international relations, should have a unified religion; the religion should be the one practiced by the king himself. So, in October of that year, Louis XIV decided to renounce

Protestantism. He issued the Edict of Fontainebleau from the comfort of his large, palatial hunting camp, located 55.5 kilometers, or 35.5 miles, south of Paris in the forest of Fontainebleau. This act, commonly referred to as the Revocation of the Edict of Nantes,[26] banned the practice of the Protestant religion throughout France and revoked the few freedoms and privileges still left to the Huguenots. It had very severe consequences for the economic and cultural status of France.

Immediately after the edict was issued, *dragonnades*, a title given to soldiers who began specialized training in 1681 for the sole purpose of containing Huguenots, and legions of Catholics attacked the Protestants in the cities and rural countryside. Pastors and the laymen of the Protestant Reformed churches were either executed or imprisoned, and thousands of practicing Huguenots were killed on behalf of their beliefs. Some of those arrested were sent to be imprisoned in Paris, while a portion were sent to be prisoners on galleons in the Mediterranean Sea. These men were used as slaves on the ships, and when they were not of use or the ships were in port at Marseilles rather than at sea, the men were locked up in cages. Alternatively, many of the remaining prisoners were shipped to French-controlled islands and regions to work as slaves in very hot, brutal climates. Protestant churches, homes, and businesses were burned. Women were raped and otherwise demeaned; their young children were taken to be reeducated and indoctrinated into a Catholic-embodied life.

Although it was forbidden for Huguenots to leave France, many did find their way out of the country to more hospitable countries willing to accept Huguenot refugees. Those who were able to find means of escape fled to countries such as Switzerland, the Netherlands, Germany,

England, South Africa, and to the English colonies of America. Soon after, the king sent death squads to these countries to seek out and kill the escapees. This effort was largely unsuccessful, as the Huguenots quickly assimilated into the cultural anonymity of their host countries and were largely unidentifiable to the death squads. Many of the persons who escaped France and fled to other countries died, not from efforts of the death squads, but from diseases already endemic to where they settled.

Chapter 1
Forming a Congregation

And so begins the story . . .

In La Rochelle, Antoine Jardeen had been a faithful, practicing Catholic his entire life until his adulthood. It was then that he began to read about and become intensely interested in the Reformed teachings and beliefs. The Reformed principles were a contradiction of what he had been taught in the Catholic Church, and were similar to those that he had already independently determined for himself while much younger.

At the age of twenty-two, Antoine married a woman; Martine was her name. He was two years her senior. When he was a young boy they were playmates, as her parents lived just three doors from his parents in La Rochelle. They became separated after both of his parents had died, and he had been taken to Bordeaux to live with a relative. But this young girl never forgot him. When he was twenty-two, they met again. She had grown from a young, gangly girl into a strikingly beautiful woman. They grew an inseparable love for one another and soon married. By 1556, they had rapidly parented three children: Tomas, Paul, and Marye, each child separated in age by only two years. A fourth child, a daughter named Molly, died when she was just three years old.

In 1561, a firebrand disciple of Martin Luther's, John Calvin, came to La Rochelle to preach his message of religious freedom just a few years prior to his death. Catholicism was the national religion of France, and although Antoine and Martine had remained Catholic all their lives, they had heard, studied, and meditated upon the Protestant teachings. What they had learned had touched them deeply and in mysterious ways. Although they were hesitant and somewhat afraid, they decided to attend the service given by Calvin. It would be a new experience for them to attend and worship as a couple. In the Catholic Church, men and women worshipped separately at Mass.

Together with their children, they attended Calvin's open-air service, which was conducted in an evangelistic setting in the public square of the city. They were afraid of what measures the Church, or even the king, might take against them if identified as being present, but despite that they still decided to attend the service. The government would certainly have soldiers following Calvin and making lists of persons whom they could identify at his services. In La Rochelle, the Jardeens would certainly be widely recognizable.

On a Sunday morning in the middle of May, people crowded the square in the center of town. Only a hundred or so people were expected, but at least five hundred came. Boats that had brought people from Île de Ré, just a few miles away across the harbor, dotted the wharf area around the harbor. They had been arriving since early morning, with their windswept, white sails fluttering in a mild, gentle breeze that was normal for the month of May. Farmers had come into town from surrounding rural areas to hear Calvin's message of reform, religious freedom, and hope. Soldiers watched with concerned interest. Tension filled the air. Everyone knew that there would surely be consequences to come—maybe not today or tomorrow, or even next week, but surely in the months ahead. First, the soldiers would confer with church officials and report to their commander, who in turn would report to the king for orders to be carried out. Certain persons would likely be marked for harassment, or possibly even execution. Chances are that a few homes in the city and the countryside would be burned, or some farmers' crops destroyed, and maybe a couple of boats might be seized . . . all just for the sake of warning the people once again of the fact that they are Catholic.

That Sunday, John Calvin preached about the wrongs of the Catholic Church; he preached about the heavy taxation levied on every person to support the hierarchy of the Church, the business of selling relics of the Church (most of which were counterfeit), and the wrongfulness of indulgences. The granting of indulgences in return for the payment of money had long been a shameful practice of the Church, accepting payment in return for the partial or full remission of sin, or for the reduction of a given number of days in Purgatory, supposedly speeding up a person's journey into Heaven. In each of the previous cases, the degree of supposed relief was dependent on the size of the monetary payment made to the church.

Calvin argued against the Catholic Church's belief that the common man could not speak to God, and that man had to have the pope pray for him or her. Of course, payment was also demanded for the pope's prayers.

Antoine and Martine were most touched that day by Calvin's preaching that man is saved by the grace of God, and not man's good deeds or efforts here on earth. This was a very emotional and defining moment for them. It was the pivotal point in their desire to leave the Catholic faith and pursue the Protestant religion, as it was for most of the people who attended the service that beautiful spring day.

There was no Protestant Reformed church in La Rochelle in 1561 for disenchanted Catholics to attend. Antoine and his brother Charles, a gentleman farmer at his *manoir état* (estate) and a partner in the boatbuilding and repair company, began thinking about how to organize a worship site for persons of the Reformed faith. Because of restrictions placed by the king and the Catholic Church on religious freedom, it was necessary to protect themselves and others of similar beliefs from suspicion of government officials, the local priest, and the prying eyes of the king's soldiers.

They decided as a beginning step that they would hold secret services in homes and businesses on a rotating basis. Each meeting, of course, needed to be kept to a small number of people in accommodation with the small homes provided, as not to attract the attention of the soldiers. Further, it was decided that persons participating in this practice would need to continue attendance at Mass consistent with the routine which they had been attending; also, the families should continue to pay their tithe to the Catholic Church. These last two steps could certainly help to keep their Reformed activities a secret from the bishop and the priest.

They would begin in a small way, involving only a few close friends and relatives in whom they had absolute trust. The first service would be held at the boatyard in one of the shops. It would be in the evening, since it was not unusual for the boatyard to be busy some nights with the craftsmen working late. Antoine believed strongly in good family values and home life; thus, he made it a practice to ensure that his workers did not work at night on a regular basis, and never on Sunday.

So, on a late Friday afternoon in the third week of August 1561, one of the manoir coachmen drove Charles and his family into the city from their home in the nearby countryside for a supposed social visit to the home of his brother. It was a quintessential dog day of summer. The sun had been intensely bright, but the heat and humidity had lessened somewhat by late afternoon with a moderate breeze off the Bay of Biscay. They were careful not to wear clothing that they would ordinarily wear to a Catholic Mass. Instead, they wore less formal clothing deemed more appropriate to a social visit with friends or relatives, as to not draw suspicion. They arrived about the time that the sun was sinking to the horizon, and a beautiful orange and pink sunset was beginning to fill the sky to the west over the bay. Before Antoine left for the boatyard, the adults had a couple of drinks of wine and Cognac. The brothers were the best of friends, and the wives enjoyed each other's company, as did the cousins.

Since having heard Calvin speak back in May, the two families had enjoyed time spent together discussing their newfound beliefs. Life seemed ever brighter. Family life was certainly less stressful, farmwork seemed less demanding, crops seemed more bountiful, the business of boatbuilding seemed to be growing and was more profitable. Tomas, the oldest son of Antoine and Martine, was now taking an active role in the business. Although his parents were suspicious of such, he had not yet told them of his engagement to be married. They of course knew that he had been seeing Margarite Légere, the daughter of Michel and Elisabeth Légere. Michel was the recently appointed mayor of La Rochelle, replacing John Gulton, a retired admiral and fanatical Catholic.

Margarite, or Maggie, as she was affectionately known to her close friends and to her parents' friends, was a very beautiful and talented woman. She was both musically accomplished and a lover of literature. She had been educated at the Sorbonne in Paris. Although her stay at the university was very Catholic, like the Jardeens, Maggie and her parents had personally studied and believed in Reformed principles.

Antoine and Charles had each invited another family to join them for worship at the boatyard. One family was the Légeres, and the other was Robert Marigot and his family. Monsieur Marigot was a highly respected, prosperous merchant of the finest clothing in the city. These families understood the necessity for secrecy and promised not to reveal to anyone else the discussions and meditations of the meetings, nor of the Jardeens' aspiration to one day have a Huguenot church in La Rochelle. Developing a following of persons with common beliefs would not be hard, but the building of a physical structure was only a dream at this point, a dream of just two families. It is important to realize that for the early Huguenots, the term "church" meant a congregation of persons with similar religious beliefs and practices, and not necessarily a building. But if political conditions ever permitted, it would be nice to have a building where large numbers could gather to worship together.

That night, after the sun was going down and the outside began to darken, the adults had wine and Cognac as all shared in the consumption of a large platter of bread, cheese, and fruit. Antoine departed to walk by himself to the boatyard. This was safe for him, as the patrolling soldiers were used to seeing him often take early evening strolls on the city streets from his home to the boatyard. The streets were already dimly lit by oil-burning lanterns, and expectedly so, the soldiers were out and watching. As he passed by, he witnessed one officer and a member of his patrol unit standing on a street corner talking in muted voices.

"Bonsoir," he called out to the patrol. He was familiar with them. Even though they seldom ventured into the boatyard, he had often stopped to chat with them. Usually, the conversation was about the weather, or about boats and the harbor. Antoine was always careful, however, to be very judicious in his comments, for the soldiers would try through clever conversation antics and slights to pry information out of him. If successful, they would then report what they gathered to the authority or the local priest. It was a battle of wits. He knew that any vital information given to them, even unintentionally, would surely pass on to Catholic officials, and from there, perhaps even through channels to the king himself.

"Bonsoir, Monsieur," the soldiers called back to him.

About the time that Antoine reached his office, Charles and his family set out with their coachman and rode to the boatyard. Martine and the children set out in their own coach, with Tomas driving. Before leaving home, Antoine had instructed all the families coming that evening to park the coaches out of sight behind one of the warehouses on the property.

Before the others began to arrive, he lit the meeting room with oil lanterns, drew the shutters over the windows, and arranged seating for everyone. Antoine would lead this first service. It was successful, and there was no reason to think otherwise, as plans for successive services would be made for the congregation to grow in steps, by each family asking another family with whom they felt they could place complete trust. This practice would continue until there were so many people in the group that it was no longer possible to meet in secrecy without being discovered by the soldiers. But for now, they felt secure in believing that the Holy Spirit was present and would protect them. The intent was to become an underground resistance movement of fervent Protestant believers; albeit, if successful, Antoine knew that it would be a difficult plan to manage.

Tonight, Tomas was especially glad to see that his fiancée had decided to come with her parents. Just the opportunity to be with her gave him this warm, unadulterated feeling and caused unfulfilled excitement within him. Besides being both very beautiful and very smart, Maggie also had a presence that incited comfort in others. She seemed to love children, and they always seemed to love her back. That was definitely a good sign for Tomas, as he was looking forward to being a father. He knew deep in his heart that she was indeed the one person with whom he wanted to spend the rest of his life. It seemed important to him to have several sons to carry on the Jardeen name and to continue the boatbuilding business, as he planned to do for his father. And who knew, perhaps there might be some sort of a political future in store for himself or for his sons. When Maggie arrived with her parents, heads turned as Tomas hurried over and gave her a tight hug and a romantic kiss. The guests smiled with pleasure.

Still embracing her, he whispered to her so quietly that no one else could possibly hear, "Do you think that this is the right time?"

"The right time for what?" Maggie asked, with an amused smile on her face.

"You know," he whispered, while stumbling for words. "About telling of our plan to be married. I have already spoken to your father."

"Yes, my dear Tomas," she whispered and continued to smile. "I think this is a perfect occasion. Let us do this to honor those who love us so very much. Tell them."

Speaking in a loud and excited voice, Tomas called for the attention of the guests. Everyone turned with anticipation and faced them. "Maggie and I have a very important announcement." He paused as his heart started thumping in his chest, his mouth became very dry, and his tongue felt like it had swollen to twice its normal size. He swallowed hard. Putting his arm around her waist, and in a halting voice, not as loud as before, he began. "As all of you must surely know by now, Maggie and I are in love. I am sure that it is no secret to any of you that someday we plan to be married. In fact, you probably have already wondered when that might happen. Well, tonight I am excited to tell you that I have formally asked, and she has accepted my proposal of marriage." With that, the guests began to applaud and shout their congratulations.

Then he continued, "Now, we are Catholic, but as all of you know, only in formality. In substance and in our hearts, we are Huguenots. That is why we risk our lives tonight by being here together with you—our families, relatives, and friends—in a spiritual communion that has been declared by the king to be unlawful. By necessity, we will be married in the local Catholic cathedral by Father Benedict, our local priest. We will ask the father for a wedding date in late October. And if Maggie's father is willing, we are asking that he later remarry us in a civil ceremony according to Huguenot creeds. We would like for that to be at Christmastime, when we return from our wedding trip, in his beautiful home here in the city."

Everyone surged toward the couple to give their blessing. The younger children were jumping with excitement and began to dance. The noise attracted the attention of a soldier who, by chance, was patrolling the street just beyond the gate of the boatyard. The young soldier came over to the building and listened just outside the door, trying hard to make out what was going on inside. He tried the door, but it was latched from the inside. Of course, he could not see through the windows, as Antoine had closed the shutters. Finally, the noise quieted down somewhat. Antoine, Charles, and Robert Marigot had poured wine for everyone, and as Maggie's father was about to make a toast to the happy couple, there was a loud rapping on the door. Antoine went to the door, and without opening it, he asked, "Who is it?"

"It is the king's police," the soldier answered. "Open up!" With as much confidence as he could muster, Antoine undid the latch and slowly opened the door, all the while trying not to show any fear.

"Bonsoir," he said to the young soldier, one whom he had never before met. "May I kindly assist you?"

"What is going on in here? Why are all these people in the boatyard? It looks suspiciously like you have gathered here for a Huguenot service . . ."

Trying to avoid the last statement, and without telling a lie, Antoine calmly explained, "No, Monsieur, we are celebrating my son's engagement to the beautiful daughter of the good mayor of La Rochelle. See, there is the mayor himself, his wife, and there is his daughter." Antoine motioned toward them. "My son and his fiancée have just announced to everyone their plans for marriage." The soldier looked at him with a puzzled stare. Antoine continued, "They will be married by Father Benedict, our good Catholic priest. Surely you know of him. They wish to be married in October. Soon, they will talk to Father Benedict to make arrangements."

"Merci," the soldier said quietly. "Congratulations to you, your wife, and your son. I am sorry to have bothered you, Monsieur. Bonsoir."

"Bonsoir," Antoine answered back. He stood in the door and watched as the soldier walked slowly away. He was unsure whether his story was convincing enough, but he knew that regardless if the soldier had believed him, the incident would be reported to his superiors. In spite of the unknown, the celebration would continue. However, there would be no church service this evening, at least not here at the boatyard.

The wineglasses were refilled several times, and toasts were made to the young couple in purposely loud voices. If the soldier was listening outside, he would surely hear and know that this was only a celebration and not a religious service.

After about an hour, Antoine locked up the building and they all left for their homes. Charles and his family would spend the night at Antoine's house. On the way, no soldiers were seen on the streets. There were only a few people out and about that evening. It was still very warm, and the humidity off the Bay of Biscay hung heavy over the city. Obviously, the king's police had decided to call it a night. No doubt the soldiers were already holed up somewhere, each with their own mademoiselles.

Chapter 2
Wedding Plans

Back at the house after the incident at the boatyard, Antoine and his brother, Charles, stayed up late talking about their plans. They knew that they would continue to be watched with suspicion for a while. Perhaps summer would not be the appropriate time to begin the efforts to start a congregation. Because of the heat and the humidity, it would surely be a hardship for people to meet indoors. To chance outdoor meetings in the city would be out of the question, even at night. They would encourage their friends to pray, to thoughtfully consider the moral and ethical principles espoused in the Reformed religion, and to hold family services in the privacy of people's homes and businesses. They vowed to be available to meet with these friends, if invited. However, they thought it best if their wives and children kept a low profile for their own safety. Their efforts for the organization of a church would best wait until after the wedding. Winter would come soon enough; the soldiers and the portly Father Benedict would spend most of their time inside, rather than outside. Prying eyes and keen ears would not be so numerous in the cold weather ahead.

Several days later, Tomas and Maggie, with her head properly covered, visited Father Benedict at the Catholic church. The father warmly received them, and invited them into a small room that served as his office. There was just a desk that had been made for him by one of the local parishioners, accompanied by a small table with a few chairs. There were wineglasses on the table, and next to them a bottle of expensive red wine. Tomas had been in the office many times when he was younger, having served the Church as an altar boy. But Maggie, who knew Father Benedict, although not as well, had never been inside his office.

"Monsieur Jardeen, it is a pleasure to see you again. You do not come by so often anymore. Oui, you are older now and have important things to do." Tomas's face began to redden, and slowly his hands began to tremor ever so slightly. He hoped that Father Benedict would not notice.

As those solicitous words were being spoken, Tomas struggled to stay in the moment as his mind raced back to when he was just twelve years old and beginning puberty. Father Benedict had sexually abused him any number of times right in this very room, and had sworn him to secrecy never to tell anyone, not even his parents or friends. The first time, he even told Tomas that if he told anyone, the soldiers would take him into the forest, remove all of his clothes, lash him to a tree, castrate him, and leave him there alone to bleed to death. He threatened that when he was dead, the wolves in the forest would eat his sex organs and then tear the flesh from his body. Tomas was so ashamed of what the priest had done to him, but he was afraid that if he refused him, he would die like the priest had described. Despite this, after all, Benedict was his priest, a man of God. Thus, his young mind supposed that there was no sin in what was going on. As an adult, his memory often flashed back to those situations when the priest would lock his office door and order Tomas to take off all his clothes. Benedict would then, unwillingly, take off his clerical garb and remove his own clothes. The priest would abuse Tomas until he was so weak and unsteady that it was difficult for him to stand. When he recovered, Benedict would order

Tomas to manually, and sometimes orally, pleasure him in similar ways.

Most often the abuse would repeat numerous times before it ended. At the end, when both were physically and sexually spent, albeit Tomas suffering more from emotional exhaustion, Benedict would place his hand on the head of Tomas and pray to God to bless this wonderful young altar boy, following the prayer with a thank-you for the personal services that the lad had so willingly provided him.

These encounters lasted until Tomas was sixteen years of age, when he went away to the university. Even though other altar boys told him of similar treatment, he was afraid to tell them that he had experienced the same abuse handed out by the priest. If he did, and they told, then word might get back to Father Benedict; he would surely die tied to a tree deep in the forest at the hands of the soldiers.

Even until the present time, memories of the events were devastating and often caused him to awake in the middle of the night, and he would quietly sob until morning. It was a burden that he knew he would carry with him for the rest of his life. He was also afraid of what might happen if he told his father. But he now took solace in believing that marital relations with Maggie would be like paradise compared to those forced and mentally painful episodes with the priest.

Tomas was brought back into the moment as he heard Father Benedict say, "I hear that you are becoming important to your father in the running of his business. He must be very proud of you." Benedict then took Maggie's hand and, bowing his head slightly, said, "And Mademoiselle Légere, how pleasant to see you again. You have become a beautiful and gracious young woman. Your father speaks proudly of you when we meet to discuss business." Even though these were words that would be expected from a priest at such a meeting, Tomas and Maggie felt a sense of nervousness creeping over them. Was it because of the importance of the moment, or was it because this man no longer represented what they believed spiritually or intellectually?

"I am just about to pour myself some wine. Will you kindly have some with me?" Father Benedict asked.

"Merci, that would be very nice," Tomas answered. He did his best to smile, but instead just managed a hard stare directed at the priest. He averted his attention to Maggie. She saw in his eyes that they were telling her she needed to speak.

"Merci," Maggie said in a quiet voice, but her stomach was tied in knots and she was not totally sure that she could handle it. She would take a glass and have just a few sips. No doubt the priest would be drinking a pleasant, smooth wine brought from Paris, and not the less-expensive local wine.

As Father Benedict was pouring the wine, he asked, "What matter is on your minds today that brings you to honor me with a visit to the church?"

Tomas and Maggie looked at each other for only a few seconds; though short, this probably seemed to last an eternity to the priest. Tomas gathered his thoughts and said, "Father, we have come today on a very important matter. Margarite and I are in love, and we want to be married. We have the blessing of her parents, and also the blessing of my parents. We are here to ask for the holy blessing of the Church, and to ask if you will perform the nuptial ceremony."

"When would you like for the wedding to happen?" Father Benedict asked.

"Father, with the blessing of the Church and your personal blessing, we would like to be married in the fall . . . we are hoping it can be in late October, preferably October 27?"

"My son, that does not give us much time," the priest said, as he handed them each a glass of wine. "Is there any particular reason for that date?"

Thinking for a few seconds, Tomas responded, "Well, Father, October 27 is a special date in my family. It is the birthday of my late sister, who died too young."

"I see," Benedict said, looking at his calendar. "Oui, I think that date will be okay. First, let me offer a toast to you, to your love for each other, to your union, to a long and happy life together with many children."

"We will drink to that," Tomas said with the best emotion that he could gather. Maggie smiled weakly, raised her glass in deference to the priest, and took a sip of her wine. It was very pleasant and smooth, definitely Parisian.

Father Benedict quickly finished his glass, pouring himself another, and asked, "May I freshen your drinks?"

With due social grace, Maggie answered for her fiancé, "Merci beaucoup, Father, you are very kind. But no, we have had enough."

Knowing that Maggie's response was meant to close the meeting, Benedict told them, "Tomas and Margarite, I must seek the approval of the pope for his blessing of your marriage. You know the communication channels within the Church . . . they are slow. They must first pass through the bishop, then through His Eminence, through the cardinal, on through to the Holy Father in Rome, and once they have been received they must then come back through the same channels to me. In the meantime, I pray that you continue your love for each other, but remember that in accord with the will of the Church, you must remain chaste and pure. I trust that you and your families will continue to support the Church and give most generously."

With those words spoken by the priest, Tomas felt like he had been punched in the stomach. He, in that moment, understood more than ever before why so many fellow countrymen were leaving the Catholic religion and following their hearts and minds into Protestantism. Martin Luther was indeed right in his allegations against the Church. Clearly, its aim was to not only control the lives of its people, but also their money! Father Benedict had been trained well in Church doctrine. The transparency was evident in the hypocrisy of the local church, as it did not do much to help the poor, but rather seemed to suck everything but life itself from them.

"Merci, Father, you were kind to see us today. We will await your reply with great anticipation." And with that, Tomas bowed his head to the priest, clasped his hands in a prayerful gesture, and bowed slightly at the waist. Maggie, taking her cue from Tomas, did likewise. They then said, "Au revoir," and quickly departed.

Chapter 3
Summer Doldrums

After the visit to see Father Benedict, the summer just seemed to drag on interminably. The humidity sweeping in off the Bay of Biscay, as always in the dog days of summer, was oppressing. Every day, like clockwork, thunderstorms seemed to come in midafternoon. Fortunately, Tomas and his father had some flexibility in their work schedule. At this time of the year they would go by coach, rather than by open carriage, to the boatyard. They usually arrived by sunrise to have the maximum amount of daylight for the workers and to protect them from the weather. By early afternoon, before the rain would be expected to begin, they would give the workers an hour for lunch. During this time, they would return home for a meal and rest. After lunch, Tomas would have the family driver carry him to Maggie's parents' home to visit. Antoine generally stayed home for a couple of more hours of relaxation with the rest of the family. They would return to work, and then near dusk, the employees at the boatyard knocked off from work. Tomas and his father would close shop for the day, unless there was urgent work to be accomplished.

Maggie was an accomplished musician and loved to play everything, from a clavichord to the harp and the violin, for Tomas. The Mersenne Clavichord in the Légere home was the very finest style available in sixteenth-century France. Several of Maggie's very favorite compositions for the clavichord were:

"Sancta Trinitas," Antoine De Févin, 1470–1512

"Prelude - Fantasie - Hors envieux," Nicolas Gombert, 1495–1560

"Gamba Gagliarda - Moneghina Gagliarda," Antonio Gardane, 1509–1569

Maggie's two baroque violins were both imported from Italy: the first one made by Zanetto Micheli, 1490–1560, and the second by Pellegrino Micheli, 1520–1607. The Zanetto Micheli was acquired when she was studying music and literature at the Sorbonne. The second one was imported for her through a business connection of Tomas's father. It was a gift to her from the Jardeen family.

Maggie loved sacred music of the Renaissance period, as well as Burgundian chansons, Parisian chansons, and the Italian and English madrigals.

Maggie's access to music was made possible by the printed music sheets which she obtained in Paris while at the Sorbonne, and music sheets now available for sale in La Rochelle. Her repertoire was improved by recreating her beloved French music on the harp that had been passed down to her through the Légere family. It dated back to the early 1500s, but had received most excellent care and played perfectly.

Each morning, Maggie practiced at least an hour on each of her instruments. Her Aunt Colleen, her mother's sister, lived on the same block as her parents. Colleen visited almost every day for tea with Maggie's mother, but Maggie knew the real reason was to hear her play her music.

Maggie longed to work in a bookstore. Her love, after her music, was literature. There was a bookstore in the city owned by an older couple who always treated her as if she was their surrogate daughter. Their own daughter had married and moved to Paris. As a result, they almost never saw her or their grandchildren. The store had grown to be very successful, but it had become too demanding for them to operate totally by themselves. They asked Maggie if she would help them out in the afternoon and early evening; these were the times when they were at their busiest. After consulting with her parents, it was agreed that she might give it a try. Their main concern, though, was for her safety. They deemed that the family driver must drive her to and from work, unless Tomas or his father's driver agreed to transport her, and that she must always be driven home by either her father or the Jardeens if she worked past dark.

She usually went to the store in the early afternoon and stayed until the early evening. Tomas's lunch break allowed him to ride with her to the store on his return to the boatyard from his meal at home. Back at the office, he busily involved himself in solving design and construction problems for the boats now in process. His skills in these matters came from his mastery of mathematics and engineering studies at the University of Paris, which came into prominence in the late twelfth century and by the mid-sixteenth century rivaled many of the best universities in Germany for technical education.

His favorite time at work was spent, though lazily, dreaming about Maggie, and sometimes about imagining boats he assumed had never been thought of before. Boats were built bigger to carry more freight, armament, and people, but expansion of trade around the world was demanding sleeker and faster ships. Of course, getting sailing speed was always a problem at this time of the year, when the wind would sometimes just suddenly die on the bay.

The bookstore stayed open until the customers thinned out. This was usually just before dark in the spring and summer. From mid-October until the end of February, darkness came earlier. In any event, the old couple who owned the store traditionally shooed the customers out who were still browsing at six thirty and locked the door. Then Maggie would stay for a while, helping them freshen up the store for the next day. At first this concerned her parents, but they knew that the owners had tasks for Maggie to do after the store closed. However, they did insist that she leave no later than seven o'clock. Tomas had an agreement with Maggie that she keep the door of the building where she worked locked after the store closed for the day, and that he would meet her at seven o'clock each evening, when her coachman would arrive to drive her home. Tomas was always punctual arriving at the store, and would knock on the window for her to let him in. The Légeres knew that their daughter would be safe riding with him.

These days, the soldiers seemed more prevalent than before he and Maggie had met with Father Benedict. It seemed obvious that the soldiers had been directed to watch the Jardeen and the Légere family members. They were especially observant of Antoine and Tomas, but gave scant attention to the two mothers and the other Jardeen children; and of course, Aunt Colleen seemed to be exempt from their pursuits. Charles and his family were also being watched. A squad of soldiers made it a point to ride by the manoir at odd times each day, sometimes stopping to talk at the front gate to the estate. Mr. Légere was also being followed on occasions from his home in the city to his office. Walking home at the end of the day, one of the soldiers would almost always pick up surveillance as he left his office, but then seemed to mysteriously disappear when he was near his home. As for Maggie, it was hard to tell whether they were watching her, since she was usually with Tomas whenever she was outside the safety of her home. However, there was usually at least one soldier lolling nearby the bookstore whenever Tomas arrived to pick her up at night. It is possible that this surveillance had been ordered by Father Benedict, but it would be very difficult for them to confirm this suspicion.

Things were beginning to make sense to Tomas. He knew that a priest had always been able to perform marriages at his discretion after counseling. He looked to receive a commitment of loyalty from the couple to God, and by proxy the Church itself, to raising the children in the Catholic faith, and he demanded a vow of chastity until after the marriage. Tomas now realized that he had never heard of a priest having to get the blessing of the pope to perform a wedding ceremony. The excuse given by Father Benedict was no doubt a ploy to give the soldiers time to investigate the families about their religious beliefs. And besides, the pope certainly had more important things to worry about than giving approval for a marriage in faraway La Rochelle. Perhaps by the time that he and Maggie had met with Father Benedict in his office, the father had already learned from the young soldier of the encounter that night at the boatyard, when they had gathered for a church service and had conveniently disguised it as an engagement party.

Maggie looked forward to Tomas seeing her to and from work. The afternoon ride gave them a few brief minutes to talk about and plan for their wedding. It was a special, albeit brief, part of her daily routine. It gave them the opportunity to take their time, hold hands, and dream about their future together.

Tomas was now twenty-two years old, and she would soon be twenty-one. They had never loved each other physically, although they had had strong urges that went unfulfilled. Time spent together at night, in the privacy of the coach especially, gave them the opportunity to hug, kiss, and look forward to their physical unions after they were married. After all, they were normal, healthy young adults looking forward to having a family and a prosperous future. God had blessed their lives, and they would have the gift of carrying on their families' legacy through traditions and business.

Hopefully, though, contrary to popular wisdom and pressure to have children immediately, Tomas and Maggie wished that, with God's blessing, they would not have a child right away. They wanted time to pursue their futures. Of course, it was assured that Tomas would take over the boatyard when his father felt like he wanted to retire. But, until that time, he would surely hang around the boatyard in lieu of doing nothing productive for his family or the people of the city. In Maggie's case, there would be old family money that would always ensure a good life for her. However, she wanted more than that. She wanted to be intellectually independent, to feel that she was influencing the lives of the people of La Rochelle and, in a broader sense, the culture of the country. She was sure that she could accomplish her goal through her music and literary interest. In fact, business in the bookstore had already increased as more and more customers sought her out to discuss literary meaning in the books and the poems that they were perusing.

Although there would be significant financial support from their families early in their marriage, they wanted some time to earn a nest egg of their own. They planned to live temporarily in a townhouse that her parents and in-laws wished to buy for them. Also, Tomas's Uncle Charles, as a wedding present, had deeded them a nice piece of land at the manoir that they could build on when they were ready for a country home.

By all appearances, the future seemed very bright for them.

Chapter 4
Strong Resolve

By late September, when the air was beginning to cool and the humidity was lessening, Tomas was told by a young man who came to the boatyard that Father Benedict would like to see him that evening in his office. Tomas was not sure, but he thought the man looked like a soldier whom he often saw with Father Benedict on the streets of La Rochelle whenever the priest ventured away from the church. However, today the man was in street clothes rather than his uniform.

"The father will see you after dark when he has had his dinner," the man fairly ordered Tomas. "Bring Mademoiselle Légere. Don't be late." With those brief imperatives the man, without giving the normal courtesies of the day, turned and walked away.

It all seemed very peculiar, but Tomas could only presume that the father wanted to tell them that he had received the okay to perform the marriage for Maggie and himself. Or perhaps the father might even have further questions for them.

Tomas hurried home to change his clothes and rushed the short distance to Maggie's house to let her know of the meeting. He rapped on the door and a servant appeared. He was cordially invited in, and was led to the tearoom where Maggie was having tea and Madame Légere was enjoying a glass of wine. Madame Légere did not rise from her chair as Tomas bowed ever so slightly to her, took her hand, and kissed it. "How lovely to see you," she told him.

"Manfried," Madame Légere said to the servant, "bring Monsieur Jardeen a glass of wine." She asked Tomas after the fact, "You would like a glass of wine, would you not?"

"Merci, Madame, of course . . . that would be most excellent," he answered. With that, the servant bowed and excused himself to pour another glass of wine. In one's own home, things were usually a bit more relaxed, but formality prevailed when in someone else's home.

However, Maggie forewent the expected formality and said to the servant, "And I will as well." And with that, she quickly got up, hurried over to Tomas, kissed him, and said, "I am so excited to see you. My mother and I were just discussing some dreary news. How nice it is for you to come over. You have made my afternoon so much brighter."

They all sat and talked for a while, exchanging information about family, friends, and what was going on around town. Because of Maggie's father's position as mayor of the city, she and her mother were always current on what was happening. Madame Légere said that the soldiers were being more active in the Huguenot community. They were warning persons suspected of Huguenot involvement to be loyal to the Catholic Church, threatening them and their families with harm. Not only had the men been threatened, but women and children had also been verbally accosted. Children had been questioned about their parents' religious practices and what their parents were teaching them. "Just last night," Madame Légere told him in dismay, "a Huguenot home in the country was burned by the soldiers as the family looked on in horror."

This was the first that Tomas had heard of a home being burned. This incited fear in him, and he questioned the reason behind this meeting between him and the father.

Why would Father Benedict send a soldier to tell him to come to the church? Besides, the father had worried about even getting an answer in time for a wedding in October. He would go to the church this evening, but he would not take Maggie. He decided that he would make an excuse that she was not feeling well. He decided to not share the information with the Légeres.

Later, back at the boatyard, he confided to his father about the meeting and what he had been told at the Légere home. Antoine was suspicious, and told Tomas that he would go with him to see Father Benedict. That evening, after they had eaten dinner and darkness had begun to settle down on the city, they left home for the meeting at the church. Antoine just told Martine that he and Tomas had a business matter and would not be gone too long. The stars were beginning to come out and the full moon was already bright, the oil lanterns on the street already lit. Besides themselves, there seemed to be only a few people out. It was pretty easy to see when two soldiers began following them, but they stayed a respectable distance behind. As they neared the church, a third soldier suddenly stepped out of the shadow of a building and confronted them. Without any of the pleasantries common in French culture, he barked out, "Why are you out tonight? Are you going to one of your Huguenot meetings?"

Antoine quickly decided that his new religious beliefs were too important to deny, so he did not answer. Instead, Tomas told the soldier, "My father and I are on our way to the Catholic church to see Father Benedict. We have an appointment."

By this time, the two soldiers who had followed them caught up to the unfolding incident. One of them was the same fellow who had come to the boatyard earlier in the day, carrying the supposed message from Father Benedict. Except now he was in his military attire, and not in civilian clothes. All three were fully armed with swords, daggers, and protective shields. It became evident to them that they had been lured into a trap. The soldier who had initiated the very reason Tomas and his father were caught up in this proceeded to ask, "Where is your fiancée? She was supposed to come with you, not your father!"

"She could not come. She is not feeling well tonight," Tomas told them. "My father came with me so that we can discuss the wedding plans with Father Benedict. If you will please excuse us, we must go on or we will be late for our appointment." And with that, Tomas began to walk ahead.

The soldier who had first accosted them pushed him back into his father, almost knocking Antoine over. "You were told to bring Mademoiselle Légere, not your father," the soldier sneered.

Antoine spoke up, "Mademoiselle Légere is the daughter of the mayor of this city. You must not fool with her. If you have a grievance, you can settle it with us."

"Shut up, you old Huguenot fool!" the soldier sharply shot back.

Quickly resolving his conscientious desire not to tell a lie and deny his acquired Protestant faith, Antoine told the soldier, "I am Catholic; my son is Catholic. We attend Mass at least once per month as required; I regularly pay our tithe to the Church. You must let us go so that we can continue on our way to see Father Benedict."

Suddenly, the two soldiers who had come up from behind grabbed Antoine and held him in a firm grip. The third soldier grabbed Tomas and threw him to the ground. All of this happened so quickly that neither Antoine nor Tomas had any time to try to defend themselves. If they had not been immediately overpowered, the outcome could have been much more serious than it was turning out.

Pressing on Tomas's chest with his heavily booted foot, the burly soldier pulled out his sword and touched the sharp point to Tomas's throat. "You are Huguenot trash. You are not worthy enough to live. You are a disgrace to France and to our king. Let this be a warning to you and your Huguenot friends." Sheathing his sword, he then said, "Next time, the consequences shall be far more serious than tonight." The other two soldiers released Antoine. Together, the three began to humorously stroll down the street, most likely on their way to the nearest tavern, where the remaining part of their night would play out accordingly with the nature of the establishment.

Antoine thought out loud, "Where are the civil police when you need them?" Then, without saying it, he thought to himself, *What could a city patrolman do against the king's soldiers? Besides, they are probably paid to look the other way and not get involved.* He didn't want to voice his suspicions, as to not encourage any more fear in his son.

Antoine asked Tomas, "Are you hurt?"

"No, Father, I am not hurt. Did they hurt you?"

With that question, Antoine gravely shook his head and responded in a low, soothing voice, "No," and then, with a pause in his voice, he said, "Let's go home to your mother."

With tears welling down his face, Tomas grabbed his father and gave him a hug. "I think that is a fine idea." They turned around and silently retraced their route homeward. Antoine and Tomas arrived home disheveled and weary, probably more so from emotion than from anything else. Their encounter on the street with the soldiers had been frightful, but had not resulted in injury. There was no doubt between the father and son that the scene was intended to scare them back into being compliant Catholics. It was undeniable to them now; the soldier who had come to the door at the boatyard had surely guessed the real reason for the four families meeting that evening in August. The priest must have had suspicions about their nonpresence at Mass, except for the minimally required attendance. Or perhaps one of their trusted friends or social acquaintances had unintentionally said the wrong thing in wrong company.

Martine was distressed to hear the news, begging for her husband and son to tell her the horrid details. "I will," said Antoine, "but first, I need a drink of our best Cognac." Tomas offered to pour the drinks for his parents and himself. While he got the glasses and opened the bottle, Antoine slowly began, in a halting voice, to relay details of the evening to his beloved wife. The younger children came into the parlor and were allowed to stay. The Jardeens thought this would be a good lesson for them, to learn the harsh reality of the times in which they lived.

After hearing of what her husband and son had to tell, Martine said that the family should thank God for bringing them safely home. She suggested they ask forgiveness for those who wanted to harm them, and ask God to protect their family in these dire times. Antoine offered a long prayer of thanks to God for protection. He acknowledged the many blessings and mercies given to him and his family. After the prayer, the younger children were shooed off to bed. Antoine, Martine, and Tomas stayed up late discussing what they should do now about pursuing their religious practices. With much doubt and little conviction, they decided to continue their worship as usual. They would proceed in their minimal Catholicism, for show only, naturally, and to work as secretly as possible to further the Protestant Reformed movement in La Rochelle. They would not say anything about the attack except to Charles. They decided not to even tell Maggie and her family. Life should continue as if nothing had happened. The only exception was that Martine agreed to stay inside the house with the children while her husband and son were at work. Whenever she had a social engagement in the afternoon or needed to shop, one of the men would come home for a couple of hours to escort her wherever she had to go. Finally, after midnight had passed and they were too sleepy to continue, the three decided to retire to bed.

Across town, in a tavern near the wharf district, the soldiers that accosted Antoine and Tomas had too much to drink and were already bedded down with the prostitutes they had met later in the evening.

Chapter 5
The Future

As September was coming to a close, the Jardeens could feel autumn gradually descending on the city of La Rochelle. The days were beginning to cool down; at night, there was a noticeable nip in the air. The approaching change of season was ever more evident in the nearby countryside than in the city itself. The trees, especially the maples and oaks, were beginning to show reflections of traces of yellow and red. In contrast, the fruit trees always seemed to pridefully hold their green color as long as possible. Charles and Paulette reported that the fall crops were looking bountiful. The usual fall rains had been keeping the crops well hydrated.

One afternoon, while walking home to escort his mother to Marigot's apparel store to buy a new dress, Tomas came across Father Benedict, who said that he was out visiting some sick parishioners. The father was cordial and seemed genuinely glad to see Tomas. "My son, I have good news for you," the priest told Tomas. "I have received a communiqué from the bishop. I am told that the Church offers blessings for your marriage to Mademoiselle Légere. Can she and you come by the church tomorrow afternoon to discuss your wedding plans?"

"Of course, Father," Tomas answered. "What time can you see us?"

The father tried to mentally plan for a time for the meeting to take place that would correlate with a soldier doing surveillance on the couple. He regained the time spent by quickly answering, "Four o'clock, tomorrow afternoon. You do remember my office, don't you?" Tomas nodded his head. The priest continued, "The bishop will join us. I will set out my best wine for you and your lovely fiancée."

"We will see you then," Tomas responded in the most courteous voice that he could muster, as his mind inadvertently shot back to those terrible afternoons in the office with the priest when he was still just a boy.

He watched as the priest began to walk slowly down the street, under a canopy of overhanging trees that were beginning to show their autumn colors. Suddenly having mixed feelings, and dizzy with the myriad of thoughts that now were racing through his mind, Tomas forgot the obligation to his mother and began to walk away, not realizing where he was going. *Is now the right time to be getting married?* he wondered. *We are young. Maggie has seemed different recently. Does Maggie really love me? Do I really love Maggie? Dad, Uncle Charles, and I are in negotiations to build a new ship. It will be the biggest and nicest seacraft that we have ever built. With our growing business, will I have time to be a good husband? Will I be a good father? Will Maggie be a good mother? Are Maggie and her family stronger in traditional Catholic doctrines, or in Reformist beliefs? Will we have to promise to raise our children in the Catholic Church? What happens if our marriage doesn't work out? Should I just end everything right now?*

Tomas kept walking and thinking as these thoughts raced and tumbled in his mind. He came to a house and knocked. In his dazed state, he had gone to Maggie's home and not to his own. Mother would have to miss going to the fabric store that afternoon. Answering the rap on the door, the servant heartily greeted Tomas. "Bonjour, Monsieur Jardeen!"

"Bonjour," Tomas replied hesitantly. "I would like to see Margarite, is she here?" He then added out of respect, "And, if it is permissible with her mother, I would like to speak privately with her."

"Oui, Monsieur. Please come in. I will tell her that you are here." The servant showed him into a small sitting room just off the foyer and said, "Please have a seat. May I serve you a glass of wine?"

Thinking that wine might quickly help him sort out what he might say to Maggie, Tomas said, "Merci, I would enjoy a glass of wine." The servant poured from a nearby crystal decanter and served it to Tomas on a silver tray. He then put the decanter onto the tray and sat it on a low table, between Tomas and the empty chair directly across from him. Then, backing slowly to the door and bowing slightly in a show of courtesy, the servant said, "I shall let Mademoiselle know that you are here."

It was a while before Maggie appeared. Tomas understood, since the servant would have conveyed to Elisabeth that Monsieur Jardeen wished to have a private conversation with her daughter. Surely that caused concern and raised questions on her mother's end.

After what seemed like an eternity, the servant escorted Maggie into the sitting room. Tomas stood and took her hand when she entered. As might be expected under the circumstance, she had a worried and puzzled look on her face. The servant poured a glass of wine for her, refilled Tomas's glass, and then asked, "Mademoiselle, will there be anything else?"

"No, that will be all."

The servant bowed his head slightly in a sign of deference and retreated, closing the door behind him. As was customary, he would be waiting just outside the door in the event that the young couple would require his services. They would just ring the small crystal bell which he had placed on the table with the wine.

"Tomas, is there something wrong?" Maggie asked, in as calm of a manner as she could muster. "I did not expect to see you this afternoon."

Taking just a few seconds—seconds that seemed like an eternity to Maggie—he responded, "I met Father Benedict on the street this afternoon on my way home." He could tell that just this little bit of information caused Maggie some anxiety. "He told me that he has received the Church's blessing for our marriage, and that he wishes to meet with us to further discuss our wedding plans."

"That is wonderful news," gushed Maggie.

Maggie would have expected at this moment that the couple would have gotten up, embraced, and kissed. But they didn't. With no initiative from Tomas for an expression of affection, Maggie said, "My love, is there a problem?"

Breaking the vow of secrecy that he had given his parents, Tomas began to tell her the story about the night when the soldiers had attacked him and his father. He related details of the warnings given that he and his friends must remain good, compliant Catholics, as well as the consequences if they did not give up their Reformed beliefs. He told her that the soldiers had planned the attack, probably at the request of Father Benedict. He told her that he did not know what harm would have come to her that evening if she, rather than his father, had been with him.

"Why have you not told me this before?" Maggie asked.

"Because I did not want to worry you."

"Worry me? These are things that a man shares with the woman that he is going to marry. Do you not trust me enough to tell me about a threat made on your life?"

At this point, Tomas made a grave mistake. He said, "I did not know if the intent was to scare me by harming you."

"You were worried about my safety, but you didn't even tell me."

"Yes, I felt sure that, aside from that evening, you would be safe."

"Why did you think that?"

"Well, with your father being the mayor . . ."

"The soldiers do not work for or take orders from my father. They work for the king. My father and mother are committed to the same religious beliefs as you and your family."

Noticing that Maggie did not include herself, Tomas felt inclined to ask, "Are you not also committed to Huguenot religious beliefs? I need to know that you're willing to give up your Catholic beliefs and become a practicing Huguenot, and by extension, agree to raise our children in the principles of the Reformed Church." Looking at the anxiety on her face, Tomas realized that perhaps this was not the right question to ask at this moment, but he knew that he needed an answer now. Maggie took pause. These were the questions that struck to the very core of her soul. She had fumbled with what her answers would be many times. But this time, the thoughts on the matter were not coming to her so easily. Since the night when they had met as students in Paris, and she had first danced with Tomas at a holiday party, she knew that he was the person whom she loved, and was sure she would one day marry. But now, with the immediacy of a wedding hitting her squarely in the face, and with the blurring realities between her Catholic beliefs and what was expected of her, she was not sure what she wanted. It would be a huge embarrassment to call off, or even postpone, her marriage, and it most certainly would bring unbearable shame to both families.

Maggie rationalized to herself, *I am young, and these doubts are surely normal. Probably all young women have these doubts.* With every nerve in her body feeling like it was going to tear apart, she thought, *I need to be strong. With God's blessing, I will make this marriage work. Together, Tomas and I will raise our children to be good Huguenots.*

"Oui!" she said to Tomas. Trying to put on a happy face, she braved a big smile and got up to hug Tomas. "Let's go see Father Benedict."

Chapter 6
The Wedding

The month of October was demanding for Tomas and his father. They had contracted with a privateer, named Auguste "Augie" Cussions, to build him a *corvair*. Captain Cussions was licensed by the French government to use an armed private vessel to raid the commerce of foreign governments. In this case, Captain Cussions needed a fast ship for service in the Mediterranean, and for duty off the west coast of Africa. In designing a ship of this type, speed was of utmost importance, but the need for heavy armament would certainly impact on the ability for speed. To grant swift acceleration, it needed to be lightweight. The choice of armament would, of course, be a choice of Cussions's. The ship would be designed around the ideas of the captain.

Cussions had received permission of King Henri III to do business with the Jardeens, for they had a good reputation and were known for high-quality work at a fair price. Successfully completing this contract would make them a leading contender along the French Atlantic coast for future work. Corvairs and bigger ships had always been built in Brest, La Havre, or Marseilles. The Jardeen brothers, together with Tomas and their design engineers, began to work diligently on the new design. The boatyard, just by the nature of the smaller boats built to date, did not have a dry dock big enough to construct the corvair. Antoine realized this limitation. However, design was everything, and this aspect could best be done by Tomas and the rest of his team.

The construction and outfitting would be subcontracted out to the Montaigne brothers at their large shipyard on Île de Ré, just a couple of miles across the harbor from La Rochelle in the Bay of Biscay. This was the basis on which Antoine sold the contract to Captain Cussions. The Montaignes were brothers of Charles's wife, Paulette.

The Montaigne brothers had already built several warships of a similar design to the corvair. Their dry dock was the right size for the job. Their engineers would be working closely with the design staff from the boatyard in La Rochelle. It was diligent work. Antoine and Charles dedicated much of their day to brainstorm with the designers, and they would go home in the late afternoon to be with their wives and children. However, Tomas would stay some nights until late hours to work with the designers to get their ideas down on paper. Sometimes, he would finally give up the idea of even going home and would just fall asleep on a cot in the office. Everyone was safe, including Maggie. On the nights Tomas could not be her escort, either her father or Antoine would pick her up and see her safely home.

A large seal of King Henri III had been posted at the gate to the boatyard. In recognition of this, the soldiers, instead of harassing the Jardeens and their workers, now were supposed to actually offer them protection. They wondered if the king had forgotten that these were Huguenots. Regardless of these concerns, they knew that they had no choice in the matter. They had the responsibility to adhere to the king's wishes. And in accordance with those wishes, they would back off. The Jardeens, it would now seem, were sacrosanct. And as well, by relationship and political importance, so were Mademoiselle Légere and her family.

Maggie and her mother were very busy planning the wedding. Her parents wanted to keep it as simple as possible, but realized that for the Church, and being such an important political family, it would have to be a bigger affair than they would prefer. After all, the whole event was being planned simply to get the marriage recognized by the Church and legally recorded in Church and government records. From the viewpoint of their true religious beliefs, the important step would be the later private exchange of their wedding vows, in the presence of their families and trusted friends at Christmastime. The Huguenot ceremony at Christmastime would be an affirmation of their marriage in accord with their Protestant Reformed Church. This civil ceremony, for the lack of better terminology, would be performed by Mayor Légere and would be recognized neither by the Catholic Church nor by the French government.

Although Elisabeth Légere did consult on occasion with Martine, Maggie's mother-in-law-to-be, wedding plans were, by French custom, largely the responsibility of the bride's family. Essentially, Tomas was expected to just show up on time and be standing at the altar, awaiting his bride-to-be as she walked down the aisle on the arm of her father, Michel.

Father Benedict had scheduled the ceremony for Saturday afternoon, October 27, at 4:00 p.m., in the downtown cathedral next to the central park. The bishop of La Rochelle would be there to assist in the wedding, but his main purpose unofficially was to see who would be present. Huguenots were still a concern to the Church, and it would be a good opportunity to see who the friends of the two families were.

The Jardeens were aware of this potential and hoped that the Church would have no idea that for the families, the wedding was more or less window dressing to cover up suspicions of their true religion. The Jardeens' idea was to fill the cathedral with people, mostly consisting of Catholic acquaintances and business associates, to make the Huguenot guests more difficult to identify. Advance word of these plans would be spread among their Reformed community.

As the date approached, Tomas was very busy trying to balance his time between seeing Maggie and the demands of his work on the corvair. The only way that he could take time away from the design effort on the privateer vessel was through the brilliant efforts of his own design team, and the engineers that the Montaigne brothers had working with them. However, as time passed, Tomas became concentrated more on his desire to work than to see Maggie. This felt contradictory to him, and he was filled with both peculiarity and guilt as his priorities shifted.

Uncle Charles and Aunt Paulette had offered the couple, and by extension their servants, their home in the country for a period of semiprivacy after the wedding. Charles's children were by all accounts grown, and were already at this point living independently in smaller accommodations on the estate. Charles and Paulette would in turn spend a few nights with Antoine and Martine, and then they would be off to Paris for a few weeks of vacation at the apartment owned with Antoine and his family. They had worked hard on the farm at the manoir this year. By the time of the wedding the fall crops would either be harvested and sold, or processed for winter and spring keeping for the Jardeen families. Antoine would be okay solely running the boatyard for that time. When they returned to La Rochelle,

Tomas and the new Madame Margarite Jardeen would go to Paris and return home in mid-December for the civil reaffirmation of vows before her father. Because Maggie had studied in Paris, she knew the city quite well. While Tomas had also studied in Paris, he did not have the time for the same type of social adventures that Maggie had experienced at her university. She could not wait to share the glories of the Parisian cultural and social scene, as seen through her eyes. There was an immense amount of adventure that waited for them, such as, but not exclusively, The Palace at the Louvre, the small cabarets, Bohemian theater and concert venues, romantic walks along the Seine River, the magnificent royal chapel of Sainte-Chapelle, which was finished in the thirteenth century with its astonishing amount of stained-glass art; and, if nothing else, the wonderful food at some of the best restaurants to be found anywhere in Europe. Paris was indeed a very special city, even in those times. It was a city of the "haves" and the "have-nots." They were fortunate to be of the class that would be able to afford and enjoy what the city had to offer.

October 27, 1575, finally arrived. Tomas was out of bed before the rest of his family. The boatyard would be closed, except for the designers. To calm his nerves, he decided to go to his office for a little while. It was still pretty dark outside. The sun was just rising across the eastern horizon, beginning its ascent over the city. As he watched this unfold, he thought instead about going down to the waterfront by the defense towers, and watching the unfolding of what was sure to be a very busy day. His heart was full of emotions. It was hard to believe that the little boy he had once been was now a grown man, about to be married to a strikingly beautiful and wonderful woman and ready to take on the world. Despite its history and many problems, right now Renaissance France seemed a glorious place to be. As he wended his way to the harbor area, the streets began to come alive. Merchants were busily getting ready to open. Many of them were sweeping in front of their store and setting up displays of merchandise on the sidewalks to sell. At this very moment, for Tomas, La Rochelle seemed like the center of the universe.

By the time that Tomas returned home, his parents and siblings were up and breakfast was about to be served. After they were seated, Antoine asked that they hold hands while he offered a prayer of thanksgiving. "Dear Father God, this family gives thanks today to you, and to your Son Jesus Christ, for the many blessings that you have given us. And for our son Tomas and for Maggie, we pray for their life together—for the children of this marriage and for their children's children. Martine and I thank you for all that we are and all that what we have. We pray for the future of our country. Touch our hearts and guide us to do Thy work. Amen."

"Amen," Martine echoed, and then signaled for the house servants to serve breakfast.

Meanwhile, at the Légere home, Maggie and her mother were still getting dressed. Her father Michel had a bite to eat and was already en route to his office at the city's administration building. There were a few important matters that required his attention, and he planned to work at his desk until noon or one o'clock. Besides, it would be better for him to be out of the house while Elisabeth busily directed the staff in preparation for the wedding reception that was to be held in their home that evening.

Later that morning, Michel received the attaché, who represented Henri III, King of France. The duke called unexpectedly on the Honorable Michel Légere to bring congratulations from King Henri on the marriage of his daughter to Monsieur Tomas Jardeen, and to present the royal gift which the king had sent for the couple. It was a silver serving tray, a silver carafe, and eight silver wine goblets; all were made of nearly pure silver and had appropriately been engraved with the date and with a replica of the royal seal. Because the moment was unexpected, Michel was taken aback and hardly knew what to say. Bowing, he managed, "On behalf of my daughter Margarite and Tomas Jardeen, her husband-to-be, please convey to the king our sincere appreciation for his most kind thoughts and generosity. This is a gift which I know they will deeply appreciate for their entire lives; their children and their children's children will always treasure it. May God protect and bless the king."

The meeting was brief. As the duke was leaving, he told Michel, "Please convey to the couple that the king would be pleased to receive them at the palace when they visit Paris on their wedding trip." Now Michel was even more puzzled. How did the king know of the plans to go to Paris? What else did the king know about them? He started to question why would he care enough to send such a beautiful gift. Of course, he himself was the civic mayor of La Rochelle, which did carry a lot of responsibility and necessitated a lot of contact with the duke, who in turn reported to the king. Then there was the important shipbuilding contract presently underway at the Jardeens' boatyard to consider. The contract with the Jardeens, although privately negotiated, was endorsed and sanctioned by the king.

"Oui, I shall convey the king's invitation to them. Please tell the king that they will be most honored to have an audience with him." Though mystified, he felt proud and bowed slightly, taking the duke's hand and kissing it. Meeting his bodyguards just outside the door, the duke paused, stepped back through the door for just a moment, and silently looked at Michel, who was now behind his desk. And then, the duke and his entourage swept down the hallway and were gone. Michel had no idea of what further he had to say, but obviously he had thought better of it. He chose not to worry. Michel knew without doubt that if it were important, he then would soon know.

Meanwhile, Tomas's mother and sister, Marye, were at the cathedral supervising the placement of flowers and arranging final details with the priest. Wedding rituals of the privileged class in the sixteenth century were not too different than those of today. The wedding rehearsal had been the evening before with the rest of the wedding party. His father, Antoine, would be his best man; his good friend from the Marigot family would be a groomsman, along with his brother, Paul, and two male cousins from the farm.

A very close married friend, just a few years older than herself, would be Maggie's matron of honor. Tomas's sister, Marye, would be a bridesmaid, as well as another of her close friends, a not-yet-married daughter of Robert Marigot and his wife. The young daughter of her matron of honor was to be the flower girl, and the young son of one of Tomas's cousins would be the ringbearer.

Maggie's mother had already had the casual mother-daughter talks with her about marriage in general, but more importantly, she taught her about the marital obligations of a woman to her husband. Maggie listened respectfully, but thought her mother should have taken into account that she was a grown woman who had studied health and biology at the Sorbonne, as it was required for all females. Besides,

Maggie had married friends with children, and sex was a frequent topic of conversation.

Similarly, Antoine had already talked with Tomas about a husband's relationship with his wife, and about what a man must do to create and keep a happy marriage. Antoine's almost twenty-five years of marriage with Martine had been extremely good ones. He loved her more than when they first wed. Unlike the custom of many French men, the idea of a mistress had never even been a serious consideration, although the opportunity had certainly presented itself many times. These were things that he wanted his son to know. He knew that Tomas surely by now already understood the intimate details of a marital relationship, but he did say to him that he was available to discuss these matters if he had questions.

Maggie was to wear a beautiful Spanish farthingale[27a, 27b] dress which the Marigot family had made in Barcelona and sent by ship just for her. The red skirt part of the dress was embroidered throughout in patterns of gold thread and was made with much fabric to create a fullness of appearance. Tight-fitting at the waist, it was worn over a corset with a cone-shaped wire cage and several petticoats to keep it increasingly fanned out as it dropped to the floor. The wire underfitting was such that it prevented her from sitting or riding in the family coach. Thus, she would have to be dressed at the church. The tight-fitting, trumpet-sleeved bodice was made of the same fabric and gold embroidery as the dress, with red sleeves matching the skirt, and was trimmed with purple-dyed puffed lace. Over the dress, she would wear a loose-fitting shawl-like coat which would hang off her shoulders. It would be pulled around and tied at the abdomen with a long, fancily woven, tasseled sash, which dropped near the floor to reveal the dress in front as inverted Vs connected at their apexes. The coat was accented with black fur on the lapels. Maggie's wedding ensemble would be accented with a beautiful pearl necklace made locally in La Rochelle, and presented to her the night before by Tomas as his wedding gift. The colors for her wedding attire were chosen to make a statement—more to the Catholic Church than to the wedding guests.

For centuries, red had meant to represent the chastity of the woman. The rich black and purple colors conveyed the upper-class social status of the family. The Légeres were a moneyed family in La Rochelle. Michel Légere and his wife each descended from families that had a very long history in the ancient province of Aunis. Prosperity had followed them down to the present time. Maggie was their only daughter, and she was to always have the best that life could afford, as would her children. Certainly Tomas and his family, already well-placed through the boatbuilding and trading industry, would prosper even further through the marriage connection with the Légere family. It seemed assured that this marriage would result in a family of nobility.

At two thirty in the afternoon, the family carriage, driven by the family's coachmen, drew up in front of the Légere home. The servant got down from the carriage, stood stiffly in his top hat by the running board, and waited patiently for the family to come out of the house. A few minutes later, Maggie came down the steps escorted by her father; her mother followed just behind them. It was just a short ride to the cathedral. They ascended the steps and paused briefly on the terrace, just beyond the portico.

Maggie stopped to embrace her mother before going inside. The seriousness of what was about to happen struck her hard. She had never undertaken anything so serious, something sure to be demanding beyond all imagination. She realized at this moment that there would be no turning back. They both had a brief cry. Composing themselves, they went to the bridal salon where Maggie, with assistance, would change into her wedding attire.

People began arriving about three thirty. Soon, all the guests were already seated forward of the rood, a dividing partition in the sanctuary. Just a couple of minutes before the four o'clock hour, Madame Jardeen was escorted to her seat by Tomas's younger brother, Paul. Then, Madame Légere was similarly escorted to her seat on the left side of the aisle by Charles's oldest son. Meanwhile, Maggie and her father waited with the wedding attendants at the door of the cathedral, ready to process down the aisle. Tomas was waiting at the altar with his best man. He was dressed in resplendent gold tights and red leggings, matching the red of Maggie's dress; his attire was completed with a luxurious, full-fitting coat with a large collar. The fabric of the coat matched the ornamental gold of his tights. Although tailored with an abundance of fabric and padding, both the coat and the tights were also lined throughout with padding to create the appearance of fullness. This design technique gave him the appearance of being larger and more muscular than he really was. The best man was resplendent in dress, but not as much so as Tomas.

As soon as Maggie had covered her head with the lace veil required for a woman to enter the church, the prelude of assorted music ended and the processional, "Las, Las, Las, Las Par Grand Delit," a twelfth-century composition by the French composer Gautier de Coincy, began. This spirited harp dance continued while the party of attendants, led by Father Benedict and the bishop, processed down the aisle and took their place before the altar. When all of the attendants were in place, Tomas and his father turned to look as the bridal march began. It was "Ronde," a piece for harpsichord by the sixteenth-century composer Tielman Susato. Maggie was absolutely stunning, and all eyes were on her as she came down the aisle holding on to her father's arm, being careful not to step on the bottom of her dress. They stopped just before reaching the altar and genuflected. Father Benedict led the bride-to-be, her father, and the assembly of wedding guests in the sign of the cross.

Then Father Benedict began, "We are gathered here today to honor the love of Margarite Légere and Tomas Jardeen, and to celebrate their union in Holy Matrimony."[28] A murmur of approval went through the church as Maggie and her father stepped forward to join the priest and bishop at the altar. Motioning to Tomas and his best man to come and join them, the priest continued, "Who gives Margarite to be married to Tomas?"

"I do," Michel said in a clear and commanding voice.

At that point, the priest took Maggie's arm from her father and placed it onto Tomas's arm. Michel retreated to take a seat on the front pew beside his wife.

After asking the couple to kneel, Father Benedict turned to face the cross-bearing Jesus, cupped his hands, and bowed his head. "Blessed Trinity," he began the prayer, speaking in Latin. *"I ask Thy blessings and tender mercies for this couple, who present themselves here today to be wed in Holy Matrimony. I pray for them a happy and fruitful marriage. May their lives be long."*

Turning back to Maggie and Tomas, Benedict blessed them with the sign of the cross. The bishop stepped forward for the Penitential Rite. He invited the entire congregation of guests to repent of their sins, and led a short liturgical ceremony in which he forgave all persons present of their sins. The congregation stood and sang "Gloria," a hymn of praise to God in the highest. He then opened a recently published Latin Bible and began his liturgy. In accordance with the custom of the Church, the first reading of the word was from the Old Testament, Genesis, chapter 2, verses 18–24. The words of this reading describe the creation of woman from the rib of man and conclude, "Therefore, a man leaves his father and his mother and cleaves to his wife, and they become one flesh." The bishop concluded by saying, "The Word of the Lord," and the congregation responded with, "Thanks be to God." The cantor then sang a psalm about love.

The second reading presented by the bishop was from the New Testament, First Corinthians, chapter 13, verses 1–8. This passage spoke eloquently of what constitutes love. He recited, "If I give away all I have, and if I deliver my body to be burned, but have not love, I gain nothing. Love is patient and kind, love is not jealous or boastful, love is not arrogant or rude. Love does not insist on its own way. Love is not irritable or resentful. Love does not rejoice at wrong, but rejoices at right. Love bears all things, believes all things, hopes all things, endures all things." Again, the bishop paused and then quickly followed with, "The Word of the Lord," and the congregation responded, "Thanks be to God."

The cantor then led the congregation in singing the Gospel Acclamation, after which the bishop proclaimed the Gospel and concluded by saying, "The Gospel of the Lord," and the congregation responded by saying, "Praise to You, Lord Jesus Christ."

Exchanging places with the bishop, Father Benedict offered a short homily, in which according to the Catholic rite of marriage, he spoke about the dignity and mystery of love and of marriage, the grace of the sacrament, and the responsibilities of married people, each to the other. And then the priest conducted the rites of marriage. "Margarite, do you take Tomas to be your husband, to love, to have, and to hold forever, in sickness and health, for as long as you both shall live? Do you promise to live your life according to the principles and practices of the Catholic Church, and do you promise to raise your children in the principles of the Catholic faith?"

"I do."

"Tomas, do you take Margarite to be your wife, to love, to have, and to hold forever, in sickness and health, for as long as you both shall live? Do you promise to live your life according to the principles and practices of the Catholic Church, and do you promise to work in unity with Margarite to raise your children in the principles of the Catholic faith?"

Tomas knew that these questions about the Church were coming. He was concerned that to affirm the question, he would lie. Given his true beliefs, he felt trapped. But for the opportunity to be married to Maggie, and praying that God would forgive him for the falsehood, Tomas resolutely answered, "I do."

Father Benedict then took their hands and joined them together, saying, "I now pronounce you man and wife. May the Father, the Son, and the Holy Spirit smile on you and bless you forever and ever! Tomas, you may now kiss your bride."

The lector stood up and read the General Intercessions, or Prayers of the Faithful. Offering the prayer "For, we pray to the Lord," the congregation of guests responded by saying, "Lord, hear our prayer." Usually the ancient Nicene Creed was recited only on Sunday weddings or on days of solemnity. Because of the presence of the bishop, it was decided that it would be recited today. The congregation was led by the bishop himself in the recitation of this rather lengthy statement of faith.

In preparation for the celebration of the Eucharist, the guests sat in their seats while the priest and the bishop prepared the altar, and the gifts of bread and wine were brought to the altar by two young altar boys, each either twelve or thirteen years old. As Maggie and Tomas collected monetary gifts for the needs of the Church and the poor and brought them to the altar, Tomas could not help but wonder if the altar boys were receiving the same abusive treatment as he was when he was their age.

Finally, the priest began, "Pray, my brothers and sisters, that our sacrifice may be acceptable to God, the almighty Father." The assembly of guests rose from their seats and stood. The bishop took over at this point and began to pray the Eucharistic prayer. At appropriate points in the prayer, the assembly offered three acclamations: the first was the singing of the *Sanctus* ("Holy, Holy"), then kneeling they offered a Memorial Acclamation, and lastly, standing, they sang the "Great Amen." Following this, the bishop led them in the Lord's Prayer. "Our Father, which art in Heaven, hallowed be Thy name . . ."

Father Benedict offered a Nuptial Blessing to Margarite and Tomas as he prayed for them, while they knelt before him. The bishop broke the bread as the wedding guests sang a hymn of praise, and then he blessed the wine. At appropriate moments, at which time a bell rang, the transfiguration occurred behind a curtain; according to Catholic belief, the bread transformed into the body of Christ, and the wine into his blood. Beginning with the newly married couple, the bishop and the priest distributed the now-holy Eucharistic elements of bread to the attendants, and to the assembly of guests as they came forward to the altar. The two goblets of the blood of Christ were drunk by the priest and the bishop.

After the completion of the Communion, and with the assembly of guests standing, Father Benedict again prayed a solemn blessing for Margarite and Tomas. The guests responded throughout the prayer with "Amen." Then, with a dismissal from the priest, the guests responded with, "Thanks be to God." Most of the service was conducted in Latin, except for the homily.

The recessional music began to play. It was "Bransle II," by the French composer Pierre Attaingnant, which had quickly become a classic. After she and Tomas had processed, Maggie hurried to the bridal salon to change from the wedding outfit into more comfortable attire. As she changed, her matron of honor waited in attendance and gathered the wedding outfit piece by piece to return to the Légere home. Meanwhile, the priest and the bishop processed down the aisle. Next to follow were her parents, then Antoine, Martine, and Tomas's siblings, and lastly, Charles and his family were led out, respectively. Finally, the guests filtered out of the church to wait outside for the married couple to appear. When Maggie and Tomas made their appearance on the steps of the cathedral, with the parents leading the way, the crowd of guests surrounded the couple and the parents to offer their congratulations and good wishes.

When at last the wedding party had departed in their carriages for the wedding reception at the Légere home, the ladies socialized with polite conversation while the husbands and the older sons went for the coaches. By now it was dark, and the lanterns on the side of the coaches had to be lit. Some of the families had a coachman to drive them to the reception. As guests arrived at the town home of the Légeres, they lined up outside and waited their turn for the house butler to meet them. Asking for their name, he would take each couple separately to the receiving line. Even though the Légeres and the Jardeens already knew each of the guests, some perhaps more closely than others, the butler still introduced them as Madame and Monsieur (last name). The introductions were very formal. Each guest was told—first by the Légeres, then by the Jardeens, and then by Maggie and Tomas—how pleased and honored they were that they honored them with their presence. After exchanging the proper amenities, the formality broke down and many hugs and kisses were exchanged.

The wedding guests were numerous, so much so that the downstairs part of the large house was almost filled. A chamber music group was playing in the ballroom, and the music softly drifted throughout the house. Bright fall flowers, such as chrysanthemums, hydrangea, solidago, and red-hot poker, were used to decorate the house. The walls were highlighted with shades of red, bronze, and richly deep browns created with the use of berries and twigs, and accented with the colorful foliage of the season, along with acorns and nuts. The contrasting fall colors that were intertwined among the beautiful artwork hanging throughout the house were dramatic against the paint and artistically designed wallpaper that the Légeres had used to recently redecorate their most beautiful home.

In each of the downstairs rooms was an ample supply of ale and the very finest French wines to please the palate. Perhaps not too surprisingly, there was also cold, fresh milk provided by Charles Jardeen from the cows at the manoir. There was an ample stash of Champagne ready for many toasts to the couple, and for the use of sealing their marriage with a wedding toast to one another. The cooks, supervised by the head chef, had worked for several days preparing the wedding feast. Because La Rochelle was so conveniently situated on the coastline of France, fresh fish, scallops, and oysters had been bought earlier in the day and prepared for the banquet. According to custom, it was said that only months containing the letter *R* provided the safest and freshest oysters. These oysters were deemed viable to eat, since October did of course have that letter. Venison and wild boar came from recent hunting expeditions that the brothers, Charles and Antoine, had been on in the deep, dark forest behind the family manoir. The most exotic dishes were pheasant and grouse from the farm. The birds were first cleaned and cooked, and then the heads and the feathers had been carefully put back on the birds. They may no longer have been able to fly, but they certainly looked very much alive laid out on the serving dishes. Bread, richly textured cheese, soft brie, camembert, and farm-fresh eggs with deviled yolks were served along with meats. The vegetables prepared for the feast were potatoes, drenched in oil and sprinkled with rosemary, and parsnips sautéed in butter and warmed in heavy, rich cream. Turnip greens were included as well, deliciously cooked with the diced roots and seasoned with mace and nutmeg, as well as baked acorn squash, seasoned with cinnamon and black Corinthian currants dried from small, sweet, seedless grapes which grew easily in the summer on Charles's manoir estate. These delicate grapes were not used for winemaking. There was freshly ground ginger, nutmeg, and cinnamon used to season a compote made of stewed fall apples, late-season plums, and cherries grown in the orchards that ringed the city. Dessert was rich torte cakes made with many eggs and much butter, filled with almonds and dried fruit, which had been wrapped for several weeks in cloth and moistened each day with liberal amounts of a delicate sherry that was always pleasing to the palate.

Before dessert was served, the guests gathered for a round of toasts. Michel led off with a brief, but warm, heartfelt tribute to his daughter and her new husband, wishing them a long life of happiness together. Antoine then offered a blessing, as did Uncle Charles. Many of their friends and associates also toasted them.

Finally, it was time to cut the wedding cake. Margarite, with Tomas at her side, would cut the first cake. Of course, in accordance with French etiquette, none of the guests began to eat their dessert until the couple had had a piece of their cake and made their wedding toast to each other, to again affirm their wedding vows.

After everyone had finished eating, Father Benedict announced that he was going upstairs to the couple's chamber, to bless and sanctify the wedding bed. While he was gone, the guests drank after-dinner cordials poured by the servants and enjoyed the nuts, fruits, and sweetbreads put out on the side tables. Finally, Father Benedict returned and announced that the wedding chamber was prepared. At eleven o'clock, after some dancing, there was a final blessing and a prayer for a fruitful marriage, and amid much clapping, whistling, and singing, the couple went arm in arm up the stairs to the room where they would spend their first night as man and wife. The party continued until the early hours of the morning with music and dancing downstairs. The marriage was consummated as many times throughout the night as Tomas was physically able, and they did so without the customary wedding sheet,[29] which they had wadded up and dropped on the floor beside the bed. Wedding guests took turns going upstairs and serenading outside of the bedroom door. Each time seemed even more intense and pleasurable to each of them than the time before. Sleep did not come easily until about four thirty in the morning.

Chapter 7
The Morning After

On October 28, 1575, midmorning after the wedding, Tomas and Margarite took one of her parents' carriages and loaded Maggie's trunk, along with a couple of smaller bags, onto it. Then they prepared to drive over to his parents' home. Michel and Elisabeth had also been invited to have breakfast with the Jardeens, but they decided to wait a while to give Maggie and Tomas a little time alone with his family.

As they rode along, the fog that usually hung over the city at this time of the year had been rapidly melted away by the rising sun. The trees were nearly bare by now. The air was crisp, so light coats and hats felt very comfortable. To them it seemed that a certain aura of mystique had settled over the city. It was something that they had never felt before. People were out and stirring about, a lot of folks preparing no doubt to go to Mass. Despite the normality of the early morning rituals, things just did not seem the same. There were no soldiers visible on the streets. Children were out playing. People were waving and greeting each other with hearty "Bonjours," even to people they did not know. The air was pleasing, with a delicate touch of a light breeze off the Bay of Biscay.

Uncle Charles and his wife, Paulette, were already staying with Tomas's parents. Besides the Légeres, the Marigots had promised that they would also come over for breakfast. The four families—correction, five families, although it seemed too soon for Tomas to think of himself and Maggie as a family—would have their own worship service. And then, they would load Tomas's baggage, say their goodbyes, and drive out to the farm for a period of secluded pleasure until time to leave for Paris. In the meantime, while the couple occupied their home, his uncle and aunt would enjoy the pleasures of the city with Antoine and Martine, and most certainly would enjoy whatever activities La Rochelle had to offer. Charles, who was very knowledgeable of naval architecture, would take over Tomas's place on the design team for the corvair.

The manoir home was always well-stocked with much food, wine, and beer. With the exception of the servants left behind to cook and clean for them, they would have complete privacy to live and love as a married couple and do whatever they wished. Right now, life seemed very, very good.

Chapter 8
At the Manoir

Tomas and Maggie visited with their families until late afternoon, far longer than they had anticipated spending. By the time they left for the ride out to the manoir, the weather was changing. It was much colder than it had been in the morning, and storm clouds were already gathering. Tomas went ahead and lit the lanterns on the sides of the carriage. The manoir was not too far outside the city, but they would have to hurry if they had any chance of arriving before darkness completely settled over their way. With the heavy clouds hanging overhead threatening rain, there would almost certainly be no moonlight or stars to guide them. His parents had insisted that the young couple spend the night with them. They could have gone back to Maggie's home, or even spent the night with the Marigots, who lived very close to the Jardeens. But stubbornness and marital independence ruled their decision. They wanted so much to be alone; they wanted to be free from the social graces and interactions that were required in being part of a company of people. These feelings were reinforced by the alcohol they had consumed that afternoon with his parents. The midafternoon brunch served by the waitstaff at his parents' home was very filling, and they had eaten too much. Afterward, the men gathered in the library to smoke cigars and drink Cognac, while the women gravitated to the parlor for wine and conversation. Tomas had not smoked but just a few times before; however, he was glad to be included as part of the adult-male legion. Very soon, though, the effects of too much food, too much drink, and the smoke from the cigars had him feeling sick. As they were nearing the edge of the city, the sun was beginning to descend at their back. The wind was whipping through the trees. The houses were becoming fewer, but those which they saw through the trees and behind tall hedgerows were certainly bigger and grander than most of those closer into the city. As they got farther into the country, the chateaus and villas were protected by high stone walls and iron gates.

Suddenly, on a lonely stretch of the road, it seemed out of nowhere several steeds carrying soldiers came racing toward them. The horsemen pulled up just in front of the carriage and gave Tomas a signal to stop. Dismounting and walking over to the carriage while the others formed a protective shield, the officer began to ask Tomas a series of questions. Where was he heading? Why was he traveling at this time of day on such a lonely stretch of road? What was he carrying in his wagon? When Tomas and Maggie identified themselves, the officer instantly recognized the names and apologized for having inconvenienced them. He, of course, knew of their wedding the day before. And, without acknowledging it, he was also aware of the work being done at the shipyard, and the king's seal that had been granted to the Jardeens, resulting in the special protection that was to be given to the family and to the Légeres. Unaware of any special order of protection, Tomas loathed to tell the officer of their plans to stay at Uncle Charles's home, with just the servants around for several weeks, before proceeding on to Paris.

With an edge of nervousness, Tomas asked the officer, "Monsieur, is there a problem? Why have you stopped us?"

"There are robbers up ahead in the forest. Several coaches have been attacked today. It is best that you turn around and go back to the city," the officer told them.

"We are going to my uncle's farm. It is only so many more miles. It is late." Then, telling a little bit of a falsehood, Tomas said, "We are tired. We want to go to bed." That last part had some truth to it, but they had no intentions of sleeping.

"Of course, Monsieur Jardeen. We will escort you to your uncle's farm."

Tomas was not sure that he believed him, but at this point he did not have any options. "Thank you, Monsieur," he told the officer. "You and your superiors are very kind to protect us in such good fashion." Thinking to himself how much things had changed since that night when he and his father were accosted by soldiers and roughed up on their way to see Father Benedict, Tomas said, "We would be appreciative for your escort to my uncle's farm." Of course, Tomas was sure that the soldiers knew exactly how to get there, but as a matter of courtesy he still asked, "Do you know the location of the Jardeen manoir?"

"Yes, Monsieur, we have been there already this evening on our patrol. The servants are safe. I have left two of my soldiers at the farm for their protection."

"Merci," Tomas said. "I know that they will feel much safer with the protection of the king's soldiers."

"Shall we proceed?" the officer asked.

Tomas slapped the horses with his whip and the wagon began to move down the road, slowly at first, and then with increasing speed. The officer rode alongside the wagon, with a soldier riding in front and a soldier riding behind them. They moved swiftly down the road for about two miles. As they were getting near the farm, Tomas could see in the dimming evening light a bunch of logs and tree limbs across the road ahead of the carriage. The initial thought that crossed his mind was that the blockage had been made by the soldiers; he and Maggie had inevitably been duped. When he brought the carriage to a stop, four dirty, bedraggled men brandishing weapons sprang out of the bushes from the side of the road. Before they could even order Tomas and Maggie off the carriage, the soldiers had drawn their weapons and engaged them in combat. Two of the robbers were quickly slain by the slashing swords of the soldiers. The other two robbers attempted to run into the woods, but a well-placed shot from the officer's gun killed one of them. The other robber escaped. Maggie looked on in horror at the carnage that now lay on the ground, and felt sick to her stomach. The officer and one of the soldiers stayed behind to hunt for the escapee. The other soldier was ordered to take the couple to the farm and ensure their safety by remaining on guard until relieved. Tomas and the soldier cleared enough of the brush from the road so that the carriage could pass. Shortly, they reached the safety of the manoir. As the officer had stated, there was already a soldier in the watchtower guarding the entry into the compound. The soldier who escorted them signaled to the guard, and they were allowed through the gate. As soon as they were inside, the soldier who had been standing guard mounted his horse and hastily sped away back toward La Rochelle, without ever addressing Tomas and Maggie.

All the servants came out and enthusiastically greeted the couple. Tomas was a frequent visitor here, and was liked very much by the house staff. A young maid who looked to be several years younger than Maggie curtsied and greeted her as Madame Jardeen. Unbeknownst to Tomas, the maid had always thought him to be really cute, with a great sense of humor, and she even had a crush on him. Though still somewhat distracted and shaken up from the previous events, Maggie and he talked with her while two male servants unloaded the carriage and carried the baggage into the house, upstairs to the bedchamber. Maggie found the maid delightful and gave her a hug. No doubt, it was a very good way to start a lifelong business relationship with the young woman, who might one day, after they returned from Paris, come to work for her and Tomas.

The next morning, the lieutenant and the young soldier, who had ridden off in such a hurry the previous night, returned. They told Tomas that the robber who had escaped into the woods had been captured, along with an accomplice. He promised that his protective squad of soldiers would be sure to check on their safety while patrolling in the area. With that assurance, the officer and his subordinate rode away.

The service provided by the soldiers in this circumstance had been very helpful, and maybe had even saved their lives. Robbers like the ones who had accosted them worked those roads with the intent to kill or wound their victims, for no apparent reason other than to rob them of their money and jewels. They were blessed not to have been harmed. No doubt if the soldiers had not been present, Tomas would have been killed beside the coach. The harsh reality of this scenario would have found Maggie in the woods raped, and her fingers would have been chopped off with a saber for her new gold wedding ring. After this tortuous chain of events, they would have most likely killed her, or worse, left her to die. Tomas was chilled by the similarities between what could have happened to him and what Father Benedict had threatened him into secrecy with all those years ago. The coincidental nature of those two potentials sat with Tomas. The former scenario, considering it involved Maggie, was almost too unbearable for him to even think about.

For the remainder of their stay at the farm before leaving for Paris, the servant staff prepared them exquisite meals and they enjoyed ambrosial wines from Uncle Charles's large wine cellar. Tomas went around the farm doing odd jobs, not because he was expected to, but because it was fun. It was a change of pace for him, and he found it to be therapeutic. He and Maggie took long strolls through the fields and into the woods. They especially enjoyed the trail that took through the woods down to the river. They would venture down to watch the beavers and river otters playing with their young, while the males worked on expanding and reinforcing their lodging. Nature, an amazing phenomenon, was something that Maggie, being a city girl, did not often have a chance to observe. Being alone in the woods gave them the chance to be romantic and talk about their future. Maggie wanted to have children, but secretly hoped for a smaller family than Tomas did. They spent many an afternoon alone in the bedchamber, and usually escaped back there very soon after eating their dinner. Of course, it was French custom in the higher class of society to eat late, and most evenings they did not finish dinner until about ten o'clock or ten thirty.

Finally, after a very satisfying honeymoon on the farm, it was time to leave for Paris. One early morning near the middle of November, the servants loaded the couple's luggage onto the carriage. The sun was just dawning from the east; it sullenly rose over the forest. It was foggy, and they thought it would be nice to go back to bed. The weather had grown more like what would be expected in the middle of fall. This day there was a drizzling rain, and though it was certainly not a great day for traveling, they knew they must begin their trip. Taking Uncle Charles's finest coach and being driven by his uncle's most experienced coachman, as well as an armed security guard who would accompany them to Paris, they set off on their wedding trip. Since Tomas would not be driving, he and Maggie would be protected inside the carriage from the foul weather that was likely to take place this time of the year. Hopefully, things would improve as they moved away from the coast toward Paris, to the northeast. Much of the travel would be along muddy trails until they got closer to towns along the way. Closer to Paris the roads would be wider, but still filled in some places with ruts. They would have to be careful not to break an axle or wheel. Tomas was not too fearful of breakdowns, for the coach was well-built. The rims of the wheel were protected with sturdy new metal bands, and the axles were hand-honed from the finest hardwood and not likely to break; however, just as an added measure of security, the driver did carry in the back a spare axle and wheel. He was more comfortable with the idea of being safe rather than sorry. During the trip, he did daily inspections of the undercarriage whenever they stopped for food and lodging. Most towns, regardless of size, would have a blacksmith shop that could do repairs; they would be unlikely, however, to find a smithy in the countryside.

It was approximately 384 kilometers from the farm to Paris, or close to 230 miles. Tomas and Maggie planned to get up each morning before dawn, eat a hearty breakfast, and be on the road by sunrise, or soon after. Before they were ready to depart, the horses would have been fed and teamed up to the carriage. They needed to travel as far as possible each day before stopping that night in the nearest town to find lodging. However, they would always look out for chateaus or villas along the road that would take travelers in. Most places were strict in whom they allowed entry; this meant that they must be clean and well-dressed. Having a driver who wore a waistcoat, tie, and a top hat certainly indicated to the proprietors of these establishments that the guests were of the upper class, and in most cases a lineage of nobility. These unspoken requirements were ones that Maggie, Tomas, and their attendants all met.

The driver estimated that they could plan to travel about sixty-five to seventy kilometers each day, depending on the weather. This would provide ample time to rest and water the horses, and give them time to occasionally dismount from the carriage and stretch their legs. They would be able to get water for the horses from troughs in the small towns along the way, as well as from creeks, rivers, and canals that generally meandered near the road.

They hoped to make it to Niort that first day. It was about sixty kilometers from the farm. Maggie and Tomas were warmly wrapped in blankets inside of the carriage. For travel, Maggie wore a wool bonnet and a hand-knitted woolen shawl; Tomas was in tight wool knickers, knee-high riding boots, a wool coat, and a hat. His face was scraggly, for he had not shaved since the day they were married. His new beard and mustache were beginning to fill out enough so that soon he would be able to begin to shape them into a style that he wanted. Maggie was not certain of his growing facial hair. She was not sure that it looked right on her husband, and it tickled her when they kissed. But she loved her man, and pretended to like it. Maybe when it had fully developed, she would change her mind. It was coming in a slightly reddish-brown color, which was close in shade to Tomas's long, curly, auburn hair.

Once they were away from the coastal area along the Bay of Biscay, the drizzling rain stopped, and the sun began to melt away the fog. But it was still a rather cold, blustery day. The extra blankets felt really good. In fact, both the driver and the guard had wrapped blankets around their shoulders for protection from the chilly wind.

About five o'clock in the afternoon, as they were nearing the commune of Niort, darkness began to settle in on them. They came upon a lovely villa to the west of town. It was a two-story farmhouse with a number of dependencies, all enclosed by a relatively high stone fence that had a locked iron gate into the yard. The owner hung an oil lantern on the gate, the green light being cast from it the result of the tinting of the glass. In France, a green lantern hung on the gate signaled to travelers that the house took in guests, and that there were vacancies for the night. A tinted amber-colored lantern would indicate that they took guests, but there were no more vacancies.

After Tomas had given his approval, the driver stopped at the gate, got down, and shook the strap of cowbells which hung on the fence beside the lantern. The gentleman of the house came out to converse with the horseman, who then returned to the wagon to speak with Tomas. The price of lodging for the night, dinner this evening, and breakfast in the morning would be three silver francs, one each for Tomas and Maggie, and a half-franc each for the coachman and the guard. The price of feeding and stabling the horses would be a half-franc, or fifty centimes. The silver franc coin had been introduced in France earlier in that year, and replaced the gold franc coin that had been in use since 1360. Tomas agreed, and the horseman reported to the innkeeper that yes, they would like to spend the night. By this time, the owner's hunting dog, a Braque du Bourbonnais, had joined them. The dog was a large, fawn-colored female with brown ears. Although not seeming aggressive, she insistently stood between Tomas and her master, keeping Tomas at a safe distance. The innkeeper let the carriage through the gate and then locked it again for the night. Once inside the house, André, the innkeeper, introduced his wife, Maureen, and showed them to their room. The driver brought in their essential baggage, along with the small, locked, iron coffin box in which they kept their money, Maggie's jewels, perfume, and Tomas's pistol. Tomas paid the innkeeper with money he carried on him. Their room had a four-poster canopy bed topped with fluffy pillows, stuffed with down and feathers from the geese on the farm and mixed with wool sheared from local sheep. There was a dressing vanity and an armoire for their clothes. The driver and guard would be staying in a sparsely furnished room in the carriage house. The stable was conveniently located to the side of the carriage house. Tomas and Maggie would eat dinner with the owner and his wife; their attendants would have their dinner in an area just off the kitchen.

Dinner was a simple but delicious meal. There was a thick barley-based soup and bread to begin the meal, followed by baked venison, killed by the owner. It had been cured in the smokehouse. There was a green vegetable cooked with some pork for seasoning, and potatoes which had been stored in the potato cellar. Venison was not a meat that Maggie particularly enjoyed, but this time it was actually very tasty and satisfying. The wine and conversation were both good. The farm had been the family estate of André, the owner. Maureen was from nearby Niort, and her mother's brother had owned the adjacent farm to this one. She had visited her uncle often, and had played with André during those visits. She had begun to attract his romantic interests when he was sixteen and she was just fourteen. She never loved anyone other than André, and they had married when she was just eighteen years old. Their two sons lived independently on the farm, and assisted in the farming duties and the winemaking. Their children were now all grown and married. Besides the two sons living on the farm, they had two daughters who married men from Paris. One of these daughters had died several years before, giving birth to her fourth child. They had three other children living nearby in the commune of Niort.

The couple was sorrowful that they did not get to see their grandchildren from Paris as often as they would like. The children usually visited in the summer, and sometimes at Christmas. However, it seemed unlikely that they would be coming this year.

Now, it was just them with their two sons, farmers just trying to make the best of life. André had been left an inheritance. Although they were living comfortably, the income from innkeeping helped to keep up the house and dependencies. Since they were located on a main road into Niort, they usually had several guests; but tonight, probably because of the bad weather in the morning, there were only Tomas and Maggie.

Although the two sons were largely responsible for running the estate, profits from the sale of the crops and the winemaking had to be split three ways. Several hectares were set aside for growing their own food, and several hectares were rented out to other farmers. They had six cows which supplied milk for drinking and cooking, as well as for churning butter. There were a number of hogs and sows, with lots of piglets. Additionally, there was a herd of cows grazing in a pretty large, fenced-in field, and bulls penned in a high fence closer to the compound. From all indications, the family was self-sufficient as to raising their own food.

André was an avid hunter and always kept the smokehouse full of meat, either hanging up, or packed in salt or sugar in wooden barrels. They also grew flowers, which they sold in town during the growing season. Up until now, the summer and fall had seen good weather, which produced bountiful flowers and plants for sale. Now they were selling fall flowers, and planning was underway for selling Noël wreaths and loose garlands at the Niort market.

They seemed in reasonably good health.

Talk eventually turned to a religious discussion; the religious symbols and meaning of the Nativity scene which would soon be displayed for Noël were brought up. From things said, Tomas suspected that they were practicing Huguenots, but he did not bring the matter up, nor did he reveal much about himself, or about Maggie and her family. Having just met these people, he felt that it was no doubt better to listen than to say too much. Besides, conversation was not limited, as they seemed very willing to share the details of their life. Tomas figured that they were just hardworking, lonely people who were yearning to see their children and grandchildren more often than seemed to be the case. Other than showing interest in the fact that Tomas and Maggie were newly married and on their way to Paris, and some discussion about La Rochelle, André and Maureen seemed content to talk about themselves and did not pry deeply into the lives of their guests.

When they came down the next morning, the driver and the guard had already eaten. While Tomas and Maggie had a hearty breakfast of buckwheat cakes with churned butter, freshly laid eggs, homemade sausage, and fresh milk that had been chilled overnight in the overflow of cold water in the springhouse, the driver tended the horses and teamed them up to the carriage. When they were finished with breakfast, Tomas and the attendants loaded the baggage and said their goodbyes to the innkeepers.

The road into and out of the commune of Niort followed the Sèvre Niortaise, a gently flowing river. It followed a course of 158 kilometers from near Sepvret into the Atlantic Ocean at Bourg-Chapon, a small town just north of La Rochelle. The commune itself lay on the banks of the river, on the slope of two hills which faced each other from opposite sides of the river. It was overshadowed by a medieval castle built by Henry II of England and his son, Richard I,[27] known as the Lionhearted. The two square towers of the castle dominated the view of the town. Near the castle stood the Catholic cathedral, construction of which was begun in the 1400s and was still not completely finished. Building of the Catholic cathedral in Niort had been delayed by the strong legions of Huguenots that had gathered in Niort from the early days of the Protestant Reformation. The growing number of Protestants had negatively affected the finances of the Catholic Church. It was also reported that Huguenots had carried out attacks of vandalism and acts of desecration on the cathedral. Reports of such behavior by Protestant brethren made Tomas and Maggie angry. They felt that violence among Christians and their institutions, regardless of one's beliefs and practices, was morally wrong and a sin in the eyes of God. They left town feeling very ponderous over what the future would hold in store for them, and all Protestants in France.

The driver expected to arrive in Poitiers by early evening. Poitiers was fifty kilometers from Niort, or about thirty-one miles. Even before the Roman influence, the area had been populated by the Celtic Pictones Tribe. During their occupation there, the Romans built baths, a large amphitheater, a burial site, aqueducts, and a large dolmen, a tomb-like structure made of stone. The Roman structures gave significance to Poitiers as a town of major importance, and possibly even as a provincial Roman capital called Gallia Aquitania.[28] By 1575, these Roman edifices were pretty much in ruins.

From 1418 to 1436, the royal parliament of France moved to Poitiers from Paris because of the occupation of the capital city by English forces. During this time, Gypsies and witches in the area were hanged in the town square or burned at the stake.

There were many Calvinist converts in Poitiers, and battles were fought there between Protestants and Catholics. One such battle had taken place as recently as 1569. In this battle, Gui de Daillon defended the city for seven weeks against the attack by the Huguenot Gaspard de Coligny, who withdrew after an unsuccessful bombardment of the city.

It was a common practice in France for the mayor and town officials to swear their allegiance and support to the king. In return, the king gave them local authority over the town. Thus, this sworn relationship gave the mayor and his officials control over the citizenry of the town. Any person who challenged their authority was challenging the authority of the king. In 1567, King Henri III, along with his large entourage of personal assistants and government officials, made a visit to the city. Some of his entourage displayed bad behavior and rudeness while there, arousing the ire of the local residents. Rather than dealing with the complaints in a heavy-handed way, Henri addressed the residents in a speech given in the town's public square. He defused the issue by tactfully acknowledging and thanking the residents for their loyalty and generous support.

Tomas and Maggie stayed at a small hotel near the center of town. The driver found a stable for the horses and an adjacent carriage house where he and the guard spent the night after having a few beers in a bar just down the street. The meal which Tomas and Maggie had in the hotel was less elegant than even the one they had the night before in Niort, but tasty. They had a beef pie and some fall vegetables. It was something like a shepherd's pie, which they had heard was a common dish in England. The local claret wine, though, was excellent. It was rather cold that night, but the wine and the warm covers of the bed ensured a good night of rest.

The next stop on the road to Paris would be Tours, located in the lower Loire Valley between the River Loire and the River Cher. From there they would travel to Paris, staying in Orleans along the way. These communes were too far apart for the driver to go from one to another in one day. It would potentially be several days of hard travel from one to the other. Paris was at least four or five days' journey. They would be required to spend some nights in whatever small country villages they came across along the way. Because of the vast distances between the cities, there was a chance of being attacked and robbed in those unpopulated areas. It would be important to find lodging every night before dark; the daylight seemed shorter each day, as the fall season was quickly advancing on to winter. It had become a race to get to Paris. Maggie was complaining in the mornings of not feeling well. She also could not seem to appease her appetite, nor could she find energy to carry herself through each day. Finally, in Orleans, she told her husband that she did not feel that she could travel on to Paris immediately; she needed to rest for a while. As inexperienced as she was in such matters, she suspected that she was pregnant. Based on discussions she had through the years with her mother, she felt positive that she was showing the quintessential symptoms. However, she was cautious in discussing her suspicion with Tomas until a physician had confirmed her pregnancy.

Tomas and Maggie found a nice hotel in Orleans that had a small apartment suite. Tomas arranged stabling and quarters for both their driver and their guard at a livery just down the street from the hotel. Maggie rested for the better part of each day, but the fresh air from an afternoon walk always lifted her spirits and seemed to make the nausea subside. Tomas sought care and eventually found a doctor with a good reputation who agreed to see her. Once she described the symptoms she was experiencing and acknowledged that she was, in fact, a newlywed, Dr. Pontel suggested that she might be with child. Maggie felt hesitant when he asked her to undress so that he could examine her. She had never been naked before a man, except for her father when she was a child and with Tomas. But she was reassured by the doctor's fatherly manner and his gentleness while doing the exam. He told Maggie that she was in the first stage of pregnancy; his consultation was that she could only be just a couple of weeks. With events now whirling around in her head, Maggie guessed that conception occurred during the stay at Uncle Charles's farm. Dr. Pontel said that she should rest a couple of days in Orleans, and then she might continue the trip to Paris. He left her with sage advice to carry with her throughout her pregnancy. His list read as follows: "Eat well, get plenty of sleep, stop travel early in the evening, and for the rest of the pregnancy, be sure to consume as much dairy as possible. So, drink a lot of milk and eat a lot of cheese. This will keep your bones strong and make your baby healthy. You will, however, need to refrain from wine." He urged her, "Be sure to find yourself a fine doctor when you arrive in Paris." And finally, he left her with, "It will be safe to have sexual relations with your husband until a month or two before it is time for the baby to be born." Then he emphasized, "Just don't overdo it!"

As Dr. Pontel spoke, Maggie's brain spun with various emotions. She knew that any doubts she felt would fade by the excitement of her parents and her in-laws. She was already experiencing relief knowing of the great joy and the love that Tomas would feel. She could not wait to tell him that he had fathered a baby . . . a real human being. Walking back to the hotel and holding hands, Maggie told Tomas that they would have to stay in Orleans for a few days; the doctor had instructed that she get rest before going on to Paris. He had suspicions, which especially stirred as she told him about her having to drink milk and eat cheese, but he did not want to spoil the joy that she would surely get from telling him. Once they were back in their little apartment at the hotel, Maggie embraced her husband. She told him how much she loved him and whispered in a voice filled with emotion, "I am pregnant with your baby."

Before she could go on, and while excitedly firing questions at her, Tomas lifted her up and laid her on the bed. The news seemed too incredulous to be true. Without thinking, he asked, "How did this happen?" This was a question that Maggie was sure she did not need to answer. He continued without pause, "When is the baby due? Are you okay? What are we going to name him?" The questions were coming too fast.

She tried to answer, "Late July . . . Yes . . . It might not be a boy . . . It just might be a beautiful baby girl."

Then, Tomas said the sweetest, most loving thing that Maggie had ever wanted to hear. "It doesn't matter whether it is a boy or a girl. The most important thing is you and the baby are healthy. You are going to be a great mother!" In that moment, she knew she truly loved Tomas more than ever, and just wanted to be held in his arms.

And then she whispered, "And you are going to be a great father."

Chapter 9
Return Home

Tomas and Maggie had a difficult decision to make. At most, they were just a few days from Paris. But they had to consider what was best for her health, and that of their infant she was carrying. They wanted very much to go on to Paris, but returning home to La Rochelle seemed the more viable option. Given the approaching winter and the knowledge that they might be snowbound if they were to return in December, they decided the trip to Paris was not a good idea. They planned to stay in Orleans for two to three days and then return home. There was a lot for them to see, some nice restaurants to try, an opera house, and even some theaters with local musicians and can-can dancers. Besides, it was probably safer at night than in Paris. Surely there would be many wonderful times ahead when they could eventually visit "Gay Paree."

Even though there was a postal rider coming through Orleans every third day, going from Paris to La Rochelle, they decided not to post a letter to their parents. They did not want to tell them yet about the pregnancy, nor did they wish to raise issues and concerns about the cancellation of the trip to Paris. They would just show up one day back home and then explain everything.

The first thing that Tomas did was give the driver and guard money to go out and find more comfortable quarters for them. He looked to either rent a small cottage or find lodging at an estate outside of town. Maggie gave her husband the names of a couple of books for him to find that she would like to read. A lot of women of the time did not read, because they did not have the education. Maggie, of course, had studied at the Sorbonne and enjoyed immensely her studies in music, literature, and French history. She was interested in countries other than France—especially Italy and Spain—but right now in her condition, reading in a foreign language would be difficult and not pleasurable.

Paris had its first printing press more than a hundred years before in 1470, and another press had been introduced in Lyon in 1473. Since then, there had been an explosion of French literature and poetry. The presses had allowed the development of humanism and Neoplatonism in French writing. The writers were showing increasing interest in love. Both psychological and moral analyses were evident in their writings. Books about the etiquette of the Italian and the French royal courts had begun to affect that of the aspiring class-conscious citizenry below the level of nobility.

Poetry that had been written until that point in the sixteenth century consisted mostly of love sonnets incorporating skillful and complex wordplay. There was also the evolution of the sonnet cycle to include amorous paradoxes. The rediscovery of Greek poets had begun to have a major influence on French poets.

One of Maggie's favorite poets, Pierre de Ronsard,[30] penned *Les Amours de Cassandre CXCIII* in 1552. She had fallen in love with Ronsard's previous works and was eager to get a full collection of his love poems.

Ronsard was born in 1524 and had a notable reputation as a humanist inspired by classical culture, but sought to create uniquely French literature. Writing with an almost musical lilt, his poetry was sensuous and romantic. Much of his work had been specially written for the royal court.

Cassandre CXCIII was at the top of the shopping list that she gave to Tomas.

While out that afternoon, Tomas saw several soldiers stopping people on the street and questioning them to see if they were Huguenots. He avoided them by ducking into shops and browsing the merchandise. Finally, he managed to find a bookery and spent a considerable amount of time browsing the shelves. He engaged in a pointed conversation with the proprietor about religious writings. During the discussion, it became clear to the owner that Tomas was a Huguenot, though he did not say. He knew that Tomas needed protection from the soldiers outside. He locked the front door and put up a closed sign in the window. He motioned for Tomas to follow him, and they went into a back room of the store. "Mon ami, you are in danger. I will take you back to your hotel in my carriage." Opening a cabinet, he took out the book of poetry by Ronsard. Giving it to Tomas, he said, "This is the only volume I have of the beautiful poetry written by Ronsard. Please accept it as a gift from me to your wife and to your unborn daughter."

Suddenly choked with emotion, Tomas fumbled for the right words. "Merci, you are very kind, but I cannot accept your gift. It is not right that you give me the only book that you have of this poet."

The owner replied, "Please, if it is God's will that I live, I will get other copies. If I am to die, it is important that you and your wife have this book." Tomas thanked him with deep gratitude, and told him he was sure that Maggie would get great pleasure from it for the rest of her life.

"But," Tomas asked, "how do you presume to know that my wife is pregnant with a girl?" The shop owner thought for a few seconds while he hastily scribbled something on a piece of paper. Smiling, he took the book back from Tomas, opened it, and slipped the paper between the pages in the middle.

Giving the book back to Tomas, he said, "My son, there are many mysteries in this world . . . some of which we may never understand. The wonder of the creation of new life and the mystery of parenthood are beyond realism. I know that you are married and that your lovely wife is pregnant with child, because I have seen you and her together several times here in Orleans. I was having dinner the other night at the café at the hotel. It was obvious that the two of you are very much in love. I overheard you talking about what to do and your decision to go home. She had the beautiful radiance that pregnant women always seem to have. Your unborn baby must be a girl, for a woman that loves romantic poetry so much will surely have many girl children. I have not been wrong too many times in my life.

"Now, we must go. It is getting late and it will not be safe tonight. The soldiers are already roaming the streets. Things may get violent when it gets dark." With some stress in his voice, he continued, "Come, hurry, out the back door." The carriage was just outside. "Quick, get in, lie down on the seat, and pull the blanket over you. No one should see you." Tomas did as he was ordered. Quickly, the shop owner locked the huge lock on the back door, jumped up onto the driver's seat, and drove off as if everything was okay. In a short time, the carriage stopped in front of the hotel. After looking around to see that no soldiers were watching, the owner whispered back to Tomas that all was safe.

Thanking the gentleman several times and tightly clutching his book of poetry, Tomas hurried into the hotel and up to his room. He wasn't quite sure of what had just happened to him, but he was relieved to be back in Maggie's arms. Everything had happened so fast that he had forgotten about the piece of paper that the man had slipped into the book. Maggie was so excited that he had been able to find Ronsard's work. She gave him a big hug, a kiss, and said several times how much she loved him.

It was nearing dusk and Maggie was already hungry. Due to the warning about the soldiers being out tonight, Tomas felt that it would be safer to have their dinner in the hotel. There were only a few people dining that night. They ordered cheese and bread to start with. Maggie ordered milk, but Tomas ordered wine for himself. Later, they ordered bowls of a hearty beef stew, more bread and butter, and some fruit. Over dinner, Tomas told his wife about his experiences that afternoon with the gift of the book, and with what the shop owner had said to him about the baby. The story she was hearing seemed so incredulous that when he told her about the prediction that the baby was a girl, she thought surely that Tomas was making it up to make her feel good. But when he told her about the shop owner quickly closing the store and driving him to the hotel, she began to worry. She wanted to meet this person who had befriended her husband.

"Please," she begged, "tomorrow, will you take me to the bookshop so that I can meet this man?"

The next day, after a breakfast of French bread, some soft curdled cheese, eggs, a piece of sausage, and milk, the driver and the guard showed up on schedule with their coach. Tomas told them that later that morning they would need to be taken to the bookstore; then, they would want to take a ride into the country to look at a villa at which they might be able to stay for a while.

Maggie had been unable to eat all of her breakfast. Just looking at the greasy sausage on Tomas's plate made her feel sick. She excused herself from the table and went back to the room to lie down. Tomas stayed behind and had some more coffee while his attendants ate breakfast.

When the waiter came over to the table to see if there was anything else that Tomas needed, he mentioned a fire in town last night. Tomas said that he had slept soundly through the night and did not know anything that may have happened. "It was the bookseller's shop," the waiter told him. "It happened so quickly. The soldiers did it. The bookseller lived in rooms above the store. They broke in and dragged him down to the street. He resisted as much as he could. Finally, they held him back while they lit torches to burn the building. He begged the soldiers not to do it. While it was burning, the shop owner was forced to confess his Huguenot beliefs. The soldiers threw him to the ground and held a sabre to his heart. They told him to stop his prayer, to renounce his Huguenot beliefs, and to swear allegiance to the Catholic Church. He refused them three times and they ran the saber through his heart. He was praying when he died on the street. Then they torched his body."

Tomas was overcome with emotion. He turned pale and was visibly shaking. Thinking to himself of how that man had probably saved his life last night, he wondered if the soldiers knew that he too was a Huguenot, and were watching for him and Maggie. Did his friend know that they were in danger? The hard realization that immediately flashed through his mind was that somehow Maggie, his attendants, and he must get out of town and back to La Rochelle, quickly and in secret. He told the driver and guard to continue with their breakfasts, and Tomas hurried back to his room with the horrendous news.

Maggie was all but overwhelmed with anguish when Tomas told her what he had heard. Near tears, Tomas remembered the piece of paper that the shop owner had slipped into the book. He grabbed it off the nightstand and fanned the pages until it dropped out. It said, "I am a Catholic sworn to the Reformed Church, and I know that you are also of the Reformed faith. Our lives are in great danger. They know about you and your lovely wife. Do not remain here in Orleans. You must leave, or they will kill you!" It was signed:

May God bless you always,
Robért, His servant, the lover of books and all things beautiful.

Maggie was horrified. She broke down and began to sob uncontrollably. After Tomas was able to calm her, they were uncertain of when they could leave the city and how they would escape without being detained. They went downstairs, and bringing the container with their money and Maggie's jewelry, they found their driver and guard waiting for them. "Let's go and look for a villa," Tomas told them in a hushed but excitable voice. He was overcome with fear for his life, and those of his wife's and child's.

After assisting Maggie into the coach and telling the guard to sit in the coach with Maggie, Tomas swung himself up beside the driver. In a quiet voice, so as not to be overheard by people standing nearby, he instructed his driver, "Drive very gently out of the city." Once they were moving, he told the driver, "Take the road back toward La Rochelle." Tomas watched carefully to see if they were being followed, but he did not see anything suspicious. They passed the burnt-down bookstore and saw bloodstains on the ground in front. A sign had already been posted. It simply read, "By order of the king." Everything that happened those days had been blamed on the king. Tomas knew that the king did not have any knowledge of what had happened the night before. But the most important issue, he mused to himself, was whether the king, if he were to know, would even care.

When they got into the forest at the edge of the city, Tomas motioned for his driver to stop. He and the driver got down from the coach and stood beside the carriage so that they could talk. The driver was about to light up his pipe for a smoke when two soldiers galloped up. Dismounting from their steeds, they addressed Tomas, "Monsieur, is there a problem?"

"No," Tomas told them. Trying not to be apprehensive, he continued, "We have stopped for a brief rest."

Opening the door to the coach, what appeared to be the senior officer asked, "Who is this woman?"

Making eye contact with the officer, Tomas told him, "She is my wife."

The next words out of the officer's mouth were, "If she is your wife, then who is the man with her?"

"He is the relief driver," Tomas told him.

"What is your destination?" the man asked, somewhat brusquely.

Without revealing the real purpose of their journey, Tomas told him, "We are staying in Orleans. It is such a beautiful day that we are taking a leisurely drive into the country. We are going to look for a nice place to dine and have some wine. We will return to the city before dark." With that, the soldiers wished them a good day, turned around, and slowly rode back in the direction of the city. After they were out of sight, the soldiers stopped to wait until dark, to see if they did indeed return to the city.

At dinner the previous evening, they had discussed matters that, perhaps without thinking, could incriminate them. He had thought that what they were discussing was a private conversation and that no one had overheard, but obviously he was wrong. Perhaps the waiter or someone else had listened. Could his driver be in league with the soldiers, or perhaps been overheard at some tavern the night before? This thinking, he thought, was a real stretch, but one could never be sure. He would have to put this out of his mind if he and Maggie were to safely return to La Rochelle. He needed the driver and the guard.

Reflecting back on their travels so far, Tomas remembered a chateau on the way into Orleans from Tours. When they had first passed by, there was an amber lantern swinging from the gate, indicating that they took guests, but that they were full at that time. It would not matter today, for it was not yet time to make a move. They would talk to the owner and see what could be arranged for several days later. In the meantime, Maggie, the driver, and he would return to Orleans as if nothing was afoot. They would not want to give the soldiers any reason to suspect that they were planning to flee from the city.

They found the chateau not too much farther down the road. There was a tall brick wall around the house, with a heavy iron gate. Out back, beyond the fence, there was a vineyard that obviously went with the chateau. It spread out in back almost as far as the eye could see; posts dug into the ground and strung wire in between the vines. The vines must have been bountiful, with luscious red or black grapes in the summertime. Now they were dormant and brown, enmeshed along the wire which held them up. Tomas imagined the hundreds of gallons of good claret wine which these vines must produce every year. The owner and his workers would be working hard during the winter to get the vines trimmed and fertilized for spring. Spring was Tomas's favorite time of the year. Everything appeared to come to life in the springtime. The air itself would seem new, and there always seemed to be new stirrings in him to achieve and fulfill the promises that life had to offer. This time around, it would be fun to watch Maggie's abdomen grow, now that she was carrying this new life that he had been a partner in creating. But at the moment, those were just dreams. The reality was that it was now getting late into the month of November 1575. He was not sure of the exact date, or even, for that matter, the day of the week; he had completely lost track of time. What he did know, however, was that he and Maggie were probably in danger and they must get back to La Rochelle.

Arriving at the inn, the lantern on the gate had changed from amber to green. Tomas rang the brass bell at the gate. The owner soon came out and, after exchanging pleasantries, invited them to come in. Eager to get the coach out of sight and hidden away in the stable, Tomas negotiated a price to stable and feed their tired horses. While the driver was taking care of the horses, the owner invited them to have some wine and a late lunch with him and his family. Gladly, they accepted, and made arrangements for the driver and guard to eat with the servants.

The owner and his wife were sure they had met Tomas and Maggie before, but that was impossible, for the couple had stayed at an inn just the other side of Niort when coming to Orleans. Perhaps, however, they may have passed on the street in town.

That day, the owner's grown son and his wife were visiting with several of their well-mannered grandchildren, including a young teenage boy and a preteen girl. The son and his family lived nearby on the estate and managed the winemaking operation. Tomas was told that another brother, who was not at the house that day, managed the grape-growing, and there was another brother who managed the farming of the other crops. All in all, the farm seemed to be a large family operation. Besides the three brothers living on the farm, they were told that there were other children in Paris and Tours. One daughter had married an Italian and lived in Venice. Her husband was an accomplished glassblower and owned half of a large, decorative glassmaking company on one of the islands in the Bay of Venice. She and most of her children had died from the plague that had recently swept through Venice. Only two of their grandchildren, both boys, had survived with their father, and were being trained in the art of glassblowing. The owner explained that the making of beautiful glassware with many different colors and designs is a skill that a person must begin to develop as a child, and is honed throughout a lifetime. Their other daughter had married an artist in Paris and had several children.

As the owners related to them about their large family, Tomas suddenly realized the enormity of responsibility with being married and raising a family. He realized that he had never fully understood the sanctity of life, and the delicate threads by which all human beings hang. He was especially glad of the personal relationship with God that his reformed religion provided him. He wondered about this family, and what religion had gotten them through so much travail. He dared not ask. If they were converts to the Reformed church, they would sooner or later hopefully say something that would confirm this; in turn, he would be invited to declare his religious practices to them.

When they sat down for lunch, the owner offered a prayer of thanksgiving; he thanked God for the many blessings and tender mercies that He had given to the family. He thanked Him for bringing Tomas and Maggie to their home, and asked for a safe journey for them back to Orleans; he thanked him for the food being set before them. He ended the prayer by thanking God for his strength and good health to serve Him. Tomas immediately recognized this as the signal, but he waited. Finally, while dessert was being served, he casually mentioned the horrific murder that took place the night before in Orleans. The owner and his wife seemed interested in the details. Tomas told them what had happened. He talked of how he had met Robért, the bookshop owner. He spoke of his kindness, and how Robért's death had etched what he knew would be a lifelong memory for him. He told them about the note, but omitted details that would imply that Maggie and he were Huguenots. It did not matter; the owner already knew. He told Tomas and Maggie, "You are in grave danger! How can I help you?" As Tomas was telling him their plans to go back to Orleans that afternoon, his driver came into the house and told him that the same soldiers whom they had seen before had stopped at the house.

"They looked around trying to see the carriage and the horses," the driver stated, and continued, "I had them safely hidden away in the stable. They pulled on the wrought-iron gate but found it locked. I am sure that they did not see me. They talked for a few minutes and then left on their horses, heading toward Orleans."

"You cannot go back to Orleans," the owner immediately told them. "You must stay here for a few days; you must stay hidden from view. They will think that they have lost you. There are enough carriage tracks on the road and through my gate that they will not suspect you are here. But you must remain in the house. Your driver and guard will stay in the house with you. My son will take care of your horses." There was what seemed like a long silence, but the pause only lasted a few seconds. The owner continued, "I have a plan to get you safely back to La Rochelle." Tomas felt a sigh of relief. "The soldiers will most likely be patrolling the main road very heavily," the farmer told him. "Theo, my son, is an expert horseman and driver. I am going to have him drive you to La Rochelle on back roads that the soldiers never use. They probably do not know that they even exist. These roads are not in as good of shape as the main road out front. We will change your identity. We have new clothes, as well as wigs, for you and your wife. You will leave your coach and take mine. With Theo, and your guard to relieve him when necessary, we will have you back home in just a few days. I have friends along the way who will take you in and give you food and lodging. Theo knows where to find them. For their safety, do not tell them your real names, or that you know me. The local soldiers know my son, but by the time you reach the next village, he will be a stranger to the soldiers farther along the route. Until you reach La Rochelle, you will only be known as Gilles. Your lovely wife will be called Justine. Theo will be known as Pierre. Once you are back in La Rochelle, Theo and your guard will return here. In a few days, your driver and guard will drive your coach back to La Rochelle. Do not take chances! Don't try to travel at night, for that will raise suspicion. Please, my son will take good care of you. He will stop for the night at places along the way that he knows to be safe, with people we can trust."

It was hard to sleep that night. Tomas had time to reflect on the terrible injustice that had happened in Orleans. His anger at the government and at the Catholic Church was more overpowering than ever. It ate at his gut. Sleep was slow to come. But when he finally did find sleep, the crowing of the rooster out by the stable seemed too early. However, the owner was there soon knocking on the door, telling him that breakfast was almost ready.

As the innkeeper had warranted, the next two days were spent entirely with them in the house while Theo cared for their horses, along with the proprietor's own horses. Theo, whom they must now refer to as Pierre, the son who would drive them to La Rochelle, came over each day to go over the details of their escape. Tomas had never been on the roads that Pierre outlined. He asked permission to bring two of his children, a young teenage boy and a preteen girl, to sit in the carriage with Tomas and Maggie. He told them that bringing the children would provide a sense of a family dynamic to the situation. This, hopefully, would alter the expectation of what the soldiers thought to find, if they were indeed so unlucky as to have the coach detained along the way. That was not likely, however, unless it happened as they neared La Rochelle. On the last night before they were to leave, the innkeeper went to Pierre's house to spend the night with his daughter-in-law and the rest of her family, while Pierre and his two youngest children stayed at the inn. They wanted to leave early. This time, they would break the rule about traveling in the dark, for it would be wise to disengage from the inn with a lower chance of being seen. The soldiers had been slowly riding by on the road out front many times over the past several days, pausing but never dismounting. Steps had been taken to ensure signs of normalcy. The Jardeens and their attendants had stayed out of sight, and the innkeeper, along with his family, had made a point of just going about their everyday activities as usual. It was a game that Tomas had learned to play well, but one in which Maggie had little skill in playing. She was afraid, and the fear showed with her increasing irritability.

The wife of the innkeeper fed them well before they were to leave, and fixed a basket of food for them to take on the trip. Pierre went out the back door to the stable and got his father's coach hooked up to the horses. Another of his father's horses was tied to the back of the coach as a spare in the case that a lead horse might break a leg in a washed-out gully, or otherwise get injured on the trip. This type of thinking could prove to be good. Tomas would never have thought of such.

Next, Tomas's guard slipped out to the barn; Pierre and he slowly drove over to the back door, getting as close to the door as possible. Tomas and Maggie, dressed in their new clothes and wearing the wigs provided to them, and the children slipped through the door, into the darkness and into the coach. As Pierre's mother and Tomas's driver, who was being left behind, waved goodbye from the door, the coach drove through the back gate; it stopped momentarily as Pierre jumped down to close and lock the gate. Moments later, they were slowly traveling down a fairly narrow path, dividing the fields of dormant grapevines. The soldiers, who were still asleep in their camp just down the main road from the house, remained oblivious. Once they were out of the field, the road continued into a trail through the forest. They went a short distance until they found that it was safe enough, protected by the woods all around them, to light the lanterns on the side of the coach. They had escaped without incident from the farm. The trail followed a small creek for at least a mile until they came to a wider, yet still backcountry, road. By this time dawn was breaking, and the sunlight beaming through the trees lit the road enough so the lanterns could be extinguished. Pierre expertly swung a left, and they were on their way home to La Rochelle.

Chapter 10
On the Back Roads

While Tomas, Maggie, and the children sat in the coach, Tomas's guard sat up on the buckboard and talked with Pierre as he expertly navigated the team of horses through the bumps and ruts on the road. They were well-dressed for protection from the cold. This morning, clouds were gathering in the sky ahead of them, and the air had a biting chill to it. Pierre asked the guard to take the reins, while he filled his pipe with tobacco and lit it. The guard politely refused Pierre's offer to share his bag of tobacco. "Later," the guard told him. "Right now, I am content to breathe the soft, aromatic smell of your burning tobacco."

Before long, they passed through a small village without stopping. Residents were just beginning to stir outside of their homes, and the few shopkeepers in the village were readying their shops to open by putting merchandise outside for display and sale. Pierre knew almost everyone there. He waved and called out, "Bonjour," to each of his friends as they drove through the village.

Storm clouds had been gathering all morning. By noon the sky was dark, and the wind had picked up considerably. Soon the rain had begun to come down, though not too hard at first. Pierre stopped and told the guard to get into the coach before he was soaked by the downpour that was sure to come. Fortunately, they made it to the shelter of a blacksmith shop in a small village near Poitou before the storm turned into a torrential downpour. The smithy, named Matthieu, with whom Pierre was well-acquainted, was glad to see them; he invited them into his home that was next door to his shop. Maggie liked him instantly. He was a big, burly man, with tousled black hair and a wide handlebar mustache. He appeared to have not shaved for several days. Although Matthieu recognized Theo on sight, he did not recognize the name Pierre. The matter was clarified when Theo took him aside and simply said, "Don't ask why, but you must call me Pierre on this trip through your village. I will tell you and your wife the details later, but, as a matter of security for me and my friends, you must not call me Theo or ever acknowledge that I came through here with a young married couple."

"I understand," he replied. "Though the soldiers do not come through often, I will remember what you have told me . . . just in case."

Just as they were finishing their conversation, Matthieu's robust wife appeared and immediately gave Maggie a big hug, welcoming her into their home and insisting that they all stay for lunch. Maggie was not feeling very well, so the invite sounded very appealing. With conversation, lunch went on far longer than they had expected. As it was still raining heavily, perhaps even heavier than when they first arrived, Matthieu asked, "Why don't you spend the night with us and get a fresh start tomorrow morning? You can have the house to yourselves, and my family will stay with friends in the village."

Before Tomas could even speak, Maggie promptly said, "Merci beaucoup, that is very inviting. We would like that very much. Your hospitality is very generous."

"Good, then it is done. I will get your bags from the carriage," the blacksmith replied.

Befuddled and with a look of surprise, which turned to consternation, Tomas did not know what to say.

"Is there a problem?" Matthieu asked.

Pierre seized the conversation and said, "Please, let me explain. There are only my clothes and the children's." Contrary to what had been agreed upon back at the inn, he decided to relate the entire story of the Jardeens, as it had been told to him, and explained his temporary name change, clarifying the issue he had just addressed to Matthieu. "So, you see," he continued, "my new friends may be in danger, and I am trying to get them safely back to La Rochelle. They had to escape from Orleans with just the clothes they were wearing. They could not go back for their bags. Fortunately, the soldiers have not yet found us."

Tomas then hesitantly asked the couple, "What is your religious practice?"

"We are Huguenots as well. We forewent our Catholic beliefs more than three years ago and now follow the Reformist beliefs and practices of France's native son, Jean Cauvin. We refuse to refer to him as John Calvin. However, by whatever name you may call him, we surely converted for the same reasons as you."

A long conversation ensued about their beliefs, during which Melvin and Agnés, Pierre's children, began to get sleepy. Finally, the wife said to Pierre, "Let's pray, and then we must get the children to bed."

His wife then quickly took charge. Addressing Tomas and Maggie, she offered, "You and the children will stay here in the house tonight. My husband and I will stay with friends, and you will take our bedroom. The children will sleep in the guest room." Calling Theo by his familiar name, she said, "Theo, you and the guard will sleep in quarters above the shop. Then we will all gather back here early tomorrow morning for a hearty breakfast of eggs, ham, fruit, and cheese. You must not travel on an empty stomach."

Theo then offered a prayer, asking for blessings for his guests, and prayed for their continued safety on the rest of their trip to La Rochelle.

By now, Maggie was sobbing. Her heart was deeply touched that these strangers were being so kind to them. The prayer had struck a chord in her heart, and she felt that the Holy Spirit was standing in the room with her. She had never felt this before, and she began a personal, silent prayer. Then, she heard a voice in her head. It sounded so real. The voice said, *My child, do you love me?* All she could do was imagine Christ speaking to his disciple Peter.

Silently, she answered, *Bien sûr, my Father, I do love you. I love you with all of my heart, mind, and soul.*

Then, she was asked the question a second time, *My child, do you really love me?*

Yes, my Father, I really do love you, Maggie answered.

And then, the third time, Christ asked her, *My child, do you truly love me?*

Yes, my dear Father, my Salvation, I believe in you, trust you, and love you with all that I am, Maggie answered. When she had avowed her love and trust for this third time, a compassionate feeling of warmth and security flooded every part of her body. Her fright at the events that seemed to be flooding her life suddenly left her, and she knew in that moment that she was indeed a child of God, that by His grace she was saved. It was the most amazing and freeing feeling that she had ever felt.

Matthieu told Pierre that he would check over the carriage, tend to the team of horses, and stable them for the night.

Maggie did not sleep well that night. She was excited, yet at the same time mystified, by what had happened to her. Did God really speak to her? It had seemed so real. It was as if the Holy Spirit had put his arm around her. Tears kept welling up in her eyes, and her heartbeat slowed to a peaceful rhythm. She now knew that whatever misfortune might happen to her in the future, she would have the strength and courage to go on. She knew that she must share the good news of Jesus Christ with other people, as Calvin had implored his followers to do. She did not immediately confide this in Tomas. She would do that back in La Rochelle, at the right time.

Chapter 11
Back in La Rochelle

The rest of the trip back home was rather uneventful. They arrived in La Rochelle after two more days of travel. It would not be long until Noël, and the city had already taken on a wonderful festive air. The windows of homes and businesses were already brightly ablaze with lanterns and candles. Boughs of evergreen were hanging on the doors and in the windows of the more affluent homes. Cold Atlantic winds, full of moisture, were blowing in from the Bay of Biscay, and people were bundled up in their warmest clothes. Women were wearing their fanciest bonnets and men were dressed in their top hats.

They stopped briefly at Uncle Charles's farm to let the guard off, and explained that his coachman had been left behind, but would be home soon.

"Why has the coachman been left behind?" Charles asked.

"Don't worry, Uncle Charles. He is very safe and protected. I will explain later. Right now, Maggie is eager to see her parents and I want to see my mother and father."

Making a quick departure from the manoir, Tomas guided Pierre straight to Maggie's home. The servant answered the door, with her father right behind him. Michel was very surprised and overjoyed to see them, but seemed puzzled by the stranger and the two children with them. "Père, this is Pierre, and these are his children. They are from a manoir just a short distance outside of Orleans." Michel, silently wondering why Pierre was at his door, offered his hand to greet him. Pierre bowed slightly in respect, and they warmly shook hands. In a very calm and reasoned voice, as if it was nothing special, Maggie told her father, "They saved our lives."

With a questioning look and without any hesitancy in his voice, he shot back, "What do you mean?"

"It is complicated, Father. I will tell you everything later. Aren't you going to invite us to come in? It is freezing out here."

"Please excuse my manners! Come in. Are you hungry? I will order refreshments," he said as he stumbled over his words.

"Yes, food and drink would be wonderful! Where is Mère? I want to see her."

"Certainly, your dear mother is in the parlor. She will be extremely happy to see her dear daughter." Michel gave Tomas a hug and said, "My son, I am relieved that you and my daughter are safe from whatever danger and misfortune may have interfered with your trip. Please take her to her mother."

And then, he warmly greeted Pierre again, and invited him and the children to come in out of the cold. Picking up each child, he thought about when Maggie and Tomas might give him grandchildren. He asked their names, and gave them both a hug and a kiss on the cheek.

Asking the butler to get warm milk and cookies for the children, Michel poured his best Cognac for the adults and proposed a toast to the couple; he thanked Pierre for his service and protection.

Michel noticed that Maggie had hardly touched her Cognac. She only sipped it once when he had made a toast. When he was refilling the glasses, he said to his daughter,

"Maggie, is there something wrong? You have hardly drunk any of your Cognac. Are you okay?"

"Father, I am fine. I am just tired from the trip," she told him. "We have been traveling all day." She started to speak again, but hesitated and stopped short of telling her parents the good news that she was pregnant. It would probably be best left to the privacy of Tomas and her, with just her parents.

"Tomas and I are going to drive over to see his parents, and will spend the night with them. Will you please be so kind as to provide lodging and hospitality tonight for the drivers and the children? We will return tomorrow. And then, Pierre will return to his home near Orleans with Uncle Charles's guard, so that they can swap their coach for Uncle Charles's." It was all very confusing, and Michel knew that there was a long story yet to be heard. "We will be back early tomorrow," Maggie promised.

It was late before they left to go to the Jardeens. There would be few people on the streets, and most of the candles and lanterns in the homes would already be extinguished. That night, the darkness seemed particularly ominous, giving Tomas an uneasy feeling. He imagined that he saw soldiers everywhere he looked. *Oh well*, he thought. *Surely it is my imagination, just my mind playing tricks on me.*

Unbeknownst to Tomas and Maggie, the soldiers had imposed a nighttime curfew on the city, after some artifacts were reportedly stolen from the Catholic church and some anti-Catholic writing had been scribbled on one of the outside walls of the cathedral. And, of course, without proof of who was responsible, the Huguenots were naturally blamed. Some prominent people, alleged to be Reformists, had been arrested and held for several days on trumped-up charges of vandalism; even worse than that were the charges of treason against the Church and the king. They were not treated badly in prison, but were held for several days without being able to see their families. This was an attempt to break them down and get a confession, but the men held firm. Finally, the men were set free, but as a fear tactic, their movements around the city were being closely shadowed by the soldiers. There were sentries watching their homes. The cause had been served. It was taken as a signal that the soldiers were serious about punishing Reformists, but at the same time were being seen as humane in returning the men to their families in time for Noël. Of course, throughout the Huguenot community, there was a deep suspicion that the church had been vandalized by the soldiers themselves. Nevertheless, it was a serious matter in which all would pay for sooner or later.

Word of the incident had reached the king through the governor of the province. In a magnanimous gesture of appeasement, the king had ordered the men's release; but he supposedly had instructed the imposition of the nighttime curfew on all the people of La Rochelle, Catholics as well as Huguenots, for anti-Reformist sentiments were running strong among the Catholics. The city needed time to, in his words, "cool down." Tomas's instincts were right. There were more soldiers on the street since the king had ordered reinforcements for the city. Why had Maggie's father not told them what was going on?

They were nearing Tomas's home when, suddenly, a soldier standing by a tree next to the road stepped out in front of the carriage and raised his hand for them to stop. Tomas obeyed, although the horses came close to running the soldier down. Regardless of whether he had adequate time to stop, running over one of the king's soldiers would have been a disaster in the making.

With his hand on his saber, the soldier fairly yelled at them in rapid staccato, "Your name? What is your business out tonight? Where are you heading?" Tomas tried to answer, but each time he spoke his response seemed to fall on deaf ears. The fact was that he and Maggie were unknowingly out on the streets after curfew time.

"Get down from the carriage," the soldier ordered.

Standing on the street, and not knowing about the curfew, Tomas asked, "What crime have we committed?"

Quite annoyed at being in the cold, the soldier yelled at him, "*Fermez la bouche!* (Shut up!)" A second soldier rode up and began to search the carriage, while the first soldier patted down Tomas for a weapon. Not finding one, he did not touch Maggie, but just asked her, "Madame, do you carry a concealed weapon?" Tomas asked again why they were being detained, but the soldier just ignored the question. It was at this point that Tomas did something very unwise. He reached out to put his hand on the soldier's arm and asked again, in an agitated voice. The soldier reacted by pushing Tomas away and screaming an obscenity at him. The other soldier grabbed him in an incapacitating hold. "Madame, you and your escort are under arrest."

They were put into their coach and the first soldier drove them to the prison, while the second soldier rode along beside the coach on his horse.

The next day, by midmorning, Uncle Charles showed up at the boatyard. And, of course, he told Antoine, "Tomas and Maggie stopped by the farm yesterday on their way into town. I know that you and Martine are excited to have them home safely."

"What do you mean? Martine and I have not seen them. They have not been to my house."

"Well," Charles told his brother, "they said that they would stop by Maggie's house and then they would go to your house. It may have been late."

"Oh, my dear heavenly Father," Antoine said with fear in his voice. "They may not have known about the curfew." He yelled at his driver, "Get the carriage! Now!" Grabbing their coats and hats, they ran out into the cold in their short sleeves. The driver was right behind them. "Let's go," Antoine instructed. "Very quickly, take us to City Hall!"

When they were there, Antoine and Charles ran up the stairs to Michel's office, and were told, "Monsieur Légere has not arrived yet. He sent word with his driver that he may not be here today. We were told that he is awaiting the return of his daughter and son-in-law from your home."

"Merci, Madame," they shouted at the woman as they rushed back to the carriage. Antoine ordered the driver, "Fast, take us to the home of Monsieur Légere!"

Michel was standing in the window, watching for Tomas's carriage, when Antoine and Charles pulled up in front of the house. Running out to greet them, he asked with trepidation and fear, "Is there anything wrong? Where are Maggie and Tomas? Has there been an accident?"

"We have not seen them," Antoine told him in as calm of a voice as he could muster.

"They left here last night to go to your home," Michel explained. "They were going to spend the night with you and come back here this morning to pick up their driver and his children." Antoine was confused. All of the children of Charles's trusted driver were grown.

"It is all very confusing. There is another driver, Pierre, from Orleans. I do not know the details. Maggie just told me that Pierre had saved Tomas and her from serious harm."

Charles could not fill in any of the details, for his guard had just let him know that he was back; the guard then immediately went to his cottage on the farm to be with his wife. Since Charles had left early that morning to come into La Rochelle, he had not yet had a chance to talk with his guard.

Antoine's suspicions were heightened as the mystery deepened. Then it occurred to him to ask, as La Rochelle was under curfew, "Michel, what time did they leave you to come to my house?"

"I am not sure, but it was after dark," Michel told him.

"Did you tell them about the curfew?"

"No." And then, thinking about the emotions of the night before, he continued, "I was so excited to see her that I did not think. It is only a short trip to your house . . . do you think that possibly . . ." Without finishing his thought, he shouted to the driver, "Take us to the governor's office!"

They were warmly greeted by Lord Bouché, who invited them into his chamber and offered wine for all of them, but they waved away the attendant.

Although by all outward appearances Governor Bouché was a good practicing Catholic and his loyalty to the king could not be questioned, he was a good friend of all these men. In fact, Bouché was the person who was instrumental in getting the contract for the Jardeen shipyard to design and build the privateer vessel.

The governor had personally interceded with the king to get favored recognition and protection for the shipyard and, by extension, the Jardeen brothers and their families. Lord Bouché certainly knew of the Reformist beliefs of the Jardeens, Michel, and his family. Back in the summer, he had confronted Antoine and asked him, face to face, if he were a practicing Huguenot. With deep conviction, and not wishing to betray his religious beliefs, Antoine answered, "Yes, I am a servant of the Lord God." From that time forward, Bouché and Antoine had many conversations about religion that always seemed to turn into the governor quizzing him about Huguenot beliefs and practices. At first, Antoine was suspicious of what was going on, but soon it became obvious that Bouché was having doubts about his own beliefs and was searching for new answers. Antoine knew that, given his family kinship to the king and the prestige of his office, Lord Bouché could never publicly betray his Catholic beliefs.

"Monsieurs, you look troubled," Bouché began. With deep conviction, he asked, "How can I help you?"

Before Antoine could subdue his emotions and find the right words, Michel excitedly exclaimed, "Our children are missing! They arrived at my house last night, back from their wedding trip."

At that point, with tears welling up in his eyes and his voice breaking, Antoine interjected, "They stopped off at Charles's farm to drop off his guard, and then they went to Michel's house and—"

Michel broke in, "Yes, they stayed at my house for a few hours. It was late. I was so happy to see them. They left for Monsieur Jardeen's house, and promised to come back to my house this morning. It was late, and I forgot about the curfew."

Antoine broke back in to explain, "They did not show up. I did not know they were in town; I did not know I was to expect them. It was only this morning when my brother Charles arrived at the boatyard and told me that they had stopped by his house yesterday. I am afraid that there may have been foul play involved."

Charles asked, "Your Lordship, can you intercede with the king's commander to find out what he knows?"

"Of course, of course, I am truly sorry for your despair," Bouché assured him. In an effort to calm his friends, he told them, "I am sure that everything is okay, and we will find them to be safe. Why don't you go to Michel's and wait? I will come there as soon as I have information."

The men thanked the governor profusely and left. With many lingering thoughts racing around in their heads, Michel told his driver, "Take us back to my house."

Meanwhile, Bouché stood at the window of his office and stared out at the people milling about on the street, exchanging seasonal greetings with one another. On the corner stood two soldiers who did not talk to each other, but rather watched the happy people in a manner that suggested they viewed them as evil; it was as if they thought that these people were plotting against both them and their country. He thought to himself, *Dear God, what have they done now?* He stepped out of the office into the adjacent room and instructed his assistant, "Kindly have my driver bring the coach. I am going to the prison. Have my guards meet me at the front door in ten minutes." Then he walked back into his office and poured himself a stiff drink of Cognac. He said out loud to himself, "These are good people. I must get to the bottom of this matter. The rule of law has to change." Then, tucking his pistol into his waistband, he put on his royal cloak and walked resolutely past his assistant. "I don't know when I will be back."

Waiting by the carriage were the driver and two of his guards in their most colorful uniforms, each armed with a caliver. This type of rifle was a light version of the arquebus, a formless matchlock shoulder gun. It was a powerful weapon used in infantry warfare. With the right musket balls, this rifle was capable, at relatively close range, of penetrating protective metal armor. The governor was well-protected wherever he went. This was routine, though, for a public official of his rank. Security had never been a major concern in La Rochelle, for the governor was generally well-regarded and admired for having done a good job. One exception was the soldiers. They were the king's soldiers and they reported to him, not to the governor, and certainly not to city officials. They were independent of provincial rule and had always resisted any interference from the governor into their affairs. But they had to give the appearance of cooperation, as the governor himself was a relative of the king.

The prison was down on the waterfront, not too far from the Jardeen boatyard, but in a seedier district that had given over to vices such as drinking, gambling, and even prostitution. The gates were opened for the governor's carriage, as it was easily recognized, and the prison guards presented arms as a salute when he was driven through. His own guards sitting inside, one on either side of Lord Bouché, remained stoic as the governor returned the salute to the prison guards with a stiff wave. It was an automatic gesture, as he was deeply lost in thought.

The prison warden was the commander of the king's police force, Attachment Number 12, a unit of the King's Battalion Number 7, stationed in Paris. The captain who greeted them stood at attention and reported, "Your Lordship, the commander is not available. He has gone into the city on a business matter. I do not know when he will return. Perhaps, it will be soon." Still at attention, he continued, "Can I be of service to you?"

"Merci, but I prefer to wait for the commander. It is a matter of extreme delicacy and importance," Bouché told him.

Still at attention and seemingly quite ill at ease relating to the governor, the captain briskly snapped together the heels of his heavy boots. "Very well, Your Lordship, you may wait in the commander's reception area. May I bring you some bread, a plate of the commander's finest cheeses, and a bottle of his fine wine?"

"That would be very nice. I would appreciate that."

With that, the captain did a swift about-face and retired to the commissary to find food and drink for the governor. All the while, the captain silently wondered, *What is so important that keeps Bouché from discussing the matter with me? He must be here on behalf of the man and woman brought in last night, on charges of violating the curfew and assault on a fellow soldier.* The arresting soldier had laughingly bragged that Tomas had only touched his arm, but regardless, he would still be charged with assault on one of the king's soldiers. This charge is a very serious crime. He continued in thought, *And the woman . . . she is just too nice. Oh, well, it is best that I keep my mouth shut and let the commander deal with this one.*

The captain returned to the reception area with cheese, a half-sliced baguette, and a bottle of beautiful claret wine. The wine was considerably the finest in the commander's collection. He then excused himself and claimed that "Duty was calling."

Chapter 12
Accusations against Tomas

It was about an hour before the commander returned. The governor was irritated at having to wait, but was careful to be patient and cordial to the captain, who returned a couple of times to apologize on behalf of the commander and to ask if there was anything further that he required.

When the commander finally had arrived he was in full military dress, with his plumed hat and military medals carefully arrayed across his chest. He gracefully bowed to Bouché, and the governor respectfully acknowledged with a nod of the head. It was only after the commander had removed his sword and pistol and gave them to the captain that he verbally greeted the governor with a rather cold handshake. He knew that the governor had not come to his office for a social visit. In fact, he was pretty certain as to what was on the governor's mind. He knew far more about the case than he would dare volunteer to Bouché.

It had been reported to the military commander in Orleans by several of his undercover spies that the Jardeen couple had been overheard talking about their Huguenot beliefs, and making what was reported to have been angry anti-Catholic comments about threatening danger against the Church and Catholic officials. Needless to say, the commander certainly understood that the accusations were overblown, but he could act only on the information as it was reported to him. And then he was told that Tomas had loitered for a long time in the bookstore that day with the shop owner. The owner had already been marked for death, as he was an ex-priest who had renounced his vows to the Catholic Church, associated with Reformists, and was guilty of evangelizing other Catholics to leave the Church. A priest was required to be celibate during his priesthood. So, in the warped logic of the Church, when a priest renounced his vows to the Church it equated to being a homosexual. Surely this was a simplistic way of looking at the relationship between priests and Jesus Christ, but it was the way in which the soldiers reasoned. His shop had been under surveillance. Tomas had been seen talking at great length that afternoon with the owner, no doubt conspiring with the "homosexual" ex-priest.

Somehow, the couple from La Rochelle had slipped away from Orleans before being arrested. How they managed to escape after being stopped on the road on their way out of Orleans was a mystery. The two soldiers who had tailed them out of Orleans and stopped them were not ready to tell. Knowing that the couple's intent was to return to La Rochelle, the commander in Orleans had sent a courier on a fast steed to warn the commander with whom Bouché was now meeting.

Charles's farm was quickly put under surveillance, as well as the Jardeen home in the city and Maggie's parents' home. Once Tomas and Maggie had stopped off at the farm to let off Charles's driver and continued on to her parents' home, traps had been set for their capture. Ordinarily, a person out after curfew, unless there were suspicions against him or her, was simply ordered off the streets and told to go home. This campaign was intended to intimidate, not kill. But in this case, the young couple had been made into examples, despite their social, privileged status. However, it had been their privileged societal position that incited this. Punishment meted out to them, a couple who had made a sham of the beautiful rite of Catholic marriage, would certainly catch the attention of the populace of La Rochelle. Their intentions were to bring the swelling number of Huguenots to their knees.

"Your Lordship," the commander asked. "To what do I owe the privilege of your most gracious presence?" He continued, "What is on your mind that brings you to my office?"

Giving up the pretense of formality, Bouché was straightforward with him and said, "Commander, you know very well why I am here. If there is any doubt in your mind, I will remind you. I am here on behalf of the Jardeen family, as well as the honorable mayor of this city. You have arrested young Monsieur Jardeen and his bride, who is the daughter of the mayor. Matters such as this are not to be taken lightly."

Taking cue from the governor's last word, the commander retorted, "Your Lordship, this is a most difficult case. It is with deepest regret that I must inform you of the very serious nature of the charges against young Tomas Jardeen and his lovely bride." Being careful not to immediately and outright implicate them in the Huguenot movement, the commander went on to explain, "Your Lordship, as you most assuredly know, our intention in enforcing the curfew is the safety of the good people of La Rochelle and to keep them safe in their homes at night, under the guise that there is likely to be trouble from Huguenot vandals. When the young couple had been stopped last night by my soldiers for breaking curfew, they would have initially been ordered off the street in the same way as everyone else. But young Monsieur Jardeen cursed at and physically assaulted one of my men. He appeared to be drunk, so he and his wife were brought here for their safety. They are being questioned. I expect that they will be released very soon."

"May I see them?" the governor asked, not so much as a question, but more as a command. The request resounded with the firmness in his voice.

Quickly trying to think of a reason to keep the governor from conversing with them, but unable to rationalize a plausible excuse, the commander retorted, "That is not possible today." This reply left himself open to further prying from Bouché.

"Why not today?"

"Our questioning them is not complete."

"Questioning?" Bouché asked, with increased irritation. "If Monsieur Jardeen was drunk last night, surely he has sobered by now. Why do you continue to hold him?"

"My Lordship, I beg you to remember that he did assault one of my guards, a member of the king's militia. That is a crime against the king himself. Surely you must understand. I would release them to you this very moment if it were just a case of being on the street after curfew, but the assault charge is very serious."

Bouché probed further. "No, perhaps I do not understand. Did Monsieur Jardeen strike your soldier? Did he injure your soldier in any way? Or, perhaps, was it just an inebriated man who resisted arrest?"

"Oh, no, Your Lordship, it was far more serious than you are imagining. Monsieur Jardeen pulled a pistol from under his cloak and threatened my men. When they tried to disarm him, he fought them, and one of my guards was injured."

The governor knew that the commander was lying. He could hear it in his voice cracking, and in the stress shown in the commander's face. Bouché now knew that Tomas and

Maggie needed a *homme de loi* (solicitor/lawyer) to represent them. He would take care of that immediately. First, he had to get to Michel's house and give him, Antoine, and his brother, Charles, a report and let them know of his suspicions.

"Thank you for the information. I shall be in touch."

The commander was not relieved. He knew that the governor would be back, and much to his dismay, sooner rather than later.

The captain had been waiting outside the door and had heard the entire conversation. After he heard the governor say, "I shall be in touch," and not wanting to confront him again, he hastened into an adjacent room. As soon as the governor had gone, he walked into the commander's office without knocking and saw that the commander was visibly shaken.

"What should we do?" the captain asked.

"Take care of the prisoner. Do so quickly; spare the woman," the commander abruptly shot back.

"As you wish, sir," the captain clicked his heels, saluted, did a snappy about-face, and left. The order was clear, but he thought it would be best to wait and see what evolved as a result of the governor's intrusion into the matter.

That afternoon, Bouché and his protective guards returned to Maggie's parents' home, where the fathers and the uncle were waiting in the hope for more pleasant words than he could bring. By that time it was late in the afternoon, and there was still important work to be done before evening. While Bouché related his findings to the families, his guards and the driver waited outside the parlor. Michel's servants were ordered to attend to their every need, so they were brought food and drink. Pierre, the driver from Orleans, joined the men. Maggie's mother kept his children upstairs, for she did not think that they needed to be exposed to what was happening.

"I am sure that these are trumped-up charges," Bouché told the men, "but the allegation of assault, whether it is true or not, is a very serious charge. I recommend that we get them a homme de loi."

"All things considered, we should." The men agreed amongst themselves and asked, "Who is the best available person that can represent them? Who do you recommend?"

"It will be very expensive," Bouché paused, "but there is only one person who should be considered. That person is François Ronsérre of Fontenay-le-Comte. François is a dear friend and a noted solicitor with friends at the law school in Poitiers. He has multiple important connections to people of notoriety in Paris."

"Cost does not matter," Antoine offered. "If I do not have enough money, I will sell the boatyard."

Charles spoke up. "My brother, this is a family matter. You can count on my support."

Michel quickly interjected, "Maggie is my blood. I will give all that I have for her and Tomas."

"As you see," Antoine told the governor, "money is not a question. Tell us more about Monsieur Ronsérre. Is he a Catholic, or is he a Huguenot?"

"I do not think that it matters. The law is above religion; however, Monsieur Ronsérre is indeed a very strong, perhaps fanatical, Huguenot. With the permission of the three of you, I will dispatch an emissary tomorrow morning to Fontenay to request him to come with great urgency to La Rochelle. I will of course let you know as soon as I know something."

There was nothing more that could be done right now. It had been a long, depressing day. Darkness was approaching.

"I think you gentlemen had better be on your way home," Bouché told the brothers. "You don't want to be out past curfew." Though it was a poor attempt at humor, there were still some chuckles around the room.

"How about you?" Michel innocently asked Bouché.

With a strange, almost painful look on his face, he adroitly replied, "Yes, I better get home as well. I am not sure that the governorship protects me from the wretched manacles of the militia."

As soon as the governor was safely back at his residence, he instructed his driver to go with one of the royal guards to the home of his diplomatic courier. His instructions to be relayed to the courier were, "At the break of dawn, ride with urgency to Fontenay-le-Comte. Find François Ronsérre and tell him that I requested he return with you in haste to La Rochelle on a matter of the greatest importance. Young Huguenot lives are at stake."

As he was dismissing his driver, the governor stopped and added, "Be careful, and be very discreet with the information I have shared with you."

"Your Honor, your orders will be carried out exactly as you have instructed." And with that, the driver and one of the guards departed. The other guard stayed behind to protect the governor's residence through the night.

Chapter 13
Arrival of Monsieur Ronsérre

Governor Bouché arrived in his office early the next morning to find that most of his aides were already present. Calling them together, he explained what was taking place with the Jardeen couple. Hesitant to reveal his suspicions, he told the aides that this was a matter of very high importance, and that their first attention should be to this. He told them that he had sent for Solicitor François Ronsérre and expected him to arrive later that day, or perhaps the next day.

"Pierre," he said to Pierre Ravenel, his diplomatic aide and a bright young lawyer in his own right, "I want you to coordinate negotiations with the prison commander to secure a release."

"Oui, Your Lordship." And then, with some hesitancy, he continued, "May I suggest that we meet at your convenience to discuss strategy and negotiating points?"

"First, we will wait for Ronsérre to hear his ideas. But for now, consider compromises, negotiating points, what we might offer in exchange for their release, and the promise of future safety and protection. I am available to discuss your ideas, but Pierre, in the meantime I would like for you to go to the prison this afternoon and meet with the commander. I will give you a letter with my seal to introduce you as my diplomatic emissary. Let him know that we will be visiting daily to ensure the safety and well-being of the Jardeens. He will be surprised to meet Monsieur Ronsérre face-to-face. However, it is probably best not to mention him today. Oh, and please go by the boatyard and see if Monsieur Jardeen will kindly allow Monsieur Ronsérre to stay at his house while he is in La Rochelle."

"Oui, Your Lordship. I shall do as you request."

Later that afternoon, Ravenel returned from the prison and reported that he had been allowed to see the Jardeens in private for just a few minutes. He reported the couple had told him that they were being kept separately in dungeon-like cells with sparse sunlight, and had been given very little, terrible food. He also said, "They are being questioned often. They were interrogated about the ex-priest in Orleans, about the route they took from Orleans to La Rochelle, and if anyone assisted them. They even had to answer questions on their marriage in the Catholic Church, and if they have Huguenot beliefs. Fortunately," Ravenel told the governor, "they are resisting giving up any information, except on the bookshop owner. Since he is already dead, Monsieur Jardeen has told the soldiers about his quest to buy a book of poetry for his wife, how the ex-priest assisted him, and of their conversation on the poet. It sounds innocent enough so far. They have been threatened, but so far have not been tortured or physically harmed.

"And, Your Lordship, the commander expressed his respect for you and thanks you for your interest in this matter."

"Surely so," the governor retorted. "The commander is only being gracious in overstating his respect and intent. Did you call on the young man's father, Antoine Jardeen?"

"Oui, I stopped by the boatyard. Monsieur Jardeen and his family will be honored to open their home to Monsieur Ronsérre anytime he is in the city. Monsieur Jardeen is obviously using his work at the boatyard to distract him from his worries and anxiety. He is submersing himself in work on the design for the corvair. His plan was to lay the keel in the spring, but with his son Tomas being held prisoner, that will surely have to be postponed."

Just as Ravenel was finishing, the diplomatic courier burst through the door with Ronsérre in hand. Without waiting for either to speak, the governor hastened over to greet them. He gave his friend a hug, a kiss on each cheek, and then warmly shook his hand. This was a traditional French greeting among trusted friends. "François, I am happy to see you. I am so glad you could come," he said.

"I am honored that you thought of me. I gather that all is not well."

"My friend, you are correct. An incident has happened to the children of two of my very close friends. They are in prison on a charge for which I know they are not guilty."

Then turning to Pierre, Bouché suggested, "Why don't you serve up some wine for all of us? I am sure that Monsieur Ronsérre must be thirsty after his ride from Fontenay-le-Comte. We will be in the antechamber. Please bring the wine and join us. You can tell Monsieur Ronsérre about your visit to the prison today." Then, he invited the courier to join the discussion.

"Merci, Your Lordship, but it has been a long day. The long ride to and from Fontenay-le-Comte in one day is tiring. May I be excused to go home and get some rest?"

"I understand," Bouché told him. "You are dismissed; go home to your family. Get plenty of rest. Will I see you tomorrow?"

"Your Honor, I will be here early tomorrow morning, ready to assist you in any way possible."

"Merci," the governor told him. "You have done a fine job, and I know that I can always depend on you." Then, turning back to Ronsérre, he asked, "Did you come by carriage, or ride by horseback?"

"I came by coach. My personal driver is waiting outside."

The courier was just walking out the door when Bouché said to him, "Would you please tell the monsieur's driver to come in from the cold, and wait here in my office?"

"Merci," Ronsérre said to the governor. "It is indeed cold today. And, as always, you are so generous with your hospitality."

The three men went into the antechamber and sat down. Several other aides dragged chairs into the room to be comfortable while they listened to the conversation. François began, "Your courier told me some about the situation between the soldiers and the Jardeen couple. It sounds serious. Please tell me what happened, in as much detail as you know."

"Well," the governor began, "my information is secondhand. I can only tell you what has been reported to me. They were on their wedding trip to Paris, but never made it there because of a violent incident in Orleans. The commander at the prison tells me that Tomas Jardeen is being held and questioned for violating curfew and assaulting one of his soldiers after they returned to La Rochelle. I suppose his wife is being held for aiding and abetting a criminal. She is the daughter of the mayor of this city. It is a most sensitive matter. Their imprisonment is not yet publicly known, but when it does, I expect there will be real anger in the city, which may erupt in violence. And it is more than likely that the Catholic church will be targeted."

"Then we must try to prevent that and work for their release," François replied. "But why do you suggest that there will be trouble here in the city?"

Bouché pondered the question. Finally, he spoke, but in a halting, uncertain tone, "There are more Huguenots here in La Rochelle than anyone would imagine. The city has grown dramatically, for there is an influx of people moving here from the rest of France. These are people who are allegedly Catholic, but are covertly coming to believe in and are embracing Reformed religious principles. The Huguenots are in the majority."

"Wait," Ronsérre asked in a somewhat startled voice, "are you telling me that the Jardeen couple are practicing Huguenots?"

"They technically are still members of the Catholic Church; however, they believe strongly in Huguenot creeds and principles. I have asked you to come here not only because you are a dear friend, but for your most outstanding legal reputation, and because you, too, are a Huguenot."

"I thank you for those very kind words. You are correct; it is no secret that I am a Huguenot. I have openly declared such." Then, after a pause of several seconds, he continued, "Are you perhaps telling me that you, too, might be a Huguenot? You . . ." He paused again for a few seconds. He hesitated to remind his friend of this, but continued in a reverential tone, "But Your Lordship, you are a relative of the king."

"My friend," Bouché told him, "you have found me out. I am one of the many closeted Catholics who believes in the Protestant movement. I am not as brave as you. It is impossible because of my kinship to the king, and my appointment as a lord and as governor, for me to make my beliefs public. Can you understand?"

"I do understand. If I were in your position, I would almost certainly do the same," Ronsérre said, raising his wine goblet in a toast. "Hear, hear, to our common beliefs. Your secret is safe with me." At that point, much to his surprise, everyone present in the room raised their goblets in salute and, in a near chorus, said, "Amen."

The governor then went on to add, "Do you remember the violent incident in Orleans, in which I mentioned that bookshop owner, an ex-priest who had publicly renounced his allegiance to the Catholic Church and left the priesthood, was brutally murdered and his body burned by the soldiers? Well, Tomas, who had gone to the bookstore for his wife the afternoon before the murder that night, had been observed talking to the owner at great length. Later that afternoon, the owner closed the shop early, and the pair of them were seen secretly exiting through the back entrance and speeding away in the owner's coach. On top of that, Tomas is alleged to have been overheard on several occasions in a public dining room commenting in a 'treasonous' manner about the Catholic Church, and talking about his Huguenot beliefs. It is my suspicion that one of the waiters in the dining room was in the employ of the militia force in Orleans. And there is no doubt that, if he were, he would have told the soldiers what they wanted to hear."

"Where did you get this information?" Ronsérre asked.

"This is information that the commander at the prison gave to Monsieur Ravenel. It is hard to tell how much of this is true, and how much has been fabricated."

"Well, we shall try to get to the bottom of this mystery. My Lordship, are you available tomorrow morning to go with me to the prison and introduce me to the commander as the couple's appointed solicitor? I will demand the opportunity to speak privately with my clients."

"Oui, and perchance, with your permission of course, Monsieur Ravenel might join us. He is a tenacious young lawyer with vision and energy to spare. I am sure that he can be of great assistance to you."

"That would be very nice. I would love to have him on my side," Ronsérre said. "Perhaps my own associate from Fontenay will not have to come to La Rochelle, or at least not come as often."

"Good. Then it is settled. Monsieur Ravenel will be assigned to be your full-time assistant on this case. Monsieur Ravenel, are you okay with this arrangement?"

"Your Lordship, I am pleased to be asked to work with such a famous legal mind as Monsieur Ronsérre. I can only hope that I will do honor to him and to you."

"Well, it is getting late, and darkness will soon be settling on us. We better get my friend to Monsieur Jardeen's house before curfew begins." With a hearty laugh, Bouché continued, "I don't want to have to hire another solicitor to secure Monsieur Ronsérre's release from prison." And then he said to all of his staff, "Go home. Get some rest. The hard work is just beginning. Be here early tomorrow morning and God bless each of you." Turning to Ronsérre, he said, "While you are in La Rochelle, you will be staying with Antoine and Martine Jardeen, here in the city. Their home is not far away. I will have my driver lead your driver there on my way to my residence, and I will meet with you back here tomorrow morning. Oh, and just for precaution, I am assigning one of my royal guards to be by your side at all times. Your best protection is to always have him visible for the soldiers."

The entourage left. The governor rode in his carriage with the provincial seal on both sides. One of his guards rode alongside the coach on a fine steed, while the other rode with him in the coach. Monsieur Ronsérre followed close behind in his coach. His assigned guard rode up front in the seat beside the driver. He was armed with a saber and a caliver arquebus.

On the way they drew stares from the soldiers as they fanned out onto the streets to begin their nighttime enforcement of the curfew. The governor would have been allowed to pass, but Ronsérre's carriage would have been stopped had it not been for the guard riding with the driver. In his fine, brightly feted uniform, he was easily identified as one of the governor's guard. That was as good as having provincial seals emblazoned on the sides of the coach. But the presence of a stranger in the city riding with the governor's guard would be noted and reported to the commander.

Maggie's parents, Uncle Charles, and his wife, Paulette, had been invited to the Jardeen home for drinks and dinner with Monsieur Ronsérre. They had also been asked to spend the night. The chef was preparing cuts of fine beef from Charles's farm. The tender beef was being prepared with a succulent sauce of wine and sautéed shallots, reduced with butter, tarragon, and lemon juice. A hearty red Chinon wine from the Loire River Valley would be served at dinner, followed by a dessert wine. Despite this decadent meal, they would no doubt be distracted by serious discussion about their son and daughter-in-law.

They were met at the door by a servant who escorted Ronsérre, the governor, and his guards into the antechamber. "Your Lordship, would you and your guests please wait here? I will announce your arrival." During that time, Antoine's driver met the two drivers in front of the house and led them to the carriage houses, where they could feed and water their horses. Ronsérre's driver and guard would be staying upstairs in the living area over the stalls, while Ronsérre himself would stay in the house on the upper level. Security would be tight during his stay here. Bouché had ordered two additional guards to watch the outside of the house during the night. That assignment would prove to be a brutal challenge, as a wintry cold front was sweeping in off the Bay of Biscay. In fact, within a few hours it had gotten so cold that the guards knocked on the door and asked if they might come inside for the night and watch from the windows. It was already after midnight that December 21, 1575, when the first snow of the new winter season began to fall. Governor Bouché, his driver, and his guard had already left earlier in the evening, and would hopefully be safe in his residence by then. He did not see any soldiers on the way. Most likely, the cold had driven them back to the safe haven of the prison, or they had found their preferred tavern to spend the night.

Michel and his wife also spent the night with the Jardeens, since Antoine, Charles, and he had stayed up late discussing the case with François and enjoyed Cognac, with the added pleasure of a few Spanish contraband cigars. They were easily bought from ship captains who had made stopovers in Barcelona and Majorca before sailing on to La Rochelle. Every possible sleeping area would be taken that night. Antoine and Charles stayed up, even after Michel went upstairs to join his wife. They talked to the guards and helped them watch for any suspicious activity outside. Nothing significant happened, except for one obviously drunk soldier who had passed by without even pausing to look toward the house. They had not seen any snow since the end of the previous February, long before the story that was unfolding in their lives. Of course, events leading up to the saga had been put into place many years before. The serenity of the snowflakes peacefully falling to the ground was a reminder to them of what an uncomplicated life could look and feel like. Finally, they gave up and settled into a couple of plush chairs, and sleep came rather quickly.

Chapter 14
Winter's Arrival

It was the first day of winter, 1575. The city of La Rochelle was blanketed in a beautiful canopy of snow that had fallen during the night. By early morning, before most people in the city had even risen from their sleep, the snowfall had stopped and moved on into the interior of France. It had been a pretty light snow with small, fine flakes; little moisture, and it was not deep. It was just a few inches, and with luck, a little sunshine would quickly melt it away. But even with just a few inches, the people of La Rochelle were famous for their confusion of what to do in a snowfall. The streets would be clogged with carriages, snorting horses, and people with flaring tempers. Ronsérre was up early, reviewing the case at hand and thinking about what alibis and rebuttals he might present at trial if he were not able to negotiate the release of Tomas and Maggie. Then, he reminded himself to always refer to her as Margarite, her given name, and not by her nickname of Maggie. With the families calling her Maggie, it was obviously going to be a hard task to get it right. Last night, the couple's parents had given him vital information on the pair, telling him about their childhood, their growing up, their personalities and weaknesses, and their educational achievements. It sounded as if each was a brilliant thinker with many creative talents. Margarite had evidently become very musically talented, while Tomas had become a skilled naval architect and engineer. He professed to himself, *What a pity it is that their lives have become so messed up . . . Surely, they are destined for great achievements and contributions to their country.* As he mused to himself, he wondered, *Why does man suffer such great acts of cruelty on others in the name of religion?* It seemed to him and many others that the War of Religion in France would never end. The king spoke of freedom for the Huguenots, a freedom that never seemed to arrive. Yet the king kept talking anyway. Ronsérre got out his Bible and read for a while. He read John 3:16, "For God so loved the world that he gave his only begotten son that whosoever believes in him shall not perish but have everlasting life . . ." And then he read in the Book of Matthew about the Christmas birth, and in Luke of the Easter story, about the trial and crucifixion of Jesus and his rising from the dead. Then, he wondered to himself, *Why? Why, with God's great love and mercy, are Huguenots being punished for believing in their own personal God, rather than a Catholic hierarchy who believe that they are the only link on earth to God's powers and greatness? However, maybe some Huguenots have perhaps gone too far in their vandalism and destruction of the Catholic Church's property, icons, and relics . . . Is it possible that Tomas was a part of these Huguenot extremists?* It was hard for him to imagine this to be the case. But he could not be sure until he had spoken privately with Margarite and him, heard their stories, and most importantly, seen their faces.

Finally, the families began to rise and appear downstairs, one by one. The Jardeens' kitchen staff had prepared a hearty breakfast of freshly laid eggs and a baked pork pie with a buttery herbal source. Charles had provided the eggs and fresh sausage meat, made from prime stock raised on the farm and brought to the house just yesterday, along with the beef which had been served the previous night. But the highlight of breakfast was the warm French bread, which had just been baked and was served with freshly churned butter and homemade jams. The aromatic coffee had just been acquired from a trader who had sailed into port from Portugal a few days before.

The coffee beans were grown in the Azores Islands; these islands were located in the Atlantic, about 1,360 kilometers from the coast of Portugal. Because of the Gulf Stream which raced up the east coast of North America, then, whipping around the North Atlantic, dipped down the western side of Europe, the islands enjoyed a subtropical climate conducive to the growing of good coffee beans. The Azores were blessed by currents of warm ocean water which always seemed to flow by their shores. The soil was rich because of the volcanic nature of the islands.

Ronsérre was deeply impressed with the excellent food that the Jardeens' kitchen prepared. His stay in La Rochelle would prove to be a most memorable gastronomical experience, if the dinner last night and the breakfast this morning were any indication of what he was to expect in the future. He was not used to having such fine meals back in Fontenay. His wife had died several years before of consumption. The children were grown and away from home. Now living alone, he had most of his meals at local dining facilities and taverns in Fontenay. Some places served excellent meals, while others were not quite as good. It was certain, though, that none were as good as what he had in the short time that he had been in La Rochelle.

By ten o'clock that morning, traffic on the streets seemed to lessen. One of the guards had already alerted his driver to bring the coach around to the front of the house. The sun was bright in the sky, and that morning seemed warmer than the previous day. The snow had already begun to melt. He would go to the governor's office, pick up Bouché and Ravenel, and go from there to the prison. Because he had been born in La Rochelle, spent most of his younger years here, and visited often, Ronsérre knew the layout of the city very well. He instructed his driver to use a back way, and they were at the governor's office in record time, having missed most of the traffic. They did see a couple of soldiers patrolling the streets, but no doubt the presence of the governor's guard by the driver's side prevented any interference from them. In fact, it almost seemed as though they were awed by the presence of one of the governor's guards riding with a stranger in town. One of the soldiers grabbed a piece of paper from his pocket and started to make notes. It was expected that this information would be passed along to his superior. It was protocol that if strangers were seen in the city or anything out of the ordinary was witnessed, it must be reported to a superior. In stark contrast to the olden days, it seemed like the city had become a police state. It was evident to him that his friend, the governor, took no part in creating this new reality. The soldiers did not report to him; they reported only to their commander at the prison and to the king.

Ronsérre met the governor and Ravenel right at the appointed time. It was decided that they would travel to the prison in the governor's carriage, since it displayed the governor's seal; naturally, this granted them more advantages. People would move over to make way, especially if one of his guards rode up topside with the driver. There were few people in the province and in the city who did not respect Bouché. They may have not always agreed with him or his politics, but they always respected him; this was a very important distinction. It was obvious that this respect stemmed from his open-mindedness and from him being a good person. Although it was widely suspected that he carried Huguenot beliefs, he was clearly not blinded by religion in his decision-making. It was widely known that he treated Catholics as fairly as he dealt with the Huguenots. It was not spoken of, and of course never possibly could be, but many people wished in their hearts that he was the king. His good reputation had even spread outside the province of Aunis to other provinces throughout France.

When they arrived at the prison, the same captain that Bouché had encountered on his first visit greeted them. As before, he was respectful and attentive to the needs of Bouché and his party. The commander was on-site, but not in his office. The captain asked them to please have a seat in the antechamber, and asked one of his orderlies, "Please find the commander and inform him that the governor and his guests are waiting to see him."

In only a few minutes, the commander came in and expressed polite regrets that he had kept them waiting, bowed, and said how glad he was to have the honor of a call from His Lordship. Bouché made the introductions. "This is François Ronsérre, a solicitor from Fontenay-le-Comte, and I believe that you know my attaché, Pierre Ravenel." The commander first bowed to Ravenel; however, the courtesy paid to young Ravenel was not much more than a nod of the head and a slight bend from the waist. The bow to Ronsérre was noticeably deeper from the waist, and longer than the bow paid to Ravenel. During the few seconds of courtesy made to Ronsérre, the governor noticed a pained look of recognition, and maybe even fear, on the commander's face.

Without allowing time for chitchat, Bouché immediately got to the point of their being there. "Commander, Monsieur Ronsérre has been hired by the Jardeen family and the parents of Mrs. Jardeen to represent the young couple. He is here to negotiate their release from prison, to represent them in litigation, and if necessary, to prove their innocence and clear their record."

"Um . . . I see," said the commander. His voice had a hint of hesitancy in it as he seemingly spit out the words.

The commander started to continue, but Ronsérre interrupted him. "Commander, I wish to have a private interview today with the couple to hear their recollection of events and view of the charges against them. I would like to first meet with them separately, and then jointly."

"But Monsieur, that is not possible."

"Why is it not possible?" Ronsérre asked. "I am their solicitor, and I have the legal right to interview my clients without you or any of your subordinates being present. It is not a privilege, but a right granted under the laws of this great country. With all due respect to your rank and your position, it is not a request; it is a demand."

"But Monsieur," the commander replied, in a subdued but firm voice, "I am aware of the law. However, you must show proof that you have been contracted, either by the couple or by their parents, to act as their solicitor. You are making demands without such evidence."

"Ah, yes." Turning to the governor, he continued, "But we do have papers."

With a nod of the head to Ravenel, Pierre reached inside his doublet and produced letters from both the Jardeens and the Légeres, handing them to the commander. Written and attested to the previous night, the decrees publicly announced the agreement for Monsieur Ronsérre to represent Tomas William Jardeen and Margarite Légere Jardeen in all legal matters against the Kingdom of France, King Henri III, and the commander himself, acting as the appointed warden of the prison in La Rochelle.

The commander took a few minutes to look over the documents and then agreed, "Oui, it does appear that the papers are in order. I will tell my captain to make arrangements for you to see the couple. It will likely be this afternoon before your meeting can be arranged."

"That is okay," Ronsérre told him. "We will leave and have lunch. What time do you suggest that we return?"

"Around three o'clock this afternoon would be a good time."

After saying goodbye, the trio left. Picking up the guards and the driver in the outer office, the governor gave the order to take them to the boatyard. If Antoine and Charles were there, he planned to invite them to lunch. He needed to see how high they would be willing to go to negotiate the release of the couple. He was sure that Michel Légere would pay the other half of the ransom, for that was exactly what it would be: a ransom.

When they arrived at the boatyard, they found Michel, Antoine, and Charles huddled together, discussing what Ronsérre and the governor might have found out.

The lunch invitation was extended. The governor said, "Come on, dear friends. We are going out to lunch. Won't you join us?"

Charles joked, "Gladly, Your Lordship, but only if you are paying!"

"Of course, you cheapskate. I know that a poor dirt farmer like you doesn't have any francs."

Everyone laughed. Antoine inquired, "Where did you have in mind?"

Bouché then brought another laugh from the men. He said, "Look, I am only paying. You gentlemen can choose."

Ronsérre spoke up, "Since His Lordship is treating, why don't we go to Antouille's Seafood Restaurant down on

Fisherman's Wharf? It is my favorite, and not too far of a drive."

Going in separate carriages, they arrived to find a fairly full restaurant. Of course, because the governor was in the party, the concierge quickly decided to seat them immediately. Bouché slipped Ravenel ten francs and whispered, "Go out and give this to the guards. Tell them to treat the two drivers to lunch across the street in the tavern, and to keep any change." As he was leaving, Antoine, who had heard the request to Pierre Ravenel, tried to give the governor money for his own driver. Bouché told him, "Please, my dear friend, do not insult me by giving me money. Your driver is taken care of." That was all that needed to be said. Despite their friendship, Antoine knew that one did not argue over such a matter.

All of the men except Michel ordered fine French beers; Michel was the lone holdout for wine. He ordered a nice, crisp Chardonnay. Bouché asked if they would like roasted oysters to start; everyone did. He said to the waiter, "Bonjour, *garçon*, a couple of large platters of roasted oysters for us. Say, my friends, would everyone like a salad to go with the oysters?" There was a chorus of "Oui."

"Okay," he said to the waiter, "we will each have a nice salad with sautéed scallops on top. Check with my friends to see what dressing they would like. For myself, I will have your French blue cheese dressing. That is the specialty, isn't it?"

Finally, when the waiter had completed taking the order and disappeared to the kitchen, Ronsérre brought the two families up to date on what went on at the prison, and told them of plans to return there at three o'clock that afternoon with the high hopes of getting to meet personally with his clients.

"But first," he told them, "we need to discuss the possibility of having to pay money to obtain their release."

"Yes, let's," Michel agreed. "We have already discussed it briefly amongst ourselves. There is no doubt that the soldiers and their commander can be bought for the right amount of money."

"Well," Ronsérre asked, "have you discussed an amount?"

"Yes, Monsieur, we have, but we would like to hear from you what you consider is a reasonable amount. You must have had similar cases before. What do you suggest?"

After having considered the question for a few moments, Ronsérre replied, "Well, that is a very difficult question. I think that since this is a local action, the king does not have to be paid. It is probably enough to just pay the commander a substantial amount, and then some for his guards. But you must understand, having to buy their freedom is a form of blackmail. Do you want this form of crime to continue, perhaps repeatedly, or do you want to fight the system in court?"

Michel responded to the question. "Right now, we just want our children freed, and we want the soldiers to let us live in peace."

"I can almost assure you their freedom either way. Of course, the easiest and most expedient way to do so is to pay money. But you don't know when they might be picked up again on another charge." He turned his attention to Antoine. "Even you, Antoine, or Charles might find yourself in a similar position on trumped-up charges. It is easy for an outsider to say, 'Let's fight them in court.' But I am not the victim, nor am I one of you. You must decide what is right and what is wrong, and what fits with your ethics and conscience."

"You make some very valid points," Antoine said. His face showed great anxiety and weariness. It was easy to see that the whole affair was taking a great toll on him.

"Perhaps you may want to take some time to think it over; talk with your wives, pray about it, and consider your values in life. It is not an easy decision. It is a great moral dilemma that will come back to you every day for the rest of your life. You asked me for a price. If you decide to pay for their freedom, I suggest eighteen hundred francs as a beginning offer, and a willingness to negotiate up to three thousand francs. I know that is a steep price, but you are buying two human lives. The commander and his men are aware of how dear they are to you and will use that to steepen the price."

Bouché broke in, "If you do decide to buy their freedom, count me in for one-fourth of the money, but you have to swear to me that you will never tell anyone, not even your wives or children, of my offer."

Ronsérre added, "Please do not worry about paying me. I am doing this pro bono. I was asked to help by my dear friend Governor Bouché, and because you are also now my friends, I refuse to charge."

"Your offers are most gracious and generous," Michel stated. Tears were starting to well up in Antoine's eyes. Michel continued, "But Monsieur Ronsérre, you are giving us your time when you could be serving clients in Fontenay. You have a livelihood to think of, too."

"Do not worry about me," Ronsérre told them. "I am living. I have been very fortunate in my legal practice and in my life. I am blessed to have enough money to live very comfortably for the years that I have left here on earth."

"But—" Charles began, but he was quickly interrupted by Ronsérre.

"If you are so determined to pay me, then let us make a covenant right here and now."

"What do you have in mind?" Michel asked.

"Let us swear to God Almighty that you three gentlemen will build a Huguenot church here in La Rochelle. With God's love and mercy, may it flourish beyond imaginable expectations. When the time is right, promise me that you will build a church and invite me to join you in worship. In turn, I will promise that you will know when the time is right. Do we have a deal?" Antoine looked questioningly at Michel and Charles. They nodded their heads affirmatively. "Your Lordship, what do you think?" he asked Bouché.

"It is a deal, Monsieur Ronsérre. We all are busy men, but we will find the time, the energy, and the money. We will make it a New Year's resolution."

"Then, is it a covenant between us?" Ronsérre asked.

"Oui, it is a covenant."

Smiling, Antoine laid his right hand in the middle of the table, and each of the men, except Bouché and Ravenel, laid their right hand on top of his. The governor smiled appreciatively and said, "May God bless and hold each of you close to Him."

With that, Ronsérre said, "My Lordship, I think it is time for me to get back to the prison for our appointment. Why don't you have your driver drop me off at the prison? You can return to your office, and have my driver and guard come to the prison to wait for me. I will return to your office when I conclude my interviews."

Chapter 15
At the Prison

The driver dropped Ronsérre at the prison shortly before his three o'clock appointment with the commander. By the time he was cleared through the guards and escorted to the commander's office, it was already three o'clock. He arrived right on the minute. The commander, enjoying a cigar, commented on his punctuality and invited him into his antechamber. Pouring himself a glass, he asked, "Monsieur Ronsérre, may I be so kind as to offer you wine? It is a very good, full-bodied Bordeaux."

"No, thank you. I would prefer to get on with the business at hand."

"A cigar?"

"No thanks, not right now. Maybe later."

"I see. Well, where do you want to begin? Do you have any questions for me or my staff?"

"It would be helpful if you gave me a brief overview of the events that led to the arrest of my clients."

"Ah, Monsieur, surely you already know of the events."

"Yes, but Commander, I would be delighted for you to tell me again. I want to hear the story from your perspective."

The commander suddenly realized that he had made a big mistake with his cordiality. He really did not personally know the full details of the case, at least not to the extent that he knew the solicitor would want to probe. Also, he did not have representation present. "I see," he managed to get out. There was an embarrassing pause. "Perhaps I should let you talk to the captain of the guard."

"No, continue, Commander. Please finish your thought. I am sure that you are fully aware of the report from your soldiers. I am eager to hear the full story from you."

"Okay. I will tell you to the best of my knowledge." Quickly reflecting to himself, the commander reviewed in his mind what he had been told and what details had been falsified. A couple of overnight binges at a local tavern had dulled his memory, especially the fine details. He knew, though, that he did not want to say anything that would lead Ronsérre into any conclusion that a trap had been sprung for the couple. The story must be *"Curfew, curfew, curfew, assault, assault, assault!"*

He began, "It was several days ago, and the couple was returning from Orleans. It was nighttime. A curfew was in effect. It was rather late when one of my soldiers stopped them for being out long past the curfew hour."

"Please forgive me," Ronsérre begged. "I am from out of town. Please inform me of the reason for the curfew, and how long it had been in effect at that time."

"Monsieur, the curfew had been in effect for several nights before."

"Had something happened to inflict a curfew being put into place? I think it is a fine idea. Now, I cannot publicly support it, but I will not oppose it."

"No, no. The king ordered the curfew."

"But why did the king order the curfew?"

"I am not privy to the wishes of the king. I do not question his reasons or his orders."

"Well, then, let me rephrase my question. Why do you think the king ordered the curfew?"

"I suppose because it is the season of Noël. People being out celebrating and drinking presents a greater opportunity for crime, an opportunity for people to be robbed, to be harmed, or perhaps even to be killed."

"Is it common for people to be killed in La Rochelle during Noël? Has anyone in La Rochelle been killed or seriously harmed thus far into the month?" Ronsérre calmly asked.

"No, none . . ." Then, taking a moment to think, the commander continued, "Yes, I remember. It was just a few weeks before. A couple was stopped on one of the streets here in the city by a few drunkards. They were robbed, and in the process the man was hurt defending his wife from the men's advances."

"Did your soldiers intervene?"

"Oui," the commander told him.

"Was an arrest made?"

"Oui, Monsieur," he told Ronsérre.

"Were the men brought to this prison?"

"Oui."

"Are they still being held?"

"No."

"What were their names?"

"One was Pierre and the other was Michel."

Obviously, the similarity between these names and those of the mayor and the governor's chief legal aide was uncanny. Not a very smart move on the commander's part. Knowing that this was a made-up story, Ronsérre began to drill. Though he was laughing inwardly, without smiling and with as much seriousness as he could possibly project into his voice, he asked, "You mean the fine mayor of this city and Monsieur Ravenel, the governor's chief legal aide, participated in the mugging of a couple of innocent people?"

"No, Monsieur, the good men you mention were not involved. Please, you must understand. I cannot remember everything. I am not the captain of the guard. I have a lot of responsibility."

"Of course," Ronsérre said. "But do you remember their given names? Surely you must remember signing their release papers."

"Oh, yes," the commander quickly replied, thinking that this provided him an outlet from his story.

Continuing to laugh internally, Ronsérre stated in a most positive manner, "Then surely you will not mind my examining the prison records for these drunkards and seeing the release papers which you signed. Let's see, that would be Pierre and Michel, correct? Are you positive of the names?"

At this point, the warden had seemingly no way to disagree. "Oui," he said.

"Would you please have your assistant retrieve those papers for me: the prison record with the report of the arresting soldier and the release papers?"

Without answering, the commander got up and left the room to talk to his captain.

He met the captain waiting just outside the antechamber and, without speaking, waved his hand for the captain to follow him down the hallway. When they were safely out of earshot, he told the captain what had transpired, even though he surely must have known that the captain had been listening in on the conversation. "What do we do now?" he asked the captain.

The captain thought to himself, *What do you mean 'we'?* But he was not so discourteous or rude to say it to the commander's face. "I am not sure, Commander, sir. This is a quagmire. We should have already killed the young Mr. Jardeen, or at least shipped him off to the Mediterranean to serve on one of the prison ships." Laughing, the captain added, "He would have quickly developed into a man with big muscles."

The commander thought about it, and then joined the captain in a hearty laugh. "Oui, you are so right."

"Commander, do not worry. Go back into the room. Tell Monsieur Ronsérre that your captain is retrieving the records from the file and will bring them in shortly."

The commander interrupted, "But you don't understand—"

"Ah, but Commander, I do understand. Let me finish."

"Continue," the commander said, in an almost subdued voice. The captain was a brilliant soldier and a brilliant thinker, but at the very worst was a bit too authoritarian. The commander often thought that he should have had the captain transferred to another duty station because of his arrogance, but his better sense always told him that he needed him. The captain had saved him too many times from impossible situations and embarrassing moments.

"Tell Ronsérre that I am obtaining the records for . . . did you say Pierre and Michel?"

"Oui."

"Sir, with all due respect, could you have been a bit more creative?"

Cringing with the anger now building up in himself, the commander shot back, "Could you have done better?"

Quickly responding, the captain urged the commander, "Please remember that Monsieur Ronsérre is the most famous solicitor outside of Paris, and maybe even the most famous in all of France. You are up against a formidable foe!"

"He trapped me. I did not anticipate that he was going to quiz me. I thought that he was here this afternoon to just interview the couple. And besides, you too are involved."

The thought immediately came to the captain's mind. *That is a problem. You never think. But,* he reminded himself, *some things are best left unsaid.* Instead, he told the commander, "No, sir, I only take orders from you." Then, to soften what he had just said, he paused and continued, "I am sure that I could not have done better. Continue the conversation with Monsieur Ronsérre, but on another topic. Shortly, I will come in and announce that I cannot find the records which you requested. 'Apparently they got mixed up in records recently sent to Paris by courier.'"

"Do you think he will believe the story?"

"I don't know, but it is the best that we have at the moment."

"Okay, okay," the commander said with a look of defeat. "At best, you are right; I should have released them, or at worst authorized you to dispose of them." He then asked himself, *Life should be a lot simpler, but can it ever be?*

Back in the antechamber, the commander explained that the captain was retrieving the records. "Monsieur Ronsérre, are there any further questions you have of me while we wait?" It was getting late. The sun was beginning to fade, and the commander was tired. "I am going to have some Cognac. May I pour you a glass?"

"Yes, please. I will enjoy a glass with you," Ronsérre told him. "But while we are waiting, let me review some details with you."

The commander much preferred to move on to new questions, but did not see a way. "I hope that I can remember the details of the case sufficiently to answer your questions," he said as he handed Ronsérre a silver drinking cup with a generous amount of Cognac.

Savoring a sip of his drink, Ronsérre said, "Commander, I have no doubt as to your being able to remember. Behind your answers, I can see a most brilliant intellect." Then he just sat for a while, smiling and making eye contact with his prey.

For what seemed like an eternity, the commander nervously tried to make small talk, but his attempts were met with either a simple yes or no answer, or just a nod of the head. Finally, Ronsérre broke what had been one of the most embarrassing and enduring four to five minutes of the commander's life. "Commander, how long have you been the warden at this prison?" he asked.

Almost too flustered to think, the commander told him, "About ten years, Monsieur."

"About ten years . . . I see . . . Could it be more than ten years?"

"Let me think. When did I receive—"

Quickly, without giving the commander time to consider how long, Ronsérre said in a rather snappy tone, "Maybe less than ten years?"

"Maybe," the commander told him.

The answer did not matter. It was of no consequence. Besides, the governor had already briefed him on just about everything that one could possibly want to know about his opponent.

The king had reposted the commander to La Rochelle from a grungy prison in Marseilles, in the south of France, because of his incompetence. He had been identified as having a drinking and gambling problem, and more seriously had been charged with dereliction of duty. La

Rochelle had only minor criminal problems, and it was hoped that lighter duties would keep him out of trouble. A tough-as-nails, no-nonsense officer had been posted from the king's personal guard in Paris to be captain of the guard, and to make sure that the commander did not make mistakes like he had in Marseilles. Another assignment for the captain of the guard was to keep tight surveillance on the Huguenots in La Rochelle and report directly to the king with written reports, bypassing the commander.

King Henri III had shown an interest in Huguenot beliefs and hymns as a child, but that interest had been squelched by his mother, Catherine de' Medici, a strong-willed Italian Catholic. As an adult he led the French army in the French Wars of Religion, and had involuntarily taken part in the plot for the Saint Bartholomew's Day Massacre, in which hundreds of Huguenots were killed.

Henri III was Catholic. Catholicism was the state religion of France. He was the king, and in an ideal world all Frenchmen should be Catholic. It was a pretty simple issue in his mind. But it was not an ideal world by any means. He believed for him to remain in power, there must be some give and take. He was willing to allow the Huguenots in some cities, most prominently La Rochelle, to have certain freedoms; but the freedoms must not get out of hand, thus, the need for tight surveillance and the presence of spying eyes. However, his dedicated soldiers should not get involved except in the more serious criminal cases, such as violence against Catholics and vandalism of cathedrals, documents, and relics of the Church. Obviously, these guidelines were being disregarded, and it seemed that the regulation of civil rights had transitioned to the authority of the Catholic Church.

There was strong evidence that the mayor of La Rochelle, as well as the prominent Jardeen family, were practicing Huguenots and Catholic in name only. But they were affluent, contributing members to French society. Thus, it was in the king's interest to ensure the success of the Jardeen boatyard, for it brought taxes to the government and international trade to La Rochelle. The display of the king's crest on the gate of the boatyard had not only presented the fact that the boatyard was favored by the king and his court, but that protection should have been granted to the owners, their families, and to the employees. Clearly, this was not being done.

Ronsérre reminded the commander of this fact. "Commander, you are aware, are you not, that young Tomas Jardeen is the son of Antoine Jardeen, and his spouse Madame Jardeen? The young monsieur is a valued employee of the Jardeen boatyard, which has been granted the seal of protection of the king himself. Monsieur Jardeen's beautiful bride is the daughter of the fine mayor of this city. The same seal of protection now applies to her and her parents. Commander, might I suggest that instead of provoking an attack on them, you and your soldiers would be best served by protecting them and ensuring their safety? You are currently unfairly charging them and imprisoning them because they have different religious beliefs than you or the king. I am sure that it is no longer a secret that they are of the Huguenot faith. It is evident that their beliefs make no difference to His Majesty, the king."

This time, however, the commander was a bit more quick-thinking. "But Monsieur, that is correct. We were trying to protect them. Remember, there is a curfew. They were out in the streets when they should not have been. The intent of my soldiers was to warn them of the dangers of being out late, and to suggest that they go home. Had they been lost or guilty of having drunk too much alcohol, my soldiers would have been glad to safely escort them to their home. Instead, the young man assaulted one of my soldiers."

"May I speak with the soldier whom he assaulted?"

"No, that is not possible. He has been transferred to another duty station."

"Please give me his name and the name of his duty station. I may need to contact His Majesty, the king, for permission to interview him."

"Do you know the king personally? I mean, do you—" the commander tried to ask. Ronsérre cut him off.

"Indeed, I do know the king. I have served as *conseiller* to the king in many legal matters." That part was a true statement. Continuing, Ronsérre bluffingly said, "I have already posted a letter about this matter to His Majesty, and it is already on its way to Paris. I am sure that the action taken against my young clients will get his attention. Of course, he may agree with the actions that you have taken, but then again, he may not. Which do you think he will choose? There is a risk here, but I am sure that these are matters that a smart man such as yourself has already considered. I trust that as a wise man, you will find it in your best interest to protect the prisoners until you know the king's reaction to this situation."

"Ah . . . yes, Monsieur Ronsérre, you do present yourself well. I assure you that the young Monsieur Jardeen and his bride, Margarite, are safe and no harm will come to them."

"I trust that no harm has already come to them."

"No, of course not."

"May I see them now?" Ronsérre asked.

"Oui," the commander replied. He quickly went to the door, opened it, and invited the captain of the guard into the room. It was no surprise to Ronsérre that the captain had been listening just outside the door. In fact, he hoped that the guard had heard everything, as he planned to question him under oath if the case should go to trial.

Addressing the captain, the commander spoke with a bit of fright. "Monsieur Ronsérre would like to have an interview with the prisoners, Tomas and Margarite Jardeen. Please provide him unlimited access to them at his convenience and ensure the *privacy* of his conversations with them." The captain noted the emphasis which his commander had placed on the word privacy. It was some sort of code suggesting he listen in on the meetings; or at least, this was the way that Ronsérre interpreted it. The captain snapped to attention and saluted the warden, "Oui, *à vrai dire, Commandant.* It is late. The prisoners are having their dinner. Would it be convenient for Monsieur Ronsérre to return tomorrow morning?"

Without giving the commander a chance to answer, Ronsérre said, "Yes, Captain, I will be here tomorrow morning early." He knew that the guards would need time to allow the couple a bath, for Tomas to perhaps shave, to change into clean clothes, and to be coached on what to say. Dinner and a good night's rest would do him fine, and besides, he needed to talk with Antoine and Charles. There were a few matters that he hoped they could clear up.

Chapter 16
Agonizing Noël

The winter solstice had passed, and already one could see the difference in the time that the sun began to set. From now until the summer solstice in June, it would be a little later every day. Ronsérre's driver had him back at the Jardeens' home before curfew. The cold front had passed on through, and it left the air a bit colder than it had been all day. That afternoon, Charles brought a small fir tree he had cut down in the woods on the farm. Together, Antoine and Martine had already put it up, and decorated it with some garland and decorations that they had accumulated over the years. The most treasured decoration, though, was a handmade one that Martine had made several years ago with the children. It was a girl angel dressed in white with golden hair, golden wings, and topped with a silver halo. Its beauty made her cry, as it brought back sad memories of the daughter she lost at only the age of three. It was terrible for Antoine and her to lose a child, a child that had been brought into the world with love, just pure, wonderful love. She had been a human being . . . a living, breathing human being, a child of God. Children were not supposed to die before their parents. Martine often wondered why it had happened to her. Why did God take her child from her? Of course, she would never understand, but she accepted God's decision. Molly was in a better place. She was with the Father, and Martine knew that someday she, too, would be with her again in eternity. She had cried most of the afternoon, until there seemed to be little left of her. After

Molly died, she prayed that she would not have more children. She simply could not bear to carry another child inside of her. So far, God had answered her prayers. She did not fully understand what was happening to her, but her mother had once told her that a time would come in her life where her body would change, and she would not be able to bear children. Some of the changes that her mother had described were already beginning to happen to her. She was now having occasions when she felt hot and flushed, and had mood swings; then, things would seem to go back to normal. Her monthly bleeding was now beginning to occur at irregular times, and was starting to diminish. As awful as she sometimes felt, the end of her fertile years was something to which she looked forward. Maybe then, without the potential for another child, she could put her loss into the background of her mind, knowing that she would never be able to completely forget. She had Tomas just fourteen months after she was married. That was late for a young, recently married French woman to deliver her first baby. She and Antoine were ecstatic when Tomas was born. She married when she was twenty years old, and he was twenty-two. He had just returned from military service in Paris, and she had been in love with him since she was a young girl. Her parents and his family were acquainted, and they lived down the street from each other. Antoine and she had played together when they were young, but he had soon grown too old to be seen with a little girl. Of course, he did not know she was in love with him even then. Even she did not realize it until later in life. She was just fourteen when he had taken notice of her a second time. She was a schoolgirl, and was beginning to turn into a beautiful young lady. She had that same golden hair that Molly had when she was born. Among her children, Molly was unique, as none of her siblings ever had the same color of hair.

Antoine and she had spent a lot of time together in their teenage years. They were all but inseparable. Antoine came from a family of seafarers. His father was a naval commander who rose to the rank of admiral in the king's navy; an admiral who, because of his brilliant knowledge of ship-handling characteristics, was placed in charge of shipbuilding and naval engineering for the navy. Antoine had inherited those same skills for naval architecture, construction, and repair of seagoing vessels. Now it seemed that Tomas was going to carry on in the family tradition. No doubt the admiral's reputation had played a large part in the favoritism being shown by the king to the Jardeens' boatyard. Due to the respect that King Henri had for the Jardeen family, it was safe to say that he did not know about the treatment being suffered by Admiral Jardeen's grandson.

Antoine's mother, Réne, had suffered for many years from a mental condition. She had periods of elation and emotional highs, interrupted by long, suffering periods of solitude and deep depression. It was a rare condition that confounded medical brains throughout Europe. Her husband's sea duty, with long absences from home, undoubtedly played a major role in the aggravation of her mental state. No name was given to it, and all mental problems were treated the same. You were simply classified as insane. Monastic asylums for housing the insane had all but disappeared by the time of the Reformation in France. This was because the Catholic Church did not view mental deterioration as being a medical problem. The Church viewed the mentally ill as having demons at work in their spirit and mind, demons to be exorcised from the body and killed. Patients were often tortured, and many died. Thousands had been burned alive as to rid them of the demons within. When Antoine was just ten years old, his dear Catholic mother went to her priest and begged for religious intervention to ease her suffering. In her confessions to the priest, she acknowledged a marital infidelity. She told him of an affair that she had while Antoine's father was at sea. It was with a married man of great wealth, political influence, and connections to the king's court. She had loved this man deeply, and he had promised to plead for an annulment of his marriage. She had promised to divorce the admiral so that they could marry, but he continued to delay fulfilling his promise. After many months, she learned that he was having intimate affairs with men, some of whom were in the hierarchy of the Catholic Church and others who were aristocrats in the king's court. Her lover insisted that these relationships go on. He told her that if she confided the affairs, he would tell the admiral and she would die the death of a heretic. It seemed that in France the Church was more forgiving to a man having affairs, even with other men, but a woman who was discovered of having committed an affair was shamed and harshly treated. The priest flatly refused forgiveness for Antoine's mother and threatened her with excommunication from the Church. Of course, if carried out, it would mean public disclosure of her sin.

The thought of public disclosure deepened her depression to a breaking point. She could not permit such a shameful embarrassment and risk the threat it would pose to her husband's career. So, she took matters into her own hands.

One day she took a boat over to the Île de Ré, on the pretense of visiting her sister. She and her sister were not especially close. They had not seen or spoken to each other for over two years. In fact, there had been an emotional gulf between them most of their life. This sister always had a great personality, had many friends, and was happily married with a large family. This was in stark contrast to herself. Antoine's mother had always been aloof, with a very prim and proper attitude. It was an aristocratic bearing. The few friends that she had had in life deserted her when she needed them the most.

She took Antoine with her. Perhaps the fact that he was an only child had been a factor affecting her mentally. She desperately wanted other children, but regardless of how hard Antoine's father and she tried when he was home from his at-sea duties, they seemed to be helpless in conceiving and keeping a baby to term. She had numerous miscarriages, each of which seemed to sink her into a deeper state of depression, especially with Phillippe, her naval officer husband, back at sea and unable to provide her with the emotional support that she so desperately craved. At that point, his assignment required him to spend a lot of time in Marseilles in the south of France, and in Calais and Le Havre, the shipbuilding ports in the north, causing him to seldom be home. It was worse than when he was in command at sea.

Her sister was very glad to see her and young Antoine. She welcomed them into her home, and for several days all went well. Then Réne suddenly blew up in anger when the conversation turned to her husband, and her sister casually asked if things were good at home. Réne took it as her sister questioning her faithfulness to her husband, or his faithfulness to her.

She grabbed Antoine by the hand and, in a rage, stalked out of the house, saying that she and her son were going for a walk on the beach to look for seashells. As they walked alone on the beach, Antoine noticed that his mother had a blank expression on her face. Her eyes had a far-off, distant look. He asked her, "Are you okay? Maybe we should turn around." His mother did not answer immediately, and instead just kept walking. He asked again, "Are you okay? Mother, please answer me." He started to cry. His mother stared at him for a long time with a look that seemed to say she was disconnected from the world.

Finally, she said in a soothing, calming voice, "My dear son, I am sorry, but I have to leave you now. I love you very much, but I must go. I hope that you will always remember my love for you." With that, she turned away from Antoine and faced the ocean in a transfixed state. She bowed her head, placed her cupped hands beneath her chin, and prayed. There was a special, unidentifiable aura that began to surround his mother, and on that cloudy day a bright, almost hypnotic light appeared over the ocean. Then, without turning back to face him, she said, "Goodbye, my dear son. I must go now." She walked slowly into the ocean toward the light, fully dressed, until she sank beneath the water and did not resurface.

Antoine began to cry out, "Mother, Mother, please come back! Please don't leave me! I love you!" Finally, his voice trailed off as he shouted one last time, "Mother, why did you leave me?" Passing out, he fell onto the sand, where he was later saved by a beachcomber as the tide was coming in, which would have soon washed his young body out to sea.

After his wife's death, Francis I, the then-king, permitted the admiral's retirement from the navy, granted him a significant pension, and promised to help him start a shipyard in La Rochelle. Philippe had the intention of raising his son, but the loss of his wife took a very heavy toll on him. It was not long before he turned to heavy drinking. When news of her infidelity leaked out from the Church, it turned to gossip around the city. One day, when he was mostly drunk in a city tavern, he happened to bump into Morrisétte, the man who had stolen his wife's affections. Both men's tempers flared, and they had a terrible argument. Each blamed the other for Réne's death, and the admiral challenged Morrisétte to a duel. Although duels were common affairs, officially they were frowned upon by the government and absolutely forbidden by the Church. "I accept your challenge!" Morrisétte told him in a highly irate tone. Given the state of their sobriety, probably neither man fully grasped the enormity of what was being proposed. But to refuse the challenge would have been a loss of honor for Morrisétte, the aristocrat. He growled, "Where and when?"

"Tomorrow, at sunrise. In the park next to the cathedral. Be there and bring your second," the admiral commanded in his authoritative naval voice.

"What is your weapon of preference?" Morrisétte asked.

"An arming sword." This was a heavier cutting sword that had been used for dueling since the practice began in France a century before. It was initially a military weapon adapted for use as a dueling weapon, and was meant to inflict deadly cuts on the victim. The arming sword had a heavy, double-edged blade, shorter than ninety centimeters in length. Because of its thicker, wider blade, it was a heavier sword than the rapier, which was just being introduced in France. This type of sword was generally used for parrying attacks, or defensive strikes against an attacker. Generally, the arming sword was not an effective weapon in thrusting. A rapier, with a longer, narrower blade and a sharp-pointed tip, was most useful in thrusting and piercing the body in a stabbing motion. Usefully, in this type of move, one or more major organs would be punctured, resulting in a great deal of bleeding and usually ending in death. But Philippe was intent on inflicting great pain and death on his adversary.

"Monsieur Jardeen, with all respect, I will be using a rapier, and my off-hand weapon will be a dagger." A rapier was a lighter, but newer, weapon that allowed more flexibility in offensive moves. The arming sword, because of its strength and size, was an effective defensive weapon because of its ability to either break the rapier by striking it, or knocking it out of the hand of the opponent.

The admiral quickly agreed that they would use separate weapons. His off-hand weapon would be a buckler, or small shield, made of metal, which would help defend against thrusting attacks. Besides, the arming sword was the weapon he had used in the navy and he had little experience with the rapier. His opinion was that the arming sword could inflict as much or more damage than the rapier.

"Who will be your second?" asked the admiral.

"I will have my brother, Count Norman," Morrisétte told him. "Who is going to witness your death?" he asked.

"My second will be my brother, Etainé, but I assure you that he will witness your death and not mine," the admiral barked back.

The two men then departed the bar and made their way to visit their brothers to arrange for the duel. By this time they were beginning to sober up, and with sobriety came the increasing fear for what might happen the next day.

Before dawn the next morning, the two men and their brothers were at the park, with their weapons readied for action. There was no sign of any soldiers and the Catholic church was silent, standing tall over the trees with a fog that had rolled in off the Bay of Biscay hanging low over the steeple. They were alone, left to settle the infidelity imposed upon Madame Jardeen and the dishonor brought to the Jardeen family.

While the seconds inspected the weapons carefully and went over rules of the duel, Morrisétte and the admiral paced nervously and did not speak. Neither really wanted to proceed, but as a matter of a man's honor and dignity, there could be no backing out. The seconds agreed that no armament could be worn. The only armament to be used was the admiral's off-hand weapon. It was also agreed that the duel would continue to the death of one or the other. The seconds would ensure that it was a fair fight, and fought within the traditional rules of dueling. The seconds agreed that the survivor and his second would afterward walk away from the scene of the fight, and that the victim's second would be responsible for the removal and burial of the victim's body. They swore that the identity of the survivor and the two seconds would never be revealed. The seconds further agreed that, other than their kinship to the participants, they had no interest in the outcome. They were present to ensure a fair fight and they would not themselves participate in it; they would not seek recrimination against each other and would remain acquaintances in the future.

As sunrise was approaching, the four men donned black masks that covered their faces, except for their eyes, nose, and mouth. Then, they put on black coats that draped near to their knees, black top hats, and gloves. Etainé had brought along the traditional bottle of fine Cognac and four goblets. When Morrisétte and the admiral had shaken hands and taken their places, Etainé poured the Cognac and made a toast to a fair fight, and to eternal rest for the victim. For one of the two duelers, this would be the last drink he would ever have. Morrisétte and the admiral, standing exactly twenty paces apart, raised their swords to salute each other. They then turned their backs to each other. Etainé ordered, "*Galants hommes d'honneur,* ready your weapons! On the count of ten, turn and face your opponent. On the count of three, approach your opponent and assume a battle position three paces away. Then, on the count of one, commence the duel."

There was a pause. By now, although nervous, Morrisétte and the admiral were both hyped up and ready to fight.

Etainé started counting backward: "*Dix ... neuf ... huit .. . trois ...* "

Morrisétte and the admiral raised their swords and took a battle stance, each staring the other eye to eye.

After another pause, Etainé continued, "*Deux . . .*" and finally, "*Un.*"

Immediately, Morrisétte rushed the admiral with an offensive thrust. The admiral sidestepped him, twisted a ninety-degree turn to the right, and quickly raised his buckler to parry off the secondary attack from Morrisétte's off-hand dagger. There was a dull thud as the dagger hit the metal buckler, and Morrisétte went stumbling past him. At that moment it would have been easy for Philippe to kill him, but it was too soon and too easy. Morrisétte regained his balance, turned, and bowed to the admiral. They each raised their weapons into the air, and when Etainé said, "Resume," they began to fight again. The admiral's act of benevolence certainly scored points with Morrisétte's second.

The men continued to fight. Because the arming sword the admiral was using was heavier and shorter than the rapier, it was difficult to mount much of an offense against Morrisétte. The admiral would have to be content with his parrying defense, hoping for the opportunity to strike the rapier with his arming sword and either break it or knock it out of Morrisétte's hand. After four or five minutes of a solid defense against Morrisétte's thrusting offense, the admiral saw his chance. He noticed that Morrisétte was not effectively using his dagger. He seemed to have tired, and his thrusts just didn't have the energy as they did in the beginning. One of Morrisétte's thrusts had torn into the sleeve of the admiral's coat and grazed his left arm. It was bleeding, but not badly.

Finally, Morrisétte made a final thrust with his rapier. The admiral this time parried to the left instead of to the right, away from the off-hand dagger. The rapier missed the admiral completely, but in the process the admiral was able to land a heavy blow to its forte, the thickest part of the blade near the hilt, with the forte of his own arming sword. The blow was so powerful that it broke the blade of the rapier. Morrisétte dropped the stub of his rapier, spun quickly counterclockwise, and attempted to attack with his dagger. The admiral was able to easily defend himself with his buckler, while taking the opportunity to launch his own offensive attack. Morrisétte danced around, ducking and twisting to avoid the admiral's sword, but soon an unlucky step put him directly in the path of the arming sword, being swung with ferocious strength. A strike on Morrisétte's right arm nearly sliced it off. The pain was so great that he dropped his dagger and screamed for mercy. The admiral was not finished. He continued to fight, landing a cutting blow to the stomach area. Suddenly, there was blood everywhere as Morrisétte fell dying to the ground.

The admiral backed away and took off his coat so that Etainé could wrap a tourniquet around his upper arm with a rag that he had brought with him. Turning to the now-dead Morrisétte, the admiral openly said, "I am sorry that it had to end this way. Perhaps it would be better if I had died, rather than you. May your soul rest in eternal peace." Etainé gave him another drink of Cognac for his pain, and then drove him in his carriage to the infirmary for a medic to clean and dress his wound.

Word was soon out on the street about the death of Morrisétte, one of the prominent La Rochelle aristocrats. It was not hard to guess with whom he had dueled. Word quickly spread to Paris. King Francis I was of course concerned, but only mildly so. A person of nobility had been killed, but engaging in duels was an act of courage and honor for men of Morrisétte's societal rank and privilege.

Words of sympathy would be conveyed to the family, but no retribution would ever be sought against Admiral Jardeen. His career and accomplishments had been too important to the French Navy. Extramarital liaisons were simply overlooked in French society, except when not handled with discretion. Francis himself had even been involved in a few during his reign as king. Morrisétte did not quite turn out as lucky. However, for the Catholic Church, it was a different matter. There was no criminal recourse for the Church, unless government officials agreed with the clerical body and civil charges were filed. In this case that did not seem likely to happen. And, because of the king's support for the admiral, excommunication of the admiral from the Church was ruled out. If the truth be told, the Church's anger in this matter was not so much at the fact that a duel had taken place and that a member had been brutally savaged. It was largely directed at the fact that Morrisétte was indeed a very wealthy man, and was very largesse in his giving to the Church. His wife and children were much less generous.

To spare young Antoine the humiliation of the gossip swirling around La Rochelle in the aftermath of the duel, the admiral sent him to live temporarily with one of Réne's brothers who lived in Bordeaux, to the south of La Rochelle. He would have sent him to live with the aunt on the Île de Ré, but the island had too many painful memories of what he perceived to be his mother's selfish act. Many nights Antoine had woken up screaming, "MOTHER, MOTHER, PLEASE DON'T LEAVE ME! PLEASE DON'T LEAVE ME . . . Don't leave me . . . please don't leave me . . ." His voice always trailed off, and then he would sob for the rest of the night.

Despite the fact that he had long ago forgiven Réne for her infidelities, life for the admiral began to spin out of control. His guilt over his neglecting Réne's emotional needs began to haunt him in terrible ways. Now he felt that he had abandoned Antoine, although at the time when he sent him away he felt that it was in Antoine's best interest. He felt increasing remorse for the killing of Morrisétte, for his was a human life that could never be brought back. Even though Morrisétte had done a terrible thing regardless, he was still at least partly responsible for Réne's death. Also, he was a child of God. It was not his job to be Morrisétte's judge and executioner. The admiral was being shunned by his Catholic brethren and the priest had told him that, by all rights, he should be excommunicated from the Church; but the idea of excommunication had been quelled at the request of King Francis.

The admiral's drinking grew worse. Many nights had been spent drunk on a bench in the park beside the church where the duel had taken place. Finally one night, after a few drinks, he took two bottles of laudanum to the park, sat on a bench, and drank them. Laudanum was a very strong medicinal drink of opium and alcohol, which was discovered just a few years before by a Swiss German alchemist. The potent opiate quickly relaxed the muscles of his body, his heart began to slow down, and his blood pressure dropped dramatically. Death did not take long. The admiral's body was found early the next day, reposed peacefully on the park bench. He was found by a young couple taking a morning walk with their young son. The husband ran to the nearby church and found the parish priest. The priest instantly recognized the body and ruled the death a suicide, rather than death from natural causes or homicide. The local civil authorities did not disagree.

Etainé tried to arrange with the priest for a Mass of Burial, but the Church was steadfast in its refusal for a Catholic service, nor would the Church agree to allow the body to be buried in the holy ground of the church's cemetery. "Why?" Etainé begged the priest to tell him. He did not get the real truth. Participating in a duel and having killed Morrisétte was undoubtedly the primary reason. But it was true that the Church's position on the taking of one's own life was essentially a form of excommunication, and a non-Catholic could not be buried in holy ground. The Church was so strong in these beliefs that not even a large monetary gift given on behalf of the dead person would make them think otherwise.

Etainé buried the admiral in the family cemetery on his manoir estate in a beautiful, hand-carved, polished, wooden casket. The grave was marked with a wooden cross made from hard chestnut. Etainé went personally to Bordeaux to retrieve his nephew, Antoine, and brought him back to La Rochelle. It was decided that Antoine would not go back to his uncle's home in Bordeaux, but would now live with his Uncle Etainé and his family. Their son, Charles, was just a few months older than Antoine. Charles was their youngest child. The age difference between him and his next older sibling was nine years, so he had always been treated almost as if he was an only child. Antoine would make a great companion for him, and indeed he did. They became so intertwined that you almost never saw one child without the other. They were so close that Antoine thought of Etainé and his wife as his parents, and definitely came to think of Charles as his brother. They were inseparable.

One day, when Antoine was almost eight years old, the wife said to Etainé, "Antoine is now our son. You, I, and especially Charles love him so much. He is a very good boy. Why don't we formally adopt him and make him a part of our family?"

He did not have to think about it. Without hesitation, Etainé told her, "I think it is a fine idea. A very fine idea, indeed. It is something that I have wanted to do, but just did not know how you would feel about it." Then, he grabbed her and gave her a very long kiss, something that he had not done in a while. The events surrounding the duel and his brother's death had taken a toll on him; quite frankly his wife, as most wives always did, suffered the consequences. It had been a long time since he had seen her so happy. "Yes, you have a wonderful idea!" he repeated to her.

That night at the dinner table, they discussed the idea with the boys. "I would like that," Antoine told them, with a half note of sadness in his voice. It was obvious that he remembered with deep grief what had happened to his biological parents. In Bordeaux, he had largely gotten over the nighttime spells that he had in the year that he was living with his father, but there were times even now when he broke down.

Charles was very excited. Hardly able to contain himself, he exclaimed, "Antoine, you will no longer be my cousin. You will be my brother!"

Etainé said, "And I have another announcement." Everyone turned with great admiration to hear what he had to say. Even his wife, Francine, was eager to see what was on his mind. He had not discussed anything beforehand with her. When he saw that he had everyone's attention, he continued. "This estate has been passed down through numerous generations over many, many years. Work here on the farm is hard, and I am getting old. Your mother and I have property in town which I had planned to sell. But I have changed my mind. I am not going to sell it. Instead, I am going to build a house on it, and we are going to move into the city."

"What will we do with the farm?" Francine interrupted to ask.

"We will turn it over to our older children, or at least to the ones who want to farm. You and I will still own it until our passing. I will continue to be available to the children for assistance, and will keep an eye on it to make sure that it is well-run and it prospers. We will divide the crops and the money from the use of the land equally. As they grow older, marry, and move away, their share will be divided among the ones left."

"What about us?" Charles wanted to know. "I love it here. This is all that I have ever known. What about Antoine?"

"Oh, you two boys are much too young to farm right now. You will be with your mother and me in our new home. And one day, when you are older and you wish, you and Antoine can jointly own the farm. But in the meantime, I want you two young men to live in the city, to have friends, to enjoy the culture of city life, to receive a fine education, to benefit from all that life has to offer, and to be all that you can be."

At this point, Francine broke down in tears. She had never loved her husband more than she did in that moment. Visions of life in the city raced through her mind. Charles was her youngest and she loved him so much, as he would certainly be her last child. She thanked God every day that Antoine had come into her life. It was sad to lose Philippe and Réne in such awful, tragic ways, but as family, they felt an obligation to provide for and raise Antoine with as much love as they did for their biological children. Antoine was such a wonderful young man, and perfect for their family.

Chapter 17
The Interview

Ronsérre had a long night. After dinner, he and the Jardeens were up again very late talking. They talked mainly about Tomas and Maggie; they wondered what had happened and why. Why did it happen to such a wonderful young couple, and why was their family being persecuted? Ronsérre could not give them the answers that they were seeking. No one could. He was unsure that even the commander and his soldiers could answer that question. But answers at this point were not the important thing. The most important things that he could do were to listen and share in their grief. The tragedies of their personal life told to him that night were too horrendous to even consider. It was impossible to imagine the loss of a young child. Ronsérre and his wife had a baby boy that was stillborn, and that was extremely hard to overcome. However, he could not imagine losing a child after several years. Several years of he or she being a part of their life, several years of unconditional love from the child, and several years of parental love for their little one consuming their hearts and souls. Antoine's story of the self-destruction of his parents was heart-wrenching. It was impossible to imagine the destruction of this man's emotional and mental state. In his mind, Etainé and his wife were saints to take young Antoine in and raise him to be such a fine, outstanding man. Ronsérre reflected on his own life and wondered, if given the same events and circumstances, what his life would be today.

The captain of the guard met him at the prison gate early the next morning when he arrived. It was a cold, bitter day, and the sky was threatening another Atlantic storm rolling in from the Bay of Biscay. The harbor was very rough, with large swells and whitecaps, and the wind had picked up dramatically overnight.

"Bonjour, Monsieur Ronsérre," the captain greeted him, with a sharp, snappy salute. "I have been expecting you."

Ronsérre knew that politeness and courtesy were the order of the day. "Bonjour, Captain, and a very fine day to you," he said as he reached out to shake the captain's hand. "It is a cold one today."

After a few moments of small talk, the captain led him and his party inside to the antechamber where he and the commander had met yesterday. Pierre Ravenel had already arrived and was waiting for him. He brought personal greetings from the governor and said that Bouché would like for Monsieur Ronsérre to stop by the office that afternoon, so that he could be apprised of his findings from the morning meeting. Ravenel made sure that the captain was listening when he said these things. Although he took special care to not say them in a threatening or hostile way, he did notice that there was a look of consternation on the captain's face, and then a subtle but certain change in his demeanor; a new air of formality and stiffness had grown in his responses. The captain had surely understood the message.

"With your permission, I will bring the prisoners—ah, I mean—Monsieur Jardeen and his bride up here to the antechamber, so that you may meet with them," the captain said.

"No, that is not necessary," Ronsérre replied. "I prefer to meet with them in their cells."

"But," the captain stuttered, "that is not allowed. It is against the rules of the prison."

"Captain, I do not wish to argue with you. Let us keep this encounter on a friendly, pleasant basis. You and I both know very well that a prisoner's solicitor is allowed into the cell block to speak with his client. I repeat to you that I wish to see the conditions under which the Jardeens are being kept. Do you understand, or shall I make it clearer to you?"

"Oui, Monsieur, you have made your position very clear. I will have to get permission from my commander. You do understand, don't you?"

"Of course, you do whatever you are required to do, Captain . . . I am sorry, but I don't think I ever got your name."

"It is Chevin, Captain Chevin, sir. Chevin, C-h-e-v-i-n, Monsieur," the captain said nervously as he backed his way out of the door.

It seemed very early in the morning, but Ronsérre at this moment felt empowered over the situation at hand, and it called for a celebratory drink. He walked over to the bar in the antechamber and helped himself to a glass of the commander's Bordeaux wine. "Monsieur Ravenel, would you care for a glass of the commander's fine wine?" he asked as he poured a generous second glass. "I am sure that the commander does not mind." He and Ravenel then helped themselves to cigars from the humidor. "I think we are going to be here awhile, don't you?" Ronsérre pondered, mainly speaking to himself. It was more of a statement than a question.

"Oui, I definitely think for a long time."

Captain Chevin finally returned to his visitors. He had been gone for only about thirty minutes, but it had seemed an eternity. It was enough time for two glasses of wine, and almost time for Ronsérre and Ravenel to finish their cigars. Chevin said that he was glad they had helped themselves, and apologized sincerely for not thinking to offer hospitality before he left them.

"I have spoken with the commander, and although it is against policy, he agrees that you might visit the Jardeens in their cells. However, a guard must accompany you and be in attendance during your conversations. I will ask the guard to station himself away from the cells so that he may not hear what you discuss, but will be near enough that you may call for him if necessary. There is a paper which you must, of course, sign acknowledging this arrangement."

"Of course," Ronsérre told him, "but first, may I review the document?"

When Ronsérre and Ravenel had read over the document, Ravenel quietly said, "I see no problem."

Ronsérre agreed, "No, I think it is okay. Let's sign it and go see our clients."

Chevin led them down into the bowels of the prison. This was not a good omen. Only the most hardened criminals were kept in dark, dank dungeons. Persons held on lesser charges were kept in less secure, more lighted areas. No, this was indeed a very bleak situation. On the way, rats were seen scurrying about, looking for scraps of food. They undoubtedly carried diseases such as the black plague that could, if bitten or badly scratched, take a person's life.

Margarite and Tomas were being kept in separate cells directly across from each other. Tomas was shackled with a chain to the thick wall of his cell. He was unshaven, dirty, and pretty much emaciated from the poor diet that he had been fed. This was common in French prisons for persons who were targeted for execution, or were simply being allowed to starve to death. His clothes were in tatters. Margarite, on the other hand, although dirty and whose clothes were torn, appeared generally healthy. Being imprisoned across from Tomas was obviously so she could vicariously experience the cruel treatment that he was receiving. No doubt the plan was to feed her well while Tomas, who was being starved, watched. It was cold in the dungeons, and neither prisoner was provided proper clothing for warmth, nor were they given warm covers for sleeping.

This was a familiar scene for Ronsérre. He had seen it hundreds of times before in prisons throughout the country. But it was a new experience for Ravenel. He felt sick to his stomach, and it was all that he could do not to vomit from the stench.

First, they spoke with Tomas. After introducing themselves and expressing regrets for the situation, Ronsérre said in a fatherly tone of voice, "Please tell me everything that has happened. Tell me what you have been accused of, and how you are being treated."

Ravenel would take notes.

"Monsieur Ronsérre, I have not committed a crime. I have done nothing wrong," Tomas told them. "My wife and I are not guilty of any crime except a belief in a personal God." Tomas continued with his story of being married in the Catholic Church so as to escape persecution by the Church. He had continued attendance and giving to the Church, despite his personal religious beliefs. In fact, he told Ronsérre, "I have not attended a formal Huguenot service other than when John Calvin came to La Rochelle, and never a formal service outside of my family get-together with friends. What was intended as a private service at the boatyard turned into a celebration of the announcement of my engagement to marry Margarite, the daughter of the mayor of La Rochelle. She is imprisoned in the cell across from me."

His voice was growing weak as he struggled to continue speaking. He talked about the encounter which he and his father had with the soldiers back in the summer. "Père and I were on our way to the Catholic church to see Father Benedict." He told Ronsérre how the soldiers had pushed him down, while one held his father in restraint. "Apparently, word of that incident made its way to the king, for soon afterward the boatyard was blessed with the king's insignia and, I thought, protection for the family."

He continued, "I was married in the Catholic Church by Father Benedict. Our wedding trip to Paris went without incident until we arrived in Orleans. It was there we learned that Maggie was pregnant with child, and we decided to return to La Rochelle when she was well rested. In Orleans, I met a bookseller, an ex-priest who left the Catholic Church and became a Huguenot. It was just a brief encounter in his shop while I was shopping for a book of poetry by Ronsard. The owner of the bookstore told me that he had been a Catholic priest who left the Church to marry and to embrace Reformist principles. We talked. He told me that his wife had died in childbirth just nine months after they were married. She had been carrying a baby girl. The priest knew the shop was being watched by the soldiers. It was late in the afternoon. He was a wise man. He cared for all people. He guessed that I believed in Reformed principles, even though I wanted a book of poetry by a Catholic poet. He guessed Maggie to be pregnant and envisioned that she would give birth to a baby girl. Then he saw soldiers in front of the store. So, he locked the door, pulled down the shades, and told me that we were in danger. He spirited me out the back door and drove to my hotel. I don't know if I was seen or not in his carriage. That night, the soldiers dragged him into the street, set fire to his store, murdered him in front of the shop, and then burned his body."

Ronsérre mulled over what Tomas had related to him. Finally, he asked, "And were you threatened?"

"No, no direct threats were made against us. We knew, though, that we were being watched. We left town with our driver to find lodging outside the city. On the way, we were stopped by soldiers, but they did us no harm. They turned around and appeared to head back into the city. We found a manoir estate that took in guests, and provided shelter for the coach and horses. We were well treated by the owners, and by mere chance they were Huguenots. Soldiers patrolled regularly past the house, even stopping to tug on the locked gate. After staying sheltered for several days, we left our carriage and horses there. The owner's son, accompanied by his two children, drove us in the owner's carriage back here to La Rochelle, on country roads that were out of eyesight. We made a brief stop at Uncle Charles's farm to drop off his driver, and then we stopped off at Maggie's house for a few hours. We left the driver and his children from Orleans, so that they could leave the next day to return home. We then left Maggie's home and started over to see my parents. We did not know about the curfew; no one told us. Probably Maggie's father, excited to see her, had just forgotten."

Tomas then proceeded to tell Ronsérre about being stopped by the soldiers on the way to see his parents. "We were not far from my home," he said. "Suddenly, a soldier stepped out into the street and halted us. Then another soldier rode up. They began to argue with me when I protested that I did not know about the curfew. I told them that we had been out of the city for a while and had just returned. They cursed at me. I put my hand on the arm of one when he made inappropriate and obscene remarks to Maggie, and started to move toward her. They shoved me and drew their weapons. Both of us were arrested and brought to the prison."

"And how have you been treated since you have been here?" Ronsérre asked.

"It was okay at first. We were in cells upstairs. In the beginning, Maggie was allowed to visit me in my cell for meals. Then one day," he paused, took a breath, and continued, "two guards came into the cell while we were together. One guard ordered her to remove all of her clothes. He told her that both the other guard and he were going to rape her, like Father Benedict had sodomized me when I was just twelve years old. I suppose this horrific reference of Father Benedict's past actions indicates that Benedict is somehow a part of this plot against Maggie, our families, and me. When she started to undress, I could not take it any longer. I began to fight the guards. I am sure that it was a setup to force me into a fight, so that they could continue to hold us and put us down here into the dungeon."

Ronsérre asked, "What happened to Maggie?"

"Maggie stopped undressing and the guards did not ask her again."

"Oui, it does sound like you two were set up. Monsieur Ravenel, have you recorded all that Monsieur Jardeen has told us?" Ronsérre asked the governor's aide.

"Oui, Monsieur," Ravenel replied with a nod of his head.

"Please, tell me about your treatment here in the dungeon," Ronsérre said.

"It has been terrible," Tomas told him. "Maggie is kept in the cell directly across from me. She can see me all the time, but we are not allowed any longer to be together. She, thankfully, is generally well taken care of, and is given good food. However, I am always very cold. They give Maggie a blanket at night to stay warm, but they do not give me a blanket. The guards feed me scraps, mostly stale bread and water—enough, I suppose, to keep me alive, but barely. A guard is always present just outside our cells, and we are not allowed to talk to each other." He struggled to continue. "I am tortured, told to strip naked, and then told to pleasure myself. If I hesitate or refuse, I am beaten and whipped repeatedly with a leather strap. Sometimes I am knocked to the floor and severely kicked in the groin. Because she is in the cell directly across from me, Maggie can witness what they are making me do. If she turns her head, she is yelled at and asked if she wants the same kind of treatment for herself. They also shackle me to the wall, as I am now. The guards always tell me that they are going to let us die, so that neither of us can ever tell about the sexual encounters that Father Benedict had with me when I was a young boy. I beg for Maggie to be released, but I was told that Huguenots have no right to be free; we all deserve to die.

"Slowly, they are depriving me of food until I weaken and die. Then they tell me that after I die, Maggie will be starved to death, just like I was."

Standing up to leave, Ronsérre said, "Merci, Tomas, for talking to me and telling me your story."

"Will you help me?" Tomas begged in a sagging, melancholy voice.

"I will do my best, son."

By now, all of Tomas's energy was rapidly being expended. And then, as Ronsérre extended his hand to say goodbye, Tomas pleaded, "Please get us out of here. We can take no more." Suddenly, with a gasp for air, he fell forward into Ronsérre's arms and breathed, what Ronsérre presumed, his last breaths.

Chapter 18
Breaking the News to the Family

It was the eve of Noël. It was late by the time that Ronsérre arrived back at the Jardeens' home. Antoine and Martine were waiting up for him, eager to hear of his conversation with their son. The house was ablaze with candles, swatches of holly, and boughs of evergreen. There was even some mistletoe hanging in the doorway. Martine gave him a kiss on each cheek when he came in, wished him a *Joyeux Noël*, and thanked him for all that he was doing. The table was all set for dinner. While they were bringing out the food, Antoine poured red wine for the three of them. The children had not come down yet.

Ronsérre did not know how he was going to break the news to the family. Without doubt, except for the death of his wife, this would be the hardest experience that he had ever had. It was almost impossible for him to speak without breaking down in tears.

Martine could tell from the sadness in his voice that the day had not gone well. "Monsieur Ronsérre, is everything okay? Has something terrible happened?"

Setting down his goblet of wine without tasting it, he said to Martine, "Please sit down. I have something to tell you." After they were seated, he continued, "It is with extreme sadness and heartbreak that I must tell you that your beloved son Tomas has died."

Antoine remained composed as well as one could expect. "Dear God in Heaven," he exclaimed. "Why, why did this have"—and then his voice cracked, and tears began to roll down his cheeks—"to happen?" Martine was crying uncontrollably. Getting up and stumbling to go to her husband, her legs would not support her. She crumpled to the floor, and had to be picked up and laid on the sofa. The servants had already retreated to the kitchen as a show of respect. Of course, the wailing and sobbing had brought the children down from their rooms, and they wanted to know what was wrong. Ronsérre took them aside, while Antoine stayed to comfort his wife.

"Your brother is dead. He died today in my arms. That is all that I can tell you right now. I am so sorry for your loss." The children were stunned. Paul, the younger brother of Tomas, took it well, but Marye sobbed loudly. None of them spoke.

Dinner plans were cancelled. A servant brought out a platter of freshly baked bread with cheese and fruit, but it was hardly touched, except by the kids.

It was a long, sad evening. Ronsérre did not go into details of what he had been told, nor did Antoine or Martine ask. They asked about Maggie and if she was okay.

"Oui, she is okay and in seemingly good health," Ronsérre told them, stretching the truth, for he had not even talked to her. But it did not matter right now. The Jardeens just needed to be consoled with some positive news. That news was certainly of comfort to them. Tomorrow, he would go back to the prison to plead for her release, and the Jardeens would go to claim their son's body and bring it home for burial.

Soon afterward, the governor arrived to express his condolences. Ravenel had briefed him on what Tomas had told them, and that Tomas had died in Ronsérre's arms as they were preparing to leave.

By the time the governor left, it was very late. Ronsérre stayed up until after Antoine and Martine had consoled themselves to the extent that they were able to go to bed. When he finally retired to his room, he was unable to sleep, lying awake most of the night, turning over and over in his mind what had happened. He wondered if he could have done more, or if he could have done something differently.

Before morning, the wind began to pick up and turned into a gale force with very heavy rain, thunder, and lightning. As he lay in bed, thinking and praying, he wondered if the storm would wash away the evil that seemed to be creeping across France, particularly afflicting La Rochelle. If circumstances such as what had been happening continued, what would indeed be the future of the country? If this was to be the future, he hoped that he would never live to see it!

Chapter 19
Day of Noël

Antoine and Martine were up early in the morning, despite having been awake most of the night in tears over the death of Tomas. This misery they felt had been brought into their lives through no fault of their own. It seemed senseless that man could kill another in the name of religion. Antoine said to his wife, "God created all mankind out of love. We are his children. Man has no right to take the life of God's creation, of one of his children . . . so why did they take the life of our beloved Tomas? Our Tomas, a young man full of strength, inner beauty, and intellect. A man who had so much to offer his country." No longer in this world did there seem to be any answers. The soldiers may not have slit Tomas's throat or thrust through him with a rapier, but they were just as guilty of murder had they taken his life themselves. "God bestows life and God takes life away; man does not have that right."

By the time they came downstairs to greet the day, Martine had somehow managed to compose herself. The storm had moved on to the east; as the rain lessened to a drizzle, it turned to a heavy snow which had left a covering of three or more inches on the ground. It was a beautiful scene, but most assuredly would cause problems throughout the day. Despite the weather conditions, there was a significant amount to be done. Martine embraced her husband and whispered to him, "Joyeux Noël, mon amour."

"Joyeux Noël," Antoine replied and kissed his wife as the kids silently crept down the stairs and, unbeknownst to their parents, clapped and whistled when they reached the bottom.

After Ronsérre came down, the servants announced that breakfast was ready. While they were eating, Ronsérre made no mention of the conversation he had had with Tomas. Neither Antoine nor Martine inquired, as they did not want to discuss it in front of the children. They would know in due time the gruesome details of their son's suffering.

They were, as French custom dictates, planning on exchanging gifts the eve of Noël. But the previous night had been so tumultuous that it did not seem appropriate to do so. After breakfast, Antoine invited everyone into the parlor, where Uncle Charles's small fir tree was located. This included Ronsérre, his driver, the governor's guards whom had been assigned to protect him, as well as their driver, the cook, and each of the servants. Antoine and Martine took turns giving gifts to each person, wishing them a wonderful holiday season as they did. Martine gave each hired help an envelope with a monetary bonus upon their departure from their home. The amount varied according to the length of their employment with the family, their marital status, and the couple's perception of the employee. They gave generous bonuses annually, an act of kindness that earned the Jardeens trust and loyalty from their employees; the couple considered them family by this point. The respect accorded to them was returned tenfold throughout the remaining part of the year in many ways.

Later in the morning, Antoine made a trip to buy a coffin in which to bury his son. Since the city was shut down for the holiday, he went to the coffin maker's home in the country just outside of town. After exchanging pleasantries and holiday greetings, Antoine told his friend the circumstances that brought him there, as best as he knew them. Although the exchange was brief, it took all the strength that he had in him. "I need to buy a coffin, burial sheet, and the necessary stuff to bathe and purify his body," he told his friend. "I know your shop in the city is closed today, so I don't know what to do."

"My most sincere sympathies to you, Monsieur Jardeen," the coffin maker told him. "Although I face death every day of my life, I cannot pretend to know what you and your family are feeling."

"Martine and I are taking it badly. We just do not understand. He was such a wonderful son, and his future was bright. No, we cannot understand. Why him?"

"Antoine, death is not for us to understand. You may never know why. Only our God in Heaven knows. I know such a simple answer will do little to soothe your soul. Tomas's life will, hopefully, serve as inspiration to others. Let us pray that, in your lifetime, you will know His plan."

"Merci for your kind thoughts and consolation," Antoine said. "I will share your words of concern with Martine and my brother, Charles. I know they will receive comfort, as I have from your wisdom; I will try to remember your words for the rest of my life."

"Well, Monsieur Jardeen, even though today is the birthday of our Lord Jesus, I am sure he will not object to me taking care of such a good friend as you. In fact, I think he would be rather disappointed if I did not offer my services in your time of need."

"Shall I follow you into town?"

"That will not be necessary," said Antoine's friend. "I make about half of the coffins here at home. Follow me to the barn and you can see what I have."

Antoine picked out a nice oaken coffin. It was a simple wooden coffin, with an empty cross beautifully carved into the lid. The Huguenot-style coffin was different from the ornate Catholic-style coffins with the carvings of Jesus hanging on the cross, which was the Catholic representation of Jesus dying for our sins. In contrast, the Protestant cross symbolizes that although Jesus had died, he arose from the dead and had life everlasting with the Father in Heaven. The Huguenots believe strongly that Jesus, the Son of God, was sent not to condemn the world, but so that the world might be saved through him.

"Will you need the service of my funeral carriage?" the coffin maker asked.

"Yes, day after tomorrow. We will take the body to brother Charles's farm in the country to lie in repose at his home, and there we will bury Tomas next to his sister and his grandfather, in our family burial plot."

"Will this be a private funeral, or will it be open to the public?"

"Oh, by all means we would like the funeral to be open to the public. Can you help spread the word among the religious community in La Rochelle, both Huguenot and Catholic parishioners?"

"Who will conduct the service?"

"I will, and I am sure that Charles will participate. Hopefully, Governor Bouché will attend and participate if possible."

"That will be fine. I will transport the coffin and supplies to your home tomorrow, so that you can prepare the body for burial."

"I will be picking up the body of my beloved son this afternoon at the prison. I will let you know if there are any complications."

"May I meet you at the prison to transport the body to your home? I will be glad to do that for you," said the coffin maker.

"That would be very kind of you," Antoine told him.

"Okay, I will see you there midafternoon."

"How much do I need to pay you?" Antoine asked.

"Do not worry, my friend. I will let you know later, but I will take only a small profit. I do not want to get rich on your misfortune. I promise that you will not be disappointed."

Antoine drove his carriage home slowly, while meditating upon how he could bring joy from his present misery. He remembered the commitment that he and Charles had made to Ronsérre at lunch; it was a promise to start a Huguenot congregation in La Rochelle. They would build the first Huguenot church in the city. At the time he swore an oath, not in jest, but only half serious. That was before Tomas died. Now, in his mind, the promise seemed to take on great urgency. This was something that he could do in memory of his son. It would be more than a sworn promise, or an obligation made for a payment of debt. He would do this for the people of La Rochelle. He knew that he would have to now delegate more of the responsibility of ownership and management of the boatyard to Charles. He may have to seek new business partners. Certainly, he knew that he could depend on Charles and his brothers-in-law from Île de Ré.

Meanwhile, Charles and his family arrived at Antoine's home. They were not expecting to hear the news of Tomas's death. Leaving his wife, Paulette, to sit with Martine,

Charles sought out Monsieur Ronsérre and asked if he would accompany them to the prison in the afternoon. "I was hoping that I would be asked," Ronsérre explained. "There may be some unfinished business to which I need to attend."

Governor Bouché, out of concern for the family, did not go directly to the prison. Instead he went to visit the Jardeen family to offer his condolences, and to help in any way possible. The governor was greeted by Antoine. "Your Lordship, you have done everything for me. I could not ask for more. It is enough that you have been here for me when I needed you. Please do not ever question yourself regarding me and my family. Just know we will always remember and respect what you have done. Our gratitude for your support and kindness will never be forgotten," Antoine told him.

"Are we ready to go to the prison?" Ronsérre asked.

"Yes, it is already after midday, and we have a lot to do with not much time," the governor stated as he turned to question Monsieur Ronsérre. "Will you ride with me in my carriage? I have some legal matters to discuss."

"Oui, Your Lordship. It will be my pleasure to accompany you."

Charles and Antoine pulled up to the prison gate, just behind the governor's coach. The guard recognized the coach, as the governor's seal was displayed along with the governor's brightly festooned guards. The driver was armed with a caliver, which was prominently displayed. The guard waved the driver to enter, but Bouché instructed the driver to stop. Motioning for the prison guard to come to the side of the coach, Bouché, agitated by the circumstances, addressed him. "Please admit the carriage behind me without delay. They are accompanying me into the prison. And please tell me, is the prison commander present today?"

"No, Your Lordship, the commander is not here today."

"Then is the captain of the guard present?"

"Oui, Your Lordship. The captain is here."

"Then send a messenger to tell the commander that, wherever he is, I wish to see him immediately. Do not waste time. Get that message to the commander now!" The governor almost exploded into the guard's face.

"Oui, Your Lordship, it will be done as you ordered."

"One of my guards will accompany the messenger," Bouché told him, while motioning to the guard sitting across from him. The guard got out of the carriage, and Bouché called out to his driver to proceed. The Jardeens followed without being stopped.

The captain of the guard received them in the antechamber. "Good afternoon, Your Lordship." Bouché immediately, without the expected pleasantries, introduced the Jardeen brothers to him. As the captain attempted to bow to Antoine and Charles, the governor interrupted. "I am sure that you know why we are here. I have asked the gate guard to send a messenger with one of my guards to find the commander and tell him that his presence is required here immediately."

The captain, clearly irritated, asked in a voice as calm as he could muster, "Your Lordship, I am sure that I can help you—"

Before the captain could finish, the governor, by now somewhat calmed down, interrupted. "Of course, we are here to claim the body of Tomas Jardeen, your prisoner being held in the dungeon who died yesterday."

"Oh yes, Monsieur Tomas Jardeen," the captain responded. "I see. Indeed, we must wait for the commander to arrive. Your Lordship, you did say that you have 'requested' that a prison messenger and one of your guards be sent to summon him here?"

"Oui, Captain, that is correct."

"Also," Antoine added, "the coffin maker will arrive shortly to transport my son's body to my home."

"Perhaps I should check to ensure that the messenger has left," the captain said. "Please have a seat and make yourselves comfortable." The captain abruptly left the room.

About a half hour later, the commander came to the antechamber with the captain and the coffin maker in tow. Without the exchange of any pleasantries, the men got down to the business at hand.

"We are here to claim the body of Tomas Jardeen," the governor told him. His strong, affirmative tone clearly showed his intense irritation and dislike for the commander. In his mind, he had already decided that the commander must be replaced. This would have to be a topic of discussion with the king on his next trip to Paris, or if the king should come to La Rochelle beforehand. The feelings of disdain were, of course, mutual. The commander was highly resentful of the governor's involvement concerning his authority in overseeing the prison. He understood that having the right friends could be beneficial; he himself had benefited from previous friendships in that manner. He surmised that the governor clearly used his leeway with the king in this, and he resented Bouché's unwanted interference into a matter that had been so perfectly planned and executed. Deep down, he knew that he would be the scapegoat for the arrest and death of the young Monsieur Jardeen. Quite frankly, he did not feel that Monsieur Tomas

Jardeen was important enough to warrant cause for his removal and disgrace.

"You may bring your funeral carriage around to the usual pickup point," the commander told the coffin maker. "Captain, have the father identify his son, sign the release papers, and then deliver the body to the coffin maker."

The coffin maker's name was Robért Marchand, but everyone simply knew him as the Coffin Maker. Robért Marchand did not like the commander at the prison. Bodies were always delivered to him dirty, unshaven, and generally malnourished to the point of emaciation. He was not looking forward to receiving the body of his good friend's son.

"No," Bouché protested. "Not the back door. I demand that the body of young Tomas be taken out through the front door of the prison."

Without hesitation, and with an urgency to resolve the matter, the commander consented. "Oui, Captain, do as he requests. It is not a problem."

"As you order, sir." The captain addressed Antoine, "Follow me, Monsieur. This will not take long." Charles and the coffin maker followed Antoine, leaving Ronsérre and Bouché alone with the commander.

The commander proceeded to follow the coffin maker out the door, thinking to himself, *Thank goodness this matter is at last taken care of.* He was called away from his thoughts by Ronsérre.

"Commander, I have another matter to discuss with you."

Turning back, the commander's calm demeanor imploded and gave way to his anger. He had enough of the Jardeens, and of their brash solicitor. "What do you want now?" He nearly shouted this at Ronsérre. Then, without stopping to consider what he was about to utter, he continued, "This case is over. You got what you wanted. The trap was a stupid idea—" Pausing for a few seconds, he got himself under control and tried to correct himself. "I mean, it did not have to come to this. You understand, don't you? He and his bride were being treated well. Tomas was being questioned in the presence of his wife. We had only wanted to find out what the bookshop owner in Orleans had told him. We wanted to know about the Huguenot insurrection in Orleans formulated by the ex-priest, and whether Monsieur Jardeen was planning one here in La Rochelle." Conveniently omitting any mention of the demands forced upon Maggie, the commander repeated his earlier story that Tomas had charged his questioners, knocking one to the ground while cursing him and trying to take his sword. The commander then stated, "If it was not for the assault and his pointing a pistol toward the soldiers, Monsieur Tomas and his wife would have been released by now."

Ronsérre listened carefully and made mental notes. "Is that why Monsieur Jardeen was shackled to the wall when I interviewed him?" Ronsérre enquired.

"Oui," he said forcefully. "We cannot allow such behavior."

"Well, surely you have not had such trouble from Madame Jardeen."

"No, of course not! She has spent most of her time here reading and praying. I surmise that she is of the Huguenot belief, the same as her husband."

"I don't know," Ronsérre lied. "Maybe yes, maybe no. You would have to ask her. They were married in the Catholic Church by Father Benedict just a few months ago."

"You fool," the commander screamed in a fit of rage. "Who do you think started the whole investigation and demanded the imprisonment? Surely you should know that Father Benedict and the hierarchy of the Church are not fools. They saw through the sham that the Jardeen family had imposed on the Church. They are Huguenots!" he screamed, as he wildly flailed his arms.

Ronsérre snapped back, "Maybe, but if so, Huguenots are to be protected by order of the king himself. Do you not know that the king's seal protects not only the boatyard, but the entire Jardeen family, his brother, Charles, and his family? In fact, by inference that protection extends to the Légere family because of the marriage between Tomas Jardeen and Margarite Légere. Commander, you are messing with something that is way beyond you, something bigger than you; this is something with which you should not want to tamper."

"Well, Monsieur Ronsérre," the commander stated in a deathly calm tone. "What do you want me to do? What do you ask of me?"

"Commander, first I am asking you to immediately release Madame Margarite Légere Jardeen into my custody today. She will be transported from prison and reunited with her family."

The commander paused to consider the request. "I don't know. That may not be possible."

"Commander, I can tell you that your career is probably already over. You are appeasing no one but yourself." Ronsérre, keeping his bluffing in check, continued, "I am quite certain that when I report this matter to our good King Henri, he will not be pleased with the actions you have taken. Knowing your past record as well as I do, I presume your remaining time here as warden will not be for long. Do you understand what I am saying? No doubt you will be transferred back to Marseilles or some other wretched prison; perhaps you might even be executed by a firing squad. Take time to meditate upon the unpleasant actions that could happen to you. For once, just do the right thing. You have made choices in this life, and they appear to have been bad ones. Why don't you now make good on your choices?"

The commander quietly pondered and stated, "I will go to my office and think about what you have requested. I will let you know before you leave today."

Ronsérre contemplated on asking for the prison records to be destroyed, but thought better of it. Their criminal records could be taken care of by a pardon from the governor, or the king. The governor had indicated in the carriage ride to the prison that he would do what he could after Maggie's release.

"Is there anything else?" the commander asked.

"No," Ronsérre told him. "Just the possibility of bringing criminal charges against you, a transfer, demotion, and perhaps a beheading on the king's order."

None of what Ronsérre was saying was very likely. It was nothing more than a threat, but it succeeded in doing the job. The color drained from the commander's face and it took on the appearance of a waxen death mask. The commander exhibited an edgy and shaken demeanor. Without saying anything further, he turned and walked slowly out of the room.

Ronsérre watched the commander's shameful exit and was pleased. He knew that he had won. To celebrate, he decided to enjoy more of the commander's Cognac, and one of the fine cigars from the Azores.

Meanwhile, in the prison's morgue, Antoine positively identified the body of his son. Tomas had been given a shave; his hair had been washed and trimmed, and his body had been bathed. There were scrapes and bruises on the body. They were the results of the torture and beatings inflicted on him. Antoine's temper was about to consume him. He was enraged that his beloved son, whom he was sure had not done anything to be arrested for, had to suffer such cruelty. It was the wrong time to think about such thoughts, but somehow, someday, vengeance would be his. What he might do would depend on what remedies his friend Bouché and the king were willing to offer.

Suddenly, the loud report of a gunshot rang throughout the prison. Praying that somehow it did not involve Ronsérre, the others stayed in the morgue with Tomas and the morgue attendant. Soon, word came from the captain of the guard that the commander had taken his own life in his office. He was found slumped over his desk. The suicide weapon was next to the body, and there were powder burns on his right hand. The commander had left a note, saying that he hoped by taking his life he made the right choice. The note further stated how he had failed his family, his colleagues, and the king, and how he wanted to make things right. The note ended with an order for the captain to immediately release Madame Jardeen.

As the captain was telling the news, Antoine thought, *Monsieur Ronsérre must have really gotten to him. He must have instilled the fear of an eternal life in Hell, rather than in Heaven.*

Antoine and Charles walked with the captain to Maggie's cell in the dungeon. She was reading a Catholic Bible. It was the only book she had been allowed to read while in there. She just stared at her father-in-law and uncle, but did not speak. The captain opened the cell door and said to her, "You are free to go. You are released into the custody of your father-in-law. He will take you home."

Her only response was, "Tomas . . . where is Tomas?"

Antoine quietly answered, "My dear daughter, Tomas is going home."

While they went upstairs to find Ronsérre, the morgue attendant and the coffin maker wrapped Tomas's naked body in a sheet, moved it upstairs, and placed it by the front door as Antoine had demanded. Two prison guards, and the guard provided to Ronsérre by the governor, now stood watch over the body.

The captain of the guard brought release papers to the antechamber, where the family was gathered with Ronsérre. There was no celebration. Their conversation was subdued. Maggie had spoken only once, asking, "Where is Tomas?" Ronsérre and Antoine signed the release papers for the release of Tomas's body, and for the release of Maggie to Antoine Jardeen.

Then, with the captain of the guard accompanying them to the front door, they went to watch the placement of the body onto the carriage. Antoine saluted as the body, wrapped tightly in the sheet, was carried out and placed inside the carriage.

The captain turned to Antoine and told him, "I am extremely sorry for the death of your son. There is nothing I can say that will bring him back to you and your family. I know that you will miss him always. I wish that things had not turned out as they did." The captain reached for Maggie's hand to express his condolences, but she pulled back from him. To Maggie, the captain simply stated, "I am sorry for your loss," and he turned and walked away. After several steps, he stopped and watched the family leave. Recalling the events of the day, the captain proceeded to the commander's office to take care of the mess that had been left to him.

When the entourage arrived back at the house, Antoine sent his driver to bring the Légeres, Maggie's parents, to his home. He instructed his driver not to divulge the information that Maggie had been freed from prison. He wanted it to be a surprise for them.

After Tomas was carried into the house and placed on his bed, the coffin maker brought in the coffin and the necessary supplies to prepare the body. This included water and a chemical to bathe the body, a vial of anointed oil for blessing the body, and fragrant shrubs and flowers which would be placed in the coffin to kill the odor from the body when it began to decompose. After expressing condolences to Martine and Antoine, deciding to return the next day, he left. Charles and the children went back out to the farm to arrange the digging of the grave, leaving Paulette to assist and comfort Martine. The governor took his leave to return home to his family, after promising that he would do everything within his power to bring the ordeal to the attention of the king. Ronsérre wanted to be of assistance to the family, but was unsure what he could or should do. At this point he felt very much like a fifth wheel, so he decided to stay in the background, but would remain available should he be needed.

It was all that Antoine and Martine could do to bring themselves to the necessary task of going back up to prepare the body. Martine broke down in hysterical sobs and wailed, begging over and over, "Dear Lord, why can't it be me, rather than my son?" It was an agonizing scene, but finally she could somewhat compose herself. She knew what had to be done. She knew she must be the one to wash the body. Antoine told Maggie that she should participate in the preparations. She still did not speak, but nodded her head affirmatively. Paulette joined them.

The Légeres had not arrived, so the family went up to the bedroom. Antoine unwrapped the naked body. Paulette poured a bowl of the water the coffin maker provided, and gave her sister-in-law a rag for bathing. While Martine was bathing her son's face, she thought that she noticed his lips and eyes twitch, but then it stopped. She knew her imagination was playing tricks on her, so she did not tell anyone and kept bathing. She watched very carefully, but saw no further signs of life, as to not give herself hope. She finished washing the emaciated body while Maggie watched silently. Welling tears finally began streaming down her face. When the bathing was over, Antoine, in a concession to Catholic practice, anointed his son's forehead with a cross made with holy oil from the vial.

When the sign of the cross had been placed on the forehead and his father was reciting the Nicene Creed, a ritual the Reformed Church believed was conformable to the word of God, there was a sudden arousal from Tomas. His arms and legs flailed. Suddenly, his eyes opened, and he tried to speak. At first, his words were garbled and were little more than grunts and groans. The family, except for Maggie, stood in rapt silence, mystified and afraid. Maggie spoke first. She bent over the body and said softly, "My dear, dear husband, it's me, Maggie, your wife. Please speak to me. I love you so very much. Tell me that you love me and that this is real; tell me that you are alive and back with me. I thank God every day for you." Then, he drifted back off to sleep.

Martine put blankets on him, knelt by his bed, and prayed for life to return to him. The family sat by his bedside into the night waiting for further signs of life, with candles lit on each side of the bed. In the meantime, their driver, along with the governor's guard assigned to Ronsérre, had returned with Michel and Elisabeth Légere. Finally, near midnight, Tomas began to show movement again and tried to call out for Maggie. His speech was clearer than before. Paulette ran to get Maggie, who had long since gone to bed after talking to her parents downstairs.

Maggie was not ready yet to tell them that she was pregnant. She just told them that the stress of the prison ordeal had taken a toll on her energy. While the food that she had been fed was not good, it had certainly been better than what the guards had fed Tomas. Finally, she was so tired that she had to find a bed to lie down for some rest.

Shaking Maggie awake, Paulette told her, "Come quickly. Your husband is waking up and is calling your name." They ran upstairs together.

"Tomas, Tomas, you are okay!" Maggie said loudly. "Thanks be to God, you are alive!" It was all that he could do to try and sit up. Although the room was crowded with family, including the Légeres, no one ventured to help him up, for they were afraid to touch him. Obviously, it was a miracle given by God that he was alive, and in their minds he must be a holy figure.

Unable to raise himself up from the bed, he fell back onto his pillow. "How long have I been asleep?" he asked. "Where is Monsieur Ronsérre? I remember falling into his arms. Where am I? Am I dreaming that I am at home, or am I in Heaven? Is everyone in my family dead?" He was beginning to ramble off questions.

Martine answered him, "My dear son, we are not dead, and you are not dead. You are alive. You are very much alive, thanks be to God. You are with us. You are home with your parents, Aunt Paulette, your wife, Maggie, and her parents. They are all here. Monsieur Ronsérre will be here in a minute. He is here in the house. Father will find him and bring him to you."

Ronsérre could not believe the incredible news. In his entire life, he had never heard of such a thing, and neither had the family. After Tomas had collapsed at the prison, he had personally checked him for a pulse. He could not feel a pulse in the wrist or in the neck, and there did not appear to be any sign of breathing.

Ronsérre was the first to touch Tomas. He bent over the bed and gave Tomas a hug without mentioning their encounter at the prison, he only expressed his happiness over Tomas and Maggie being free and well. Everyone took turns sitting on the side of the bed, showering Tomas with love until Antoine suggested it might be too soon for Tomas to bear all the manhandling and "womanhandling."

Maggie directed all her attention to her beloved husband. She lovingly looked at him and began to speak. "Tomas and I have wonderful news for you." All eyes were focused on her in wonder as she smiled and said, "I am with child." While looking into the faces of her loved ones, she announced, "Tomas and I are going to be parents." Everyone in the room began to cry with excitement and questions. Maggie informed them that she found out in Orleans. Questions and answers continued throughout the night until everyone was too tired to stay awake. Antoine volunteered to sit with Tomas, so the rest could get some sleep. Maggie argued for the privilege, but was overruled because of her delicate condition.

Before going to bed, Martine stopped by the kitchen and informed the servants, who had been huddled awaiting news from upstairs. She told them Tomas was alive and sound. Martine happily shared the news that she and Antoine were to become grandparents. She had no hesitancy in telling the servants, for she considered them family. Martine, being overjoyed by the evening events, gave her last instruction for the day. "All of you get some rest now. Do not worry about breakfast." Although she knew that it would not happen, she told them, "We will be sleeping late. Why don't you take the day off? Spend it with your families. All is well at last." Finally, she gave each of them a hug and a kiss on the cheek. "Thank you for all that you do. May God bless each of you, always!"

Chapter 20
The Day after Noël

It was midmorning when people began to wake up, dress, and gather downstairs. Because the staff had been given the day off, Antoine and Charles decided to try out their cooking skills. They cut several loaves of raisin bread prepared for Noël, and put out some cheese and jelly. They sliced some apples from the fruit bin in the cold cellar and poached them in some sweet red wine, serving them over hot cereal made from grain grown that summer on the farm. Everyone liked their coffee strong, so they put in a few extra scoops of crushed beans.

Of course, Maggie and Tomas were the center of attention. The Légeres had stayed over and hardly gave anyone else time to talk to Maggie. Antoine and Martine were eager to spend time with Tomas. Ronsérre certainly understood, and did not mind being left out of the conversations. After breakfast, he and Charles retired to the parlor to talk privately about whatever legal steps, if any, should or could now be pursued. Charles was convinced that a pardon from the king would not be enough to satisfy the family. "I cannot speak for my brother, Antoine, and his wife, Martine," Charles said, "but I feel confident that nothing less than an admission that Tomas did nothing wrong will be acceptable to them."

"Ah, Monsieur," Ronsérre told him, "I would also hope for that, but I think it is unlikely that the king will find his own soldiers guilty of misdeeds . . . at least, not publicly."

"What do you suggest?"

"In the springtime, I will be making a trip to Paris for both business and pleasure. I will have an audience with the king, and I shall argue these points with him. You must remember that France is still a Catholic country, and that the king's power and authority rests almost entirely on the satisfaction of the Catholic Church. This whole affair will be an embarrassment to the Church and its leaders. I think that to keep the Church officials happy, a pardon is the most that the king can do."

"But don't you agree that Tomas is innocent of the charges brought against him?"

"Oui, I am quite sure that he is innocent, and I am sure that a number of heads are going to roll. Of course, I only mean that as a figure of speech. They won't have to face the guillotine. But the prison system here in La Rochelle will be reformed, a new commander will be appointed, and the captain of the guard will be transferred. I will try to convince King Henri to give our good governor the authority to appoint the new staff at the prison."

"That would be a positive step, for sure."

"Yes, it could be the beginning of a new era for the Huguenots here in the city."

"But Tomas's life is ruined," Charles rebutted.

"No one, except the Légeres and anyone that you or Antoine have told, know anything that happened to Tomas. I am certain that any prison records pertaining to his case have already been destroyed, or will soon be, by the captain. As far as the captain is concerned, he has never heard the names Tomas and Margarite Jardeen."

Charles agreed, "You are probably correct in your analysis."

"I plan to travel back and forth to La Rochelle. I love this city, you know. This is where I was born. I will let you know when my trip to Paris is planned. Perhaps you and your wife would like to accompany me. There is much to do there."

"Oui, I know. Maybe we shall, for it has been a long time since we visited Paris. We will talk about it. I can hardly remember the last time we had a leisurely walk around the city, or along the banks of the Seine. Antoine and I do have a place in Paris, although we seldom visit. It is not far from the palace at the Louvre. You are welcome to use it while in Paris."

"You are very kind, but I do have a daughter in Paris who would be offended if I did not stay with her."

"Ah," he agreed. "You must stay with her. Maybe Paulette and I will see you there."

The conversation turned to other topics as family members joined them in the parlor. Tomas came in. He was weak and had to be steadied by Maggie coming down the steps, but his condition did appear to have improved over the course of the night. Maggie reported that he had eaten a good breakfast.

"How do you feel today?" Uncle Charles asked.

"I feel like I need to be doing something," Tomas told him. "Of course, it is wonderful to be together again with Maggie. It was a terrible ordeal, but I am alive. Thanks be to God. I feel that I must somehow find a way to repay His mercy. Right now, I am quite uncertain as to how I can do that. I pray for him to speak to me and tell me what I can do."

Listening to the conversation, Ronsérre knew. He kept silent and just smiled. The answer would surely come, but it was an answer that Tomas must figure out on his own.

"Uncle Charles, how is the design of the corvair coming?" Tomas asked his uncle. "I suppose that the plans are all finished."

"Well, almost," Charles told him. "We are pretty far along, but there is still plenty of work for you. We have missed you. The work has been slowed without your creative mind. We are looking forward to you being able to rejoin us at the boatyard, but first you need to regain your health and strength."

"I can't wait to get started; however, Maggie and I need some time alone. It's our time to reconnect with one another; it's our time to fall in love once again."

"Of course," Charles told him. "You will know when the time is right. We also have to discuss building your new home on the farm."

"Uncle Charles, Maggie and I thank you so much for your kindness and generosity. We have looked forward to doing that for a long time. However, we have decided that for now it is best we stay in the city. We will visit you often on the farm."

"We want to find an apartment for now," Maggie interjected. "Maybe we will build the home in a couple of years? We hope you understand."

"I do understand. I understand completely," Charles told them. "Both of you are very special to me. I will be ready when you are."

By then, Antoine and Martine had come into the room.

Ronsérre announced, "I have some loose ends to tie up here in La Rochelle, but I will be returning to Fontenay in a few days. Charles will tell you about my planned trip to Paris in the springtime. In the meantime, I will be back soon."

"Monsieur Ronsérre, on behalf of the Légere family and of my family, we thank you from the bottom of our hearts for all you have done for us. We are certain the outcome would have been tragic, if it had not been for you. It would have been likely that our son and daughter-in-law would not be alive, or would have spent the rest of their lives exiled as slaves on some remote island. Be assured that the vow we made to you will be remembered. We are not certain as to how we'll proceed, but we believe the way will be manifested for us to succeed."

Ronsérre knew those were hard words for Antoine to say, and even difficult for Tomas and Maggie to hear. He pondered for a moment and said simply, "My friend, I know that it will be done in due time. Now I have to prepare to go to the prison. I have unfinished business there."

Arriving at the prison gate, the guard on duty informed Ronsérre the captain was expecting him, and would be waiting for him in the antechamber.

Ronsérre wondered silently to himself, *How did the captain know I was coming today? I did not tell him that I would be here today.* In fact, Ronsérre did not know he would visit until that morning, when he had talked to Charles.

As he wondered, a voice spoke to him as he entered the prison walls. *Go forth, My son. Do not be afraid, I am with you always.*

The captain was indeed waiting for him, as the guard had instructed. "Monsieur Ronsérre, how fortuitous that you came today. I suspect that we have things to discuss. Please sit down."

"Merci," he told the captain while he extended his hand. "Both of us have been through a tough ordeal that we probably wish to erase from our minds."

"Oui, it has been unpleasant," the captain said as Ronsérre took a seat. "Please excuse me for a minute," the captain said softly. "I need to excuse my aide and the guard so that we can speak privately."

Ronsérre thought to himself, *Now comes the demand for money.*

Returning, the captain offered a glass of Cognac and a cigar. "Oui, but only if you join me in the pleasure," Ronsérre answered.

The captain started the conversation. "Monsieur, I hoped that you would come today as I have issues to discuss with you; but first, you must promise me that what I say to you will be kept strictly in confidence between you and me."

"I do agree," Ronsérre replied. "But you also have to swear your secrecy to me."

"I promise," the captain said, "anything said here, today, will go with me to the grave."

"So, what do you have on your mind?" Ronsérre questioned. He was deeply puzzled. At this point he felt that he must have missed something. "Do you wish to be paid money?" he asked.

"Monsieur, please do not insult me. I do not ask for money. If anything, I should be paying you. You have something much more valuable."

"I apologize, truly, I meant no offense. I do not understand, but please go on," Ronsérre told him.

"First, let's talk business," the captain replied as he took a good, long taste of the Cognac. "My talking to you is outside the bounds of my authority, but I am troubled by what has happened. I am sorry for the arrest of young Tomas and his bride Margarite, and I am sorry for the treatment that they received here at the prison. It was a trap set for them."

Ronsérre sat straight up in his stair and listened intently, but kept silent while the captain continued. "My commander learned from a soldier who rode a fast steed from Orleans about the Jardeen couple being on their way back home. The messenger told him the details of the activities of the ex-priest who owned the bookshop there, and the clandestine meeting between him and your Tomas. The ex-priest was supposedly guilty of luring parishioners from the Church and inciting hatred and violent action against the Church. As they were being watched in the bookstore, the priest suddenly closed the shop, spirited Monsieur Jardeen out of the back door into his coach, and sped away. Monsieur Jardeen was overheard on several occasions talking to his wife about their Catholic wedding being a 'sham' to cover up their true Huguenot beliefs. He was also alleged to condone violence and civil disorder against the Church here in La Rochelle. The commander was told that Monsieur Jardeen and his wife did not take the main road back to La Rochelle. It is believed that they must have taken primitive back roads that added several days to their trip home."

Ronsérre interrupted, "Do you believe these allegations?"

"As a soldier serving my commander and the king, it is not my duty to believe or not to believe. It is my duty to follow orders," the captain told him. "Please, let me finish."

"Please, do continue."

"My commander told this information to Father Benedict, the priest at the cathedral. Do you know him?"

"No, but I have certainly heard of him," Ronsérre grinningly told him. "I have not yet had the pleasure of personally meeting him."

The captain laughed and said, "Well, you are a bright man and no doubt know the rest of the story. The commander was pressured by the Church to arrest the couple. I stated to my commander that we cannot simply arrest someone without proof that they have committed a crime. He instructed that we create a scene and provoke young Tomas to commit a crime for which he could be arrested."

"What good was accomplished by the arrest?" Ronsérre inquired.

"None, Monsieur, nothing was gained by the arrest. There was no assault. No crime was committed."

"I am sure that the family, if you should choose to tell them, would be relieved to know the truth. Would you be willing to tell them that much?"

"Let me think about it," the captain replied.

"Oui, please do. If you decide to speak to them, you know where to find them."

Ronsérre stood to go. He was about to say goodbye when the captain said, "Monsieur, please, can you stay a while longer? I wish to discuss a personal matter with you."

Ronsérre was bewildered. He was unsure whether to tell the captain that he must leave, or whether he should stay. He was pleased with what the captain had shared with him so far, but he could not imagine what the captain had on his mind of a personal nature that he wished to share. "Certainly," he told the captain as he hesitantly sat back down.

"Monsieur Ronsérre," the captain began, "I have found you to be an honorable man with good ethics and morals. You impress me as a good Christian man who has happily found peace and humanity in your dealings. You have centered your everyday life around God. You have friends who care a great deal about you. I want your kind of life for myself."

Ronsérre listened carefully to what the captain was telling him.

"I am an unhappy person," the captain continued. "My entire life has been centered around the military. My father, his father, and his father before him all served the royalty as military officers. And now, I too serve the royalty in the king's militia. The acts which I have been required to carry out as a soldier have sometimes been contemptible. I have killed and tortured people . . . many I believe were innocent of the crimes of which they were accused. Sometimes it felt as if the devil owned my soul. I feel I am living not to do good in this world, but to work evil and misery on human beings. I sometimes feel that I am both the judge and the executioner; you and I both know that cannot be."

Ronsérre remained silent, but looked at the captain with empathy and nodded his head, as if to understand.

"The Catholic Church has not given me comfort. As a young boy, I was taught to believe in a kind, benevolent, loving God, and I believed that. But God did not speak to me, and I could not speak to God. I was taught that only the priest was worthy to speak to God and that I must confess my sins to the priest, who would then pray to God for my forgiveness. I have confessed my sins many times over to Father Benedict and have begged for a new life, but he insists that I am doing a good job as a jailer. He says that I am serving God and the Church by continuing what I'm doing, and not to worry. He claims that any work done on behalf of the Church cannot be a sin. He told me that my soul is secure as long as I did my duty to serve the Church. I ask myself, 'What am I doing to serve the Church?' I might be serving the Church by allowing Father Benedict to have control over my life. Yet, is what I'm doing in accordance with what God would have me do?"

"How does your wife feel about what you are doing?" Ronsérre asked.

"I do not see my wife and children very much, as I spend most of my time here at the prison. However, they do not seem to have any religious beliefs at all. They have not attended Mass in a long time, and she does not wish to discuss religion with me."

"Do you see your marriage as being a happy one?"

"I cannot say for sure," the captain told him. "I have had my number of affairs, and I feel sure that she has had lovers. But I do not condemn her. I love her very much, but the military life puts a great strain on a marriage. I have been away from home so much. And when I am at home, I have not been much of a husband or father. I often feel like doing what the commander did . . . just ending it all," the captain confessed in a soft, hesitant voice. He was near tears.

"How have you dealt with these feelings?" Ronsérre asked him.

"I have not dealt with them very well at all," the captain told him, after taking a minute to reflect on the question. "I have dealt with them by letting alcohol control my life."

"I see," Ronsérre said, pulling on the chin hairs of his gray beard. It was a comforting habit of his whenever he was deep in thought.

Unsure of where to go in his confession of faith to Ronsérre, the captain took a chance. "Monsieur Ronsérre, I am guessing that you have renounced the Catholic faith. You have embraced the Reformed teachings of John Calvin. Am I correct?"

"Yes, Captain, you are correct, but only partially so."

"What do you mean? Can you please explain?" the captain asked with great curiosity.

Now it was Ronsérre's time to explain his religious beliefs. "We are alike in certain ways. I, too, was raised in the Catholic beliefs, and I came to have doubts similar to yours. It was while I was studying law that I questioned whether there was a God. I did not receive comfort from the Church's religious beliefs or practices. When my wife was sick, and I knew that she was going to die, I wanted God on a personal level. A God that I, and not the priest, could pray to, one who would hear my prayers and my confessions of sin. I wanted a merciful, loving God and a simpler religion for the common man, who spoke French and not Latin. I did not want the heavy taxation of the Church. I wanted to give to the service of God beyond money with my own service and knowledge. I yearned to serve mankind for the sake of doing so, and not under the pretense that I would be denied the promise of eternal life otherwise. I believe in receiving heavenly reward through the grace of God. Can you understand what I am saying?"

"I think so," the captain said quietly. "I want what you have found!"

And then, the two men sat silent for a long time and enjoyed another glass of sweet, burning Cognac. Then, Ronsérre said, "It is getting late, so I must go. I will be returning home in a few days. Come to Fontenay if you need me, although I will be back here in the city from time to time."

"Merci beaucoup, Monsieur. Today has been meaningful. I will pray to God and ask for his blessings on you, on me, and on my family."

Taking a chance, Ronsérre told him, "You know that you can speak with Mr. Jardeen's father about your doubts. Go in peace to him. I am sure that he will give you wise counsel."

As Ronsérre was going out the door, the captain stopped him. "Tomas and his wife, Margarite, can rest assured that their reputations are safe. I will personally take care of the matter. I will call on the parents very soon."

"I know you will," Ronsérre told him, and then he turned and left.

Chapter 21
Return to Fontenay-le-Comte

One evening in the week after Monsieur Ronsérre had gone back to Fontenay, there was a knock on the door at the Jardeen home. Antoine was mystified when he answered the door to find a tall gentleman in a military uniform. "Monsieur, may I help you?" he asked.

"Oui, Monsieur Jardeen. My name is Captain Daniel Chevin. I am the acting commander of the prison where your son and his wife were held. It is pertinent that I speak with you and your wife about a matter of great importance. May I come in?"

At first Antoine thought that he recognized the officer's face, and quickly remembered the captain when he told him his name. "I am here by myself, and I mean no harm to you. Monsieur Ronsérre suggested that perhaps I should call on you. I had hoped that you would be glad to hear the information that I am bringing to you, and that I could have the opportunity to offer my most sincere apology for what has happened."

The mere mention of Ronsérre's name immediately softened Antoine's lingering uneasiness. "Yes, please come in." Ronsérre had not told him about having met with the captain, or to expect a visit from him. Antoine was prepared to put what had happened behind him, but he was now eager to hear what Chevin might have to say. "Please have a seat," Antoine offered when they were in the parlor. Picking up a small crystal bell, he rang it, and in a few seconds one of the servants appeared. "Would you notify

Madame Jardeen that we have a visitor, and ask her to join us in the parlor?"

"Oui, Monsieur, right away. And may I bring you and your guest a bottle of wine? The Cognac is satisfying on cold winter nights such as this," the servant told him.

"That sounds very good. Also, would you prepare a tray of brie, fruit, and some bread?"

A cargo of foreign wine and fruits had arrived in port the previous day, and Antoine had been able to buy directly from the merchant ship's captain. "Is there anything else you would want?" he asked Captain Chevin, in a show of French courtesy.

"No, what you suggest sounds very good," the captain replied. "Thank you for your generosity."

The servant bowed and then retreated to find Madame Jardeen.

"If it is not too much to ask," the captain said, "perhaps your son and his wife, if they are here, could also join us." Word of Tomas's amazing recovery had spread. "I am sure that they will want to hear what I am about to tell you."

"Yes, they are here." Ringing the bell again, another servant appeared. "Please ask Tomas and Margarite to join us in the parlor."

Knowing that there was a guest in the house, Martine took time to freshen her face with some powder and brushed her hair. As she aged, she felt increasingly less attractive, and spent more and more time trying to maintain a younger appearance. When she came into the parlor, the captain stood and Antoine made the introductions. Chevin was stunned by the grace and classic beauty of this woman. She gave the captain a slight curtsy, he bowed to her, and then he gingerly took her hand, kissed it, and said,

"Madame, it is a great honor to meet you. I am glad that your husband agreed to see me."

Social civility was the order of the day in sixteenth-century France, especially in the middle and upper classes of society. But Martine had no idea what this was all about. Her husband had not told her that a guest was expected, and she had no idea who this man was, or why he was in her home.

When Tomas and Maggie came in, they needed no introduction to the captain of the guard. Tomas asked in a rude tone, "What are you doing in my parents' home? Why are you bothering us? Haven't you already ruined our lives enough?" Antoine was taken aback by his son's rudeness. However, he could only imagine what terrible ordeals had been inflicted on his son and daughter-in-law on the orders of this man, or what he might have personally done to them. So, he remained silent and decided to see where everything was heading. Tomas turned and started to leave the room. Maggie did not. "Come on, let's get out of here," he said to her.

"No, I think I will stay," Maggie told him. "I want to hear what our 'friend' has to say. And I think you should also stay, and show some civility."

Tomas was angry at his wife, but he agreed to stay for a while.

By this time, the Cognac and tray of food had arrived. Although the captain had decided to cut down on his drinking of alcohol, it seemed impossible to give it up completely. The only water safe to drink was well or spring water, or water that had been boiled. Precautions had to be taken when drinking water from public sources. So, wine, beer, and Cognac were the drinks of choice at the time for which France was well-known. One glass of Cognac, some cheese, and fruit was all that the captain would have that night. The conversation went on for a long time, as the captain retold the information that he had shared with Ronsérre. "I want you to know that I have taken the liberty of destroying all records of your imprisonment," he announced to Tomas and Maggie.

"Why did you do that?" Tomas asked, somewhat puzzled.

Without mentioning Ronsérre's name, the captain said, "It was suggested to me by an angel that I should do what I could to clear your names of the false charges; I should do it for your honor, your future, and your children's future."

"Won't you be jeopardized if this information is found out? Is there not a serious risk in telling us this?" Antoine asked.

"I don't think so," the captain told him. "I believe that you and your family are honorable people. Yes, I am taking a chance, but I feel certain that the secret is safe with you."

"Thanks be to God," Antoine exclaimed. This comment opened up the opportunity for the captain to ask about Huguenots' beliefs, and then the conversation swung to religion. Without demeaning the Catholic faith, Antoine explained the concepts of Huguenot beliefs: a personal relationship with God, and people taking responsibility for their own beliefs and relationship with the Lord. When all was said, the captain affirmatively told the family, "I want that. I crave to have the joy in my life that you have. What can I do?"

"Well," Antoine told him, "it would be difficult for you to be a member of the militia and to practice Reformed principles at the same time."

The captain mulled this thought for several minutes before he answered. "I agree. It would be impossible for me to remain in the service of the king, but it is important that I find a new life, a new spiritual one. One where I find God and He becomes the center of my new life."

"Are you willing to leave the military?" Antoine inquired.

"Yes, I am willing to do that, no matter the consequences. I am willing to die if necessary."

"You should not make this decision tonight. Think about it, pray on it, and let's stay in touch. I will gladly help you in any way I can, but this must be our secret."

The captain graciously thanked the family for having given him their evening and left. Antoine and Martine watched as he drove off in his carriage all alone. It disappeared into the blustery night, with a light snowfall surreally swirling in the air.

Chapter 22
Life after Prison

Tomas and Maggie did not seem to suffer any long-term ill effects from their time in prison. Tomas was recovering physically and mentally from the torture, and the malnutrition suffered from the poor diet. However, they did not seem ready to talk about the experience. Maggie was showing healthy signs of pregnancy, morning sickness followed by intense cravings for certain foods, especially in late afternoon and early evening. One of the first orders of business was to get her thoroughly checked out by one of the local doctors. From there, they could arrange for a midwife to continue care, and to ultimately birth the baby.

After several weeks, Tomas rejoined his father and uncle at the boatyard. Maggie spent most of her time at her in-laws' house, where Martine ensured her comfort and well-being. Some days, the Jardeens' driver would deliver her to her own parents' home, or her father would have his driver pick her up. Often, her mother would arrive to spend the day with Martine and Maggie. It seemed that all of the women's lives were filled with joy and happiness at the prospect of a grandchild.

The baby was expected to be born sometime near the end of July 1576; it was now the spring of 1576. Tomas and Maggie wanted to find a home of their own in the city, and to be settled in it before the birth. There certainly wasn't time to have one built. A small, but attractive, home became available for purchase about midway between Tomas's parents and her parents. It belonged to the older couple who owned the art gallery and bookstore, and had employed Maggie before her marriage to Tomas. They wanted to sell the businesses and move to Paris, to be near their children and grandchildren.

The asking price of the home was 475 pounds, including most of the furniture. Having assisted the owners for several months, Maggie also decided that she would like to own their businesses. Music, books, and art were her passions, respectively. Her plan was to take over what had been a prosperous business and make it grow even bigger, despite her impending motherhood. She did not see that as a problem, as she was sure that she would probably have plenty of help from the *grand-mères* in taking care of the baby. The problem was that it was neither lawful for a woman to own property, nor was it acceptable in French society at the time for a woman to work outside of the home — especially in a business where she would be meeting the public and perhaps be in a position of having to have business dealings with men, and as a result be alone with them in a store. Therefore, a sale of the business to her was not possible. Tomas was not a rich man, and could not possibly finance the purchase of the home and businesses himself. In fact, without support of his and her parents, he and Maggie would have had a difficult time making ends meet. However, it was well-known in business circles that Tomas was a hard worker, and that surely someday the boatyard would be his, as none of Charles's sons had yet shown any interest in boatbuilding. Thus, it was decided that Tomas would borrow his share of the money for the purchases from a local banker, through whom Antoine and Charles conducted their financial interests, and that some assets of the boatyard might be selectively used as security for the loan. Antoine, Charles, and the Légeres could easily make the purchases outright by spending their own money. Both families agreed, however, that it was necessary to get the young couple established by Tomas assuming partial financial responsibility in the transaction. In addition, they each agreed to become partners with the couple by partially financing the purchases. Maggie's father, who was very well-liked by the citizens of La Rochelle, consented to purchase the building next to the book and music store, and operate it as an art gallery with Tomas as his partner. The name of the gallery would be Légere's Gallery of Fine Art, and the other business would be simply named Books and Music for All People.

The Gutenberg press, invented between 1440 and 1450 in Germany, had rapidly spread throughout Europe, and books had become widely available. Reading was a passion among the literate middle- and upper-class citizens of La Rochelle, and there was a special love of French literature and poetry. Reading books also gave the average literate citizen a glimpse of what was going on in areas of France other than La Rochelle and, to some degree, what was happening in the rest of the world. Books had already been written about the adventurers exploring the New World across the ocean, and about the politics and economies of England, Italy, and Spain.

Maggie was determined to play an important, but not so visible, role in the success of the businesses. The existing help would stay on and Maggie, although not officially an owner, would become the business advisor to her father, and to the Jardeens. Much of this effort could be done from home. She would decide the artwork to be bought for resale, and what books and music were to be carried. She would be unpaid, but Tomas's draw from the profits would be adjusted to cover both his and her salaries. Maggie would work in the stores only when Tomas or one of the parents or in-laws were present.

The Church had begun to crack down and demand attendance at Mass, and other special services. The demand applied to everyone, except a blind eye would be turned for persons known to be Huguenot, even though they were generally faithful about attending their own services held around the city in stores and persons' homes. This leniency or relaxation of enforcement could no doubt be attributed in part to what had happened to Tomas and Maggie.

Word of the prison scenario for the Jardeens had leaked out, as well as Tomas's miraculous recovery. It was probably wild and ill-conceived to think that it could be kept a secret. Also, in a way it was a blessing that it did become known, for it forced the Church and the government to begin easing the restrictions on Protestantism. It was on January 5 that King Henri III formally renounced his Catholicism in Tours in favor of his former Huguenot faith. There was no proof, but it was believed at the time that the episode of the Jardeen couple in La Rochelle was a contributing factor to his dramatic slap on the Catholic Church. Then, on February 3, Henri fled Paris and returned to Béarn in southwestern France, where he took command of the Pyrenean Huguenots.

In early May, the Fifth War of Religion was ended by the Edict of Beaulieu, issued by Henri III. This edict gave the Huguenots the right of freedom of worship throughout France, except in Paris, and granted the establishment of Huguenot garrisons in a number of cities in France. The general and tax amnesty declared under the Edict of Beaulieu brought many new Huguenots to La Rochelle, and spurred the growth of business development for the city. This was sure to impact on the businesses that the Jardeens and the Légeres were proposing to buy, although it had little impact on the boatyard since that was not a consumer industry. It solidified the families' plans to buy the bookstore and the art gallery.

In the spring, Antoine, Charles, and Michel became energized in their vow to Monsieur Ronsérre to begin a Huguenot congregation. The first service was to be a public gathering the second Sunday in June, in the square where John Calvin had first preached when he visited La Rochelle. Ronsérre came from Fontenay for the service, and stayed with Maggie's parents rather than at the Jardeens. Doing so served several purposes, such as the opportunity to get to know them better. He had little contact with them when he was in La Rochelle at Christmas, working on the case. Getting to better know the mayor of the city would not be a bad thing. The positive aspect of that opportunity was dashed when he learned of Michel's plan to resign. Secondly, although the Jardeens were well-known, speaking at the Huguenot rally as a guest of the mayor would lend more status and significance to what he was going to say. Antoine certainly agreed with these suppositions. This time around there was no curfew, and Governor Bouché did not need to assign him a guard.

Since Mayor Légere was to be personally involved in the rally, everything had to be done legally. Antoine obtained a permit from the city office, and Father Benedict was notified. Benedict asked that the service be conducted concurrently with the Catholic Mass at the cathedral. The supposed reasoning behind the request was that Benedict wanted to prevent his parishioners from attending the Huguenot service. Despite Father Benedict's earlier demand that parishioners attend Mass, he knew that many were staying away and probably associating with the

Huguenots. This was not a new phenomenon. One of the complaints that had long been leveled by the Church was that the Huguenot Reformists were siphoning members away from the Catholic Church. Antoine quickly agreed to the request, as there was nothing to lose. Besides, the "thinkers" in the Catholic Church had already left the faith and associated with the Reformists. The church in La Rochelle was left primarily with just the poorer, illiterate members of society. The others left in the church were the very rich and societal climbers. The Huguenots consisted primarily of the French middle class, such as the merchants, bankers, businessmen, the artisans, and other contributing members of society.

Of course, Father Benedict did report to his bishop that the meeting was being planned. The bishop made plans to have several Church officials attend the gathering to make sure that Catholics not already on the list of converts, or possible converts, attended, and to make sure that the Church and its beliefs and practices were not held up to criticism and scorn. This did not seem a problem to Antoine, for his message was not intended to savage the Catholic Church, but to deliver comfort and peace to people who were seeking a personal and peaceful relationship with God, rather than through a person anointed by man to intervene for them. "I see no problem with what you requested," he assured Benedict.

The meeting in the square was planned for the first Sunday in June. One day, he stopped by the prison to see Captain Chevin. He had run into him several times on the street since that meeting when the captain came to his home. When they had bumped into each other, their conversations had always been cordial; Antoine never brought up matters of faith, as not to compromise the captain. He could tell that

Chevin was appreciative of his respect for privacy and confidentiality. When he next saw the captain, Antoine handed him a piece of paper with a note informing him of the planned gathering.

"Oui, I am already aware of your meeting," he told Antoine. "Father Benedict has already alerted the new commander, and has requested surveillance by the soldiers. I have been told by my superiors to be there, but not in uniform."

"I am glad that you will be there." Antoine smiled broadly and told him, "I am sure that there will not be any trouble."

"No, there will not be trouble," the captain promised.

Chapter 23
The Gathering

The weeks leading up to "The Gathering in the Square" were especially busy for Antoine and his brother, Charles, as well as for Tomas. There was a home life to maintain, a boatbuilding business to run, an estate to oversee and farm, plus the finalization of the business transactions with the older couple, who would be turning over their home and business on June 30. It was almost too much to handle at one time. Michel Légere's contributions to the organization of the Huguenot rally had to be handled with a spectrum of discretion and decorum. His position as mayor of La Rochelle made him a highly visible public servant, the same as the governor, and as such he would be crossing an ethical line to openly promote Reformist principles over the national religion. It was a quandary that would end with his resignation. That dramatic step would happen when the purchase of the art gallery was finalized, or perhaps even later, when the business was up and running successfully.

Monsieur Ronsérre arrived back in La Rochelle the week before "The Gathering." That was the name by which the event was being promoted, and already it was the name to which it was commonly referred to by people around the city. Antoine had originally envisioned an audience of perhaps twenty-five to thirty people, fifty or sixty maximum. But even within a few days of it being announced, over 150 friends, and even more people whom he hardly knew, told him that they would be there. A factor which he had not considered was that word of the gathering could spread beyond the borders of La Rochelle, and people were likely to come from nearby cities and towns.

On the Saturday before the gathering that Sunday, La Rochelle was indeed a busy place. People were streaming into the city without any place to stay. Hotels and inns became filled to capacity. Local Huguenots, those with extra beds, were offering hospitality in their homes and offering to sleep out-of-towners in their carriage houses and quarters above their stables. Strangers were even sharing beds, and some out-of-towners slept that night in their coaches.

The next day, people began arriving at the square by early morning in order to be assured of a good spot near where the speakers would be delivering their messages. Boats were arriving from Île de Ré. Most people from the island traveled in groups on schooners. The schooners' white sails were puffed out in the gentle breeze blowing across the harbor. But some came in smaller boats rowed by muscular men, most of whom were fishermen or laborers.

There was little that could be done at this point. By midmorning, there were already several hundred people spilling out of the square. It was surreal. It was similar to a mob scene, but without the noise and unruliness of a mob. People were courteous and talked to each other in civilized ways, telling each other what being there meant to them. Many were openly praying to God to be with them and the speakers; they prayed for the success of "The Gathering." Antoine, Charles, and Ronsérre circulated among the crowd greeting as many people as possible, thanking them for coming and saying to each, "May God be with you," or "May God bless you." People whom they were able to greet were overwhelmed with emotion, and thanked them profusely for what they were doing. Many could not hold back their tears. There were those that were crippled, or disabled in some way, and asked to be cured. They were told that only God and his son, Jesus Christ, were the healers of the faith and of the body.

The service was not long. Antoine spoke first and welcomed everyone. Without going into detail as to why, he explained that he, his brother, Charles, and a friend had made a vow to Monsieur Ronsérre to begin a Reformed church in La Rochelle, and that this was the first step in fulfilling that promise. A prayer was offered in which he thanked God for the "opportunity for people to be assembled in openness and without fear of intimidation, to pursue their dream of freedom of religious principles and worship." With these words being said, a yell of approval came from somewhere in the crowd, and then there was a widespread breakout of tumultuous joy among the worshippers. One person standing near the speaker's stand pointed toward the sky and called for everyone to look up. To everyone's surprise and joy, a cloud had suddenly appeared in a shape that seemed to be the face of Jesus. Antoine told the crowd, "I am sure that God is smiling down on us today. He is pleased that you are here." It continued to hover over the assemblage for the rest of the service, and then broke up with the gentle breeze blowing at the end.

As he had promised Father Benedict, there was no mention of the Catholic Church, no mention of government repression, except for the brief mention of "intimidation" in his opening prayer, and no mention of the misfortune that Tomas and Maggie had endured. John Calvin was mentioned often, and recollection was made of his earlier visit to La Rochelle when he had preached in this very square. Obviously, some of the people in the crowd, or their parents and grandparents, had been there to hear Calvin speak, for there was a roar of approval that went up and people began to clap in appreciative approval. Monsieur Ronsérre was introduced as being a "famous solicitor from Fontenay-le-Comte and a longtime disciple of Reformist teachings and practices." Ronsérre came to the podium and made Antoine and Charles proud with a powerful oration of personal belief and witness. He talked like a father to his children about the teachings of Calvin and the doctrines of grace. He ended his sermon declaring the principle of predestination, "God will grant eternal salvation to every person on whom he has mercy, regardless of the unrighteousness of the person, or good deeds done," and went on to say, "Eternal life is guaranteed for all those who accept Jesus Christ as their Savior. Go forth and multiply in the faith. And remember, a church is not a building. A church is the people who share common beliefs, values, and who choose to worship together. The building is just the structure in which we gather to worship."

Charles closed the rally by assuring the crowd of the vow made to Monsieur Ronsérre to build a church in La Rochelle. "It will be a church of the people. People like you and me worshipping together, forming small groups to worship in homes, in stores, in your businesses, wherever you feel safe . . . and may God's love and compassion shine down on each of you, today and always!

"I promise you that one day, in the not too distant future, there will be a building where we all can worship together." A roaring cheer, loud enough to be heard at the cathedral, went up from the crowd gathered together that day.

After the service was over the people remained in the square for a long time, greeting each other, discussing what they had heard that day, meditating, and praying for a new life. Captain Chevin, not in uniform, was one of the last to leave. His heart had been deeply touched that day, and he wondered if there was any way that he could help Antoine and Charles in their noble effort.

By midafternoon, with darkening skies, a thunderstorm began to roll in from the west. Soon the winds had picked up considerably, and there were rolling swells and whitecaps on the bay. Sharp streaks of lightning lit up the harbor, followed immediately by loud claps of thunder. People on the street scurried for the shelter of their carriages. Most of those who had come from Île de Ré were still in La Rochelle, window-shopping and buying from the few merchants that had blatantly opposed the law and opened that afternoon. Chevin had instructed his men to turn a blind eye to events that afternoon. Actually, there were very few soldiers out, and those who were made it a point to patrol away from the shopping area of the city.

A torrential rain had begun to fall. Unfortunately, though, some of the people who had come in small boats from Île de Ré had already left, and were caught on the bay in the middle of the storm. Two boats capsized in the storm, and the people in them were lost to the perils of the sea. Of those who died were Catholics who were coming for the service at the cathedral; the other family were Huguenots who attended the gathering. The loss of life on both sides was unfortunate.

Word soon began to spread in the Catholic community that the drownings occurred because of the wrath of God; the Almighty was displeased with their having attended a Huguenot rally. In fact, Father Benedict hammered on this theme for some time in his preachings, with no mention of the Catholics who drowned when the second boat had capsized.

Chapter 24
Life Changes

Now that The Gathering in the Square had taken place, Antoine and Martine were looking forward to some peace and relaxation. They knew there was nothing that they could do to quiet the gossip on the street about the drownings that occurred in the harbor after the service that Sunday. Tomas and Maggie would be moving into the house they had purchased, and they would be opening their new businesses soon afterward. Maggie and the expectant grandparents had to prepare for the arrival of the baby. Martine was sure that the bookseller in Orleans was correct when he told Tomas that the baby would be a girl. Friends would ask how she could be so confident in this statement. "Because of the way that she is carrying it," Martine told them. "She is carrying it low." Of course, her belief was based on folklore of the time, and yet the old midwife had confirmed her suspicions. The midwife was now stopping by several times a week to see Maggie, feeling her abdomen and checking the baby's heartbeat with an oddly shaped tin cup. It was two funnel-shaped cones, connected by a common stem. This was a device that her own son, the inventor, had made for her many years before. She would place one cone on Maggie's abdomen, and listen for the heartbeat with her ear on the other cone.

"*Ça va bien. Vous avez un beau bébé!* (Fine, just fine. You have a healthy baby!)" she would always assure Maggie. After the midwife left, Martine, Paulette, and Elisabeth, if she was there, would always joyously put their ears to Maggie's belly and try to listen for themselves.

Whether they heard the heartbeat or not, they would mock in the same voice as the midwife, "She was right, you do have a healthy baby." The three women would start giggling.

As the end of the month neared, the deal was done on the purchase of the house for Tomas and Maggie. The purchase of the businesses would be completed on the last day of the month, and the old couple would stay in the house for two weeks without payment of rent. That was part of the agreement of sale.

Preparations had to be made for moving, but the grandparents forbade Maggie to take part due to her pregnancy. The three families would handle all the details. Charles had arranged for some of his farmhands to go and retrieve some of the possessions the families were donating to the young couple. They didn't need much, as the older couple's furniture came with the purchase. The elderly husband and wife would just be taking their clothes, personal possessions, and memories of a long and happy marriage in their home with them to Paris. They already had an apartment set up and waiting for them in Paris.

Once Maggie and Tomas moved in, Martine sent several of her servants over to cook and clean until Tomas was successful in hiring someone willing to take over the duties. Maggie's servants loved both Tomas and Maggie dearly, and several had family members that they recommended for the job. Tomas and Maggie interviewed candidates and picked the sister of one of the servants employed by the Légeres. One was all that Tomas could afford to pay at the present time, but he would hire more later when Maggie and he were better established. After the baby arrived, they planned to hire someone to help care for him or her when Maggie wanted to be out and the grandmothers were not available.

Michel's resignation from his job was effective June 29, the day before he was to officially become a business owner. The papers had already been signed, but money would not exchange hands until the next day, when Michel would be able to participate and the proper documents were filed with the city.

It was agreed that the purchases included buying the goodwill of the businesses. This included the turnover of customer lists, account records of debt owed, and receivables outstanding. Also, an inventory of books, music, and artworks was part of the final arrangements. As it turned out, the couple had paid all their debt before selling the store. Charles and the parents agreed among themselves that the right thing to do would be to collect the receivables, minus a small fee for their collection effort, and send the money to the couple in Paris. The next day, in the evening of June 30, 1576, after the old couple had finished their last day of business, signs went up in the windows saying, "Under New Ownership" and "Help Wanted."

The families gathered the same evening for a celebration, all but Tomas and Maggie. They went to their new home, so Maggie could retire to bed early. Carrying the baby, coupled with the constant movement and kicking in her abdomen, was tiring. It thrilled her to feel the baby kick, for it always reminded her that she was carrying a new life. Many times during the day, she would pause and think, *Thank you, dear God, for Thy creation.*

The next morning, Antoine, Charles, Michel, and Tomas were at the shops early to open for their first day of business. When people on the street saw that they were open, most came in to greet their old friends and browse. Many bought books, although patrons at the art gallery were few. That was expected, as the artwork was considerably more expensive than buying a book, or even a couple of books. Tomas and his father slipped away by midmorning and went to the boatyard, to ensure that everything was operating smoothly.

After a week of this daily routine, Antoine realized that there were too many demands on him. The success of the boatyard was personally more important to him than the shops. He felt divided, for he sincerely wanted the shops to succeed for the sake of his daughter-in-law. His brother, Charles, could not continue to spend full time at the bookshop, as he too was important to the boatbuilding business. The farm, especially, seemed to suffer without him since he and his wife had turned it over to his children. On top of this, they were contemplating having a new home built in the city, so that Charles would be closer to the boatyard. There were several choices needing to be made. Central to all of them was the hiring of a good, strong manager: a manager to take over the operation of the farm, a manager to take over the bookshop, or a manager to oversee the boatyard while they were doing other things. The person would have to be intelligent, creative, loyal to the business and the family, and above all he must be honest. After much consideration and discussion with Charles and Tomas, it was decided that Antoine would sound out Captain Chevin at the prison.

Luckily, one day not long afterward, the captain and his wife came into the store looking for some books for their children. He was not in uniform that day, as it was a day he took to spend time with his spouse. They were going to do some shopping, and then have lunch in town. The two had spent the day together to reconnect in an effort to save their marriage; both wanted and needed it desperately. "Captain, I have a personal matter to discuss with you. It is probably not best to speak on this matter at the prison. Can you and your wife come to my home this evening?"

A puzzled look came across the captain's face. "Of course," he told Antoine. "But must it involve my wife?"

"Oui, I think that your wife would want to hear what I have to ask you. It is a matter of great importance to both of you. I would tell you more if I could. Perhaps you will be pleased when you hear what I have to say, or perhaps not. Only you will be able to make that decision. Will I see you this evening?" Antoine asked.

The wife looked questioningly at her husband. He nodded his head affirmatively. She then said, "Oui, we will come to your house. What time?"

"Why don't you come for dinner at seven o'clock?"

The captain paid for three books, then his wife and he strolled out of the store, hand in hand. Antoine felt positive he was making the right decision. He felt very optimistic, for he was sure that he was about to change two people's lives for the better.

Chapter 25
The Business

That evening at the Jardeen home promised to be a busy one. Martine left the store early. She went next door to the art gallery first to invite the Légeres to join them for dinner to talk with Captain Chevin and his wife. Then, she had her driver take her home. She needed to tell the kitchen staff to expect six guests that night for dinner, and to generally take charge in preparation for the evening. It had been a long and tiring day. The store had been very busy, which kept Antoine and Tomas from going to the boatyard at all that day. Most people who had been into the store bought books, but Martine could not help but wonder how many of them would actually be read. Antoine and she knew most of the people who came in, and she considered how many books were sold out of obligation to patronize the store. Meanwhile, over at the art gallery, business was slow for Michel. The art inventory was expensive. It was more serious, formal artwork that probably only the wealthier would truly appreciate. And besides, artwork was something that a person either liked or did not like. Individual pieces of art might grow on a person over time. He expected that customers would stop by the gallery just to browse the paintings, but his hope was that over time a particular piece of artwork might begin to appeal to a person, as time has a way of creating new perspectives. Michel made a good effort to speak with nearly everyone who came into the gallery, and tried to find out their interests and likings. What he discovered was that the rich who lived in the chateaus and villas in the countryside were generally very interested in what he was offering, but were slow to spend their money. He knew that the *nouveau riche* were quicker to spend their money than those with old money. The very rich, whether they fully understood or appreciated the formality of art, craved the nobility that said formality endowed on them. He discovered, unsurprisingly, the lesser rich of that social class and the middle class seemed more interested in realism and lighter artwork, such as paintings of the countryside, of flowers, or of fruit. They enjoyed the subjects of a more everyday nature, things that were light and airy. These types of paintings brought cheer into their lives. Maggie had told him this on many occasions, but for now he was stuck with the inventory that he had inherited. He would sell this art well in Paris, or perhaps in Lyon. Down the road, after the baby was born, he would have to get Maggie into the store a few hours at a time to go over the inventory of paintings, and discuss how they could turn over the stock and get fresh new paintings in for sale, paintings more to the liking of his customers. Michel was typically a shrewd businessman, but he was really doing this for Maggie's sanity and future. Though it was unusual in 1576 France for a woman to be involved in any way in business, Maggie was no ordinary woman. She was extremely bright and forward-thinking. In fact, so much so that he had recognized it at an early age and had worried about how she would fare as an adult in a largely male-dominated society. Her mother was different. She was willing to take a back seat and be led. He had bought this business for Maggie to give her the opportunity to lead and be fulfilled. But in doing so, he also had other motives. One was to protect Maggie, and the other was to steer her in a direction that did not overtly conflict with the stereotype that Frenchmen had of the woman's place being in the home, and not out in the open world. For some time, at least until Maggie had become known and accepted to the people of La Rochelle, he would have to be the person out front and perceived as the business owner. Another motive was to provide an outlet for his wife to develop socially, and he thought placing her in an alliance with Maggie would be of mutual benefit to both of them. Finally, he wanted, along with the Jardeens, to establish a strong Huguenot presence in the business community of La Rochelle.

That night, during dinner at the Jardeens' home, Michel found out for the first time what Antoine's plans were for bringing Captain Chevin into a management role at the bookshop. Books were more important to Maggie than art, and he feared that the plan would somehow diminish her role in a business that was being created for her. He sat silent for a while wondering, *Why has my friend Antoine not consulted me on this before?* A number of thoughts raced through his mind. *Chevin has not yet demonstrated to us a strong conviction of Huguenot beliefs. Perhaps he needs time to get his beliefs in order. And anyway, he does not have business experience. Perhaps he does not have an appreciation for the business.*

Then an inner voice seemed to speak to him: *Michel, Antoine has not betrayed you. He is carrying out My will. By giving this man a second chance in life, he is bringing him closer to what you want from him. There is room for both him and your beloved Maggie in the business. Let Me handle this.* Michel was puzzled and, at first, uneasy. A voice had never spoken to him before like this. The voice continued, *Michel, if you love Me, then trust Me. All will be well.* Strangely, these words brought comfort to him, and things suddenly began to come into focus.

Yes, Antoine is my friend. He always has been my friend, and I should not begin now to doubt him. No, I shall not pretend to judge another man and his commitment to God. Chevin has said that he wishes to embrace my beliefs. It is not my duty to mark the progress of his religious beliefs. No, Maggie does not have management experience, and the captain does. I may not be happy with what he did to Maggie and Tomas, but his experience as a military officer and as captain of the guard has no doubt made him a driven, disciplined, results-oriented person. He is more than ready to step in, take charge of a business, and drive it to success. The piece of the puzzle that Michel did not see could play an unknown final part of God's plan.

The captain and his wife were overwhelmed at the offer. No demands outside of those of management were made of him. Antoine explained that the business was purchased for the benefit of Margarite and Tomas. "How do you feel about a woman owning a business?" Antoine asked the captain in a point-blank, matter-of-fact way.

"That is not a problem for me," Chevin spoke. "It might be a problem for the rest of France, but not for me." Continuing, he said, "I have a wife. She is sitting here beside me, and my opinion on whether I accept your offer will be influenced by what she thinks. Despite how society views the role of women in marriage, or in social and civic business affairs outside of the home, I see my wife as an equal to me. I have changed . . . France will change. I have two daughters. I can only hope that someday I may be able to offer them an opportunity such as the one that you are offering to me."

"Let me be a little more direct," Antoine responded. "How do you feel about actually working for a woman? To be more specific, how would you feel about working for my daughter-in-law? Remember, this is a woman who was your prisoner in jail. Could you, and would you, listen to her guidance and carry out instructions that she might offer you?"

"Yes, that will be different from everything I have ever experienced before." And then, smiling broadly at his wife, he added, "Except at home." Everyone in the room chuckled as his wife tried to protest. "But," he continued, "the more important question is, how would Madame Jardeen feel about me working for her?"

"Madame Jardeen can speak for herself. Can you please answer the captain's question?"

Martine looked at her husband with a quizzical expression, as if to convey, *What am I supposed to say?* She was not yet used to having Maggie addressed as Madame Jardeen, and realized that she was going to have to get used to sharing the title with her daughter-in-law.

"Monsieur Chevin," Maggie answered, "I suffered emotional distress from confinement at the prison. Emotional stress that I don't think you can possibly understand, and from which I may never totally recover. My husband, Tomas, suffered physical abuse and near starvation for something of which we were not guilty. But my husband and I, and certainly our parents, are forgiving people. You have apologized for what happened. We understand your duties and your loyalty to obey orders. Strangely, I see that as a good quality in you. It is something that we will need to make the business a success. I would be glad to have you join us in making that happen."

"Madame, I appreciate your trust and your forgiveness," Chevin told her. Then, turning back to Antoine, he said, "How much are you proposing to pay me?"

"What do you think would be a fair amount?"

"Your question is a complicated one."

"Why is that?" Antoine asked.

"In addition to my regular service pay, I am paid extra for housing, a food subsistence, plus an extra amount for serving the militia force at the prison."

"Well, can you tell us how much that adds up to?"

"It is a comfortable living," Chevin answered politely. "I prefer to wait to answer that question. We can negotiate."

"Yes, you are correct. We can negotiate. Give it your full consideration," Antoine told him. "I promise you that if you are successful in helping to make this business grow, there will be great rewards down the road for you and your family."

With that, Antoine broke up the dinner meeting by saying, "We are eager to move ahead. Please give us your answer as soon as possible."

As he was leaving, Chevin and his wife were seen by a pair of prying eyes hidden away in the shadows of the trees. One of his own soldiers was hired by Father Benedict to follow the captain and report back to the Church on his contacts. Benedict was still seething over the tragic loss of the prison's commander. He felt betrayal from Tomas and Margarite Jardeen's freedom, granted by the captain. He failed to carry out the orders of the Church, and therefore was little more than a heretic. Besides, he had been seen at The Gathering, and he did not attend in uniform. His sighting at the bookstore buying books just added flames to the talk that was already circulating among Church officials that the captain was a practicing Huguenot. *What a shame!* he thought when he heard news of the captain's recent choices. The Church's mole in the militia force reported the social visit with the Jardeens. Despite past loyalty to the

Church and having faithfully served the wishes of Father Benedict for so long, these indiscretions could not be tolerated. The priest decided that he would ask his bishop to intercede up the hierarchical ranks of the Church to plead the case to the king for the removal of the captain, or for whatever remedy that His Eminence felt to be best.

Benedict did not realize his low standing in the Church's hierarchy; he never had. It did not help that he had not been successful in the persecution against the young Jardeen couple. Excuses were not acceptable. It was not enough for him to offer that the case fabricated against Tomas and Maggie was not strong, nor that the Jardeen family was protected by the king's franchise given to the boatyard. Perhaps the handling of the captain would be presented to the king in due time, but right now something must be done about the Father. That week, Father Benedict was called to the office of the bishop, who offered him Cognac and a cigar. They chatted for a while; in the meantime, Benedict got up several times and poured himself more drink. It was at this moment that the bishop knew what had to be done with the alcoholic priest.

"Father," the bishop told him, "for the betterment of the Church here in La Rochelle, I have decided that I am going to ask the cardinal to arrange for your transfer to another position. I appreciate your dedicated service to this church and to this city, but I believe for your own good it is time for you to have the opportunity to function in a new area."

At this point, Benedict was sort of in a half-drunk state. It was hard for him to focus on his boss, and was doubly hard for him to decipher in his mind what the bishop had just told him. "I . . . I don't . . . I don't understand." He wanted to stand up to confront the bishop, but his head was pulsating, and he knew that he was unable at this point to rise out of his chair.

"I think that it would be best to send you to the abbey in Avignon for rehabilitation. You know very well, and I know for certain, that you have several issues that you need to personally come to terms with. Your drinking may be the least of your problems. It is no longer possible for you to continue to serve here."

"What have I done?" Benedict begged of the bishop. He began to rage. "You must tell me what I have done!"

"Father Benedict, please, I am trying to spare you embarrassment. I am saying that it is in your best interest, and in the best interest of the Church, for you to be transferred where you can receive help."

At this point Father Benedict lost all sense of respect for his bishop, and for the courtesies required between a subordinate and his superior in the Church. "You must tell me what I have done," he screamed at the bishop. "I need to know!" he demanded. "I have a right to know; tell me!"

"Father Benedict, besides your drinking problem, you are guilty of showing an unnatural and unacceptable sexual interest in the young boys of this church. Early on, you sexually abused young Tomas Jardeen when he was only twelve years old, and continued to abuse him until he was sixteen."

"That is not true. Who told you that? Did Tomas tell you? It is his word against mine. Who do you believe—a young boy, or your loyal servant? I am a man of God! I have never . . . I would never—" And then the bishop interrupted him in midsentence.

"Father, there is no use," the bishop firmly told him. "There is clear evidence of your guilt. I have read the notes of the abuse in your journal, notes that you yourself made."

"You have no right to read my journal!" Benedict shouted. "Where did you get it? It is an invasion of privacy to read my journal."

"No, Father Benedict, it is not an invasion of your privacy. The journal belongs to the church; as your bishop, I am entitled to read the records of the church. Your critical mistake was noting such affairs in an official record belonging to the church."

"But—" Benedict sputtered.

The bishop cut him off. "My mind is made up. As of this moment, you are suspended from all pastoral duties. I will conduct all further Masses until a new priest is assigned. You are to have no further contact with the parishioners of this church. You are confined to your residence until your transfer is arranged. One of the cardinal's protective guards will soon accompany you to Avignon."

In a full state of rage, Father Benedict found the strength to rise from his chair, and with the bishop silently watching, he walked over to the bar, poured himself another drink of Cognac, and drank it in just a couple of swallows. And then he poured another. Perhaps it revived him, or perhaps it just made him crazier, there was no way of knowing.

Before turning back around to face the bishop, he reached inside his robe. With the hand still inside his robe, he paused and reflected as the bishop's words raced through his brain. *Yes, I do have an unhealthy interest in the boys of the church. That is a weakness of my character, and a transgression for which I can never be absolved*, he thought to himself. *Perhaps my skills in taking care of the running of the church are not perfect, but one cannot question my loyalty and faithfulness to the needs of my parishioners. Have I overstepped my authority? Maybe, but I have been a loyal servant and have faithfully done the bidding of my superiors.* He told himself, *I am guilty of abusing young boys. I hate the Jardeens. They tried to fool me with the sham wedding of the son and that woman he married. I cannot be made a fool of . . .* And then he thought to himself, *The bishop himself was aware of my plan to have the couple arrested . . . or was he? I am too drunk now to remember. I only helped set the trap for their arrest. Was I also responsible for their treatment while jailed? They were Huguenots! They should have been exiled as slaves to an island or prison ship . . . or just simply executed in prison. They were lucky their punishment was only to the extent that it was.*

Then, slowly pulling his hand from beneath his robe and spinning around, he flashed a pistol. The bishop saw and began to plead with him. "Don't do it. Put the gun down. It is not worth it. Please, give me the gun." There was a sudden, loud blast, followed by another shortly after. The shots echoed throughout the cathedral.

Chapter 26
Aftermath

The soldiers determined the incident in the bishop's office to be a murder-suicide. There was simply no way they could suppress the news of what had happened.

Within hours, everyone in La Rochelle found out, whether they knew the details or not, that both men were dead. There were mixed versions of what had occurred. Half of the population correctly believed that Father Benedict had shot the bishop, and then turned the gun on himself. Some believed that the bishop had shot the priest, himself the next to follow. There were those who believed that the priest had shot the bishop and, in a rage of guilt, climbed the steps to the top of the bell tower and leaped to his death.

There were other stories as well, but few came even close to having it right. The most ridiculous thought-up scenario was that the bishop and Father Benedict had struggled in a jealous fight over one of the nuns and the gun fired, accidentally killing the bishop; in the horror and embarrassment of what had happened, Benedict did the proper thing and shot himself in the head. Obviously, this was incorrect, as the bishop was found slumped over on his desk and not lying on the floor. It was undeniable, however, that Father Benedict had murdered the bishop. Then, after putting another piece of ammo in his gun, he turned it on himself. This was substantiated by the fact that Benedict lay on the floor with the gun lying next to his right hand, which had gunpowder on it.

The people were suspicious of whether the king's soldiers were correct, or if they were simply trying to cover up to save the Church's hierarchy embarrassment and shame. It really did not matter. Both men were dead and, regardless, the blame for both deaths would be placed on Father Benedict.

A high burial Mass was held for the bishop. The cardinal of the province of Aunis presided. Hundreds of people attended the Mass, so many, in fact, the crowd spilled out of the cathedral into the street and park outside. In addition to members of the Catholic Church and the Aunis bishopric, several persons from the Huguenot community dared to attend. They did so largely out of curiosity, but also in protest of a crime in which a religious leader was murdered. They might not agree with all the bishop's beliefs and teachings, but nevertheless he was a man of God and was to be respected.

It was a long funeral Mass with twenty-one priests and higher Catholic clergy from churches near and far, either paying their respects or actively participating in the conduct of the service. Incense was burned and Communion was served. As was customary, the transubstantiation of the Communion bread turning to the body of Christ, and the Communion wine actually becoming the blood of Christ, were conducted behind a curtain which completely surrounded the priest who was in charge of the elements. Each person, except the Huguenots, came forward to receive the bread. The cardinal serving the Communion refused bread to anyone whom he knew was not a confirmed Catholic. This was not unexpected, as all the Huguenots present at the service were familiar with the ritual, for many were former worshippers in this very cathedral.

Parishioners came with their heads bowed and their hands clasped, as if in prayer. Each genuflected before the crucifix of Jesus, and then crossed themselves before receiving the bread from the cardinal. Opening their mouths, the cardinal laid a piece of unleavened Communion bread on their tongues. After everyone had received the bread, he and other clergy present drank the wine. The Mass ended with a commemoration of the bishop's earthly services to the Father, and with a plea for the taking of his soul to Heaven in eternal rest. Finally, his body was taken to a nave in the cathedral and encrypted in an above-floor vault.

There was no service for Father Benedict that day, or ever, for he had committed a murder and that was one of the deadly sins. He could not be buried in the cathedral, nor in the Catholic cemetery behind the cathedral. He had committed this sin and had done unmentionable acts, which were not public and would never be known. The record of these transgressions would be sent to Rome and sealed in the heavily guarded vaults of the Vatican forever.

The cathedral and the Catholic cemetery were sacred places, and reserved for persons of the Church's choosing. He was buried in the public park near the cathedral. Many of the parishioners, although most did not like Benedict, felt badly about the treatment being accorded to him; but they did not dare complain openly to the cardinal, nor would they be allowed to claim the body and give it a decent burial in a non-Catholic cemetery. To have done so would have put them into direct conflict with the hierarchy of the Church, and subject to punishment. Some, though, did have friends and colleagues in the Huguenot community to whom they spoke to about the treatment meted out to Father Benedict. Acting on their deep religious teachings and objections of inhumanity of man against man, a group including Charles and Antoine got together to claim the body of the priest. They gave him a proper burial, in a casket paid for by the Jardeens, in a small, nondenominational cemetery outside of the city.

The cardinal was enraged when he found out what had happened. It would be difficult, if not impossible, for him to ever find out which members of the Church had gone against his ruling. The Huguenots involved had sworn secrecy among themselves, pledging not to tell who in the Church had approached them. The cardinal insisted that the captain of the guard at the prison must demand his militia to detain the Huguenots involved. Captain Chevin refused, telling him that there was no direct evidence to implicate any of the Huguenots in a crime. "I can tell you who they are!" the cardinal raged at the captain. And then, he proceeded to tell the captain the names of a dozen or so people whom he was positive were involved. Without naming Charles, he strongly accused Antoine Jardeen of being involved.

"No, with all due respect, Your Eminence, you are wrong," the captain lied. "I was drinking in a pub here in town the afternoon that Father Benedict was taken to his grave and buried. Antoine Jardeen and his brother, Charles, were in the pub drinking and eating most of the afternoon, discussing business. I can vouch that Antoine was not involved. Therefore, I cannot be sure that any of the other persons you name were involved. I am sorry, but there is nothing I can do. It seems to me that giving a person a decent burial is not a crime. Perhaps you should be honoring, rather than condemning, those persons who had the courage to place the priest in a proper grave."

The cardinal had never been spoken to like this before. At first, he was enraged that Chevin had had the audacity to speak to him in such a manner. He was used to having his orders obeyed immediately, and not having them questioned. But the captain seemed to show no anger or malice. He was calm, self-assured, and not afraid. *Perhaps,* the cardinal thought silently to himself, *I am too used to having yes-men around me who are afraid to say no. Men who are afraid of my authority and power over them, and men who are afraid to offer alternatives to my thoughts.* Taking a moment to think about what the captain had told him, he realized that the captain had perhaps done him a great service. It was at that moment that he came to see that the Church made men into a certain type of people. Parish priests were generally not well-educated. *It is only the hierarchical figures of the Church, such as myself, who have had the education at the best schools and who are most likely to take problems and logically reason them out to a good solution,* he silently thought to himself. *But I, too, am guilty of being too quick to make false assumptions and come to senseless conclusions.*

"Captain," the cardinal, with a look of pain showing in his face, slowly told Chevin, "you are correct. I now realize that the important question is not whether some Huguenots dared to question my policy. The fact is, they laid to rest a troubled soul who may or may not have committed a crime. We are not sure of his guilt. My bishop died, yet I am not sure whether he was shot purposely by Father Benedict, or if he was accidentally shot while taking it upon himself to try and stop the father from killing himself. I am sure that it is a fact that we will never know for certain. I guess that the right thing to do would be to exhume him from his grave and rebury him in a Catholic cemetery."

"No," the captain told him. "Do not move him. Father Benedict is resting in peace with his God. I am sure that he was buried with respect this time, and though the people who reburied him may not have appreciated his beliefs, they no doubt respected him as a human being and his position as a man of God. It doesn't matter where he is buried. Please let his body remain in peace wherever it is now. His spirit is with God."

The cardinal was now confused. The few brief words spoken by Chevin had a great impact on the cardinal, who responded, "Captain, you speak with reason and sanity. I will consider what you have told me. In the future, it will be my goal to try to promote peace among men and women of all faiths, and to ensure respect for civil law and for proper Catholic law within the powers given to me by God and by the Church."

The person who spoke those words was Cardinal Benédict (the French form of the Latin Benedictus, *meaning "Blessed"). It was later determined that Cardinal Benédict was an uncle of Father Benedict, the deceased priest from La Rochelle. By 1628, Cardinal Benédict was the chief conseiller to the infamous Cardinal Richelieu, and one of the few advisors who opposed Richelieu in his determination to lay siege to La Rochelle and wipe out the Huguenots forever. For his non-support, Richelieu had Benédict executed.*

In August 1576, Margarite Légere Jardeen delivered a healthy, bouncy baby girl, whom Tomas and she named Elisabeth Marye. The labor was long and painful, but uncomplicated. When Elisabeth finally presented herself, the midwife started to proclaim her usual mantra, but together Maggie and the grandmothers, almost on cue, cut her off and laughingly chortled, "It's a fine, fine baby!"

"No," the midwife firmly told them. "*She* is a fine, fine baby girl!" Tomas was waiting outside the birthing room and heard the women's cries of joy. He grabbed his father and gave him a big hug.

"Thank you for all that you and Mother have done for me and Maggie," he told his father. "I love both of you with all my heart. Thank you for being great parents." Then, tears began to flow down Tomas's cheeks. It was at this moment that he realized what it really meant to be a father. It was almost too deep of an emotion to fully understand. *But I am getting there*, he thought to himself.

Captain Chevin resigned his commission as a soldier of King Henri III and joined the employment of the Jardeen and Légere families as the manager of their new retail businesses. This caused some consternation in the community, but people were apparently quick to forgive and forget, for the families were respected throughout the city for their integrity and contribution to its economy and culture. The respect was indeed earned, and was held by members of the Huguenot community, as well as most Catholics. If the Jardeens and the Légeres could forgive the captain, then who had the right to question what they had done? The book shop and art gallery were each blessed with the royal insignia after King Henri had visited the shops on a trip to La Rochelle later that year. The businesses continued to grow and prosper. The takeoff at the art gallery began when Maggie was able to come in and evaluate the stock of paintings. The high-priced paintings inherited from the previous ownership were exhibited in a private section of the gallery, and new paintings were bought from budding artists in the maritime and wine-producing regions of France. The style of the paintings, along with the outdoor scenes of beautiful landscapes, flowers, and fishermen hard at work, were things that people living in La Rochelle seemed to care about and appreciate the most. Paintings depicting the magnificent twin fortress towers of La Rochelle, constructed a century before, were very popular, despite their having served as the prison. The towers were impressive in construction and lent a majestic view to boats coming into the harbor.

Business was taking off at the boatyard. Design of the three-masted corvair was completed by the middle of 1577, and construction of it had begun at the dry docks on Île de Ré. The king, as well as Captain Aubie Cussions, the entrepreneurial financier jointly financing the construction with the French government, was well-pleased with the plans conceived and developed by the design team put together by Antoine and Charles. The design had progressed rapidly once Tomas had recovered and was able to return to work. Antoine had freed up a lot of his time by hiring Captain Chevin to manage the sale of books and music. Antoine and Charles were beginning to look forward to the day when they could retire as active partners in the boatyard. They saw the necessary work ethic, intelligence, and knowledge of the business in Tomas and had visions of him someday becoming the active partner, while they assumed the role of silent partners. However, it would not be at this time. Tomas was still a young man and not ready to assume the leadership role.

Construction of the corvair began in the large dry dock on the Île de Ré in the summer of 1577, and was expected to be completed by the fall of 1580. A number of the workers from the boatyard in La Rochelle moved to Île de Ré to be part of the shipbuilding workforce. Others opted to remain living in La Rochelle and take the ferry every day back and forth to the island. The intense pressure of design was over.

Antoine and Charles, the nobleman and the gentleman farmer, were now free to pursue other projects and interests. Since Tomas had been the principal architect of the corvair, he was given authority to oversee the construction, to ensure that it complied with the plans and proceeded on time. The cousins who owned the shipyard on the island would manage the construction itself. It was a nice family working relationship, and things went smoothly. The protection given by the king to the Jardeen boatyard in La Rochelle was extended to the shipyard on the Île de Ré.

Elisabeth Marye Jardeen was then almost fourteen months old, and attempting to walk and talk. Her first year of life had been fulfilling for Maggie's parents, and for all of the Jardeens. Everyone, including Tomas's siblings, seemed to revel in bonding with her. She brought deep meaning to and renewed vitality to everyone's life.

Not everyone was happy with Captain Chevin's decision to leave the military and the Catholic Church to work for Huguenots. A lot of people were seemingly envious of the success he was having in the business world. Threats were made against him. But he had many friends in the militia, and they protected him. It was not that he sought their protection, as he felt quite capable of taking care of himself. Even though the bookshop and the art gallery were supposedly protected by order of the king and the display of the royal crest, anonymous threats were made against the businesses, owners, and employees. Because of the various threats, which many people presumed originated with the Catholic Church, the soldiers patrolled the streets heavily both day and night. During the day, a soldier was usually loitering in the stores and could be found in the gallery innocently looking over the books, or supposedly admiring the art. At night, there always seemed to be a couple of soldiers within visual distance of the businesses. Chevin, still called "Captain" and "sir" by the men whom he had commanded, was generous in rewarding the soldiers for their protection. A few pounds were slipped to them every once in a while, or an occasional meal or drink helped to ensure their loyalty. In fact, the soldiers began to just turn a deaf ear to the complaints of the priest who had replaced Father Benedict, and of the new bishop. The Church had become infuriated at the freedom being allowed the Huguenots, and the bishop made an unveiled threat that some people were going to pay dearly.

Cardinal Benédict implored the new bishop to tone things down, but the bishop, young and ambitious, continued to rage his private battles. The priest at the church reported to the bishop, and thus took his cues from him.

King Henri III was born in 1551 in Fontainebleau, a son of Henri II and Catherine de' Medici. He was a learned man who delved deeply into religious issues. However, under pressure from his parents, Henri became Catholic. As king, he strongly supported the Catholic Church, but deep in his heart he had the attitude of "live and let live." La Rochelle and the other Huguenot strongholds were far from Paris. Paris was considered, obviously so, the most important city in all of France. Most Parisians were overwhelmingly of the Catholic faith. This city was the scene of the first major discord between the religious sides. It began as incessant acts of personal violence of Catholics against the Huguenots, and revenge acts of vandalism by the Huguenots against Catholic churches and cathedrals, as well as against statues of Catholic saints and other property. There was danger of things spiraling out of control. The unrest soon spread to the Huguenot havens, such as La

Rochelle. Despite the relative peace that had existed for so long in La Rochelle between the people, the bishop's firebrand type of leadership provoked animosity in the city. The Jardeens and the Légeres were seemingly being spared. There were many reasons for this. Primary among the reasons was no doubt the goodwill that they incurred by being voices of reason in the midst of the ugliness. They spoke out against the violence swirling around them. In their Reformed ministry, they were careful not to slander the Catholic Church and spoke simply of "the rights of man to possess personal beliefs and pursue personal religious freedom." Finally, they were giving voice to peace among "brothers." Regardless, the Catholic Church was not happy, but realized that matters could be far worse. Besides, the bookstore carried books on Catholicism, and most of the parishioners were customers there; the gallery was selling artwork that did not offend anyone. For the most part, Catholics loved the paintings being sold as much as anyone. Also, the Légere family, as well as the Jardeens, were recognized for the charity they sponsored that was blind to religious views. Simply put, the charity money collected from businesses and individuals was for all people of the city who needed assistance, regardless of religious belief. It was a kindness that touched many lives and was deeply appreciated. Although done in strict confidence, there was no way of hiding the identity of the people behind it. Again, the Catholic Church wished that it was the Church who was the moving force to help its own, but they had deep appreciation for the Jardeens and the Légeres for their unselfishness in helping Catholic parishioners as well as the Huguenots. It was an act of human decency that was soon applauded, even by King Henri and the government of France. In the fall of 1578, Henri III came to La Rochelle and presented the Legion of Honor, France's highest award for contributions to French society, to Antoine Jardeen, Charles Jardeen, and Michel Légere. He did this fully knowing that they were activists in the Huguenot community. Cardinal Benédict mandated that the new bishop be present at the award ceremony. The bishop chose to be present only because his cardinal would be attending. Cardinal Benédict spoke after the king and offered the "profuse gratitude of the Church to the good work that these men were doing, for the community and for all of mankind."

There was no doubt in his sincerity when he spoke these words. The bishop took his cue from the cardinal, and without being overly profuse, more or less mimicked Benédict's words. After all, both families were still carried on the Church's rolls as parishioners, and they still contributed as expected to the Church. The apparent love affair with the Jardeen brothers and the Légere family finally ended the next year, when a butter tax was enacted by the local government on behalf of the Church to pay for the construction of a new cathedral in La Rochelle. The Jardeen brothers became vocal protesters of the levying of a tax to support a state church that was already flush with funds. Insult was added to injury to believe that the need for a new cathedral was prompted by serious talk in the Huguenot community of plans to build the Reformed Church of La Rochelle. This talk had supposedly been stirred by none other than the Jardeens in fulfillment of the promise made earlier to Monsieur Ronsérre. Although violence was not the intended goal, once again there was some vandalism carried out against the Catholic church when the bishop reacted and protested the building of a Huguenot church. The church was defaced, but the damage was minor. Probably more serious was the defacing of statues of saints. The head of Saint Paul was decapitated, and was later found in a back alley in a run-down section of the city. The brothers begged the Huguenot community to exercise self-control and stop these crimes. They argued that vandalism was dealing a deadly blow to the efforts to have their own church. The fact that vandalism was being carried out against the Catholic church was denied throughout the Huguenot community. Most of the Huguenots in the city believed that the vandalism being reported was minor, and that it was being perpetuated by the Catholic Church itself as leverage to enforce the collection of the tax. The rhetoric on each side grew consistently louder and more insidious until the tax was repealed. Little money had been collected in the short duration, as most of the Huguenots and a majority of the Catholics in the city had refused to pay it. The effect had been largely to grow the divide between the hierarchy of the Church and the Huguenot community; this divide did not seem to yet exist between the Huguenot community and the Catholic parishioners. In fact, the imposition of the tax had an opposite effect on the relationship between the two communities than had been hoped for by Catholic leadership. By this time, Cardinal Benédict had already been made the cardinal of Lyon, an elevated promotion that promised a path to Paris. His replacement was largely untested, but was viewed as being more resistant to Huguenot freedoms than Benédict was. Together, the new cardinal, the relatively new bishop, and the local priest had conspired to arouse the parishioners against the building of a Huguenot church. Instead, the butter tax had resulted in quite a few Catholic parishioners refusing to make any further contributions to their church, and allying themselves with the Reformists. A further result was the increased trade with Huguenot-owned businesses, and increased friendliness and tolerance in everyday interaction on the streets. In summary, the tax had exactly the opposite effect and outcome from the one that was expected by the Church.

The Jardeen brothers, along with Michel Légere, began to raise money and gather building materials for their new church. The prosperity of their businesses was a big contributor to the cause. A parcel of land was acquired in a nice part of the city, just a few blocks from the Catholic church. Plans were made for a building that would accommodate 250 worshippers. When the number of worshippers outgrew the capacity of the building, they would begin to hold multiple services until the church could independently afford to expand. The intent of these three men was to facilitate the construction of the church, but not to be the ministers, although they would certainly aid and promote the ministry in any way possible.

Groundbreaking for the new church was in March 1579. Monsieur Ronsérre came from Fontenay-le-Comte for the ceremony and was honored as the founding father of the church building. Ronsérre, however, made it clear to the people gathered that the real heroes were the Jardeen brothers and Michel Légere, not himself. For the first time, it was publicly made known the story of the imprisonment of Tomas and his wife, and how that experience had changed the lives of their parents and their uncle. For the first time in the memory of those present, a woman took charge of a church service and gave the homily. Margarite Légere Jardeen stood proudly at the speaker's outdoor dais with her toddler daughter, Elisabeth, at her side and professed how proud she was of her parents, in-laws, and of the spiritual aspects of her marriage bonds to her husband, Tomas. She spoke of the grace and beauty that results from having God and His son, Jesus, become an integral part of everyday life.

When the church was about half completed, the search began in earnest for a respected reverend to head the congregation. Monsieur Ronsérre suggested that the Jardeens travel to the city of Angoulême, the principal city and capital of the province of Angoumois. It was a distance of about 201 kilometers (about 125 miles) between the two cities. Even though the road they would be traveling on was good, the trip would take several days and be rather arduous. It was the fall of 1579. The weather was nice, and the air was coolish; however, at night there seemed to be a mystic chill in the air. The foliage of the trees had already turned their brilliant red and orange colors. Because the men had decided to take their wives along on the trip, Governor Bouché offered up several of his guards to accompany them. For comfort, they traveled in two coaches instead of riding together in one. This was not only for the safety of the travelers, but also to afford the party the appropriate distinction of social and economic standing when meeting with the young Reverend Jacque Daniel Horry. Horry was a noble and honorable name of a very wealthy and influential family in the province of Angoumois; the history of the family had already spread to La Rochelle in the province of Aunis.

In the ninth century, Pépin, the king of Aquitaine, created the county of Angoulême in the province of Angoumois. Because of his loyalty and service to the king, Amōs Hori, an ancestor of Jacque Horry (by the 1500s, the spelling of the family name had been changed), was ceded a large estate in the new county and given a title of nobility. The Hori family had grown and prospered financially, similar in many respects to the way in which Charles

Jardeen was now managing his manoir estate back in La Rochelle.

Monies accrued from farming their estate and the selling of timber from the forest had enriched the Hori family beyond reason. Hunting fees were levied by the family for the right to hunt in the forests on their land, and they sold the resin collected from the pine trees. Having acquired ownership to most of the buildings in the town of Angoulême, the family eventually got ownership of most of the businesses there. In the meantime, the land baron's holdings in the country grew through battles won over neighboring landowners. As the family finances increased, a greater share of their wealth was expected to be paid to the king. In return for their "gifts" to the king, the political force and armed might of the government was at the ready to assist the family in whatever way was needed; the family did not hesitate to ask for these favors. Despite the acquisition and growth of wealth and power, the Horry family were generally good people, as far as one could expect land barons to be. They treated their tenant farmers very well and were active in the practice of their religious faith. In fact, the Horry family financed the construction of the first Catholic church in Angoulême.

Their break with Catholicism came in the mid-1500s, when Joshua Horry, Jacque's father, had been figuratively delayed by the Church with imposition of a special tax on his property and a demand for him to deed a rather large piece of it to the Church. Joshua had already been introduced to the principles of John Calvin, and had studied the statement of principles which Luther had posted on the door of the church in Germany. The beliefs of Luther, and the even more stern and dogmatic Calvin, made good sense to him. He reached a compromise with the Church on their demands for money and land, but from that time forward Joshua remained Catholic in name only, as he became a strong believer in the Reformist teachings being widely preached by the Huguenots.

When Jacque was eighteen years old, his father sent him to the university in Geneva, Switzerland. It was there that young Jacque was immersed in the teachings of the Reformed Church and came to the decision to become a minister. This was exactly what his father wanted for him. In 1563, as soon as he finished his university studies, Jacque enrolled in seminary in Geneva, where he had the privilege of attending several guest lectures by John Calvin before Calvin died in 1564. In 1578, Jacque Horry returned from Switzerland to his native Angoulême upon the death of his father. Joshua had left his vast estate and business interests to his four children. Jacque, however, had no interest in maintaining the land. It was agreed with his siblings that he would remain in the ministry and permit them to manage the business affairs of the legacy that their father had left. And since he would not be taking an active hand in managing the family affairs, he would forego a portion of his share of income. Being a close-knit family and realizing the importance of Jacque's work, the arrangement proved satisfactory to his siblings. It was agreed that Jacque would maintain one-fourth ownership of the estate, and would have one of the homes that his father had built on the land, but would receive only one-eighth of the yearly income from all of the business operations, while the other half of his share would be divided up evenly among his three siblings. This seemed complicated, but it gave Jacque and his family lifelong interests in the estate, and provided him more than a substantial income to live a very comfortable, luxurious life, if he so chose. Comfortable, yes. It would enable him, along with his meager ministerial salary, to enjoy the things of life important to him, to be able to be generous in his support of the needy, and to pursue worthy charitable causes. However, the luxurious type of life was not what Jacque wanted for his children and grandchildren. He wanted happiness, good health, and success for them.

When Antoine and Charles met with him that day in 1579 in Angoulême, it quickly became obvious that Jacque Horry was the person who they wanted to bring to La Rochelle to lead the new Huguenot church under construction. He showed himself to be a powerful witness to God's work here on earth, to the importance of belief in a personal God, and a witness to the saving grace of the Lord Jesus Christ. At the end of the day, after they had met for eight hours straight, only taking a short break to eat lunch with their wives, they were mesmerized by what he had had to say. They invited him to come to La Rochelle as the senior minister of the new church. And he agreed.

"I am honored to be asked," he told them. "I am sure that my family and I will come to love La Rochelle as much you so obviously do. I pray that I will bring honor and dignity to your church, so that I may lead it to grow and prosper while doing the Lord's work."

It was agreed that Antoine and Charles would find a suitable home for the Horry family in La Rochelle for occupancy within the next six months, and that the Horrys would begin to prepare for the move.

Privately, Jacque and his wife planned to keep their home on the family estate in Angoumois and use it as a vacation home, as a home for one of their children when grown and married, or perhaps one day to live retired, where their future grandchildren could come. Whether this was a realistic dream or not, only time would tell.

Chapter 27
Construction of the Church

Construction on the new Reformed church in La Rochelle proceeded smoothly, despite some vandalism and stolen building materials. As opposed to before, it was the new Protestant church being vandalized, rather than the Catholic church. Huguenots in the city blamed the Catholics, and the Catholic hierarchy contended that the misdeeds had been done by the Huguenots themselves, to discredit the Catholic religion and create bitter feelings toward Catholic parishioners. At least, those were the official allegations being made by each side. This was the same familiar story told, except in reverse roles, for the desecration of a Catholic church or relic anywhere in France. Fortunately, the number of these incidences was few. Responsibility was hard to pin down. Certainly, the common people on the street, regardless of religious persuasion, continued to get along well with each other. Huguenot-owned businesses continued to prosper with the support of the Catholic parishioners, and the number of Huguenots in civil service and the military grew. The king's militia in La Rochelle had long since been turning a blind eye to religion, no doubt because of a continued allegiance to Captain Chevin. Overall, times seemed good, even though the Catholic Church was still the national church of France. All people were supposed to show solidarity of the nation by being faithful to the Catholic beliefs.

Jacque Horry made several trips to La Rochelle to ensure that construction on the new church building was proceeding smoothly. In fact, on most of his visits, he tried to make it a point to pay a courtesy call to the Catholic bishop and the local parish priest. Although they did not greet Horry's arrival with enthusiasm, they were always generous in their showing of cordiality and hospitality to him. There was little else they could do, since more than 50 percent of the population in the city were now Catholic in name only, and most of these were openly practicing Huguenots. There was a question as to whether the new church structure could accommodate all the Huguenots in the city, as well as those who would be expected to come from Île de Ré.

Finally, Reverend Horry moved his wife and five children, two sons (ages fourteen and ten) and three daughters (ages eighteen, sixteen, and twelve), to La Rochelle in April 1580. They moved into the manse, a home purchased near the church being built. Renovations had been made to the home. It was a large house with an expansive yard for the children, and an office and library for the minister.

The dedication of the Huguenot church was on the last Sunday of June 1580; the first church service was to follow four Sundays later. Reverend Horry worked almost without stopping from the time he first came to La Rochelle, but the time between the dedication and the opening church service was especially intense. There was much to do to try to pull the small, private congregations worshipping in various homes and businesses into the unified church's congregation. They were also in the process to set up a committee, which would select persons to be ordained as elders of the church. These elders would serve as the governing body of the church. A committee needed to be established to deal with the financing of the church's debt, even though it was rather small thanks to the covenant made between Ronsérre, the governor, the Jardeen brothers, and Michel Légere, along with support from the other prosperous businessmen and advocates of the cause. Another committee was developed to draft the covenants and creeds of the church, as well as to handle plans for the first service. One important policy agreed to for inclusion in the church's covenants was the stipulation that church members, including the minister and his family, would be allowed to drink alcohol in the privacy of their homes and in public dining places, but that it was not to be excessively consumed. Already, there was controversy about this stipulation. It would be a hard covenant to obey, since the water in La Rochelle was not yet completely safe and the definition of "excessively consumed" would be difficult to define.

Much of the available water was polluted by underground salts and the seawater from the Bay of Biscay. Some wells were safe, while others were contaminated. Water was not yet available in all parts of the city, and where it was available, it was not always potable. The public water supply, or what there was of it, was collected in a large cistern fed by reconstructed ruins of a Roman aqueduct, which brought water down from the hills of the province of Aunis. The aqueduct sloped steadily downward toward the Bay of Biscay at La Rochelle. At first, residents of La Rochelle, if they did not have wells on their property, had to collect water from the several cisterns in buckets, or collect it from a freshwater bog slightly inland from the sea.

In the rural countryside, manoir estates, such as the one owned by Charles Jardeen, received water from sources such as springs and nearby creeks with the use of windmill-driven pumps. Charles's manoir had easy access to water, thereby enabling him to make wine for himself, Antoine, Michel, and even some for sale. His wine was largely made from the pineau d'Aunis grapes, one of the several species which he grew in the vineyard on the farm. A red claret wine made from this grape was imported as early as 1456 into England by King Henry III, son of Henry Plantagenet and his wife, Isabella of Angoulême.

This red wine would be the Communion wine at the church, although unfermented grape juice would be available for the few who might prefer it to the wine.

Public water to homes and businesses in the city started to be developed by 1650 with the use of pipes made of stone, or in many cases, from cast iron. By the 1670s, primitive plumbing fixtures such as sinks and toilets were becoming available for families that could afford them. Although it was a project started years before, progress on the water supply and indoor plumbing had been slow until the term of the forward-thinking Mayor Légere. He put great emphasis on getting this project finished and spent considerable money on it. The system was just being completed when he left office to become an art dealer.

The bishop and the local parish priest were invited to the dedication ceremony at the church, but they each politely replied that they had prior commitments and would be unable to attend. That was expected, but they had been invited anyway, just as a matter of courtesy.

Monsieur Ronsérre came from Fontenay-le-Comte for both the dedication and the first service. He congratulated the Jardeen brothers for their choice of Reverend Horry to be the pastor. Ronsérre, now in his early forties, also informed the Jardeens and the Légeres of his retirement and sale of his legal practice. The most surprising news, though, was that he would be moving to La Rochelle.

Upon hearing the news, Governor Bouché immediately issued an invitation to Ronsérre to serve the governor in a legal advisory role once he was relocated. Without hesitation, he replied to the governor, "Your Lordship, your kind offer will no doubt speed up my plans. You may have me here in La Rochelle sooner than I had expected."

But Antoine broke in and laughingly said, "But, Your Lordship, he will not have much time to serve you, for he is going to be a full-time conseiller for the new church."

Bouché quickly, almost without even taking time to think of a reply, and with a broad smile on his face, replied, "Monsieur Ronsérre is so tireless and so brilliant there will be enough of him to share with you."

Maggie Jardeen agreed to take on the responsibility of church musician. A church choir had not yet formed. So much like in the Catholic Church, one person would lead the congregation in songs of praise while Maggie would play the clavichord or harpsichord. There were many fine voices in the congregation, and hopefully the responsibility for hymn-leading would pass around among willing volunteers. At least six people volunteered to lead the singing at the dedication; Martine, Antoine, and Monsieur Ronsérre were among them. It seemed appropriate, though, for Ronsérre to do it because of his deep, carrying voice, and the fact that he was the force that had driven the establishment of the church in the first place. The men's honor was at stake. They firmly believed that a covenant made was a promise to be kept, and this was the fulfillment of the covenant they had made at a lunch.

The dedication service went very smoothly. An extraordinary number of people attended the service; no doubt many came out of curiosity. The boxed pews were crowded, and people were standing in the aisles and the narthex of the church building. A certain peace descended over those in attendance. It seemed almost mystical. Many people reported that as they gazed at the empty cross hanging on the wall, they felt relief from the problems of their lives; they felt a presence of the Holy Spirit descend upon them, something that most of them had never experienced before in their Catholicism. God was speaking personally to them. The service began with the singing of "O Come, Thou Holy Spirit," a twelfth-century Latin hymn which had become very popular in France, both among Catholics and Protestants. It was perhaps one common element that seemed to bind all people together. Words are from an unknown author.

> *O Come, Thou Holy Spirit, come!*
> *And from Thy celestial home*
> *Shed a ray of light divine!*
> *O Come, Thou Father of the poor!*
> *O Come, Thou Source of all our store!*
> *O Come, within our bosoms shine!*

A prayer of thanksgiving was offered for the new church building, and for the people who had gathered together that day to celebrate the blessing and gift of God. A plea was made that this be a day for new beginnings for all the people of the city, and that God's work be done in accord with the plan that He had for them. The memories of Martin Luther and John Calvin were invoked, and a homily was given which reviewed the principles of faith prescribed by these men.

Antoine, without denouncing the Catholic Church or the government, told the story in a matter-of-fact way of how his son and daughter-in-law were imprisoned because of their faith, but were spared death by an officer with moral principles. "That officer sits among us here in this church today," he said. Without naming Captain Chevin, he went on to relate how the former soldier had found a passion for life and for freedom of the soul. "This person has found a God that he can believe in, a God who is a personal experience for him, and of Jesus Christ, the Son, who died on the cross for our sins," Antoine said. He then turned to look at the empty cross hanging over the altar. With that proclamation, an aura seemed to envelop the church, and suddenly there was a din of chatter as the congregants began to share their emotions with each other.

Antoine went on to tell of the immeasurable assistance lent by Monsieur Ronsérre, who had come from Fontenay-le-Comte to help secure the freedom of the two young people, and of the promise made to him to build a Huguenot church in La Rochelle. Then Ronsérre was invited to come forward to address the congregants. As he made his way to the pulpit, he was met with great applause and mutters of appreciation from the people. He spoke only briefly.

"I just want to thank the two Jardeen brothers and their families, plus Michel Légere and his wife for the great trust they had in me, and for their commitment to the vow made to me in seeing the construction of this church completed. No doubt it would not be here today if it weren't for these courageous families. And I want to thank the unnamed persons sitting here today who made contributions of their money, time, and talents to help make this all possible. Now, please permit me to introduce your new pastor, the Reverend Jacque Horry, who moved here with his family from Angoulême." Before inviting Reverend Horry to step up to the pulpit, he went on to describe a few facts about him: his education, the churches he had served, and a brief introduction to his religious views and beliefs. "I know that you are going to treasure him and his family, and be blessed by his service to you. Reverend Horry, will you please step up to the pulpit and meet your congregation?"

As the reverend made his way to the front of the church, the congregation stood and politely applauded their appreciation and welcome to him. There were many shouts of "Thank you!" and "God bless you!" as he made his way down the aisle. After tributes to those persons who had worked so hard to found the church, and thanking his wife and children for their love and support, the reverend gave a homily on listening to God in one's daily life and being faithful to following God's word in one's relations with mankind.

He closed the service by leading the congregation in the Apostles' Creed as spoken in the Reformed Church: "I believe in God the Father Almighty, the maker of Heaven and earth, and in Jesus Christ, His only begotten Son . . ." A statement of beliefs written by early Christians sometime between the fifth and ninth centuries, the Apostles' Creed was not a passage from the Bible, but was accumulated from a collection of biblical references. As originally written, the creed stated a belief in the "holy Catholic Church." This statement of faith was not intended to mean the Catholic faith as such, but instead meant all Christian churches. But for the first time in a church service in La Rochelle, and perhaps for the first time in the history of the Reformed Church, the expression of belief in the "holy Catholic Church" was omitted. Instead was substituted a profession of belief in the "church universal." Each of the interpretations were intended to signify "a one or universal church for all Christians" (Galatians 3:26–29). It continues,

"You are all sons of God through faith in Christ Jesus, for all of you who were baptized into Christ have clothed yourselves with Christ. There is neither Jew nor Greek, slave nor free, male nor female, for you are all one in Christ Jesus. If you belong to Christ, then you are Abraham's seed, and heirs to the promise." The omission of "the holy Catholic Church," whether meant as a slight or not, was taken as such by the Catholic priest as offensive. If it was indeed meant as a slight, it long bred contempt within the Catholic Church, and was not soon to be forgotten.

A more succinct meaning of this doctrine is probably best expressed as, "The spiritual solidarity and bond which binds together the faithful on earth and those in Heaven."

Chapter 28
Tragedy

The rest of 1580 was relatively quiet. At first, there was quite a bit of fluster as the new Huguenot church got launched. The Reformed Church of La Rochelle was now officially a being with a life all its own. In the twelve months ahead, through the generous contributions of its members, and without any pressure from Reverend Horry or the people who were so instrumental in founding it, the church became debt-free. Those who could afford it were most magnanimous in their gifts. Many of the less fortunate gave generously, and in several cases more than they could really afford, for many of them came back for assistance through the charity efforts of the Jardeen brothers and the church. It often seemed like a revolving door, there was money coming in and money going out just as quickly as it came. But the job got done!

At first, despite the perceived slight now uttered regularly by the Huguenots, the Catholic priest in La Rochelle and the hierarchy of the Catholic Church pretended to ignore the presence of the Huguenot church just a few blocks away. It was desperately coping with a declining attendance, and declining monetary gifts by the parishioners who remained loyal. Despite the attempt to live in peace with the Reformists, it was increasingly becoming obvious that the Huguenot church was a threat to the prosperity of the Catholic church in La Rochelle. The same effect was beginning to be felt in other Protestant communes throughout France. There promised to be many ills and dark days ahead.

On the second Sunday of February 1581, there were a large number of people in attendance for the service at the Huguenot church. In fact, the hard pews of the church were full. There were babies to be christened, and it was a baptism day for the youth of the church. These were always joyous days for the members. There would be visitation afterward and celebrations in the homes, as members would pay social calls on the families celebrating the religious experience of their children. There would be the opportunity that day for families to share their religious ties with other families, and to fulfill social commitments with simple gifts for the children.

That day, however, an unexpected and horrible thing happened. Antoine Jardeen, the senior elder of the church's governing body, called the session and was just beginning to speak on the congregational life of the church, when a lone man silently entered the church and walked rapidly to the front. As well-dressed as the others in the church, people assumed that he was a latecomer looking for a seat up front. Unchallenged, he began to shout and demand the opportunity to address the congregation. Quickly, the ushers and other men of the congregation were rising from their seats and beginning to move toward the front of the church. Antoine stepped down from the pulpit and approached the man, asking what he wanted. The man pulled a gun from under his doublet and pointed it at Antoine while shouting, "I want you dead! You are a traitor to the one Church of God." At that moment, Tomas, sitting on the front pew, leaped from his seat. Surprised, the gunman spun around to his side and fired his weapon as Tomas lunged toward him. The bullet from the gun hit him in the chest and he crumpled to the floor, having died almost instantly. Simultaneous with the gunshot, another member of the congregation flew into the back of the gunman, knocking him to the floor, and three others jumped into the melee, wrestling the gun from him. Antoine Jardeen was not hurt. Everything had happened so fast. The fact that his life had been spared by the sacrifice of his son was a blur in his mind that was awakened with the wailing of the new widow, Margarite Jardeen, and her young daughter. The noise in the sanctuary had risen to an almost unbearable level, as people began to offer prayers and talk amongst themselves. Many of the people were sobbing uncontrollably. Reverend Horry tried to encourage everyone to leave the church, but his pleas went unheard and, for the most part, unheeded. Monsieur Chevin made his way out of the church and reported the shooting to several soldiers loitering just down the street. The militia force made it a practice to keep an eye on activities at the Reformed church, as they did at the Catholic church. It was a commonly acceptable routine to which Horry and the elders of the church did not object.

The soldiers from the street did not recognize the gunman, and neither did Chevin. But, although he could not immediately put the pieces together, he knew that he had seen this man before. For his own safety, the soldiers quickly led the gunman from the church into Chevin's carriage, and whisked him off to the prison. During the next week, he was interrogated extensively, but he refused to provide any useful information and remained almost mute. The few words he uttered were garbled, like those of a madman. He carried no money or identification. No one came to visit him, except people from the church, and they did so out of curiosity of who this man was who had committed such a heinous act of inhumanity. The stranger ate very little and probably survived mostly through the intake of fluids.

In the meantime, the funeral for Tomas Jardeen took place on the second day after the incident, at the family's cemetery on Charles's estate in the country. It was a small cemetery completely enclosed by a stone wall, to discourage trespassers and keep out predatory animals. The entrance was by stone steps built onto one side of the wall to ascend, and mirroring steps on the other side to descend.

There was a large turnout for the funeral service held at the Reformed church. The families kept up a stiff outward appearance, although those who knew them well could tell that on the inside they were devastated. Other than Reverend Horry, who conducted the funeral, two other persons got up to speak. Uncle Charles, while sobbing and with a cracking voice, spoke first. He told the story. "I am the brother of Antoine Jardeen. I know that everyone here today knows and loves the Jardeen family and the Légere family. Each of them holds a special place in our hearts and minds. They are friends to every single person in this city, regardless of their religious beliefs or affiliation." With those words, echoes of "Amen" resonated throughout the church, from Catholic parishioners who chose to attend this service to their Huguenot brethren. After pausing for a minute, he continued, "And I know that today there is a very special place in your hearts for the young and courageous Tomas Jardeen, who gave his life in order to save that of Antoine Jardeen, his father." Charles stopped for a moment to wipe the tears from his eyes. "Before I share some of Tomas's life with you, let me tell you about his father. Antoine is my cousin, as well as my dear brother. His mother died when Antoine was very young, then his father died shortly after, and Antoine came to live in our household and was adopted by my parents. There is much to tell about the bond of love that existed between my family and the family of Antoine. There is much I could tell you about the love that still exists today between me, my wife, my children, Antoine, and all of his family. I am the godfather of the man whom we are going to bury today. I care as much about his widow, Margarite, and his young daughter as I do my own family. I hope all of you will give them the love and support which they will need in the weeks, months, and years ahead. And I plead with you not to ever forget Tomas, who was so full of life and vision for the future. His life was indeed one that was robbed from each of us long before his time!" At this point, Charles began to sob and was able to finish only with the words, "But, we must continue . . ." The words slowly faded away as silence enveloped the sanctuary.

Then, Captain Chevin, resplendent in his former military uniform and sitting with the family members and Monsieur Ronsérre, rose and asked permission to speak. Striding briskly to the pulpit, he gave his name, and although almost everyone in the church by now knew him and his story personally, he identified himself as a soldier and former captain of the guard at the prison.

"I want to take a few moments to tell you about a remarkable young man, who each of you are here today to mourn. As captain of the guard at the prison here in La Rochelle, I was ordered to see that the young Tomas Jardeen and his bride, Margarite Légere Jardeen, die for alleged conspiracy against a church that represents beliefs different in many ways from those that you practice. The responsibility was not something that I wanted, but was instead a duty placed on me because of my position. Thanks to the Honorable Monsieur Ronsérre, who is here with us today, my efforts were stalled. My life was messed up by alcohol, and no firm religious beliefs to save me. My own marriage seemed doomed, and I was seriously considering taking my own life. Then, something wonderful happened. I met Antoine Jardeen, the father whom young Tomas died trying to save. I saw a thoughtful man who was forgiving and considerate of others . . . a family man who deeply loved his wife, children, and above all loved his God. Monsieur Jardeen was unlike the father who was never present for me. Through him, I saw great value in the lives of Tomas and his bride, Margarite. I began to want what this family had. I wanted to personally know God. I wanted the strength, courage, and love that comes from knowing God, and the redemption that comes from knowing and believing in his Son, our Lord Christ. My life has turned around. I have it all. Thank you, Tomas and Margarite, and thank you, Monsieur Jardeen, for giving me the chance to find myself and to know your God."

By the time Chevin finished, there was not a dry eye in the church, not even among the hardest of hearts. The congregation knew enough not to sullen the dignity of the reason that they were there. The silent "Amens" spoken after his eulogy were in the hearts of the people.

Chapter 29
Trouble Ahead

On the twelfth day after the tragic shooting at the church, the Catholic bishop was seen going through the prison gates and did not come back out for several hours. Not much was thought at the time about his visit to the prison. There were Catholic prisoners held there, deeming it normal for the priest and Church hierarchy to visit. Perhaps in this case, the bishop had business to conduct with the prison commander. Reason indicated that it was not an event of great note, that is, until several nights later. At one of the local bars, a soldier went on about how the bishop had visited the prisoner who had shot and killed the Huguenot, and that the bishop had met with the prison commander in his office. He reported that he then overheard the commander talking to the captain of the guard. The commander allegedly told the captain, "The prisoner will be transported on Sunday out of here to the regional prison in Angoulême. It will happen during the Huguenot church service, so as not to attract notice." And in an emphatic voice, he told the captain, "Talk to our man and make sure that he never gets there alive."

Clicking the heels of his boots, the captain snapped back to salute his superior. "As you command, sir!" Not returning the salute, the commander turned with his head bowed and, in a seemingly dazed state, slowly began to descend the steps to his office.

Early the next morning, in the darkness of the predawn sunrise, the captain rode out of the prison gate on a speedy steed and headed out of the city. The captain understood it was a given that the hands of the militia force must not be implicated in the matter.

The story was overheard by two Huguenot friends who were having a leisurely dinner that evening in the bar, and naturally they would report the details of the story to the Reverend Horry. They quickly finished their dinner and, without staying for their usual after-dinner Cognac, headed off to visit the reverend at his home. The reverend was unsure of what to make of the story that the men told him. He asked them to not tell their story to anyone else, for he worried that the knowledge of these members would present the opportunity for them or the church to be accused of being part of whatever might happen.

After spending the night turning the matter over in his mind, Horry drove over to Monsieur Ronsérre's house the next morning. On the way, he stopped to see Antoine Jardeen. The famed solicitor had bought a home near that of the Jardeens'. Antoine's driver was waiting with the carriage to take Antoine to the boatyard, but Horry caught him just as he was coming down the steps. He told Antoine, "I have something very serious to discuss with you. Do you have time to go inside and talk in private?" Signaling to the driver to wait for him, Antoine walked back into the house with the reverend. Telling his wife that he needed privacy, he and the reverend went to the parlor. Dismissing the servant who appeared, Antoine told him, "The reverend and I need to be alone. Ensure that we are not interrupted. I will ring if I need you."

"I will be just outside," the servant replied, as he exited the room and closed the door.

"Jacque, tell me what is on your mind. It must be very important for you to be here so early in the day."

The reverend related the story that had been told to him the prior evening by the two church members. As he spoke, he could see increasing anguish in Antoine's face. The loss of a child was something that no one who had experienced it would ever get over, and it was a heavy weight for him to carry. Antoine sat without interrupting until the reverend was finished.

"Do you think this story was told by a drunken guard?"

"I thought the same thing," Horry agreed. "The men told me that, although the soldier was having a drink, he did not appear at all to be intoxicated; it was more like something that was bothering his conscience, and he needed to tell someone . . . you know, like a plea for help."

"Have you told anyone besides me?" Antoine asked.

"No, you are the only person I have told. I was on my way to speak with Monsieur Ronsérre."

"Oui, I think it would be good to talk with Ronsérre." Ringing for the servant, he rightfully observed, "The introduction of the Catholic Church into this matter does present complicating angles, but I think that we could have surmised as much. Perhaps most important is the order which the commander gave to the captain of the guard. You are from Angoulême. What do you know about the prison there?"

"It can be a very rough place," the reverend told him. "But it's not like it used to be."

There was a knock on the door. "Come in," Antoine called out to his servant. He instructed him to go with his driver to Monsieur Ronsérre's home. "Tell him that the reverend and I have an important matter to discuss, and bring him back to us."

"As you wish, my master," the servant said, and quickly retreated, closing the door behind him.

"As I was saying," Horry continued, "the judicial system in Angoulême has gotten pretty easy on civil injustice. The Catholic hierarchy is behind most of the wrongs being committed." He acknowledged the pain that the Jardeen family had experienced, and was careful not to make a comparison to the system that had wrongfully incarcerated Antoine's son and daughter-in-law.

Leaving the discussion hanging, Antoine asked Horry, "Jacque, I know that you know who killed my son. He is from Angoulême, isn't he? Please tell me, for I must know. Tell me the truth!" he pleaded. "When he dies, I want to be there to see justice done, to see the pain in his face as I saw the pain in the face of my son, and the pain that I now see every day in the faces of Margarite and my granddaughter."

The reverend sat and thought back over the murder of Tomas. In his mind, he could think of three persons in Angoulême who could possibly be connected to the case, but one especially stood out; however, he could not be sure. He thought it better to remain silent. As he gazed at Antoine, the usual façade of strength that had always shown in his friend's face just seemed to melt away before his eyes. Quickly, considering his thoughts, he said, "My dear Antoine, it is better that you do not know this man's identity right now. Trust me, you will know in due time."

Just then, there was a knock at the door, and Antoine quickly wiped the tears from his eyes with his hands. "Monsieur Ronsérre," the servant announced from the other side of the door.

"Please bring him in," Antoine answered, and although still dazed from the conversation with the reverend, while feeling weak and unsteady on his feet, he stood to greet his friend. As the servant was about to leave, Antoine said to him, "Please, prepare some coffee and Cognac for us."

"Oui, my master, shall I mix them?" the servant replied.

"Merci, that would be a nice treat on a cold winter morning such as today."

Reverend Horry tried to retell the story of what he had learned to Ronsérre, but the telling was a bit chopped up, as Antoine would nervously break in with questions and comments of his own.

But the conversation was soon interrupted when the servant brought in the coffee. "My master, it is your favorite drink," he announced.

"And just what is that?" Ronsérre politely inquired, with a broad smile on his face.

Before the servant could answer, Antoine spoke up. "Surely, François, you can answer your own question. It is your favorite, coffee and Cognac steeped with cloves and cinnamon."

Winking at the reverend, Ronsérre smiled and said, "Of course, I do remember. I have had the witch's brew a few times before here at your house."

"If you do not like it, why do you drink so much of it?" Antoine laughingly replied.

"Oh," Ronsérre said, "you are going to cause the kind reverend to think that I am a wicked man."

"No, you are not the wicked one; it is our dear friend, Antoine, who is plying us with alcohol," Horry said as he took another sip of the brew and smiled with deep satisfaction.

Then, getting back to the business at hand, Antoine asked, "Can we really believe that the Catholic Church was behind the murder of my son?"

"That is a good question," Ronsérre pondered, while stroking a newly grown goatee. "If we can rely on the story of the informer, then the evidence quickly leads you to believe that. But what if the killer is just a fanatical Catholic who was, in fact, just intent on killing you because of your involvement in organizing our church? Perhaps because of your charity work, or for some other reason? You do realize that you and your brother have been intruding into matters which some consider to be within the province of the Catholic Church. Matters such as gifts of food, clothing, and financial support to its parishioners. The church does not take lightly to such intrusions across religious lines. What if the killer was intent on murdering you for some personal reason, not a hired killer . . . but someone with a grudge against you? Maybe he is a person with a mental disturbance? The Catholic father could have been at the prison as a compassionate visitor to a fellow Catholic. We may never know."

"Of course, you are right, we may never know, but there is one thing I do know," Antoine told him, with heavy emotion welling up in his heart. "I will never give up trying to find out. My dear granddaughter cries for her father, and her mother has been scarred forever by the violent loss of her husband." Then, unsure of himself, taking a few moments to compose his thoughts, Antoine continued in a voice barely above a whisper, "Perhaps it would have been better if Tomas had just contracted some terrible illness or disease and died, or had just gone to sleep one night, never to wake up again." And then he broke down completely in uncontrollable sobbing.

The meeting ended minutes later when Reverend Horry offered a prayer, thanking God for the friendship bond of the three men and asking for comfort, mercy, and blessings for the Jardeen and Légere families. Before closing, he prayed that God would lead them to insight as to the identity and true motive of the killer.

The men all agreed that it was hard to figure out the reason why man commits violence against other men. At the door, as he was leaving, Ronsérre offered, "I will be in touch. I have contacts who might be able to help." As the reverend was driving Ronsérre to his home, he said to him, "You need to begin with the Catholic Church."

The next Sunday, Monsieur Ronsérre did not attend church, nor did Antoine Jardeen. They stood on the street beside the prison, with a clear view of the prison gate; they were not too close, and yet not too far away. For all appearances, they could appear as just two locals talking about the weather, local gossip, or whatever. Not sure of what time the prisoner would leave for Angoulême, they presumed that the transfer would happen during the time that the Huguenots were attending church. If it did, then the intoxicated soldier would have been telling the truth about what he said that he had heard. About fifteen minutes after the service would have begun at the Huguenot church, there were signs of increased activity at the prison gate. Three prison guards walked out of the prison and hurriedly crossed the bridge over the protective moat, to the huge iron gate that closed off the prison from the world. The guard at the gate allowed the soldiers to proceed to the gatehouse. After a couple of minutes passed, a coach appeared and crossed the bridge to the gate, where it stopped. An armed soldier riding with the driver got down from the carriage to talk to the four soldiers waiting at the gate. He and the three guards, who had walked to the prison gate, conversed for a few minutes. Ronsérre and Antoine could not hear what was being said, but the waving of arms and hands was animated. There appeared to be some problem that needed to be resolved, and the four men walked back across the bridge into the prison, leaving the prisoner shackled and manacled in the carriage with just the unarmed driver and the lone guard at the gate. A disheveled, poorly dressed man appeared on the street, seemingly to have come from nowhere. Appearing to be lost, he crossed over to the guardhouse and started talking to the guard. There was little doubt that he was hitting up the guard for a handout. Suddenly, another man crossed the street and approached the carriage from the blind side, unseen by the guard, and flashed a pistol. He grabbed the handle of the door of the carriage, jerked it open, and fired at point-blank range as the prisoner screamed for mercy. The driver jumped down to the street on the other side of the coach. Without any intervention, the stranger fled down the street to safety, while the shooter fled in another direction. The hit had been made, and of course, neither the shooter nor his accomplice were caught.

With the man who killed Tomas now dead, the case would be officially closed. The ruse had been cleverly planned. On the surface, it would appear that the militia force was innocent of any involvement. After all, the guard had been left by himself at the gate. He could have chased after the killer, but because the driver of the coach was neither qualified nor armed to guard the gate, the gatekeeper could not leave his post. It all happened very quickly. Although the militia forces later pretended to conduct a search of the city, neither the shooter nor the stranger were found.

Back at Ronsérre's house, Antoine asked, "My friend, what do we do now?"

"I am going to Angoulême," Ronsérre told him. "I think I know who the assassin is, or at least I have contacts there who will know."

"Shall I go with you?" Antoine inquired.

"No, I must go alone. There may be great danger involved."

Three days later, Ronsérre set out on his trip from La Rochelle to Angoulême. Captain Chevin advised him not to take the main road, because it was being carefully patrolled by soldiers. So, he went south along the coast for quite a distance and then took a lesser-traveled road, from the coast east toward Angoulême. Hidden in a secret compartment in the flooring of his carriage was quite a bit of money. He knew that most of the information that he might get would have to be bought. Not even his driver knew about the mission of the trip, or about the money. One could not be too careful, especially when traveling off the main roads. Also, extreme cautiousness had to be taken, being a stranger in a city where no one, except a few legal associates from your past, would know you.

Monsieur Ronsérre arrived in Angoulême early afternoon on Saturday. After securing lodging for himself and the driver, he took a stroll around the city, making sure to go into stores and stop people on the street to ask directions. He had been to the city a few times in his life, and was comfortable in finding his way around. But the walk gave him the opportunity to engage the locals in conversation, for them to see and hopefully remember his face. But most importantly, it provided him the opportunity to find out something about them. Ronsérre had an outstanding memory, and a special knack for drawing out of people important details and relationships. That evening, before he went to dinner, he sat down in his room and recorded names and important data in his journal about each of the persons he had conversed with that afternoon. Even soldiers he met on the street had been willing to unknowingly give him useful information. Angoulême was a middle-sized city, not any larger than La Rochelle. And like La Rochelle, most citizens knew most everyone else, or knew who could give him information. But unlike La Rochelle, Angoulême was not a designated Protestant commune. Thus, the population was probably no greater than 35–40 percent Huguenot. He would attend services tomorrow at the Reformed church, and shake as many hands and admire as many babies as possible. He would not deny that he was from La Rochelle. He would pose under the cover of being in town to see if it was suitable for retirement. He hoped that persons would ask about the shooting incident at the Huguenot church in La Rochelle. That would certainly open the opportunity for some probing questions, to see if they had any information important to his real mission in Angoulême. If he learned little there, he would plan to attend the Catholic service the next Sunday. Surely the priest at the church would not refuse him Mass, since he was from out of the city and unknown to the good father.

However, that is what happened. "Monsieur," the priest told him when he arrived, "I must request that you leave, for you are not welcome here." The priest refused to give him an explanation or reason. When Ronsérre hesitated, the priest told him, "Either leave now or I will have you removed by a *gendarme*." Not wishing to attract attention, Ronsérre left the church by a side door. How did the priest know who he was? Or did he hear of the encounters with all the strangers in town? For the rest of the day, he turned over and over in his head the idea that someone from his past had seen him, recognized him, and informed the priest. Or, perhaps, the priest was someone from his past. It was impossible, though, for him to pinpoint anyone, for no doubt there were hundreds of people who might have reason not to like him. That was simply the nature of the legal business. And besides, he was well-known as a Huguenot.

Or, he thought to himself, *there is more to this than meets the eye. Just maybe, the priest has information that he does not want me to have. But*, he wondered, *why would a guilty person call attention to himself by denying me a Mass and the blessings of the Lord?* That night, he lay awake until the early hours of the next morning. Besides turning the events of the time since he first met the Jardeens over in his mind, he tried to sort out the various other legal cases that he had handled in his career. There were too many, though, and his memory, although acutely sharp and reflective, did not serve him well enough to remember all of them, nor all of the people whom he had met in his lifetime. But the priest who had refused him Mass was not old. Surely, if he had encountered him before, he should at least remember the face.

A couple of days later, Ronsérre was in a local drinking establishment in Angoulême, having a few glasses of Cognac, when a Catholic priest came in with two of his friends for drinks. It was not long before the camaraderie among the people in the tavern included Monsieur Ronsérre, who had previously been drinking alone. The man dressed in priestly garb introduced himself as Father Damien.

"Are you the priest at Cathédrale Saint-Pierre d'Angoulême?" Ronsérre asked.

"Oui," Father Damien told him. "And these are my associates," he said. "This is Father Benoît, and this is Father Thibaut."

"I am most pleased to be acquainted with you." The priests sat silent, and Ronsérre knew that they were expecting to learn his name. "I am Auguste," he lied.

Knowing that they had never seen him around town, they asked, "So, Auguste, what is your business in Angoulême?"

"Mostly vacation," Ronsérre told them. "I am recently retired, and thinking about relocating here to Angoulême."

"Really now, where are you from?"

"Originally from Paris, but most recently from Orleans," Ronsérre told them. This was a convenient truth, for his memory of Orleans from his days at the university there, and many business trips back on legal cases, would serve him well. It was becoming difficult to remember the several stories that he had told around Angoulême, and to relate them to which persons to whom he had told them. This was the story that he was sticking to from now on, he decided.

"My late wife and I faithfully attended services at Cathédrale Sainte-Croix." Again, he lied. But he needed to gain the confidence of these priests, and he knew that they would know this cathedral. In fact, he had attended service there when he was first a student at the university. However, even though he had not attended since he was introduced to the beliefs of the Reformed Church, he knew the progression of priests who had faithfully served the cathedral.

"So, then you know Father Timothée, non?"

Ronsérre considered whether they were being straight with him. Quickly reflecting, he remembered that Father Timothée was the priest the last time that he was in Orleans. That was several years ago. *No matter*, he thought to himself. *I am on safe grounds.* He replied, "Oui, I am acquainted with Father Timothée."

"All of us in the Church mourn the passing of Timothée," Damien told him. "How is the new priest enjoying his assignment?" Damien asked. There was a long pause.

Seeing that Ronsérre did not know of Father Timothée's death and did not know the name of the priest who replaced him, he said, "I can never remember his name. It is a strange one."

Ronsérre, feeling trapped, tried to provide himself a little wiggle room. He responded as calmly as possible. "I'll be frank, since the death of my wife, I have not attended Mass in Orleans. I spend most of my time in Paris with my son and his family, and time in Lyon with my daughter and her children." He did not mention La Rochelle, and of course, he conveniently left out the fact that he left the Catholic Church a long time ago.

Shooting a wink to his associates, Father Damien said, "Let us enjoy another drink before we three priests have to get back to the business of the Church." Signaling to the waiter for another round, Damien said to Ronsérre, "I believe you said your name is Auguste. Is that not so? Well, Auguste, we must not let this new friendship languish. You will stop by the church to see us, won't you?"

"Of course, of course," Ronsérre pledged. "I am sure that we will meet again. Perhaps soon?"

After Damien and his cohorts left, Ronsérre stayed on in the tavern, all the while limiting his consumption of Cognac so as not to the point of losing his ability to think. When the place was near empty, the owner came over and introduced himself. Ronsérre invited him to sit down.

"Who are you?" the owner asked, almost in a whisper. Ronsérre did not answer immediately, as he was not sure what the man was really asking him. Would Auguste suffice, or was the man asking something deeper? Was he being exposed?

"Listen, it is none of my business, but I met you at the Huguenot church. And now I overhear you telling the priests that you are a Catholic from Orleans. At the Huguenot church, you identified yourself as Jacque from La Rochelle. Why do you tell two different stories?"

"It is involved," Ronsérre told him, "and a very complicated affair." By this time, all the customers had gone.

"Why don't I serve us up some food?" It was more of a statement than a question. "You can tell me over dinner."

"I don't know," Ronsérre said, as the owner got up and headed toward the kitchen.

"Look, you are hungry, and I am too," the owner replied. "Tonight, the dinner is on me."

While the owner was gone, Ronsérre sat and thought about how he was going to get out of this situation. He thought about getting up and slipping out the door. But that would cast even more suspicion over himself. Perhaps by staying, he could get valuable information; surely the tavern owner knew most, if not all, of the people in the town.

The tavern owner returned with two large bowls of stew, prepared with an abundance of venison and wild boar killed on one of the nearby country estates. His wife brought out a large plate of bread, cheese, and fruit. She went back to the kitchen and quickly returned with a bottle of hearty tawny Port wine, surely from Lisbon, and two glasses. Obviously, she was not invited to stay and dine with her husband. Addressing Ronsérre directly, she smiled and asked, "Monsieur, is there anything else that I may get for you?"

"No, merci beaucoup. This is lovely. You are most kind. I am sure that it will taste as wonderful as it smells. Again, thank you."

As she bowed and turned to retreat into the kitchen to eat her dinner, clean up, and wait for her husband to go home, her husband said, "My dear, would you please lock the door? My guest and I want to talk privately, and I do not want more customers tonight."

Chapter 30
Confrontation

Ronsérre and the tavern owner began their dinner while the wife locked the door. "Merci," the owner said to her as she passed their table on her way to the kitchen. "We have important business and do not wish to be disturbed."

The stew was delicious, and the tawny Port was surely the very best Ronsérre had in a long time. Obviously it was from the owner's private collection, and not the everyday wine which would commonly be served to the customers. At least it was certainly more robust, but smoother, than the wine that he had earlier in the evening. However, that in no way suggests that the previous drink was not also good.

"Monsieur, tell me your real name," the owner said. "I know that the names that you have been using are false."

"Why are you doing this?" Ronsérre asked. "I am a stranger. Why do you take such an interest in a stranger?"

"Are you not a Huguenot?" the owner inquired, as he stared Ronsérre squarely in the face. "You cannot deny your religion. I am sure that you do not remember me, but I remember you. You were at my church the first Sunday you were in town."

"How do you know my travels?" Ronsérre asked.

"My dear friend, that is an easy question. The people in this city are very close to each other, and they are a very suspicious sort. There is little that happens here that I do not know. Remember, this is a drinking establishment, and most of the business in town, at least the important business, is discussed here. I am a good listener. What I hear stays with me. This is the way I keep alive."

"I see," Ronsérre said, speaking in a matter-of-fact way.

The owner went on. "You have been asking questions around town which have aroused suspicion. Did you not try to attend the Catholic church this last Sunday, but were turned away? Your veil of secrecy is very thin. I overheard your conversation tonight with the priests. Obviously, they were playing you for a fool. I suspect that your life's in danger. Let me help you find what you are looking for, before they kill you."

"Who are they?" Ronsérre asked, trying not to show surprise or fear.

The owner laughed, almost sarcastically. "Who do you think?"

"I do not know," Ronsérre told him. "You tell me, and I will no doubt have fulfilled my mission of being here."

"Well, then you must tell me who you are and what you are trying to find. You must tell me the truth. We are both Huguenots—you can trust me to be your friend. Think about it. I will get us some more wine. Would you like some more to eat?"

"Merci, that would be very nice," Ronsérre told him. If he was going to continue to drink, the food would help to keep him sober. Obviously, tonight he would need a very clear mind.

Chapter 31
Disclosure

"My real name is François Ronsérre. I am a retired solicitor now living in La Rochelle. I am here to find information about a recent murder back in La Rochelle. Do you want the long story, or a more concise version?"

"Please, my friend, tell me as much as I need to know so that I can help you."

So the two men sat for several hours while Ronsérre told him most of the story of Tomas and Margarite being imprisoned. He led on with the murder in the church, and how the killer was then murdered as he was being transported from the prison in La Rochelle to the main prison in Angoulême. "We have a witness, a soldier, who tells of a meeting at the prison between the local Catholic bishop and the prison commander, in which the plot was allegedly laid."

"Do you know for sure that the meeting actually took place? Surely you must know that soldiers often have a penchant for bragging to make themselves seem to be more important than they actually are, especially ones who have been drinking enough to brag in a public tavern. I know from personal experience how they sometimes overly embellish stories here in my own tavern."

"No," Ronsérre told him. "I believe that he was telling the truth. All of my investigation so far would suggest that he is telling the truth. My evidence points to a hired assassin, one probably right here in Angoulême. I believe that the Catholic Church is deeply involved."

"My friend, you are treading into very dangerous territory. Why are you putting yourself in the face of such danger when you are retired? Isn't this a matter for the police?"

"Ah, Monsieur, you do not understand. You see, Tomas was not the intended victim. The intended victim was my very good friend, Antoine Jardeen, the father of young Tomas. Through Tomas's intervention, the killer left a young, bereaved widow and a small daughter. She will never know the love of her father, will never see his face again, and will always wonder what could have been . . ."

"And what do you think I can do for you?" asked the owner.

"You can help me unravel the mystery," Ronsérre told him, talking softly to conceal what he was about to say from the owner's wife, who probably had her ear to the kitchen's door. "I have an informant who has provided information that has so far proved to be true. All events have happened as he said they would. His story implicates the priest in the Catholic church in La Rochelle, and potentially ties him to an assassin here in Angoulême. As you no doubt know, I was asked at the Catholic church here to leave the service, supposedly by a priest, or by anyone dressed in priestly garb. The person was not one of the three priests whom I met here this evening. I am fairly positive of that."

"What do you mean the three priests who were here this evening?" the owner asked in a quizzical voice. "There were not three priests here this evening."

"But they introduced themselves as priests," Ronsérre explained, trying to hide his shock.

"I am sorry, my friend, but there was only the priest from the church and his one associate," the owner insisted.

"Could the other be the person who asked you to leave the Mass?"

Stopping to think, Ronsérre said, "Perhaps, perhaps." Then, pausing to review his memory of that day, he flashed back to the man he presumed to be a priest standing over him and threatening to call the soldiers. "Yes," he told the owner, "I think you might be correct. I believe that one of the men here tonight could be the same person I encountered at the Mass. Can you identify him for me?"

"His name is George Miguel Morrisétte. He is believed to have a criminal past. No one is sure of where he came from. He just appeared in Angoulême one day a couple of years ago, as a wanderer with no job and no family. No one knows for sure, but it is rumored that he served prison time in Lyon for the murder of a prominent financier there. He started doing odd jobs at the Catholic church in return for shelter and food."

"Listen," the tavern owner explained. "It is getting very late. I know a soldier you can trust. He knows about the misdeeds going on at the Catholic church here in Angoulême, and he knows also about the murder in Lyon. He and two of his subordinates are doing all that they can to clean up the misdoings of our Catholic church. What you tell them will be kept strictly confidential."

"I don't know," Ronsérre skeptically told the tavern owner.

"Well, it is the best that I can do for you. I can have him here tomorrow night during the dinner hour. I will have a private table for you in the corner. Trust me, I would not do anything to put you or your clients in trouble."

"Okay," Ronsérre agreed. "I will be here."

Chapter 32
The Next Day

Ronsérre arrived safely back to the hotel. It was after midnight. Not being sleepy, he stayed up for several hours, reading and mulling over his encounter with the tavern owner. *The information that the owner gave me might well be critical to understanding the whats and whys of my questions. But even more important at the moment is whether the soldier and his associates can be trusted. Will my safety, and that of the owner and his wife, be endangered? It seems like the best opportunity I have to get to the bottom of the attempted murder of Antoine. There seems to be no motive except against Antoine's Huguenot beliefs, or can there be some other reason?*

The thought kept coming back to him as he pondered the situation. *Was the assassination the plan of one man? If not, then who could be the other members of the cabal that wanted Antoine eliminated? There are no obvious answers. Maybe the soldier whom the tavern owner suggested would be able to clear things up. In the absence of any better plan, and under much uncertainty and consideration,* Ronsérre finally concluded, *I will just have to trust my instincts.*

Finally, very late at night, he laid his pistol on the table beside his bed and tried to go to sleep. Sleep, however, did not come easy. Although he tried to put matters out of his mind, he was restless, and kept waking up and then dozing off again. Shortly after, he was awakened by a loud rapping on his door. Ronsérre called out, asking who was there, but there was no answer. He grabbed his pistol and went to the door. Cocking his pistol and preparing to defend himself, he slowly opened the door. There was no one there. Stepping into the hallway, he saw a man loitering in the shadows at the end of the hall, but he could not get a clear view of the person. As he began to walk toward the figure, the man darted down the steps and out the front door of the hotel. No doubt the person was just a hired hand trying to scare him. But how did the man know which room was his? Most likely, the hotel desk clerk had been paid for information for the room number.

He went back to his room, locked the door securely, and got back into bed. The incident was unnerving, but he felt safe in his room. Anyone who tried to get into his room again would be dealt with in a very harsh way. Ronsérre slept through most of the morning before rising and shaving. It was a rainy, foggy morning. As he was dressing, he decided that he would skip breakfast and just have lunch in the hotel's restaurant. Entering the dining room, he noticed a man sitting by himself at a front table with his back to the window. He was just having a drink and not dining. This obviously gave the person a clear view of everyone in the restaurant. As Ronsérre ate, he noticed that the man stared constantly at him. When he was paying his tab, he asked the waiter if he knew the person. Before the waiter could answer, the man got up, went outside, and walked briskly away from the hotel. Ronsérre threw a few coins on the table for a gratuity and ran out the door after the stranger. He noticed the man loitering in front of a store just several doors down the street. He decided to go in the same direction, pass the man, and see if he would be followed. That was indeed the case. Deciding to confront the individual, putting his hand on the pistol inside of his tunic, Ronsérre turned around and started to walk toward his stalker. He called out to him, but the man fled down the street and out of sight. No doubt it was the same man who had knocked on his door in the middle of the night. Things began to get very interesting. By that point the rain had ended, and the sky was brightening up. He spent most of the afternoon browsing a couple of bookstores and an art gallery, with the intention of reporting back to Antoine on the competition in Angoulême. There was no further sign of the stalker. All seemed well once again, but he sensed trouble ahead.

Ronsérre, feeling the effects of being on his feet all afternoon, decided to return to his room for a rest before going to the tavern to meet the informant. Back at the hotel, he found a note tacked to his door which read, "Be careful, be very careful! You don't know who is watching you!" He folded the note and put it into one of his pockets. At first, it was distressing, but then after locking his door and relaxing a bit, he felt that someone was just trying to scare him off the investigative trail, or to scare him out of town. Caution and sharp eyes would have to be the rule the rest of the stay in Angoulême.

Although the city was not large, and the tavern was not far away, he realized if he walked that he would be returning after dark, probably a little woozy from the alcohol that he would no doubt consume that evening. It would be better to be on the safe side. He would have his driver deliver him in his carriage to his supposedly clandestine meeting at the tavern. This time, though, in addition to his pistol, he took his short-barrel caliver, which was a product of the late 1500s. By this time, the caliver had replaced the heavier arquebus. It was a muzzle-loaded, short-barrel, smooth-bore, matchlock firearm for which standard-sized ammunition was available. It was fairly lightweight, with a hooked butt and a short trigger perpendicular to the stock. He took a bag of bullets with him.

He left the stable at six o'clock and was soon at the tavern. Secreting the caliver in a special hidden compartment in the buggy, Ronsérre was immediately noticed by the owner as he entered the tavern, who motioned him to a dark corner table, away from the crowd of people already enjoying their beer and wine. It was noisy, and the soldier had not yet arrived. Soon, though, a tall man in civilian clothes came in, and was immediately brought to the table where Ronsérre was seated. An introduction was made by the tavern owner. The informant was introduced simply as Johann. Ronsérre assumed that this was an alias for security purposes. "Johann, may I offer you wine or Cognac?"

"Oui, Cognac, s'il vous plaît."

Speaking to the owner, Ronsérre said, "Please bring two glasses and a bottle of your finest Cognac." Ronsérre made a request to the owner: "And bring a third glass if you can join us. Also, serve the two gentlemen at the next table who came in with Johann. Put it on my bill."

"I am sorry, it would not be wise for me to join you with people watching. I will have my wife bring you dinner, and I will join you when everyone has left. Please, you and Johann have a good conversation. He has much to tell you."

"I fully understand. Please join us at your convenience," he told the owner.

During a brief and awkward silence, Ronsérre studied Johann's face and body movements, and did not feel any tension between them. "Permit me to introduce myself," he finally said to Johann. "My name is François Ronsérre. I am a solicitor originally from Fontenay-le-Comte, and more recently from La Rochelle. I am seeking information about the attempted assassination of a very good friend of mine, and the murder of his eldest son who left a grieving widow and a young daughter—"

At that point, Johann suddenly interrupted. "We must change seats. I need to be seated facing the crowd. I am going to pretend to leave in order to relieve myself. While I am gone, please take my seat, and when I return I will sit in your place. Please understand. I will be gone just long enough for you to make the switch. Be casual about it. Try not to arouse attention. I will explain when I am back. Are you carrying a weapon? If so, put your hand on it, just in case."

With that, Johann got up from his seat and walked casually, taking time to look around the room at the crowd of customers, and then disappeared. He was only gone a few minutes. In the meantime, Ronsérre quietly switched drinks, stood up as if to speak to someone, then quietly returned to the table and took the seat in which Johann had been sitting. He was pretty sure that no one had noticed except for three very formidable-looking men sitting at a nearby table. Returning, Johann paused briefly and spoke to the three men, then sat down in the corner seat as planned.

He spoke very quietly. "I left a note this morning on your door to warn that you are in very grave danger."

Suddenly, Ronsérre turned very pale and began to wonder, Has the tavern owner set me up? Has he placed false trust in Johann?

"Listen," Johann told him. "I already know of what you have to tell me, and I suspect that a brilliant mind such as yours has already figured out most of the story. But there are details that you cannot already know. But first, let me tell you that the persons who planned the attack on your friend and who hired the hit man are in this room right now.

Do not worry, as I have three other soldiers with me who are armed and will reinforce your security."

At that point, the owner arrived with brandy glasses and the Cognac. It was one of the finest that France produced. He brought several fine Spanish cigars for each of them, too. "Please, my friends, enjoy. My wife will be out shortly with a delicious meal. It is my gift to you." And then he walked away, making it a point to remain constantly in the room, specifically near Ronsérre and Johann, but trying not to attract attention to himself.

Back at the table, Johann asked, "Monsieur Ronsérre, do you know why your friend was the target of an assassination attempt?"

"My friend and I have ideas, but we don't know for sure."

"Then perhaps I can shed light on the matter. Listen carefully. There are many things that you cannot possibly know."

Chapter 33
The Explanation

"First of all, the person who planned the murder is a Frenchman by the name of George Miguel Morrisétte. Have you ever heard that name?"

"No, I do not recall."

"Well, George Miguel Morrisétte is a half brother to your friend, Antoine Jardeen," Johann said.

"How is that possible?" Ronsérre pleaded with dismay. "That cannot be!"

"Non, Monsieur, it is not as improbable as it might seem. You see, Monsieur Jardeen's mother was a very attractive woman. Monsieur Jardeen's father was a naval officer at sea for long periods of time. She met a very handsome man of the upper class, with ties to the royal court. What started out as possibly a onetime liaison turned into a prolonged affair. Madame Jardeen loved this man very much, and became pregnant with his child. Her lover begged Madame Jardeen to take steps to abort the pregnancy, but she refused. By the time that Admiral Jardeen returned from sea duty, he did not wish to embarrass his wife, so he proposed to support the child as if it was his own. In the meantime, while her husband was stationed ashore, Madame Jardeen became pregnant with Antoine. But before Antoine was born, she learned that her husband was also guilty of past infidelities. To make matters worse, her lover was having intimate affairs with important men of nobility, and with members of the king's court. She slowly became mentally disturbed over the love triangle that she believed was of her own creation. To further the tribulations, Antoine's father, being at sea once again, was not home for the birth of Antoine. At her request, she turned custody of young George Miguel over to her lover when Antoine was not even a year old. Antoine was never told of his half brother. Over a period of years, her mental illness progressed until Antoine was a young boy. And, of course, I am sure that you must already know that she took her life on Île de Ré in the presence of young Antoine."

"It is a fantastic tale," Ronsérre said.

Before Johann could continue, the wife of the tavern owner brought their dinner: a bisque of mussels and oysters, seafood platters with assortments of delicious broiled shrimp, clams, and fresh fish; and a new bottle of wine.

While they were eating dinner, Ronsérre asked Johann why it was in his interest to come forth with these details after someone had already been murdered.

"You are the only person that has ever shown interest in the case. I feel a moral duty to tell you what I know. Monsieur Morrisétte is a very dangerous man. He is a killer, and he has plans to kill you—he may even try this very evening. If this is indeed the case, do not worry. You are well-protected!"

"Why me?" Ronsérre asked.

"Of course," Johann went on, "you remember that the admiral killed his wife's lover in a duel, and then took his own life by drinking laudanum containing a heavy dose of opium. The result of the story so far is that young George was left a total orphan in the world. Young Antoine was taken in by the admiral's affluent brother and was presented with every opportunity that life could offer. Of course, the illegitimate son of Madame Jardeen was deeply angry at and envious of his half brother. After his father's death, George existed by begging for food, sleeping on the street or in deserted buildings, and stealing to support his drug and alcohol habit. No doubt Antoine met him any number of times as he wandered around La Rochelle, trying to stay alive. Finally, he found himself in Lyon, living on the street. By this time, Italian financiers had emigrated to Lyon and had largely taken control of the banking system. As well, they influenced the arts and almost all aspects of the culture. Besides controlling the Catholic church, they lived in luxury, raised taxes on the poor, and had close associations with the king.

"Needless to say, the Huguenots living in Lyon were in a minority and were being persecuted rather severely by the business community, especially by the Catholic church. Supposedly a prominent Huguenot, who felt that he had been unfairly treated in business dealings with a certain Italian banker, hired Morrisétte as an assassin to kill the banker. Monsieur Morrisétte was apprehended and held in prison while awaiting trial."

"As he should have been," Ronsérre interjected.

"But you do not understand, Monsieur. George Miguel Morrisétte wanted the best legal mind in the whole of France to defend him. That person was you, and you refused him. You may have had good reason, but still you refused him. He vowed that one day he would seek revenge on you for his life of poverty and crime.

"Both you and Antoine Jardeen were intensely hated, and Morrisétte swore that one day he would kill the two of you.

"Due to popular sentiment, he was released from prison after about five years. He came to Angoulême and lived by doing odd jobs for the Catholic church, including certain intimate, personal favors for the priest and bishop. And then the name of Antoine Jardeen came back into his life. Monsieur Jardeen and his adopted brother Charles, with the support of the mayor and the Honorable Governor Bouché, were instrumental in the building of the Huguenot church in La Rochelle. This took many parishioners from the Catholic church. This affected the stability and wealth of the La Rochelle church, which concerned the bishops, cardinals, and even the pope in Rome. Also, the Jardeen brothers were actively assisting the poor, in both the Huguenot church and in the Catholic church. Their reputation for doing good things was spreading. The Jardeen boatyard had been given official recognition of the king, thereby protecting both Jardeen families, as well as the Légere family. The priest in La Rochelle was upset at the reputation that Monsieur Jardeen was building for himself, at the expense of his leadership and reputation, and was concerned with the dwindling attendance and finances of the Catholic church. The priest there made a trip to Angoulême to meet a friend of his. That friend was the priest of the Catholic church here. The case was made that there would be no evidence trail to the Church.

"Monsieur Morrisétte was hired by the Catholic priest in Angoulême to take care of the matter. With money from the church in La Rochelle, he hired an assassin here in town to kill Antoine, and his brother, Charles, if he had the chance. But, of course, Antoine was the most important target. The assassin made a mistake of attempting the assassination in a crowded church rather than on the street, or in an invasion of the Jardeen home. And evidently he did not expect Tomas to be sitting in the front pew of the church. I, of course, do not support what happened. I can only tell you that everything about the plan went wrong. The Catholic church here petitioned the prison in La Rochelle to transfer the assassin to the prison in Angoulême. They knew the day that he would be transferred, and the time that he would be at the gate of the prison. A hired gun was found here in town and sent to La Rochelle to kill the assassin, so that the truth would never be made public. That is wrong, and my companions and I vowed to tell the truth if ever asked.

"And then," the soldier continued, "your appearance here in Angoulême, asking questions of people on the street, posed the opportunity for Morrisétte to carry out his longtime wish to also kill you, for refusing to represent him in the murder case in Lyon."

Ronsérre asked, "Did you know beforehand about the plan to kill Antoine?"

"There were hints of some sort of planning going on at the church, but suggestions were not strong enough to indicate against who, where, or when. It was decided to keep a silent watch on the suspects. We were fooled by the fact that either Morrisétte hired a hit man, or the priest here hired one. I am extremely sorry for the death of the son of your friend, but it seemed that there was little that we could have done."

"I do understand," Ronsérre told him. "I appreciate your honesty and willingness to step forward with the truth. How much payment do I owe you?"

"You owe me nothing," Johann told him. "It is a weight off my chest. Just give my regrets to Monsieur Jardeen, and to the widow, for the loss of Tomas."

As the two men rose to shake hands and say goodbye, a loud shot rang out. Ronsérre whirled around to see Morrisétte, standing just a few feet away with a pistol in his hand. The pistol was pointed directly at him. Blood was already streaming down Morrisétte's arm, where he had been hit. The bullet had been fired by the tavern owner, and Morrisétte's pistol hand was shaking. As Ronsérre was reaching into his tunic for his own pistol, Morrisétte managed to fire. The bullet went through Ronsérre's loose tunic and hit Johann, grazing him mildly in his left side.

Then, quickly, there were two more shots. Both shots from two of Johann's associates hit Morrisétte, one in the neck and one in the back. He wheeled around as a shot from the third associate hit him directly in the heart. With that shot, he died instantly. The local Catholic priest and his remaining companion ran out of the tavern. Later that evening, they were detained on the street near the cathedral. The associate pulled a pistol from his tunic and pointed it at the soldiers. He was shot. Then the priest reached inside of his tunic, and was also shot. Both died later at the prison where they were taken.

The commander of the prison in Angoulême told Ronsérre the true identity of Johann: his captain of the guard. With a wink of the eye, he stated, "My investigation of the incident reveals that my captain and three of his officers just happened to be in the tavern, off duty, having a few drinks. The captain bumped into you and was engaging in casual conversation. My officers reacted to a dangerous situation in line with their police duties. The tavern owner is authorized to carry a pistol, to protect himself and his wife from robbery and other crime. We believe that he acted to save your life, and no charges will be brought. That is the end of the case. The records will be forever sealed."

Ronsérre saluted the commander, and the salute was stiffly returned. Then the commander asked, "When are you returning to La Rochelle?"

"I think I will spend a couple of days more here. Perhaps I will look for some old friends to visit."

"Well, when you are ready to go, pay me a visit. I will send a couple of guards to ride with you for your safety."

"Merci beaucoup, Commander. I will be in touch."

Chapter 34
Accosted by Thieves

It had been just over four weeks since Ronsérre had left La Rochelle to go to Angoulême. It seemed like he had been gone forever. He missed his home and, most of all, his friends. Times were tumultuous for the Huguenots throughout France.

The commander at the prison in Angoulême sent two of his guards to escort him and his driver to La Rochelle. Considering that the commander was no doubt a Catholic, he wondered why the courtesy was being extended to a Huguenot. The guards took turns, one riding atop with the driver and one sitting with Ronsérre inside the coach.

It was very strange, but Ronsérre was deeply grateful for the protection, and even more so to have people with whom to converse. He tried to keep his religious beliefs off the table, but the soldiers seemed interested in his Protestant beliefs. No accusations or belittling words were ever exchanged. The soldiers wanted to know much about him, his life, and his work as a solicitor. Conversely, Ronsérre got to know them extremely well. They were open to telling him about their lives, how they came to be where they were, and their aspirations for the future.

There was one potentially dangerous incident along the way. They were about halfway to La Rochelle, on a road in the middle of a forest, and dusk was fast approaching. A trio of robbers, armed with knives and guns, halted the coach and demanded money. However, the robbers withdrew and galloped off on their horses when the guards flashed their weapons at them.

The trip home took just four days, with them staying each of the three nights in country inns along the way. Although the prison commander had given the soldiers money to cover their travel expenses, Ronsérre was determined to pay for their accommodations and food. After all, they were accompanying him for his protection. And besides, they were good company.

Once in La Rochelle, the guards were dropped off at the prison, where they would be treated very well and given a coach and several horses for the trip back to Angoulême. Ronsérre thanked them for their company and wished them well for the future. He told them, "I will certainly be back in Angoulême sometime, and will make it a point to see you then."

"Monsieur, it will always be our pleasure."

As he drove home that night, he wondered if the conversations he had with them would, in any way, sway their beliefs and hopes for the future.

The next morning, he arose early to a rather chilly and stormy day. There was very little food in the house, and no cook or servants. They had been dismissed with pay while he was away. So he decided that he would stop at a small restaurant on the way to the Jardeen home and have some boiled oats, perhaps some eggs, sausage, toasted homemade bread, and naturally a lot of coffee. It was so good to be home again, and to have slept in his own bed. Over breakfast and the aromatic smells coming from the kitchen, he pondered on how much he should tell Antoine, and what Antoine's reaction was likely to be. *I must be tactful*, he reminded himself repeatedly. *But then again, I have a duty to be honest with my friend. I should tell the story just as it was told to me.*

When he knocked on the door at the Jardeen home, a servant familiar to Ronsérre answered it. He could not remember the servant's name. So he just said, "Sir, would you be so kind as to tell Monsieur and Madame Jardeen that I am here and would like a conference with them?"

"Monsieur Ronsérre, there has been a most tragic event in this home since you left on your trip."

Ronsérre's instant reaction was shock. What flashed through his mind was numbing. "Tell me that it is not possible."

"Non, Monsieur. It is with deep regret that I must tell you that Madame Jardeen is deceased. She became very depressed and unstable over the loss of her son Tomas. Monsieur Jardeen ensured that she saw the best doctors in town, but her condition worsened. A decision was made to admit her to an asylum, but in the meantime, she found an opiate and took a strong enough dose to take her life."

Tears of sorrow began to roll down Ronsérre's face, as he felt a strong urge to cry and shout out in anger, but he restrained himself the best that he could. "I am so sorry. Please tell me how Monsieur Jardeen is faring."

"Monsieur Jardeen is taking it very hard," the servant said. "In the same manner as his wife was, he too is now depressed. He has aged considerably, and says very few words. He finds it difficult to console his children, and no longer regularly goes to the boatyard. However, his brother, Charles, has been of great comfort to him."

"I suppose that now is not a good time to see him," Ronsérre volunteered. "Would you please ask Monsieur Jardeen to have a courier notify me at my home when he feels well enough to see me?"

"Oui, I will, Monsieur. Thank you for your service, and for coming here."

With those parting words, Ronsérre stumbled down the steps and walked in a daze to his coach. He envisioned that night would be one of heavy drinking. On the way, he stopped at the home of his chief servant to let him know that he was back in town. The servant would then contact the others and inform them to return to work.

Chapter 35
The Meeting

Early in the morning, the second day after arriving home from Angoulême, Ronsérre received a caller at his front door. It was a courier sent by his friend, Antoine Jardeen. "Monsieur," the courier addressed him, "Monsieur Jardeen has been told that you have returned. If it pleases you, he requests that you meet him at his boatyard office at ten o'clock, tomorrow morning."

"Please tell Monsieur Jardeen that I will be there promptly as he requests, and please give him warm greetings from me."

"I will do that, Your Honor." And with that, the courier excused himself and left in his carriage.

Ronsérre watched as the carriage drove out of sight. He wondered about the condition and well-being of his dear friend.

After conferring with the kitchen staff about food, wine, and grocery supplies needed, he instructed the driver to drive one of the kitchen chefs out for what was needed. No payment was necessary, as his food supplier ran an open tab on him, and he paid monthly.

Before retiring to his study, he asked for a glass of Cognac and one of his fine cigars. A servant said, "Oui, Monsieur, I will take care of that right away."

As the Jardeens did with their employees, Ronsérre enjoyed a most excellent relationship with his staff. He was always respectful of them, and they of him. They were paid well and given ample time off to be with their families.

Ronsérre often paid their medical bills when their wives or children were sick, and permitted them to take home food when the need was expressed. One thing that he did not allow, though, was the absence of alcohol from his wine cellar. He kept personal records on incoming alcohol and what was consumed. This practice was not so much about money as it was keeping his workers sober and able to work. He intended on fostering a good family life for them rather than, perhaps, an unpleasant one.

As Ronsérre sipped on his Cognac and enjoyed his Spanish cigar, he mentally relived the details of his experience in Angoulême. Somehow, his mind had blocked the remembrance of any specific threats to his personal safety. *I went to Angoulême on my own initiative. Antoine did not ask me to go, but on the other hand did not stop me.* Therefore, the more he thought about it, he decided, *I must keep the explanation to Antoine brief. I must concentrate just on the aspects of what Johann told me about the attempted assassination, and the accidental murder of Tomas.*

That night, Ronsérre did not sleep well. Sleep was slow in coming, and he awoke several times from nightmares that included the imprisonment of Tomas and Maggie for a crime they did not commit, the attempted assassination of Antoine, the accidental murder of Tomas, and his recent experience in Angoulême. Also, the news of Martine's apparent suicide weighed heavily on his mind. The depression she suffered and her complete mental breakdown were things he found hard to imagine. Her mental state almost mirrored that of Antoine's mother, a depression undoubtedly brought on after her affair with the duke and birth of a son for whom she later surrendered her parental rights. One parent loses her son to murder, and the other loses her biological son by the death of parental rights. One was as difficult to deal with as the other.

Early the next morning, Ronsérre awoke to the enticing aroma of brewing coffee, freshly baked bread, eggs being prepared, and sausage cooking. Instantly, he imagined, *Surely this will be the best breakfast I have ever eaten, but I must remember that I need to eat lightly, for I am planning to treat Antoine to lunch.* However, contrary to his best intentions, when Ronsérre sat down to eat and the food was served, he ate with great exuberance.

His driver came in for instruction on when to have the carriage ready, and to find out where he would be driving Monsieur Ronsérre that day. He was told to bring the coach, rather than the carriage, around to the front steps. It was a short distance to the boatyard, and they would make it by ten o'clock. The courier who had delivered the message from Monsieur Jardeen had been specific about the time, and Ronsérre was a person who was obsessive-compulsive about being punctual.

"Oui, Monsieur," the driver responded as he turned to leave. It only took a few minutes to team the horses up to the coach and come around to the front of the house.

A servant advised him when the driver had pulled up to the front door. "Merci," Ronsérre replied to the servant as he opened the door to his home, descended the steps, and was assisted by the driver into the coach. "Please don't drive fast," he told the driver. "Just make it a leisurely trip, but get me to the boatyard at ten o'clock."

On the way, Ronsérre got lost in deep thought, reliving his life since he had been asked by Governor Bouché to come to La Rochelle and defend Tomas and his wife. *The events I have been involved in and the ones which affected me directly are surreal.* He reached up and closed the heavy curtains of the coach, making it almost dark. He bowed his head and asked God for strength, courage, and compassion.

As they approached the boatyard, the driver had not heard the bell tower ring ten o'clock yet, and knew that Monsieur Ronsérre, besides not wanting to be late for an appointment, did not like to be early. So he drove around the block a couple of times before pulling up to the front of Monsieur Jardeen's office. By the time the driver assisted Ronsérre from the coach, he knew that they were on time, as the sundial at the Catholic church showed ten o'clock and the bell tower rang ten times.

Ronsérre instructed the driver, "Please stay nearby. I will need you to drive me and Monsieur Jardeen to lunch, most likely in about an hour or two." Then he walked quickly up to the door of the office and rapped several times. At first, there was no response. After a few seconds, he rapped again, this time heavily. Monsieur Jardeen did not answer the door. Instead, a young man, one of the office workers, came to the door. Ronsérre was taken aback. The young man could be a twin of young Tomas; he was roughly the same age, same build, same color of hair . . . in other words, as close as possible to Tomas, but not Tomas. It was at this point that Ronsérre realized the desperation in the lives of Martine, and now Antoine. He would bet that this young man had been hired by Antoine to replace Tomas in his life.

The young office worker led Ronsérre to the meeting room, where he had been instructed by his boss to bring him, and asked Antoine if there was anything else he could do for his guest and him.

"Non," Monsieur Jardeen told him, "you may be excused. I am sure you will find office work that needs to be done."

The young man bowed slightly to Ronsérre, then to Monsieur Jardeen, and said, "As you wish, Monsieur." He turned quickly and retreated to his work.

Ronsérre was again taken aback, this time by the appearance of his dear friend. He had changed so much in the weeks since he had left for Angoulême. He was using a cane to get around, and his hair was almost completely gray. He had bags under his eyes and was much thinner. He guessed that Antoine had been wearing the same clothes for several days, as they were rumpled and dirty.

Ronsérre put his arms around his dear friend, and tears began streaming down Antoine's face. It was a while before he could speak. Then Antoine muttered, "I am so happy to see you. You don't know how much I have needed you. With the exception of Maggie, her parents, my granddaughter, my children, my brother, Charles; and Governor Bouché, I would surely not be alive to greet you today." With that, his tears turned to sobbing. Without going into detail, Antoine tried to continue. In a whisper, he said, "You may have heard that my beautiful wife, whom I loved so much, is dead. I cannot talk about her right now. If not for my granddaughter and my two children, I would also now be dead. But they have kept me alive."

"I am so sorry," Ronsérre told his dear friend.

"Your mission to Angoulême was important to me and my family. I thank you for going. I hope all went well," Antoine told him. "Perhaps you will tell me what you have found?"

"Oui, my friend, I have much information for you," Ronsérre replied, while at the same time thinking to himself, *Non, I shall not tell him too much.*

There were several comfortable-looking chairs in the room, with a table between them. On the table was a decanter of Bordeaux wine with two glasses. "Please," Antoine said, motioning to the wine. After they had a glass of wine, Antoine passed over a silver tray with several cigars made on the island of Majorca, off the coast of Spain. They were fresh off a merchant ship which had anchored just two days ago in La Rochelle. They had been given to him the day before by a sea captain friend who had sailed directly from Majorca to La Rochelle. The bouquet of the imported tobacco was robust and aromatic. It was just what Ronsérre needed. Maybe it would calm him as he told the tragic story of what he had found out.

"Put the rest of them in your pocket—my gift to you!" Antoine offered. "Now tell me of your findings."

As they sat across from each other, Ronsérre carefully examined Antoine's face. He saw deep sadness, almost despair. Antoine's cheeks had tears rolling down them. Wondering what he was thinking, Ronsérre began. "My dear friend, tell me . . . do you remember as a child if there was another boy in your home, perhaps a brother?"

"Oui, there was a brother."

Ronsérre questioned, "Tell me everything you remember about him. What was his name?"

Antoine told him, "His name was George."

"Did your parents just call him by his first name, or did they ever call him Jardeen?" Ronsérre asked.

"Oui, my mother did."

"Did she refer to him as Jardeen when your father was home from his naval duties?"

"I cannot remember George ever being home whenever my father was home," Antoine replied. "I remember that he always seemed to be visiting one of my relatives whenever Father was home, with the exception of the last time Father was home to visit. I remember my parents arguing about my brother, and then George mysteriously disappeared with his clothes. His name was never mentioned again. Whenever I asked about him, I was told that he had been sent away to school. That is all I can tell you, for that is all I know. I never saw him again."

"Antoine, the fact is that George, in reality, was not really your brother. He was a half brother. Before you were conceived, and your father was at sea, your mother was very lonely and desperate for love and affection. She was, in fact, looking for an intimate relationship with a man, but not with just any man. Your mother was of the privileged class. She met a man who was very handsome, and had close ties to those in power. That man was George's father. Just before your father was home for the last time, your mother found out that her lover was having affairs with other women, and even with other men. This she could not tolerate. So, when your father was finally home and met the boy, he was very forgiving of your mother and wished to keep the boy as his own. Your mother would not consent to that, as she felt betrayed and embarrassed by the fact that her lover was unfaithful to her. She demanded of your father that he be sent to her onetime lover with a long letter, explaining her feelings and depression over her betrayal and public embarrassment; she did not wish to have further contact with him or the child. Your father delivered the child to his father. Shortly thereafter, your father had to return to sea duty. Your mother knew that she would not see him again for a very long time. Once again lonely, depressed, and filled with anger over the infidelity of her former lover, she decided to take her life. That is when she took you to Île de Ré and walked into the Bay of Biscay, leaving you on the beach. Please don't blame your mother, for she was badly mentally ill."

Antoine just looked on in disbelief at what Ronsérre had just told him. He did not speak.

Ronsérre continued, "There was no way for anyone to contact your father, with his being at sea. You went to live with your aunt and uncle on Île de Ré. The next time your father was in La Rochelle, he learned that George's father was often cruel to his son, not providing food and clothing for him, and not sending him to school. Your father met George on the street one day, begging from strangers. He tried to talk to the boy, but George would not talk with him, nor would he accept any money from your father. The boy, thinking that it was your father and not your mother who had sent him away, hurled vile obscenities at your father. That was the last time your father ever saw him.

"Several weeks after that, your father and George's father accidentally met in a tavern and got into an argument. One challenged the other to a duel, and the challenge was accepted. Of course, you know the outcome of that situation. As a result of what happened to your mother and the depression that led to her suicide, as well as the way that the man was now treating his son, your father had little remorse for killing him in the duel. However, in the days to follow, your father did begin to feel guilt. He began to drink heavily, much more than usual, and became desperately depressed over the loss of your mother. This led to him taking his life by drinking laudanum."

Antoine had a look of desperation on his face. "There is nothing you did wrong," Ronsérre tried to assure him. "Absolutely nothing, feel no guilt! You were too young to know."

"Is there anything else that you can tell me?" Antoine asked.

"Oui, my dear friend. I attended a Huguenot church in Angoulême, and decided to also attend the Catholic church to get a feel for any tension or anti-Huguenot rhetoric. At the Catholic service I was asked to leave, or else the gendarme would be called. It was a very strange experience. I had apparently been seen around town. I believe the church knew of my Huguenot passion, as if they had someone watching me. After all, I was a new stranger in town. Then one night, I was having a drink in a local tavern. There were three men at a table, watching me very closely. When they left, I inquired of the owner as to the identity of the men. He told me that one of the men, the one in clerical garb, was the priest at the Catholic church, one was his associate, and the one whom I recognized as the person who had ordered me to leave the service was a drifter. This vagrant had been taken in by the Catholic Church, and did odd jobs in return for food and lodging. Being that I was the last customer in the tavern, I talked with the owner and had reason to believe that he, too, was a Huguenot. He said that he had seen me at the Huguenot service I had attended. I related to him your misfortunes, and asked if he knew who in Angoulême might have hired the assassin that made the attempt on your life. He told me that he had a contact, and for me to return the next evening during the dinner hour. When I arrived, he sat me at a table in a corner. Very shortly afterward, another person arrived. He identified himself as a nonuniformed soldier and said he had information of interest to me. I asked why he wanted to help me. He said that, due to events in Lyon and unfulfilled justice, he and his three nonuniformed associates sitting at a nearby table felt they had a moral duty to assist me. I offered money, but it was refused. The first thing he told me was that the man whom I was seeking was sitting across the room at a table, with the local priest and his alleged associate priest. I was told that the other person with the two priests was your half brother, George Miguel Morrisétte. He told me an attempt would probably be made on my life that evening in the tavern, but not to worry because he, his associates, and the owner were armed. The information that he gave me was astonishing. He told me that the man who asked me to leave the Catholic church was George Morrisétte from Lyon; he was a beggar there who was hired by a Huguenot businessman to kill an Italian banker over a financial matter, and somehow had escaped justice. I asked why he had not been arrested in Angoulême. I was told that it was because of his connections with the local Catholic church, and his personal relationships with the priest and his associate."

"Things are starting to become clear," Antoine interjected. "Please continue."

"The most important part of the story is yet to come. Later, at the restaurant, I will finish my story. Remember, I invited you to a seafood lunch. The lunch is on me."

With a gleam in his eyes, Antoine told him, "This is an unexpected treat." It was the first time that day Ronsérre had noticed any real sign of joy in Antoine's demeanor.

The coach was waiting for them at the door.

"Take us to the seafood restaurant by the wharf," Ronsérre told the driver. When they arrived, he gave the driver money and told him to eat his lunch wherever he pleased. "Just be back in two hours," he said to the driver.

They each ordered beer, oyster stew, and paella. A Spanish captain had introduced them to this seafood dish, and it was one of Antoine's favorites. This restaurant made the very best, probably in all of France. Of course, it was made from local, fresh seafood from the Bay of Biscay.

As they ate, Ronsérre asked, "Is now a good time to finish the story of my saga?"

"Oui, my friend, please continue."

"The officer told me that George, with the support of the local Catholic church and possibly with the knowledge and support of the Catholic church in La Rochelle, hired the assassin who tried to kill you and was responsible for the death of Tomas."

"Why did the handyman, whom I don't even know, want to kill me?" Antoine asked.

It was obvious that Antoine's mind was not totally clear on what he had already told him, so he repeated much of the story.

"My dear friend, that is no doubt the most important question to be asked. Why did he mark you for assassination in Angoulême? He wanted you dead because of what happened early in your life. That man is George Morrisétte, your half brother, the son whom your mother conceived with her lover. His achievements and success in life have not been great. Your mother abandoned him, and his father essentially abandoned him. Your father, being a naval admiral much admired by the king, was in stark contrast to his father, although of upper class. After your father killed him, he was left with nobody. You moved from your aunt and uncle's home in Bordeaux to be adopted by your Uncle Etainé and his wife, Francine. Both you and Charles have achieved much—education, business success, wealth, respect of your families, and respect of the king. If he had been raised as a Jardeen, then he too would also have these things. But that was not to be. George blamed your father, and not your mother."

"It is indeed a sad combination of tragic misunderstandings. My father was a very forgiving man, and would have provided for George the same as he provided for me," Antoine reflected after a few seconds of silence.

"My dear friend, George is no longer a threat to the Jardeen family. He was killed that night in the tavern as he attempted to shoot me. The soldiers and the tavern owner saved my life."

"Why," Antoine asked, "would he want to murder you?"

"I am told that after the incident in Lyon, he wanted me to defend him against murder charges. For several reasons, none of which I can remember, I would not take the case. He believed that it was because of my being Huguenot and his being Catholic. The Catholic church in Lyon took him in and provided him safe haven, until he escaped to Angoulême and took up safe haven in the Catholic church there. Also, I am sure that he found out that I was in Angoulême asking questions on your behalf."

"And that brings this case to a close, does it not?" Antoine inquired.

"Non," Ronsérre told him. "It is imperative that you leave here today, and from this moment on heal yourself. Regain your health. Repair your mind. You are right. You can forgive, but not forget. Reunite with your children, with your brother, Charles, and his family; with the Légeres, and with Maggie. Love your granddaughter. Build your business. Grow the Huguenot church. Continue your mission to help the people of La Rochelle and defend France in your heart and spirit. Make these your objectives, and become strong again."

At this point, Antoine started to sob openly, almost as a child. "I will try. I will try; I will pray to God for strength, courage, and compassion in my life. I can do these things only with the help of God."

"Then may God be with you always," Ronsérre told him as they hugged.

"I forgive my mother and I forgive George. However, I will never be able to forget the misfortunes that he inflicted on my family," Antoine reflected, in a low voice filled with much sadness.

Chapter 36
Family Affairs

In mid-1581, when Monsieur Ronsérre returned from his investigative trip to Angoulême and met with Antoine Jardeen to debrief him on his findings regarding the murder at the church, he found his friend quite emaciated from eating very little, depressed over the death of his son Tomas and the suicide of his wife, Martine. Antoine was mystified at the identification of the person behind the killing of his son as being his half brother, whom he really did not ever get to know.

With assurances from Ronsérre, Antoine began a regiment of forcing himself to eat well, sought medical counseling for his depression, and threw himself back into leadership at the boatyard.

In 1581, King Henri III was on the throne of France. Born in 1551, Henri was the third son of Henri II and Catherine de' Medici, both of whom were strong Catholics. Although Henri practiced Catholicism throughout his life, as a child and young man he studied and memorized Huguenot beliefs and customs. By entitlement, Henri became *duc d'Anjou* and was given command of the royal army by his brother, King Charles IX. As commander of the army, he led several battles against Huguenot leaders. In May 1573, Henri was elected king of Poland, where he ruled until May 1574 when his brother, King Charles, died. Henri escaped from Poland, despite having been captured by Polish authorities, and returned to France to succeed his brother as king.

After assuming the throne of France in February 1575, Henri stiffened government restrictions on the Huguenots.

In the beginning of 1576, Huguenots began to assemble resistance to Henri's restrictions on their civil and religious liberties. They began to unite their forces in opposition to the deprivation of their freedoms. Over thirty thousand Huguenot soldiers, commanded by Alençon, brother of Henri III, assembled near Paris. The large size of this army convinced Henri to begin conciliatory peace talks with the Huguenots. These negotiations led to the concessions of the Edict of Beaulieu. The concessions of this edict angered the Catholics. The Holy League was formed to protect their interests. Because of the intense protests of the Catholics, Henri resumed warring against the Huguenots. But weary of his spending extravagances, the Estates General refused to give him money to carry on hostilities. The Peace of Bergerac, signed in 1577, temporarily ended hostilities, and the Holy League was dissolved. Slowly, freedom and justice were being returned to the Huguenots. By late 1581, such justice was exemplified by the revelations of the captain of the guard in Angoulême to Monsieur Ronsérre, and by the courtesies extended to him, an acknowledged Huguenot, from the prison commander.

During the year 1582, Antoine returned to full health and his normal mental state. As he improved, he gave more and more of himself to his duties at the boatyard. By 1583, construction of the fast three-masted corvair, designed by the Jardeen boatyard and built on the Île de Ré under the supervision of the Jardeen design team, was completed. It weighed 360 tons and was armed with thirty cannons. King Henri and Augie Cussions, the named captain of the vessel, visited La Rochelle for its commissioning. During his visit, Henri appointed Antoine as director of the National

Maritime Board. Antoine accepted on the condition that the board be run from La Rochelle. In addition, he was made *duc de Rochelle* and promised new contracts for shipbuilding. Charles was made a lord for his outstanding ownership of the manoir at La Rochelle and unselfish service to the agronomy of the region. Both were highly praised for their aid to the poor, without regard to religion. It was highly unusual for honors such as these to be given to Huguenots.

In the winter of 1584, Antoine, having recovered from his state of depression, was very lonely and started to find interest in eligible women close to his age. At a party one night at the governor's home, he was reintroduced to Madame du Bouché, the sister of the governor. Although he was long acquainted with her from the days before he married Martine, she met and married a nobleman, and moved to the city of Nantes. That husband died in late 1583 of pneumonia, and she had recently travelled to La Rochelle to visit her brother. The party was given in her honor.

Madame du Bouché remembered Antoine from her youth, and he certainly remembered her beauty as a young woman. She had been brought up to date by her brother about Antoine's situation, and the honors bestowed upon him by the king. They spent most of the evening talking, and enjoyed good wine and Cognac. Before he left that evening, he planned to take her to dinner the next evening. After several evenings together and having met his children, Charles and his family, and, of course, Monsieur Ronsérre, she was falling in love with Antoine, and she knew that the feelings were mutual. In May of that year, Antoine proposed to her and she accepted. On July 2, 1584, they were united in marriage at the Huguenot church. She had long converted to the Reformed faith, although her first husband had remained Catholic in name, paying his tithe like Antoine had done all of his adult life.

Both of Antoine's children, as well Charles and his family, loved and admired her very much. Although he would never forget Martine, she made Antoine a very happy husband. They were very prominent in the social circles of La Rochelle and attended cultural events as often as possible. They were invited to many social occasions at their friend's homes, as well as hosting parties in their own and Charles's manoirs.

The Jardeen children, Paul and Marye, were now mature adults and had been placed in positions at the boatyard; Paul was director of operations and Marye was appointed as administrative director and director of business planning. Captain Chevin, because of his outstanding success at the bookstore and art gallery, was brought to the boatyard as the senior management official and director of marketing and customer relations. Michel Légere and Maggie took over full management of both the bookstore and the art gallery. These businesses were prospering very well.

These changes in business operations were discussed with Charles, as he was the key figure in proposing and working out the shifts of responsibility. Both he and Antoine were eager to go at a slower pace, and the manoir was becoming more important to Charles as it reduced his need to travel into La Rochelle so often. He, as well as his children, felt an obligation to farm the manoir and keep it in good repair and reputation. His children enjoyed living in the homes that had been built for them at the farm. They knew that one day they would inherit the manoir and would be given noble titles.

Also, these new organizational structures would give Antoine and his new wife, as well as Charles and Paulette, greater opportunity for travel and enjoyment of the finer things that hopefully life would offer. No doubt the apartment in Paris would now have frequent visitors, and of course they would be able to get the courtesy of free passage on sailing ships to foreign countries as a courtesy of their many ship captain friends.

A major event happening in the year 1584 was the death of François, brother of Henri III. This led to Henri IV becoming the successor in line for the crown upon the death of Henri III. Catholics were infuriated at the prospect of the future king being a Huguenot leader. Consequently, the Holy League was reprised under the leadership of Henri, *duc de Guise*.

In 1585, Captain Chevin's wife suffered a severe stroke and died just eleven days later. During that time she lay in a coma, without speaking and hardly moving. After a respectable period of mourning his loss, Chevin and Maggie began to see each other. In the fall of that year, they were married. Maggie's daughter, Elisabeth, had always seemed to love Captain Chevin and his children. And even though he was married, Maggie had admired and repressed desire for the captain.

Soon after they were married, Maggie became pregnant with Chevin's child, and in September 1587, she gave birth to a healthy baby girl named Madeline. Her daughter, Elisabeth, and her stepchildren, now in their teen years, were excited to have a baby sister.

With his new responsibilities at the boatyard, and with the assistance of the Jardeens and the Légeres, Chevin and Maggie were able to buy a large town home in La Rochelle. When she was healthy and physically fit to again take on the pressures of the two businesses with her father, her mother, Elisabeth, lovingly took care of the baby.

When Henri III died in August 1589, he left no heirs. His marriage to Louise of Lorraine produced no children. Both of his brothers, Francis II of France and Francis, duke of Anjou, each predeceased Henri. The only legitimate heir to the throne was Henri IV, the Protestant king of Navarre, who was a cousin of Henri III. Of course, the Catholic League, led by Henri I, the duke of Guise, was influential in the fight against the appointment of a Protestant to the kingship. Charles, cardinal of Bourbon and a Catholic uncle of Henri IV, was appointed king until the time that Henri IV agreed to convert to Catholicism.

Chapter 37
Marriage of Elisabeth Marye Jardeen

In the spring of 1597, Elisabeth Marye Jardeen, the daughter of Tomas and Maggie Jardeen, was almost twenty-one years of age when Jean-Baptiste, the oldest son of the Reverend Jacque Horry, began to pay serious attention to her. Although he had been a secret admirer of Elisabeth ever since his parents moved with him from Angoulême to La Rochelle, he was too shy to openly express to her how much he was in love with her. He missed her dearly when she went to study at the university in Poitou. By the time that she returned to La Rochelle, Elisabeth Marye had matured in the mold of her mother into a very beautiful woman with a similar love of literature and music, especially the religious music with which she had grown up. By the middle of summer, Jean-Baptiste asked her to marry him. Her reply to his proposal was, "I wondered when you were going to ask me!"

In early September of that year, they were married in the Huguenot church in La Rochelle, France, by the same Huguenot pastor from Angoulême who had christened Jean-Baptiste when he was an infant. Reverend Gaillard had traveled to La Rochelle as a friend of the Reverend Horry, and stayed in the Horry home until after the wedding. Before the wedding, Elisabeth Marye sought out her mother. Thanking her for being a great mother, Elisabeth confided how much she had missed her father while growing up. Although she did not remember him, she always imagined what a great man he must have been, and the father that without doubt he would have been if he had lived. At that point, both mother and daughter broke into tears and hugged each other.

"Oui," Maggie told her, "he would have been a wonderful father."

"I know that Daddy has always looked down on me from Heaven," Elisabeth Marye whispered tearfully into her mother's ear.

"And your father is looking down and smiling on you right now. I know that he is proud of what a beautiful woman you have become, and of your talents."

"Mother, my talents are your talents. You have instilled a love within me of all the things you treasure so very much. I pray that I will always honor you in everything I do and everything that I think."

"My daughter, you have already made me proud! And may you be as proud of your children as I am of you!"

And then Maggie whispered, with tears flowing down her face, "My daughter, I hope that one day France will be free of the hatred that killed your father, and that people of different religions may live peacefully together. I am sure that it will not happen in my lifetime, but I pray it will during your life ahead. I will pray for you and Jean-Baptiste every day for the rest of my life here on earth."

With these words from her beloved mother, Elisabeth broke into uncontrolled sobbing and managed to say to her mother, "My love for you is infinite. I will always remember and love you, and will pray for your happiness and welfare. Remember that I will always be ready to help you, whatever your need."

The wedding was on a Saturday afternoon. Reverend Gaillard commenced the marriage ceremony according to

Reformed Protestant religious liturgy[31] by saying, "Our help is in the name of the Lord, who made Heaven and earth."

And after a short pause, he followed by reading, "God, our Father, having created Heaven and earth, and all that in them is, made man in his own image and gave him dominion over the beasts of the field, over the fish of the sea, over the fowl of the air, and over every living thing that moveth upon the earth. And after he had created man, God said, 'It is not good that the man should be alone: I will make him a help mate for him.' And the Lord God made woman, bone of his bone, and flesh of his flesh, signifying thereby that they two were one.

"Wherefore our blessed Lord, when the Pharisees came unto him, tempting him and saying unto him, 'Is it lawful for a man to put away his wife for every cause?' He answered and said unto them: 'Have ye not read, that he which made them at the beginning, made them male and female, and said, "For this cause shall a man leave father and mother, and shall cleave to his wife: and they twain shall be one flesh?" So, then they are no more twain, but one flesh. What therefore God hath joined together, let no man put asunder.'

"And the apostle Saint Paul, who commandeth marriage as honorable in all, saith: 'So ought men to love their wives as their own bodies; he that loveth his wife, loveth himself. For no man ever yet hated his own flesh, but nourisheth and cherisheth it. Likewise, let the wife see that she reverence her husband, and submit herself unto her own husband, as it is fit in the Lord.'

"Seeing, then, that this holy covenant of matrimony, which God hath ordained, is of such authority and obligation; it is not to be entered into unadvisedly or lightly, but reverently, discreetly, and soberly, in the fear of God, and with holy purpose to live therein in all purity, according to His will."

And then, after another pause, the reverend, addressing the couple, said, "Jean-Baptiste and Elisabeth Marye, are you willing to enter into the holy state of matrimony, which God hath instituted? To live together therein, according to his commandments? And do you desire to make known here, before God and this congregation, this your purpose?"

Reverend Gaillard then paused for them to answer. While looking each other in the eyes, they both answered, "Oui."

Then, the reverend said, "God confirm and bless your purpose. Let us pray.

"O, eternal God! The author of every good and perfect gift, we thank Thee that Thou hast ordained the institution of marriage; we beseech Thee to send Thy blessing upon these, Thy servants, who are now about to be joined together in this holy estate. Give them a just sense of Thy presence, of the obligation, and of the covenant they are about to make. To the end that this solemn service may have a wholesome influence upon their affections and conduct throughout life, to the glory of Thy name, through Jesus Christ, our Lord. Amen."

Addressing Jean-Baptiste, Reverend Gaillard asked, "Do you acknowledge here, before God and this congregation, that you have agreed to take, and that you now take, Elisabeth Marye Jardeen for your wife? Do you promise to love, honor, and protect her? To maintain, comfort, and cherish her, in health and in sickness, in joy and in sorrow, in prosperity and in adversity? To lead a holy life with her, being faithful unto her in all things, as is the duty of a good husband according to the word of God?"

Jean-Baptiste looked deeply into the eyes of Elisabeth Marye and answered, "Oui."

And then the reverend said to Elisabeth, "Do you also acknowledge here, before God and this congregation, that you have agreed to take, and that you now take, Jean-Baptiste for your husband? Do you promise to love, honor, and obey him? To maintain, comfort, and cherish him, in health and in sickness, in joy and in sorrow, in prosperity and in adversity? To lead a holy life with him, being faithful unto him in all things, as is the duty of a good wife according to the word of God?"

With tears of joy welling in her eyes, she looked at Jean-Baptiste and answered, "Oui."

At this point, with a broad smile on his face, Reverend Gaillard said to the couple, "In testimony that you, Jean-Baptiste, and you, Elisabeth Marye, do advisedly and solemnly ratify that all that has been declared and promised by you. Do thou, Jean-Baptiste, acknowledge and avow this woman as thy wife, by delivering unto her a ring in token of thy faith? And do thou, Elisabeth Marye, in a like manner receive the same, as a pledge of his faith and as a witness of thy vows?"

Jean-Baptiste took Elisabeth's left hand and placed a ring upon the fourth finger of her hand. Then Elizabeth Marye placed a wedding band on Jean-Baptiste's ring finger. Reverend Gaillard then placed their right hands together and said, "You are now man and wife! Those whom God hath joined together, let man not put asunder. Let us pray to God, our Father, for His blessing upon these, His servants."

And then Reverend Gaillard offered the closing prayer: "O almighty, all-merciful, and all-wise God, we pray to Thee on behalf of these persons who have entered into the holy matrimony of marriage that Thou wouldst vouchsafe to them Thy Holy Spirit. Send down Thy blessing upon these, Thy servants, whom we bless in Thy name. Enable them to observe surely and to perform faithfully the vows and covenant between them made, mutually edifying each other, to live together in purity, concord, and piety. Give them grace to reverence and serve Thee, and to contribute to the advancement of Thy glory, the honor of the gospel, and the welfare of Thy church. Favorably hear us, O Father of Mercy, in the name and for the sake of Thy dear Son. Amen."

Then, the benediction was offered. "God, the Father, the Son, and the Holy Ghost, bless, preserve, and guide you. May you be filled with all spiritual benediction and so live together in this life that, in the world to come, you may have life everlasting. Amen."

And with that, the couple turned around. Elisabeth took her husband's arm, as he offered, and they and the attendants processed down the aisle to the back of the church. There, they thanked their parents and their guests as they started to exit the church. Finally, when all the guests were outside, they went out to their coach, which took them to the manse for the reception.

During the reception, Jacque Horry and his wife took them aside to talk. They told the couple that if they were interested, the home in Angoulême was theirs for as long as they might want it. Jacque also told them that half of the income that he was receiving from his siblings for his part ownership in the manoir would now go to them, and that he had renegotiated the contract to restore him to a full share. His compensation would be made equal to that of his siblings. At the point that Jean-Baptiste might want to be productive in the operation of the manoir and its vast farmland, he would give his full share and compensation to him and Elisabeth Marye. However, Jacque told them that use of his home in Angoulême would be temporary, and they would be expected to build their own house at the manoir at some point.

Hearing this, both Jean-Baptiste and Elisabeth Marye were overwhelmed with joy. Sobbing, they were hardly able to say "Thank you," as they gave the parents long hugs and kisses.

Chapter 38
Events Leading Up to the Siege of La Rochelle—A Chronology of Succession

May 12, 1588

The Catholics of Paris, tired of what they perceived as moderate conciliatory policies toward the Huguenots, had a spontaneous uprising against King Henri III.[32] Called the Day of the Barricades, this uprising was led by the duke de Guise (the leader of the Catholic League), with support of Spain's ambassador to France. In the violence that ensued, the duke gained control of Paris, and Henri III, with royal forces, fled to Chartres. The duke was then in complete control of the city. He was offered the Crown of France, but he refused.

From a position of strength, the duke de Guise[33] forced Henri III to sign at Rouen the *Édit d'union*. The terms of this edict forbade the king from concluding peace with the Huguenots and forced him to forbid public office to anyone who refused to swear their allegiance and faith to Catholicism, to never leave the throne to a prince (Henri of Navarre) who was not Catholic, to grant amnesty to the Catholic League for all actions taken then or in the past, and to grant the League and its troops secure and fortified sites.

The duke continued to rule Paris until August 1589.

December 23, 1588

King Henri III is encamped on the outskirts of Paris at Saint-Cloud with his cousin, Henri IV[34] of Navarre. Together, preparations were being made for a joint invasion to retake control of Paris. By now the Spanish Armada had been defeated, and Henri's concern about Spanish support for the Catholic League had abated. Henri III invited the duke de Guise[35] to his council chamber. Louis II, cardinal of Guise and brother of the duke, had already arrived and had been shown to an anteroom adjacent to the king's bedroom to await the arrival of his brother. When the duke arrived, he was shown to the anteroom, where first he was murdered and then his brother, the cardinal. Further, to ensure that no contender for the throne was left to oppose him, Henri had the duke's son arrested and imprisoned.

August 1, 1589
Jacques Clément, a fanatical friar dressed as a priest, infiltrated Henri III's[36] entourage under the pretense of delivering important papers to the king. Telling the guards that he had a secret message for the king, he was led to Henri. Henri motioned the guards to stand back, so that the "priest" and he would have privacy. As the friar neared Henri, he pulled out a knife and quickly stabbed the king several times in the stomach. As he lay dying, Henri implored his cousin, the legitimate heir to the Crown, to convert to Catholicism, and urged the officers of the royal entourage to support him for the Crown.

The people of Paris, mostly Catholic, were elated at the news of Henri's death. He had not been a good ruler. The Huguenots did not like him, for in their view he had, despite some concessions, continued his father's deprivation of religious freedom and continued the religious wars of the sixteenth century. On the other side of the argument, the Catholics of France believed that he had betrayed them by what they perceived as a conciliatory policy toward the Huguenots. The country as a whole disliked him, for he was weak and ineffective as a monarch. His extravagance had brought the kingdom to the brink of bankruptcy, despite imposing increasingly higher taxes on the populace. He was effeminate and was alleged to have experienced intimate relations with minions who surrounded the Crown. This was especially annoying to the Church, although similar practices were known to have occurred among the hierarchy and ministry of the Catholic Church itself. The premeditated murder of the duke and cardinal of Guise was a final act which the Catholic populace could not accept. Henri III, the last of the Valois kings, was interred at the Basilica of Saint Denis in Paris. Henri III was so intensely disliked that later, during the French Revolution, his body was disinterred from his tomb at the Basilica of Saint Denis, desecrated, and thrown into a common grave. It is unclear as to whether this was an act of Catholics or Huguenots.

Henri of Navarre

Henri IV,[37, 38] although now the legitimate heir to the throne of France, was not able to succeed Henri III immediately upon his death. His coronation was desperately opposed by the Catholic Church, the Catholic League, and the Catholic populace of France.

August 4, 1589

While still encamped at Saint-Cloud, Henri of Navarre declared that he would, in the future, consider a conversion to Catholicism. That promise, combined with two major military triumphs against forces of the Catholic League in September 1589 and March 1590, showed military might and began to positively sway opinion in his favor. In the summer of 1590, Henri IV executed his plan to take Paris, but found that the League's forces would not be easily conquered. The League favored Henri IV's Catholic uncle, Charles, cardinal of Bourbon, to ascend the throne rather than Henri. Charles was crowned and continued to rule until 1593.

July 25, 1593
After the death of King Charles, the cardinal of Bourbon, the Estates General met in Paris to plan who the next king of France would be. While the assembly was meeting, Henri IV declared at the Basilica of Saint Denis his decision to convert to Catholicism. His decision was strongly encouraged by the duke of Sully, a Protestant, and by Henri's Catholic mistress.

The phrase "Paris is worth a Mass," commonly attributed to Henri IV, may not have actually been spoken by him, but is possibly attributed to the Catholic populace in an attempt to sully his conversion to the Catholic faith, which they believed to have occurred for the wrong reason.

February 27, 1594
Henri of Navarre is crowned king of France in a Catholic ceremony on this date in the city of Chartres, France.

March 24, 1594
King Henri IV makes a triumphal entry into Paris.

September 17, 1595
Support for Henri IV as king and ruler of France was solidified when Pope Clement VIII, standing in the portico of Saint Peter's in Rome, declared Henri free of all excommunication. This papal absolution nullified all

measures proposed earlier at Saint Denis upon Henri's conversion. It was made after much negotiation and bargaining among the hierarchy of the Catholic Church in Rome. Over the next several years, Henri won the allegiance of many members of the Catholic League with kindness, rather than force, and brought hopes for the end of the religious wars.

Henri was especially sympathetic to the causes and beliefs of the Huguenots. In the interest of promoting civil unity, Henri on April 13, 1598, issued the Edict of Nantes, granting the Huguenots freedom of religion in selected areas of France and substantial civil rights throughout the Catholic nation. The decree officially ended the religious wars of the sixteenth century in France.

An English Translation of the Edict of Nantes, Translated from Public Domain Source

"Henri, by the grace of God, King of France and of Navarre, to all to whom these presents come, greetings.

"Among the infinite benefits which it has pleased God to heap upon us, the most signal and precious is his granting us the strength and ability to withstand the fearful disorders and troubles which prevailed on our advent in this kingdom. The realm was so torn by innumerable factions and sects that the most legitimate of all the parties was fewest in numbers. God has given us strength to stand out against this storm. We have finally surmounted the waves and made our port of safety—peace for our State. For which his be the glory all in all, and ours a free recognition of his grace in making use of our instrumentality in the good work . . . We implore and await from the Divine Goodness the same protection and favor which he has ever granted to this kingdom from the beginning . . .

"We have, by this perpetual and irrevocable edict, established and proclaimed and do establish and proclaim . . . That the recollection of everything done by one party or the other between March, 1585, and our accession to the crown, and during all the preceding period of troubles, remain obliterated and forgotten, as if no such things had ever happened . . . We ordain that the Catholic Apostolic and Roman religion shall be restored and re-established in all places and localities of this our kingdom and countries subject to our sway, where the exercise of the same has been interrupted, in order that it may be peaceably and freely exercised, without any trouble or hindrance; forbidding very expressly all persons, of whatsoever estate, quality, or condition, from troubling, molesting, or disturbing ecclesiastics in the celebration of divine service, in the enjoyment or collection of tithes, fruits, or revenues of their benefices, and all other rights and dues belonging to them and that all those who during the troubles have taken possession of churches, houses, goods or revenues, belonging to the said ecclesiastics, shall surrender to them entire possession and peaceable enjoyment of such rights, liberties, and sureties as they had before they were deprived of them . . . And in order to leave no occasion for troubles or differences between our subjects, we have permitted, and herewith permit, those of the said religion called Reformed to live and abide in all the cities and places of this our kingdom and countries of our sway, without being annoyed, molested, or compelled to do anything in the matter of religion contrary to their consciences . . . upon condition that they comport themselves in other respects according to that which is contained in this our present edict.

"It is permitted to all lords, gentlemen, and other persons making profession of the said religion called Reformed, holding the right of high justice [or a certain feudal tenure], to exercise the said religion in their houses . . . We also permit those of the said religion to make and continue the exercise of the same in all villages and places of our dominion where it was established by them and publicly enjoyed several and diverse times in the year 1597, up to the end of the month of August, notwithstanding all decrees and judgments to the contrary . . . We very expressly forbid to all those of the said religion its exercise, either in respect to ministry, regulation, discipline, or the public instruction of children, or otherwise, in this our kingdom and lands of our dominion, otherwise than in the places permitted and granted by the present edict.

"It is forbidden as well to perform any function of the said religion in our court or retinue, or in our lands and territories beyond the mountains, or in our city of Paris, or within five leagues of the said city . . . We also forbid all our subjects, of whatever quality and condition, from carrying off by force or persuasion, against the will of their parents, the children of the said religion, in order to cause them to be baptized or confirmed in the Catholic Apostolic and Roman Church, and the same is forbidden to those of the said religion called Reformed, upon penalty of being punished with especial severity . . .

"Books concerning the said religion called Reformed may not be printed and publicly sold, except in cities and places where the public exercise of the said religion is permitted.

"We ordain that there shall be no difference or distinction made in respect to the said religion, in receiving pupils to be instructed in universities, colleges, and schools, nor in receiving the sick and poor into hospitals, retreats, and public charities."

Although major concessions were granted to the Huguenots, the Edict of Nantes reaffirmed Catholicism as the official religion of France. Huguenots were required to continue paying a tithe to the Catholic Church, and were required to respect Catholic holidays and Catholic restrictions on marriage.

Upon reading the Edict of Nantes, Pope Clement is alleged to have screamed in rage, "THIS CRUCIFIES ME!"

Despite all his political efforts, Henri was generally not liked because of continued religious tensions. Catholics felt that he had conceded too much to the Huguenots, and the Huguenots, of course, believed that he had not gone far enough. However, in the time that Henri remained king, most Huguenots prospered by rising to prominence in the military, in business, and in holding important civil-service positions. At least to the Huguenots, Henri became known as "Good King Henri." But because of his liaisons with the women of Paris, Henri was unfortunately given the dubious title of "The Green Gallant." Although his lifestyle was a commonly accepted practice for men in all of France's history, and even in the day of Henri among members of the Catholic Church, it provided the Church itself an opportunity to be critical of him.

May 14, 1610
After several foiled attempts on Henri IV's life in 1593, and again in 1594 by unnamed assailants, in 1610 François Ravaillac, a Catholic fanatic, stabbed Henri to death while his carriage was stopped on the Rue de la Ferronnerie in Paris. Henri's son, Louis XIII, who was to succeed him, was only nine years old at the time. Marie de' Medici, Henri's

widow and the mother of Louis XIII, served as surrogate regent for Louis until 1619, when Louis came of age and assumed the kingship, but with close monitoring by his mother.

Chapter 39
Cardinal Richelieu[39] and Marie de' Medici[39]–Tyrants or Not?

Armand-Jean du Plessis, later to become known as *Cardinal et duc de Richelieu*, was born to an important, but lesser, noble family in Poitou. Through marriages to members of the legal class, the family had rapidly risen in social and political prominence. His father, François, had become the chief magistrate serving King Henri III, and his mother was the daughter of a *conseiller* of the Parlement of Paris.

Henri made a land grant to the Plessis family of the bishopric of Luçon in Poitou with a very large mansion on it, an almost palace-like structure; François was made the feudal landlord, or the seigneury of Richelieu, in Poitou. Richelieu was the name of the valley in which Poitou was located.

Armand-Jean was just five years old when his father died, leaving an estate that had financially drained the family's resources and had been mismanaged during the Wars of Religion, which ended in 1598. As he grew older and realized the poverty of his family, young Armand-Jean was determined to restore the estate and the honor of his family.

Unrest at the cathedral of Luçon threatened the revocation of the grant to the family, unless a male member of the family was consecrated a bishop as soon as possible. Henri, the eldest son, had succeeded his father as seigneury of Richelieu. The other brother was a Carthusian monk, an order of silent, closeted monks and nuns whose mission was built on contemplation and silence.

Because Armand-Jean was not yet at an age to be consecrated at the completion of his studies, he required special dispensation from the pope to pursue his studies of theology. He was fixated on success, very studious, and put all else aside in his quest to become a priest. In 1607, at the age of twenty-two, he was consecrated as a priest and assigned to the see of Luçon as bishop. At the cathedral, he was greeted with hostility. The diocese was wrought by the continuing Wars of Religion; the clergy and staff were demoralized.

Quickly, he began to put into place the reforms promulgated by the Council of Trent. To the liking of the people of Luçon, Armand-Jean Plessis was the first bishop to write in French rather than Latin. He was hardworking, earnest, and intent on putting an end to social and political divisiveness. He was a cleric to whom the common person could relate.

Henri IV had been murdered in 1610. The rightful successor to the throne was his son, Louis XIII. Louis was only nine years of age when his father died. Meanwhile, Marie de' Medici, the second wife of Henri IV, was appointed as regent for her oldest son, Louis XIII. His mother, the daughter of a noble Italian ruling family, had very limited political skills, and her abilities to rule France were certainly questionable.

While married to Henri IV, she was aware of her husband's marital affairs with other women. At the same time, he was jealous of her very close political relationship with a transplanted fellow Tuscany nobleman named Concino Concini. After Henri's death, and while regent, she became allied with Concini to the extent that he had a prominent role in the decisions she made for the government of France. One of her first actions as the ruler of France was to make void Henri's policy on Spain. This action returned the Habsburg dynasty to a position where they could freely meddle in the French affairs of government. At the same time, she and Concini were freely spending government revenue on unnecessary things, such as the design and building of a Florentine-style palace in Paris. She sent an architect to Italy for the purpose of measuring in detail a palace in Florence, which served as a blueprint of the Luxembourg Palace she would have built for herself. She and Concini also enriched themselves with money belonging to the French government, and made embarrassing concessions to French nobles who were in an uprising over high taxes. The nobles wished to have greater control of the government, with their own interests and personal gains in mind.

In 1614, Marie was involved in a dealing in which Bishop Plessis found himself embroiled as an intermediary. His conciliatory negotiations in the matter and release of Marie of all claims resulted in his being appointed as a clergy representative from Poitou to the Estates General of 1614.

However, even after Louis came of age that year at thirteen, his mother continued to rule for another three years until 1617. During this time, the nobility of France strove to continue their control of her rule for self-benefit and position. In April 1617, a palace revolution overthrew her as regent, and her son acceded to the throne as Louis XIII. His first actions were to have Concini assassinated, Concini's wife, Leonora, beheaded and burned for sorcery, and his own mother exiled to Blois. In February 1619, Marie escaped from prison in Blois and started a revolt against the government. Once again, Plessis worked as a mediator to have the king allow her to set up court at Angers. In August 1620, she started a second rebellion for control of the government. Again, Plessis obtained favorable treatment for her from her son, Louis XIII. In 1622, Marie was readmitted to the King's Council, where she rewarded Plessis by working through the Church to obtain a cardinal's biretta for him. Then, in 1624, she persuaded Louis to make Cardinal Richelieu his chief minister.

Undoubtedly, the things that Marie did for Richelieu were meant to be a quid pro quo. However, Richelieu was determined not to be dominated by her. He rejected the Franco-Spanish alliance, which she brought about immediately after the death of her husband, Henri IV, and he began to ally France with the Huguenot power structure. These actions enraged Marie, and by 1628 she was Richelieu's worst critic and enemy. She began to press the king to dismiss him. Instead, the king stood by the cardinal. Finally, in 1631, Louis banished his mother to exile in Compiègne, France. From there, Marie escaped to Brussels and never returned to France. In 1642 she was a penniless, destitute woman.

As to his relationship with Richelieu, the king did not personally like him. However, in many ways Louis did not have the education or experience to be an effective ruler. But he saw these qualities in Richelieu. He also realized that Richelieu, although he did not always agree with the rule of the king, swore absolute loyalty to the throne.

Richelieu had always had the desire to be king, but he had enough reasoning power to know that his dream could not and would not ever be fulfilled. He realized that the position of chief minister to the king would be the zenith of his quest for power, and that if ever, he must establish his legacy for control of the government.

Although Richelieu came to have an uncertain feeling that the Huguenots were being allowed an increasing amount of power, he was willing to overlook his concerns while he was busy securing his own career, and domination in other matters of state and international affairs. However, after a period of turning a blind eye to the Huguenots, it became clear to him that the Huguenots were fast becoming a state within a state. As the chief minister he saw that, with the exception of Paris, the power of civil government and military control in most of the cities in France were shifting into the hands of the Huguenots. However, he tolerated their rising influence until Huguenot leaders allegedly negotiated to bring England, a longtime enemy, into another war with France.

Many parties were at fault for what happened to La Rochelle in 1628. The monarchs of France had historically been weak rulers of the affairs of the country. Louis XIII was no exception. Having appointed Cardinal Richelieu as his chief minister was a negative step. Although Richelieu was an efficient planner, manager of the affairs of state, and proclaimed absolute loyalty to the king, he believed in monoreligious freedom for the country. He let his Catholic faith cloud his perspective of what was right for France. Louis was too weak of a ruler to recognize this. Consequently, the road down which Richelieu was leading him was dangerous. The siege and ruin of La Rochelle was a huge mistake, from which even to this day many Frenchmen believe that their country has not completely recovered. The huge contributing middle class of France was exterminated or forced to leave the country forever. This included the productive members of the business communities throughout France, as well as many of the creative writers, professionals, people of science and medicine, artists, musicians, people of the theater, et cetera.

Over time, Richelieu became almost a proxy king as Louis abdicated more and more of his royal responsibilities to the cardinal. Subsequent to the assassination of Henri IV, the country under the regency of Louis's mother, Marie de' Medici, began the return to pro-Catholic politics. At the same time, the position of the Huguenots was being weakened. Affairs became so dramatic that a rebellion resulted from the organization of Huguenot resistance, led by Henri II Duke of Rohan and his brother, Soubise.

In 1621, government forces besieged Saint-Jean-d'Angély, a city near La Rochelle, and subsequently a blockade made access by water to La Rochelle impossible. These difficulties ended with a stalemate and the signing of the Treaty of Montpellier, which was officialized in October 1622. The signatories to the treaty were King Louis XIII and Henri II Duke of Rohan. It temporarily ended hostilities between the Crown and the Huguenots. It reaffirmed the terms of the Edict of Nantes and pardoned Henri II. Most importantly, access to La Rochelle was restored and the Huguenots were able to retain their forts and troops.

However, in 1625, the Duke of Rohan and his brother, Soubise, incited a second Huguenot rebellion in La Rochelle. This conflict ended with government forces capturing Île de Ré. This was a flashpoint for the king. At that time, the king decided the Huguenots must be subdued once and for all. In what he hoped would be the last time, Richelieu, demonstrating his loyalty to the king, declared the final suppression of the Huguenots to be the first priority of the country.

In 1626, relations between France and England soured even further. The Anglo-French treaty of 1624 failed when

Richelieu negotiated a secret treaty with Spain, leaving England by itself in the vise between the Austrian House of Habsburg and Spain. Meanwhile, France was building a strong naval force, which England saw as a clear threat to its security.

In mid-1626, England dispatched an envoy to France with the intent of starting a rebellion, and hopefully to trigger another Huguenot uprising by Rohan and Soubise. In June 1627, England landed six thousand men on Île de Ré to aid the Huguenots in an uprising. This act of aggression against France was the start of an armed conflict. In August 1627, the king of France began to surround La Rochelle with seven thousand soldiers, and reinforced government fortifications near the city. In September of that year, Huguenots fired first on government troops at Fort Louis.

Chapter 40
Siege of La Rochelle—1628

After the attack on Fort Louis by Huguenot troops, warlike clouds began to darken over La Rochelle. Federal troops began to isolate the city. Berms were built, trenches were dug, forts and walls were strengthened, and new ones were constructed. In April 1628, erection of these fortifications was completed and manned with thirty thousand French troops under the direct command of Cardinal Richelieu. By this time, although closely guarded, Huguenots and many Catholics began to escape La Rochelle for other cities not being threatened, with the intent of possibly returning when the conflict would be over. Others began to leave La Rochelle while they could find seaward passage to other countries. Escape routes, though, were heavily guarded by the troops.

Finally, the government began the construction of a rampart, extending fourteen hundred meters into the channel leading into the port of La Rochelle. This would prevent supplies being imported into the city. The rampart, a barrier of very large, heavy, wooden beams, was constructed on top of a foundation of sunken ships filled with old cannons, cannonballs, heavy stones, miscellaneous rubble, and riffraff. At first, as it was being built, a few ships were able to transgress past the rampart, but this became impossible once the blockade was completed. The ships in port had to be abandoned by the crews. If the crew members were from foreign countries, they were sent home if they were Catholic. If they were Protestant, then they were retained in La Rochelle and roughly treated, like the rest of the Huguenot populace.

Foreign powers where Catholicism was the principal religion participated in the actions against the city of La Rochelle. The Netherlands, although a Protestant country, became mercenary. Dutch ships were rented to France to transport its soldiers. However, religious Catholic services were not allowed to be conducted on these Protestant ships.

During the siege, Spain provided symbolic assistance in France's struggle against the common enemies, those being the Huguenots and the Dutch. And, of course, France always seemed to be at war with England.

England sent two more naval expeditions to assist the Huguenots, but these flotillas did not meet with success.

Richelieu personally commanded the French troops in the four-month Siege of La Rochelle, which lasted until October 1628, with the surrender of Huguenot forces defending the city. In laying waste to La Rochelle, Huguenot citizens, as well as Catholics who were determined to be nonparticipants in the Church, were given the option of recommitting to the Catholic faith or face imprisonment; or, even worse, they could be executed. Any Huguenots who took up arms against the French forces and were captured were executed by firing squad, or a bullet shot to the back of the head.

By the end of the siege, the population of La Rochelle was largely decimated, and most of the city destroyed. Among those dead was Captain Chevin, whom the French troops had been ordered to search out and kill. Governor Bouché was arrested, but he escaped execution and was released. Although long suspected by the government of being a Huguenot, Bouché was an efficient governor, as he had never overtly demonstrated Huguenot beliefs to more than a few close friends, had always been most respectful to the king, the cabinet, and to the courtesans; and he always regularly attended and participated in Catholic Mass. Michel and Elisabeth Légere, on the advice of the governor, had managed to escape on the last vessel sailing from La Rochelle before the port was shut down. No one, not even their beloved daughter, Maggie, or Elisabeth's sister, Colleen, knew their destination.

Of course, the exception could have been the governor, but he resolved to tell no one and never admitted to advising them to escape by ship.

One of the first casualties in the siege was the Reverend Horry. His wife and children were spared, for they escaped back home to Angoulême before the battle for the city began. Bouché had had one of his coaches, marked with his seal and guarded by two of his armed guards, deliver them back to the Horry estate.

Monsieur Ronsérre was also hunted; unbeknownst to Richelieu, he was in Fontenay-le-Comte attending to his legal practice before turning it over as part of his retirement.

In the case of Antoine and Charles Jardeen, members of their families, including Maggie, who was now a widow for the second time, and her aunt, Colleen, were saved by the soldier force of La Rochelle as a favor to the Catholic bishop and the local priest. They were apprehended, but instead of being taken to the prison, they were taken to the church in the middle of the night and turned over to the clerics. Secreted in numerous hidden chambers of the nunnery, and in the underground labyrinths of the church, their daily needs were provided by the Sisters of the Order of Saint Margaret. This was done in sincere regard to the service the Jardeens had provided to the needy Catholics of La Rochelle, and to the fact that they had continued to pay their tithes to the Church. Most importantly, despite their Protestant evangelizing, they had remained cordial to the Catholic clergy and had never publicly besmirched the Church. This protection was freely given, and no expectation of further commitment to the Church was made or expected. No record of the Church's kindness was ever recorded or spoken of outside of the families.

The bookstore and the art gallery were burned to the ground, however, not before the French forces confiscated all the artwork for transport back to Paris. Some of the art was displayed at the Louvre, the cathedral of Notre Dame, the cathedral of Sainte-Chapelle, Versailles, the Basilica of Saint Denis, and the Basilica of Sacré-Cœur.

During the siege, no doubt wondering where the Jardeens had gone, Richelieu took up residence at Charles's manoir home in the country. His senior officers took over the city home of Antoine and Jacqueline. Of course, the servants at these homes were safe, as they were necessary for tending to the needs of Richelieu and the officers. There was no evidence to lead Richelieu or his senior commanders to believe that they had ever embraced the Huguenot beliefs and creed, nor any proof that they ever participated in any Huguenot religious service. Unbeknownst to Richelieu, the servants' tithes to the Catholic Church had always been paid by the Jardeens.

The servants fully understood that to survive, they must serve their "guests" well. Most importantly, they understood above all else that, even under the threat of death by the officers that they served, they must not reveal the whereabouts of their beloved employers.

Perhaps the worst piece of physical destruction wrought on La Rochelle was the construction, under the supervision of Richelieu, of what seemed like the impenetrable barricade to prevent ships from departing or entering the harbor. This construction cut the city off from the rest of the world, preventing food and other necessary goods from being imported. Even if goods could be imported, there was no money to pay for them, as Richelieu had confiscated as much gold and silver as he could find and had destroyed the equipment to coin and print new money.

The most tragic damage done, of course, was the number of citizens killed throughout the city. Besides those who died at the hands of Richelieu and his army in collateral damage from the fighting, there were dead bodies resulting from executions by the troops. As well, many died later of disease wrought by starvation, and water sources purposely contaminated by Richelieu's troops. In addition, deadly illnesses were contracted from the decaying corpses. La Rochelle was left a decimated city, but in it were survivors full of hope for recovery and restoration. These survivors included both Huguenots and Roman Catholics.

Chapter 41
Return of the Money

Eight days after the troops had withdrawn from La Rochelle, Captain Cussions attempted to sail into port. When he sighted the blockade dead ahead, the channel was still wide enough for him to swing his ship around 180 degrees and head back out into the Bay of Biscay. Then, sailing north and close into shore, he spotted a cove carved deep into the beach. His maritime chart showed the depth of the cove to be extensive. He took a chance and decided to attempt to anchor sufficiently far into it, as would be necessary to safely go ashore in the ship's dinghy. Getting as close to land as he thought he could safely navigate, the crew dropped anchor and raised the international flag for anchorage.

By this time, it was ten o'clock in the morning. Two of his crewmen rowed him ashore, with instructions to return to the ship and watch for the signal of a lantern at dusk to return and pick him up.

After he watched the dinghy returning to the ship, he came up to a road and began to walk south into the city. He estimated that the hike would be about three miles. After walking at least a mile, a coach drawn by two horses pulled up beside him.

Hollering down from his seat, the driver asked, "Bonjour, Monsieur, would you care for a ride into the city? I am by myself and can use your company."

"Merci beaucoup, you are most kind to offer." As he climbed up to the driver's bench, the driver said, "My name is Matthew. What is your name?"

When he got up into his seat, he told the driver, "My name is Cussions, Captain Cussions. That is my ship you passed, anchored in the cove about a mile up the road."

"Well, Captain, where can I take you in La Rochelle?"

"I am going to the boatyard at the harbor for a visit with the Jardeen brothers."

"Of course, I know the boatyard well. Are you a friend of Antoine and Charles?"

"Oui, I have known them a long time. I have sailed my ship many times into La Rochelle."

"Well, I have some business which I have to conduct in the city myself. Will you need a ride back to the cove later today?" Matthew asked.

"Non," Cussions told him. "I will probably be staying in the city later than you. I am sure that the Jardeens' coachman will drive me back to the cove. Oh, I almost forgot to offer you money for driving me into the city. How much do I owe you?"

"Please, I did not offer you the ride for money. I stopped and asked you to ride with me. You do not need to pay me. Bringing you into town was the least that I could do for a man walking a lonely road."

"That is very kind of you. Perhaps we will meet again sometime and I can repay my debt to you with some kind deed of humanity."

At the boatyard, the brothers were excited that he was back in La Rochelle, but wondered where he left his ship.

After they had caught up on what had happened in the almost five months since they had seen him, the three of them sat down to talk. Over some mediocre wine from the farm and cigars that the captain brought with him, the brothers related what had happened in the siege: the tragic deaths of Chevin and the reverend, the escape of the reverend's family, which was orchestrated by the governor, and the escape of the Légeres by ship.

"How did the governor and you gentlemen escape being captured?" Cussions inquired.

"The governor was arrested and then released, after the bishop at the Catholic church falsely attested that they had never had any suspicions of his being a Huguenot and that he was a registered, practicing Catholic."

"Well, what about you and your families?" Cussions asked, not letting them slip by without answering his first question.

Without going into detail, Antoine just smiled and said, "We have friends in high places," and then he paused without going any further. Cussions took the pause as a clue not to probe any further, and he moved on to the subject of the money that he had kept for them.

"I have the chest of money that you left in my safekeeping. It is on the ship, safely tucked away in a place that only my first mate and I have access to; even he does not know what is in it. I have checked the security of the chest every single day since you turned it over to me. The seal is unbroken. I did not deposit the money in banks in other countries, because I feared the troubles going on here in La Rochelle and throughout the country might devalue your money, especially if there might be Huguenot-minted coins in it. You will find the chest exactly as you gave it to me. I would like for both of you to meet me tomorrow morning on the ship, have breakfast with me, and then count your money in the privacy of my cabin."

"There is no need to open the chest and count the money," Antoine quickly replied, and Charles affirmed. "There is no one we trust more than you. If you say that all of the money is there, then it is. What percentage of the money do we owe you for your safekeeping?" Antoine looked the captain directly in the eyes as he asked the question.

"You are being foolish," Cussions answered. "You are insulting me."

"Charles and I do not mean to insult you. We have to pay you somehow. Charles and I have discussed this matter. If you will not accept money, may we offer you a one-third partnership in the export-import business that we are planning to start? That is, when the harbor is clear, and ships can get in and out of port, or perhaps we might operate off of Île de Ré, or out of Brest."

"I am very humbled by what you have done for the people of La Rochelle, and for what I know you will do in the future," he told the brothers. "I have done business with you for a long time. I know that you trust me, and you have my solemn oath that I trust you. I trust your morals and your business ethics. The answer to your question is yes, I will be glad to be a partner. I can bring the most honest ship captains to move your merchandise in and out of whatever port you locate our business, and I can ensure that our goods will be delivered as contracted to whatever country they are supposed to go. As you know, honest captains are the secret to success in maritime business."

"That would be a blessing," Antoine told him. "But of course, you understand that we have to wait until the harbor is clear and vessels can safely navigate the harbor to and from the Bay of Biscay."

"We are hoping that the king will agree to foot the bill to clear the harbor," Charles quickly offered. "But it is doubtful."

"Do you really believe that the king can or will do anything?" the captain asked with a questioning look on his face. "Who is running this government, Louis or Richelieu? It seems to me that the king takes his orders from the chief minister. So why would Richelieu permit the harbor to be cleared when he is the one who ordered it barricaded and fortified?"

The brothers could not disagree with the captain's logic. They just nodded their heads in approval. With the king beholden to Richelieu, it seemed that as far as the government was concerned, La Rochelle was a forgotten city.

Antoine pondered as he sat silently for a few minutes, and then asked, "Without government money and support of the king, what can we, as individuals, do to clear the harbor and get this city on the road to recovery?"

Charles and the captain stared at Antoine with a helpless look. Finally, the captain answered, "I have a plan. I can round up the captains and crews from several ships to help us. We can buy explosives from England and blast the sunken ships from the channel. I can undoubtedly persuade some Dutch engineers to come and disassemble the rampart. We can then blast the foundation out of the channel."

"Sounds like a good plan," Charles agreed. "But it will be an enormous undertaking. What about the abandoned ships that are in the harbor right now and can't get out?"

Antoine broke in, "Remember, I am the director of the maritime administration. Hopefully, records are available for every ship that has entered the port of La Rochelle over the past fifty years, containing each name, country of origin, and the name of each captain, as well as weight, draft, and cargo. If Richelieu did not have them destroyed, the records will be at city hall."

"But Michel is no longer our mayor, and Governor Bouché has not appointed anyone to replace him," Charles reminded him. "Besides, I don't know who is left at the municipal building. I know that at least four persons from there were killed in the siege."

"Yes, that could be a problem, but we still have Bouché." Taking the opportunity to rub it in with the captain, Antoine, slowly and with some stress to his voice, repeated what he had said before. "You know that it does not hurt to have friends in high places."

Without giving Antoine the benefit of letting on that he had noticed, the captain interjected, "If you can get the information, I can track down the captains and have them come claim their ships as soon as the channel has been sufficiently cleared."

"We should get started as soon as possible," Antoine offered. "In the next several days, we should see the governor and outline our plan to him. In addition, even without specific details, we should probably share our plan with the Catholic bishop and the priest. We need all the cooperation we can get. I am sure that they have as much interest as we do in restoring the city."

The captain asked if they could have their coachman drive him to the cove. "I need to be back there by dusk."

"Of course," Charles told him. "Antoine and I will ride with you so that we know exactly where to meet you tomorrow. We look forward to having breakfast with you."

"Tomorrow, be sure to bring a coach large enough and with a sufficient chassis to support the weight of the chest.

Remember to be at the cove by nine o'clock, at the latest. My boatswain will be there to meet you and bring you out to the ship."

It was near dark when they arrived at the cove. The captain took the lantern from the side of the coach and waved it back and forth about ten times toward the ship. Soon they saw the dinghy coming into shore.

As they waited for the dinghy, the three men stood around and talked. Cussions told them about the breakfast which they could expect the next morning. Pretty quickly, the conversation turned to the businesses damaged or destroyed during the siege. Cussions asked about the seafood restaurant down by the waterfront. It was a place he always enjoyed eating at when he was in La Rochelle.

Antoine bowed his head and could hardly speak. Charles took over. "Captain, it is with great sadness that we must tell you that the restaurant burned to the ground. It was a gruesome act of the French troops. One night, when the restaurant was full of patrons, the troops marched in during the serving of dinner. The customers were ordered to immediately go outside. When they had evacuated the restaurant, the owner and staff were rounded up and made to sit while soldiers strapped them to the chairs and tied their feet to the chair legs. Then the soldiers poured flammable liquid around the restaurant and set fire to it. The customers outside were prevented from trying to douse the fire as it started, and were prevented from leaving the scene. They were forced to listen to the loud screams of agony as the workers inside burned to death."

"Why?" Cussions asked.

"There is no answer to your question," Charles told him. Just as he said this, the dinghy arrived to pick up the captain. No one spoke. The brothers shook hands with the captain and assured him that they would be at the cove the next day at nine o'clock. Cussions got into the dinghy, and the boatswains rowed back toward the ship.

The coachman drove the brothers safely to Antoine's home in the city, where Charles decided to spend the night because of the possible dangers after dark on the road out to the farm. And besides, if he went home, he would have to leave very early the next morning to make it to the cove by nine o'clock. The damage to the house caused by French officers was not serious, but repairs were still going on. Antoine was spending nights at the farm until repairs could be made, but tonight wisdom seemed to dictate that they stay in the city. The servants had been put on paid leave, so it was good that they were going to have breakfast with Captain Cussions. The coachman spent the night in a room upstairs, as did Charles. Antoine slept in the master bedroom on the first floor.

The next morning, they were up early to find that the coachman had already been out to the stable to feed and water the horses. He hitched them up for the trip to the cove.

They arrived at the cove and spotted the dinghy being rowed in to pick them up. The coachman was given instructions to remain at the cove and watch for their return. Antoine told him that he should expect them around noon.

After they were part of the way to the ship, the coachman unhitched the horses and tied them to a tree, with a long enough rope so that they could move around.

The captain greeted the brothers once they were on board; he took them to a private dining area where he and the first mate usually had their meals separate from the rest of the crew.

As promised by the captain, the breakfast was more than ample. There were eggs, both scrambled and fried; delicious sausages; thick, fried pork slices; boiled seasoned potatoes, freshly baked bread with jam, all the coffee they could drink, as well as cheese and assorted dried fruits.

After they finished eating and had their third or fourth mug of coffee, it was getting late. The captain had already asked the first mate to supervise having the chest brought topside, the dinghy hoisted up to the main deck, the chest placed onboard, and most importantly, to remain with the dinghy until the brothers were ready to leave.

At eleven, Antoine thanked the captain for his hospitality and told him that they must depart very soon.

"When will we see you again?" Antoine asked.

"I plan to be back in early December with the explosive material and equipment that you will need to begin clearing the harbor. In the meantime, I hope to fortify a warehouse on Île de Ré with a cache of explosives, black gunpowder, fuses, and mechanical equipment which we might need."

The dinghy was lowered by winches, with the boatswains and the brothers in it. Once it was released from the hooks holding it, they rowed toward the drop-off point where the coachman was waiting. When he spotted the dinghy, he hitched up the horses and opened the bonnet at the back of the coach. With the effort of the two crewmen from the ship, the five men working together got the chest into the bonnet.

Once the dinghy was headed back to the ship, the coachman closed and locked the bonnet and began the drive; however, this time the coachman took them to Charles's manoir, rather than the house in the city. The money would be safer at the manoir behind high walls and a moat, rather than exposed to workmen in the city.

Chapter 42
Governor Bouché

The day after the captain returned their money, Antoine and Charles dropped by the governor's office to arrange to meet with Bouché. He was not available, but his staff courteously made an appointment for them to meet with him the next morning.

The brothers arrived the next day at the appointed time. The governor was extremely glad to see them. He had already learned of their being housed during the siege by the Catholic church, despite the effort to keep it secret. He was relieved that the church did what they had, for surely everyone in the Jardeen families would have been among the first to be searched out and punished by Richelieu. He did know that Captain Chevin and the Reverend Horry had been executed. Expressing his sympathy to the brothers about these deaths, he asked if they had details of Monsieur Ronsérre, on whether he was killed, or he was in hiding somewhere. He did, however, know that Michel and Elisabeth Légere had left on the last ship out of La Rochelle. He continued to feign that he did not know where they were headed to resettle. He believed that it would be England, but he felt that it was best that he did not know for certain. If asked by anyone in Paris, he would tell them that it was Greece or Austria. With these details out of the way, he finally said, "I am so glad to see you. I have been very worried about your safety and your whereabouts. After the siege, I have come to realize that our lives hang by a thread, and we must each live every day to fulfill our dreams, do no harm, do good, and live the ordinances of our faith. I want you to know that you, gentlemen, are great examples of my belief."

Charles answered for himself and his brother, "Your Honor, you can never fully realize what you mean to the Jardeen families . . . not only for your defense of my nephew, Tomas, and for Maggie and her parents, but also for the many political things that you have done for us."

Listening to his brother, Antoine became emotional. He could not speak, but instead he just nodded his head affirmatively. Thanking them, Bouché expressed his appreciation for their safety, and then asked, "What brings you to my office so early in the morning? Do we have issues that need to be discussed?"

Antoine answered, "Yes, Your Honor. We have a very serious issue to discuss with you."

"Well," the governor responded, "if it is as serious as you make it sound, then perhaps we need to discuss it over drinks and a fine cigar."

"Oui, but it is only morning." Antoine added, "However, if you are going to indulge, then how can we refuse? We must join you."

Waving to Ravenel, his legal assistant, he held up four fingers and instructed him to bring a couple of bottles of the finest Cognac, and a box of the finest Spanish cigars from Barcelona. He then added, "I want you to sit in on this discussion."

As they drank and smoked, they got caught up on matters of the siege and, of course, on local gossip. Finally, the conversation came around to what was happening in Paris at the highest levels of government. "Quite frankly," the governor told them, "nothing good." And then, to the surprise of the brothers, he said, "The king is inept and does only what his chief minister tells him. Although I hate Richelieu for what he did to this city, without him at the king's side the country would now be broke and unable to pay its debts. Of course, you should never speak these words outside of this office, and I hope that you will forget who said them."

"Well, that is pretty common knowledge. People are talking," Antoine told him.

"I know that people are talking," Bouché said in a very quiet, thoughtful voice. "But it would be in your best interest if you gentlemen never echo these thoughts, not even to each other. There are too many eyes and ears around; if either of you said these things to the wrong person or persons, word would spread right to Paris quicker than a wildfire in the forest. The risk would be almost overwhelming to you and the members of your families. I must have your solemn word."

"Your Honor, you have our most solemn word," Charles told him.

Antoine took a deep gulp of his drink and said, "I, too, pledge to never repeat what you have said."

Bouché took a deep drag on his cigar, blew out the smoke, and said, "Now, let's get down to what is really on the minds of you two fine gentlemen."

The governor moved over to his large, ornate desk. The brothers sat in front on opposite ends of the desk, with the governor's legal aide in the middle between them.

Bouché started, "I have some matters to discuss with you, but first let me hear what is on your mind."

With a nod from Charles, Antoine began. "Governor, Charles and I are concerned about the amount of physical damage that Richelieu and his troops did to our city, and more importantly, what they did to our harbor. At the present time, vessels any larger than a small watercraft cannot navigate into or out of the harbor. We are cut off from the rest of the world. Food cannot be imported. Since the crops were burned, local farmers find it hard just to feed their own families, much less to help meet the needs of people in the city. People are desperate. Many who survived the siege will no doubt soon die from malnutrition, or outright starvation." As he spoke, Ravenel took copious notes. The governor sat with deep emotions showing on his face.

Antoine continued, "Your Honor, do you know if the king is prepared to send engineers to clear the harbor and rid us of that terrible rampart which Richelieu built?"

"You pose a very difficult question," Bouché answered. "I have just returned from Paris. I did bring up the subject with the king, but he just ignored the question. No, I am quite sure that given the country's monetary situation, he has no plans for anything in La Rochelle."

"Your Honor, we can, of course, concentrate on only one thing at a time. You may think that the project we propose is self-serving for our boatyard, as well as for the import-export business which we hope to start. Besides the ships sunk in the channel, there are sunken ships and a rampart blocking the inner harbor, as well as ships afloat which are unable to sail out to the Bay of Biscay. In time, unless we can get them to their rightful owners they, too, will sink and rot at the bottom of the harbor." After pausing to catch his breath, Antoine continued, "Docks and piers need to be repaired; some may actually need to be torn out and rebuilt, and warehouses must be repaired or rebuilt. Before the siege, you know that this city was the main shipping port on the west coast of France. When these things are taken care of, the shipping world will return to La Rochelle."

"You are quite right in your thinking," Bouché told the brothers. "Do you have a plan to accomplish this without the assistance of the government? I do not foresee that kind of undertaking on the part of the government. Remember, we were defeated by the army of the king. Richelieu would have destroyed every building and killed every person in this city if it were possible."

Interrupting the governor, Charles said, "Your Honor, as a matter of fact we do have a plan, and it may not cost as much as you might imagine."

"Please, go on."

Charles began, "As you know, my brother and I have been blessed to have been very successful in our adult business life." Without going into detail, he continued, "Before the siege, we took steps to protect our financial assets. We do not propose spending all that we have to solely take on the mission of restoring the port. There are other ports nearby that are undamaged and would love to have us relocate to their city, but we love La Rochelle and want to see it prosper once again."

Antoine broke in, "We have a friend who is the captain of a trading ship that, for a number of years and up to near the beginning of the siege, made regular trips to La Rochelle. This week, he anchored outside of the harbor, rowed a dinghy into the beach, and found us."

Then, without mentioning the matter of the security of their money, Charles offered, "We chatted about the problems surrounding the port. The captain is willing to help us get the rampart dismantled, and the ships anchored in the harbor returned to their owners once it is safe for them to sail. He can buy black powder to blast the sunken ships from the outer channel. When it is cleared, if French engineers are not made available by the king, he will hire a team of Dutch engineers to come here to dismantle that monstrous rampart. Then, he will bring more black powder from other countries to blast the sunken ships from the inner channel and to demolish piers that are beyond repair."

"I see, and what does he want in return?"

"There are things that we can offer him other than money." Without telling the governor that a deal had already been struck, Antoine said, "It would be a private business deal between Charles, myself, and the captain. It would not require any payments by the French government, nor would it use any financial assets of the city. I suggest you talk to the Catholic bishop and the local priest to inform them and assess their interest in the restoration of the city. For their support and recommendation to Richelieu and the king, Charles and I will double our monthly tithes to the Church; although at this point, if they speak about it to Richelieu, we would appreciate the promise not to connect our names to the plan."

"Why not?" Bouché asked.

Speaking up, Charles explained, "For one thing, Richelieu must already know that Antoine and I are practicing Huguenots. Secondly, the nunnery secretly housed our families during the siege. No doubt this saved us from execution. You somehow already know about it, but publicly this is not to be mentioned again. No demands were made on us to return to the Catholic faith. The bishop even suggested that we can better serve the community by remaining active in our Huguenot church. I cannot speak for Antoine, but I will always support the local Catholic church and its congregation in mutual ways of benefit."

Bouché just sat in silence and stared at the brothers with a questioning, concerned expression on his face, but did not immediately speak. After pausing to give the governor a respectable amount of time to speak, Charles continued, "Your Honor, if you agree that our plan is a feasible project to undertake, we suggest that you adopt it as your own; discuss it with the king and obtain his okay to proceed. It might also be pertinent to explain that it will surely help the balance of trades between France and the Mediterranean nations, French-controlled territories, and the developing colonies of America, as well as Mexico, Canada, and the South American countries. It will be a winning situation for all concerned. I have no doubt that it will only lead to good things for your political status and recognition."

The governor listened without interruption. When Charles finished, Bouché quietly mulled over the proposition. Then he spoke up and said in a very sincere tone of voice, "Charles, Antoine, you have presented your case well. I deeply appreciate your concern for this city. What I am about to say might seem like a form of blackmail, and if so, you will be correct; but do not doubt that I am serious. I will do as you have asked on the condition that one of you will agree to allow me to appoint you to replace our mutual friend, Michel Légere, as the new mayor of the city of La Rochelle."

The brothers stared at the governor in stunned silence. Not sure how to properly respond, Antoine finally spoke up and said, "Governor, I am honored for your offer, and I am sure that Charles is as honored as I am. But let me first pose a question to you. Given the number of Huguenots imprisoned or executed during the siege, what is the number of practicing Catholics now left in the city, as compared to the number of Huguenots? I suspect that the

Huguenots are vastly outnumbered. Therefore, in the interest of peace and harmony, why don't you consider appointing an influential Catholic leader to a fixed mayoral term of your choosing? Say, for a two- or maybe a three-year term of office, and then have a public election and let the people of La Rochelle choose their own mayor? If the Catholic church can do what they did for us, we can certainly work with them."

"In the ideal world, that would be a wonderful idea," Bouché responded, "but as governor of this province, the king has invested me with powers to appoint local public officials. France is not yet a democratic republic."

"Oui, and he apparently gives Richelieu the power to murder them," Antoine sarcastically retorted.

"Yes, I understand your point, but 'what is' is what it is. We don't have elections in France. As I said, this is not a democratic republic. I have to abide by the rules of the monarch."

"Yes, you are quite right, but since the chief minister is trying to solidify France as a totally Catholic union, don't you think the king would be appreciative of your appointing a Catholic leader right now instead of a known Huguenot?"

"Do you have a particular influential Catholic in mind?"

"No, I don't have any one person in mind, but I am sure that the bishop could be of assistance in identifying someone with whom the three of us can feel comfortable. Or, on the other hand, the Church may defer to you to pick the best person for the job."

"I will consider what you have told me," Bouché told him, "but I know that I would prefer someone whom I can fully trust, such as either one of you two fine gentlemen."

"We will think it over, and perhaps we can get back together in four or five days," Antoine conceded. Charles nodded in agreement. "But in the meantime, it would be helpful if you would meet with the bishop on the matters we have discussed today."

"Good," Bouché said, this time with relief in his voice. "And thanks to both of you for your thoughtful insight, and your offer to be a partner in the reclamation."

After they left the governor's office, Charles asked Antoine, "Do you see yourself as mayor of La Rochelle?"

"No, but if pressed on the issue, I might agree to serve for a few years for the good of the city; but on the other hand, maybe not. I want more than anything to get the boatyard running again and get the channel cleared out. What about you?"

"I don't know," Charles told him. "I am somewhat taken aback that we were asked."

Pausing for a bit to think about it, Antoine told his brother, "I am not at all surprised. Ever since Michel resigned, the governor, without coming right out and asking, has given numerous hints that have led me to believe that these thoughts have been rolling over in his mind."

Chapter 43
King's Approval

True to his word, Governor Bouché carried out the commitments that he made to the Jardeens. Coincidentally, when he met with the Catholic clergymen and brought up the subject of replacing Michel Légere with a Catholic, he was astounded that they, without hardly pausing, mentioned the names of Antoine and Charles Jardeen. When quizzed about their recommendation, the bishop told him, "One of the brothers would absolutely be the best person to appoint. It doesn't matter which one. They have already done much for this city and its people, both Catholics and non-Catholics. They have provided relief in many ways for the needy. They have provided food, shelter, clothes, and even money without regard to religion. In fact, I would not be surprised if they have assisted and given to the needy of this city more than this church has been able to contribute."

Back at the office, Bouché penned a letter to King Louis XIII explaining in detail the deaths caused by Richelieu and the federal forces. Also, he wrote about the extensive damage wrought by government forces to the businesses, homes, seaport, and the channel in La Rochelle. In it, he suggested a private initiative to reclaim the city and the harbor if the government could not undertake undoing the damage. He ended the letter by asking for the king's thoughtful consideration and a quick reply. It was posted to Paris by courier, with instructions to await and return to La Rochelle with the king's reply. The courier, of course, was given money for lodging, food, and miscellaneous expenses.

The courier returned in fifteen days with a written reply from the king. It was addressed to "The Royal Governor of La Rochelle," affixed with the king's wax seal.

Bouché did not open the dispatch for a while. He asked his coachman to drive out to the manoir and bring the brothers to his office. When the coachman returned with the Jardeen brothers, they were led into a meeting room where they had to wait for the Catholic bishop, who was invited by the governor. When everyone, including his legal aide, was finally together, the governor came in and took a seat at the head of the table.

"After I originally met with you more than two weeks ago, I posted a letter to the king explaining our dire situation regarding the damage to the city and to our port. Without repair to the damages from the siege, the city of La Rochelle will not survive. Without economic means to support the people of La Rochelle, there will surely be a mass exodus of people leaving for other towns that have been left unaffected. If you will bear with me, I shall read to you the king's reply."

My Dear Royal Governor Bouché,

I am sorry to be tardy in responding to the letter you posted to me concerning damage to La Rochelle businesses, and to its seaport. The siege was conceived by His Eminence, Cardinal Richelieu. My goal was to only show support for the Catholic Church, to remind the Huguenots of the Catholic heritage of France, and to provide the opportunity to return to religious solidarity with the majority of their countrymen. I did so with the hope of erasing the division separating our people.

Richelieu was only authorized to send a small federal force to La Rochelle to search out and bring to justice the vandals damaging the Catholic properties in the city, as well as those persons physically attacking the Huguenot church.

I did not authorize a military force so large, nor did I know that His Eminence, Cardinal Richelieu, planned to personally take control of the forces. He certainly did not have orders from me to execute or imprison anyone because of their faith.

As for restoration, France does not have the money at the present time to undertake the repair of homes and businesses, nor to clear the channel and rebuild the docks. However, you have my permission to proceed as you see fit with private funding and labor, as you suggested in your letter. The best I can do at the present time is to send one or two engineers to La Rochelle to advise in the harbor work. Inform me when you are prepared to get started.

As to your suggestion regarding the appointment of a new mayor, you have the authority to name a person of your choice. I suggest that you discuss this matter with the Catholic clergy, as well as the Huguenot leaders in the community. I am confident that you will make the right decision. I have great esteem for your administrative and decision-making abilities.

Seal **Louis XIII**

Nothing was said by the king regarding the Huguenots of La Rochelle entering into a treaty with England in 1627. This treaty had caused Richelieu much grief. In desperation and a desire for revenge, he sought for a complete extermination of the Huguenots in question.

"Now, gentlemen, before we proceed with further discussion on the matter of clearing our harbor, I would like to settle the matter of appointing a new mayor. You have heard that the king has given me permission to make an appointment. Your Holy Reverence," he addressed the Catholic bishop, "would you please confirm for the Jardeens your answer to me when I consulted with you on the appointment of a Catholic?"

"Your Honor, you did indeed offer the appointment of a Catholic, giving myself and the priest here the opportunity to nominate several persons of the Church for your consideration."

"Did you agree to nominate an individual or individuals from the Catholic congregation?"

"No, Your Honor, I told you that I nominate either of the two Jardeen brothers sitting here at this table."

Expressing much surprise, Antoine pointedly asked the bishop, "Why did you not nominate someone from your congregation?"

"I will tell you what I told the governor," the bishop said, all the while looking at the Jardeens. "I told him that La Rochelle was primarily a Huguenot city before the siege and, I believe, with recovery will again be primarily a Huguenot city. The office of mayor requires a person with outstanding administrative abilities. There is no doubt that either you or your brother are the most qualified for the position. Your ethics, morals, and principles are above reproach. In fact, that was demonstrated by your advising the governor to bring your plan to me and wanting to involve our Catholic church here in La Rochelle in the restoration. I also told the governor that you two gentlemen, through your charitable efforts, have helped meet the needs of the poor and needy without regard to religious ties. You have already done more than the Church could afford to do."

"Well, are either of you willing to accept the responsibility?" the governor asked.

Charles quickly spoke up. "My brother, Antoine, does a masterful job of running the boatyard. I am a partner, but Antoine is the moving force behind the business."

Everyone looked at Antoine for an answer. "Yes, Your Honor, I will agree to serve as mayor for a small term. After three years at most, I will insist that the position rotate to a Catholic. Bishop, do you agree to my proposal?"

The bishop stammered. "Personally, I do agree, but it is unknown what will be in three years, or where I will be to see that my promise today will be carried out."

Without further discussion, the governor asked, "Can we get together in perhaps a week to discuss moving ahead on the harbor issue, and how to proceed from there? Monsieur Ravenel, would you please prepare a charter of appointment and arrange a meeting to take place a few days hence for Monsieur Jardeen to take the oath of office and meet his staff?"

"Your Honor, I will do as you have requested."

"Please coordinate your affairs with Monsieur Jardeen." And with that, the governor announced the meeting to be over. Afterward, he invited the participants to stay and enjoy some refreshments.

Chapter 44
Swearing into Office and Public Duties

Five days after the meeting with Governor Bouché, with hardly any fanfare except for the consumption of too much wine, Cognac, and cake, the governor administered the mayoral oath to Antoine. Present were Elisabeth's sister, Colleen; Maggie and her now-beautiful adult daughter, Elisabeth Marye; her stepchildren from her marriage to Captain Chevin; Charles and his wife, Paulette; and Antoine's second wife, Jacqueline Chevalier Jardeen. The bishop and the local priest were invited, but they declined, instead opting to later hold an introductory reception at the Catholic church after the next Sunday's Mass.

For the occasion there was a delicious, hearty *gâteau aux fruits sec* (fruitcake) baked by Maggie from a handwritten recipe handed down from her Great-Grandmother Légere. The recipe included an assortment of dried and candied fruits, such as apples, pears, and dried grapes from Charles's farm at the manoir. Layered on top were sun-dried coconut and candied pineapple chunks, imported from the Canary Islands before the siege and stored in Charles's food cellar. The cake had been wrapped for three days in a cotton cloth wrung out daily with Spanish rum.

For the next several weeks, Antoine split his time between attempting to get his boatbuilding business running again at full speed and getting acquainted with his new official duties of the city. There were a lot of records and policies to review, many of which he had to consult with mayoral aides for explanations and suggestions for the actions Michel had planned concerning the matters. Without realizing it, his understanding of the duties and responsibilities became clearer each day he went into the city and spent time at the office.

He found time was scarce for doing both jobs. Although the boatyard had nearly been shut down since the siege and the blockade, he retained most of his skilled employees who worked in the machine shop and the wood-crafting shop. He only had to stop by once or twice a week to review the inventories of various parts and meet with the supervisors on what needed to be done. The demanding part was the administrative side, such as finding workers from the remaining populace of La Rochelle who had the capabilities and potential for the difficult business of the boatyard.

In early December, his friend, the ship captain, reappeared after anchoring again in the cove. At the boatyard, he found Antoine and told him, "Since I was here last, I have been to Venice with stops in Morocco; Barcelona, Spain; Lisbon, Portugal; and Valletta Malta." Then he reached down in a bag and took out four bottles of Portuguese tawny Port wine, and two boxes of Spanish cigars. "These are for you and your brother, Charles. Split them. The cigars should last you a very long time."

"Merci beaucoup, my friend. Contrary to what you believe, between Charles and myself, these will not last as long as you think. I know what you have given me before."

"Monsieur Jardeen, these are even better. The tobacco is imported from the French West Indies, and the cigars are made in Barcelona and on the beautiful island of Majorca.

"Malta has long been an international trading port. During the days of the Moors, alcohol was forbidden on the island. Afterward, during the short French rule and then a lengthy British rule, alcohol was reintroduced. At the present time, alcohol is imported from foreign French territories, and from Barbados and Puerto Rico. It may be the premier hard liquor in the world, as well as the cheapest. I have on my ship two barrels of the best that Malta has to offer. I can have one of the barrels rowed to the beach, if you will send a wagon to bring it into the city."

"Again, merci beaucoup," Antoine told him in a most gracious manner and bowing slightly. "I am honored that you have such high regard for us brothers. We will have to work out a time to go out to the beach. Meanwhile, you must be a guest in my home."

The captain responded and thanked him, "Normally, I would look forward to staying in your home. I am sure that it is magnificent. However, I have to return to my ship each evening to check on my crew and ensure that all is well."

"I understand. Perhaps next time, when you return with the explosives and we begin our labor of restoration, you can meet and enjoy the hospitality of my family. Right now, I am staying in my brother's manoir, while my home here in the city is restored from damages inflicted by Richelieu's commanders during the siege. Hopefully, by the time you return, the restoration will be complete. So far, work is not being completed as fast as I had hoped."

"Before I go back to my ship for the night, may we discuss the harbor work to be done?" the captain asked.

"Do you think forty-five days is sufficient to get the blasting material and supplies, plus a crew of seamen laborers to supplement the workmen that I can enlist here in La Rochelle?" Antoine asked.

"Yes, and I can be here sooner."

With that, they shook hands and Antoine arranged for his coachman to drive the captain out to the cove.

Chapter 45
Channel Clearing

For the next forty-five days, Antoine spent a portion of each day accommodating his mayoral duties. This involved a substantial amount of time conferring with Governor Bouché and coordinating with his own staff. So far, cooperation and teamwork among the staff were excellent, and the give-and-take between mayor and the staff made working conditions a lot less tense than they could have been. The staff seemed to understand that Antoine needed to spend time at his boatyard, and they worked hard to make sure that time away from the office was available to him. Everyone wanted to help him get a firm footing in the job, but they realized how vital it was to the city to get the harbor cleared. So, in a certain sense, they viewed the harbor issue as part of his mayoral duties. Although the subject matters which they discussed centered primarily around civic issues, clearance of the harbor was also a designated topic that circulated in their meetings.

While in his mayoral office, Antoine began to research city records for the names of the ships still afloat inside the barricade, and the ones still seaworthy, regardless of any damage they may have suffered in the siege. Antoine noted the names of the countries in which each ship was registered. Bills of lading kept a good idea of what each ship was transporting, as well as any indicated ammunition and explosives on board. This would be vital information to know before workers went crawling around in the bowels of the ships. He hoped that his research would prevent anyone from being killed while doing their job. For the ships still afloat, it would be necessary to know the owners' names in order to contact them once the channel was clear of undersea wreckage, thus allowing the owner with his crew to reclaim their ship and sail it out of the harbor. If they found ships unfit for sea travel, they would be towed or sailed, if possible, to the deepest water off the coast in the Bay of Biscay or beyond. Otherwise, they would be sunk or torn apart at the shipyard on Île de Ré for the lumber.

The rest of the forty-five days were given over to recruitment of labor from the city. The siege had left La Rochelle destitute of manpower to undertake the projects Antoine had planned. The water would be cold for the rest of the winter. Thus, the first project would be demolition of the floating rampart built by Richelieu at the mouth of the harbor. It was fortified with massive wooden beams anchored upright to an extended wooden platform, built on top of a row of sunken ships in the channel. They were evenly spaced every 6.096 meters along the platform, and were each an equal number of meters high.

Dismantlement of the uprights would be done on the platform using a system of ropes and pulleys. The pillars would be pulled from the platform onto land using a system similar to the one used by the druids in moving huge pillars of stone hundreds of miles in England for the construction of Stonehenge.

The second project would be to remove the wooden platform on which they had stood piece by piece, starting with the end farthest out in the channel, and moving the heavy timber nearer to shore with the same Stonehenge method used in removing the very heavy and bulky pillars. A section of the platform measuring 45.72 meters long would remain accessible for future use as a fishing or docking pier. Blasting sunken ship wreckage from the channel would have to wait until the spring and summer, when the water would be warmer for divers.

In midwinter, with the aid of two naval engineers sent by the king, the visible part of the barricade was removed in a matter of four months without any serious injuries or accidental deaths. At this point, the engineers expressed an interest in staying until the harbor was completely cleared, and work had at least begun on rebuilding the docks and warehouses. At the mayor's office they composed a letter to King Louis XIII updating him on the work done so far to remove the rampart, and asked his permission to stay as long as necessary to assist in the full recovery. Governor Bouché agreed to forward their letter by special courier to the king, with his recommendation for approval.

Two weeks later, the courier returned with the king's written response, congratulating the engineers and the locals on their success. King Louis approved the request of the engineers to stay, as long as they could be useful in the restoration of the city and not just the harbor.

A survey of damage to the docks and warehouses began immediately. Although some areas sustained heavy damage, none of the warehouses nor the docks were destroyed completely. In the engineers' opinions, everything was considered repairable. However, the time to complete the restoration would take at least a year. The exteriors of the warehouses were constructed with stone, which substantially withstood the bombardments of the siege. The damage was mostly to the interior walls and beams supporting the roofs. Since the harbor could not be cleared right away, it was decided to repair the warehouses first and then the docks. Wood salvaged from the rampart could be used for most of the repairs, and any new timber needed would be shipped in after the port was reopened. It was satisfying to know that they could restore a lot of the damage with the resources that were salvaged from the rampart.

Work on the warehouses was completed by August 10. For some time, Antoine's captain friend, as well as the French Navy, offloaded shipments of explosives at the deepwater port of La Pallice, just six kilometers west of La Rochelle. From there, the explosives were taken by smaller boats to the point on the beach where Antoine's hired hands would pick them up and cart them into La Rochelle for storage. Just ten days after the work that could be completed was done, work began on the sunken ships supporting the rampart. Underwater inspection revealed that the rampart's base was made up of stacked sunken ships filled with ballast, sometimes two high. In the deepest part of the channel, they were stacked three high.

Explosive charges were set, starting in the middle of the channel, and the blasting continued for three weeks. Every day the sound of blasting shook the city continuously throughout the day, from early morning to near dark. A navigable opening was finally made in the rampart. Heavier pieces of the blasted ships sank and lay on the bottom of the channel. These pieces were further blasted later on to break them into smaller, lighter pieces, making them easier to pull from the water. Flotsam which floated on the surface was picked up by scows, taken to a remote area of Île de Ré, and burned.

The navigable ships in the inner channel were then sailed to Île de Ré and the port of La Pallice, to remain until the ships were claimed by the owners. The non-navigable ships were blasted in place with bags of gunpowder. In some cases, the amount of powder needed for the blasting was minimal, as many of the ships contained explosive materials such as gunpowder, cannonballs, and small-bore ammunition, which aided in their destruction. The sunken ships also contained the decomposed bodies of the crews. In each case before the blasting occurred, a service of remembrance and prayer for eternal life were said by both the Catholic priest and an elder from the Huguenot church.

All in all, completion of the harbor clearing was completed by mid-November. Ships started bringing in new timber to complete work on the warehouses. This work was completed by February 1, 1630.

With the harbor being cleared, the engineers turned their attention to repairing and rebuilding homes for the people of La Rochelle. Workers from Île de Ré, La Pallice, other nearby towns, and rural communities came to La Rochelle for construction jobs. Work began on rebuilding the Huguenot church, businesses, restaurants, and taverns.

Major restoration to the city was finished in a two-year period. By the summer of 1632, the boatyard was reopened, and the import-export business operated under the direction of Charles and Augie Cussions, the ship captain partner. Antoine's children, together with one of Charles's sons, took over the management and operation of the boatyard. This left Antoine free to pursue his mayoral duties.

When the restoration was largely complete, Governor Bouché unexpectedly died of a heart attack. Soon after the death of Bouché, the king visited La Rochelle for a memorial service. Not knowing that the governor's religious beliefs were secretly in the Reformed faith and not Catholicism, he presided with the bishop in a memorial service for Bouché at the Catholic church. Although the bishop and the priest knew the secret, neither of them revealed it to the king.

During his stay in La Rochelle, Louis and his entourage stayed with Charles at the manoir house. While in the city, he appointed Antoine as the lord governor of La Rochelle. Upon recommendation of the clergy, he appointed Guilford Dion, a lay leader in the Catholic church of La Rochelle, as the new mayor. This was more or less in concert with the wish Antoine had expressed in the meeting among Bouché, the bishop, the priest, and Charles, including the request that he be a Catholic.

Chapter 46
New Beginnings

After the labor on the harbor and warehouses was completed, the naval engineers wanted to remain in La Rochelle. They admired the will and determination of the people who survived the siege, finding this mindset refreshing. The Jardeen brothers had shown a strong leadership role in the redevelopment effort and had worked long hours to make it a reality. Although the engineers were parishioners of the Catholic faith, they had come to admire the Huguenots and what they believed. One way or another, they planned to make La Rochelle their new home. Toward the end of the reconstruction of the business establishments, a courier arrived with a letter from the king requesting an update on the progress of their work, suggesting that, unless there was further work to do, they should return to Paris. After discussing the matter with Governor Jardeen, they responded to the king that the port of La Rochelle offered strategic potential for the establishment of a naval base. If built, in time it could become the main naval base on the west coast of France. With more blasting and removal of all the underwater wreckage, warships would have a deepwater channel into the base. The value of the base would, of course, be a tremendous asset to the government, and economically to the city itself. If the king, in his great wisdom, would allow them to remain for an undetermined time, they could make the base a reality.

The letter was reviewed and endorsed by Governor Jardeen, and given to the courier to take back to Paris.

Three weeks later they received the king's reply, approving the request and an allotment of money for the project. The money would be paid every three months, after receiving receipt of documents detailing progress of construction and proof of money spent on each completed project of the base. Louis signed off on his reply with the words "Keep Me Informed!"

The engineers, delirious with excitement, began to make plans to move their wives and children to La Rochelle. Over the next four months, the engineers worked to restore two town houses damaged in the siege. The residences repaired were in the neighborhood of the town house belonging to Michel and Elisabeth Légere.

The Légere home remained vacant, as the couple had not returned to La Rochelle after the end of the siege. With grief, the people who knew them feared that they had been robbed or killed on the ship they departed on from La Rochelle. Some believed they may have gotten sick on the ship or in some faraway land, or perhaps they just decided to settle in England, the Netherlands, Scandinavia, or one of the Mediterranean countries. Nobody, not even Colleen, the sister of Elisabeth, or their daughter, Maggie, knew their whereabouts. It was easy to assume the worst fate for them, as it seemed unlikely that they would simply abandon Maggie and their granddaughter, Elisabeth Marye. This thinking led to the possibility that they had been hunted down and assassinated by one of the king's agents, who may have been paid a bounty to seek out and execute Huguenots fleeing France. At this point, the fate of the Légeres was a deep mystery, and the possibility existed that they may never be found.

Because the Légeres had been gone so long, Governor Jardeen persuaded the new mayor to claim the house as city property and let one of the engineers move into it rent-free. If after three years the engineer was still living in La Rochelle, the city would consider deeding the property to him and his family.

Maggie was happy living in the beautiful, estate-style country home, which Charles and Antoine had originally built at the manoir for her, her daughter, Elisabeth Marye; and for Aunt Colleen. The same deal was reached with Colleen for the other engineer and his family to move into her town home. In the meantime, Antoine worked out an arrangement whereby the city agreed that the house formerly owned by the Légeres would be exempt from city taxes for three years.

The taxes for the house owned by Colleen would continue to be paid by her, since she was now living at the manoir farm rent-free.

The engineers got far more from this deal than they had expected. Nothing of value was left from the siege for Maggie to recover. All of her musical instruments had been destroyed; paintings in the house, as well as her beloved books, had been taken by the troops back to Paris. Most of the furniture in her parents' house and in Colleen's house had been destroyed. Anything spared was moved to their new home at the manoir.

The engineers left to go back home and bring their families to La Rochelle. They promised to return in one month to continue the necessary work to repair and fix the homes that had been damaged. Then labor would begin on the restoration of the businesses in the city. While working on the reclamation of the city, they looked for used furniture and home supplies that people were offering for sale or donating.

When all the work for the reconstruction of the city was completed in 1636, they began to make plans for the naval base in La Rochelle. The site chosen for the base was a large cove off of the channel, not very far south off the waterfront district. It was a deepwater site, where ships would be able to moor safely to a pier or drop anchor in the cove. The advantage of this site was its proximity to the waterfront district, as it was protected by a rather wide barrier of land and forest from the Bay of Biscay. This would offer security to the base, and ships docked there were less likely to be bombarded from enemy ships in the bay.

The naval base was dedicated by King Louis XIII in 1638, the same year that Elisabeth Marye Jardeen Horry gave birth to a baby son. The name given to the baby was Jean-Daniel Horry, Jean after her husband and Daniel being the middle name of the baby's grandfather, the Reverend Jacque Daniel Horry, who would not sacrifice his principles for the sake of his life. The reverend had been determined by Cardinal Richelieu to be a heretic. On order of the cardinal, Reverend Horry had been executed by a firing squad, blindfolded with his hands tied behind his back. Gunfire was heard frequently during the days of the siege as Huguenots were being executed. Antoine and Charles would have certainly met the same fate had they not been taken in and hidden in the Catholic church until after the siege, and Richelieu had departed the area.

Shortly after the naval base and staffing of the facilities were underway, operational plans were made for naval ships to begin arriving and departing on a daily basis. Naval Captain Richârd Montaine, the senior of the two engineers, was promoted to admiral and assumed command of the base. The other engineer was made a naval captain and given second in command of the base. The officers became close friends with Antoine and Charles. All of the repairs that had to be done on naval ships were done at the boatyard or at the shipbuilding company on Île de Ré, which the Jardeen brothers were at that time half owners. They invested ownership into the company to prevent closure in the future due to possible efforts to blockade the channel in La Rochelle. It also gave them access to a large dry dock for building bigger ships. In the back of their minds, Antoine and Charles pictured keeping the headquarters of the import-export business in La Rochelle and having a huge warehouse on Île de Ré, located directly on the waterfront with a large wharf for merchant ships to dock. This would facilitate the loading and unloading of their goods.

Meanwhile, the Huguenots who had fled La Rochelle at the beginning of the siege were now beginning to return safely to their homes in the city; although many were never seen or heard from again. Monsieur Ronsérre had found two attorney partners to take over his law firm in Fontenay-le-Comte. With the buyout money, he returned to La Rochelle. With great sadness from all who knew him, Ronsérre died unexpectedly just six months later from natural causes. He was buried in the cemetery on Charles's estate. No one knew where to find his children, so there were only the Jardeens to mourn him. The Catholic bishop and the priest attended the service, and asked permission to present a short eulogy about him. With the death of Ronsérre, Governor Jardeen appointed Monsieur Ravenel of his staff to be chief counsel for the province of Aunis, as well as for the city.

In 1640, Antoine died at the remarkable age of eighty-five from multiple medical conditions, primarily due to complications of stress from taking on too many obligations of business and civic duties. The stress culminated in his coming down with pneumonia, followed shortly by a major stroke. It was unheard of for a person, even the healthiest, in his time to live so long. His body was embalmed and buried a week later in the family cemetery next to that of his beloved wife Martine. Many citizens of La Rochelle, including the Catholic bishop and the priest, attended the funeral at the Huguenot church. The bishop gave a short eulogy at graveside remembering Antoine as a fine father, a fine citizen, and an honest businessman that all citizens of La Rochelle, including Catholics, would miss.

No greater compliment could be said about anyone.

By this time, all of Antoine's children were grown; none were living at home. Jacqueline continued to live in the house with the aging kitchen and waitstaff, as well as the coachman whom she and Antoine employed. But, lonely and heartbroken at the loss of Antoine, she too soon passed away just five months later, at the age of eighty-two.

Seeming like their empire was suddenly crashing down, Charles took control of the boatyard and realigned the staff to where their talents and expertise were most needed. Simultaneously, Charles began working several hours a day with Captain Augie Cussions to grow the import-export business. Cussions was also made available to the boatyard for consulting on maritime construction and repairs.

The king offered Charles the governorship, but he politely declined it. With the passing of his brother, Charles knew that the strain of politics, both locally and court politics in Paris, would be too much for him, as it had been for Antoine. When Charles declined, Monsieur Ravenel was appointed to the governorship, and one of Monsieur Ronsérre's associates from Fontenay-le-Comte was appointed to become the chief counsellor to Ravenel.

After Jacqueline died, Charles and Paulette approached Antoine's two living children to discuss what to do with the residence in the city. Paul, the oldest sibling, urged his uncle, Charles, to give the house to his sister, Marye, who by this time had become indispensable in the management of the boatyard and had not yet found time for marriage. Charles, knowing full well of her contributions, agreed. But when offered to Marye, she turned it down saying, "There are too many memories of my mother, my father, and my brother, Tomas, for me to live there. I am grateful for your consideration, and I will always be grateful, but I am happy staying with a friend."

In December 1638, Maggie became a grandmother to Jean-Daniel Horry.

In the spring of 1641, long after the siege had ended and people were returning to the city, Maggie decided to reopen the art gallery and bookstore in La Rochelle. She found that running a business at her age was a near impossibility. Afraid that the stores would fail at her age, she wrote a letter to Jean-Baptiste explaining her dilemma, and begged for Elisabeth Marye and him to move to La Rochelle and accept a managing partnership with her in the two businesses. The letter was delivered by courier to them in Angoulême, with instructions to the courier to wait there for a reply. Happily, the courier arrived back in La Rochelle two weeks later with a written reply. The response was, "Yes, very soon."

She made plans to retire to the manoir estate and live with her Aunt Colleen, who at her age surely needed assistance. She would give the house she owned with Captain Chevin to her daughter and husband. Having her grandson nearby promised to be a great joy. Six weeks later, Jean-Baptiste and Elisabeth Marye arrived with their toddler son, little Jean-Daniel. Upon arrival, they begged Maggie to live with them rather than move back to the manoir estate. They convinced her they needed her to take care of Jean-Daniel while they were working at the stores, and that they needed her close by for guidance in the businesses.

Elisabeth Marye pulled her mother aside and told her that she must stay, and that she might have the master-bedroom suite on the first floor while Jean-Baptiste, the baby, and she would have their sleeping quarters on the second floor. So it was agreed.

However, soon after Elisabeth Marye, with her husband and her young son, relocated to La Rochelle, her mother began to exhibit strange, erratic behaviors. It seemed as if Maggie was beginning to worship as a mystic. She kept very much to herself, showed little interest in the businesses, gave very little attention to Jean-Daniel, and quit attending church. The final rearrangement of her life was that she gave complete ownership of the businesses to her daughter and son-in-law. Most days, she would have her coachman take her out to the manoir estate, where she would disappear into the woods and kneel in prayer for several hours at a time. Finally, she began lighting candles and speaking in tongues at the family cemetery.

Within a year, Maggie seemed to have completely lost her mind; she did not keep herself clean and for the most part had quit eating. She kept praying for the safety of her parents, and sometimes acted out the role of the mother who never returned to her. Most alarmingly, she talked about spirits appearing to her and strange voices in her head. One morning, she did not appear for breakfast.

Elisabeth Marye went to her room to check on her and found that she had died during the night. Unbeknownst to her daughter as to what the French troops had done with her stepfather's body when he was executed during the Siege of La Rochelle, she buried her mother in the family cemetery next to the grave of her beloved Tomas.

Four months later, without any family left, Maggie's Aunt Colleen died of what appeared to be a lonely heart, despite Charles and his family paying close attention to her. She was buried in the family cemetery next to her beloved Maggie.

Very early in 1641, Elisabeth Marye became pregnant again, and in November of that year gave birth to another baby boy. This baby was named Jean-Michel after his father and his great-grandfather, Michel Légere. And then in 1644, after thinking her childbearing years were over, she birthed a precious daughter. In the meantime, the businesses that she and Jean-Baptiste took over from Maggie revived, and quickly outgrew the success enjoyed before the siege.

In 1645, Charles was an old man with health issues. He was having trouble getting around and needed assistance for bathing and dressing. He no longer was able to travel into the city, the boatyard, or to the business office of import-export. Each of his children declined offers of partnership in the businesses. Arrangements were made to make Antoine's son Paul, who had been educated at the famous business school of the University of Fontainebleau, the president of the boatyard with a 51 percent controlling interest. Captain Cussions was made a 49 percent owner as vice president, with the additional duty as head of the design department. Antoine's daughter, Marye, who was educated at the University of Poitou, was made president of the import-export business with 51 percent ownership and

Augie was made vice president with a 49 percent ownership. By this time, Marye Jardeen had married one of Captain Chevin's sons and given birth to a baby boy.

All of the affairs of the manoir estate had been given over to Charles's children, as they had wished. In respect of Charles's contributions to the boatyard and the import-export business, they were to each receive a negotiable percentage of profit from those businesses. Chevin's children additionally were to receive 3 percent of the profits from the bookstore and art gallery. Paul and Marye were to receive a negotiable amount of the profits from the manoir estate; this could either be taken annually as cash, taken as an equitable amount of food and wine produced on the estate, or taken as a subsidy for residency on the estate.

In the fall of 1645, during the time that the foliage of the trees was the most beautiful and the weather was beginning to get a certain crispness, Charles passed away. It happened suddenly one day in mid-October of a heart attack, while the coachman was giving him a grand tour of the estate in one of the family coaches with his wife, Paulette, and his two sons. He was buried on a Saturday afternoon in the family cemetery near his beloved adopted brother, Antoine. Antoine's wives, Martine and Jacqueline; nephew, Tomas; and niece, Maggie, had also been laid to rest there. Immediately after his burial, arrangements were made for workers from the farm to redo the enclosure of the cemetery. The one wall, with steps allowing persons to climb up and then down into the cemetery, was removed. The two walls that connected to that end were vastly extended, allowing for the addition of space for new grave sites. The wall which was removed was replaced with a high new wall and heavy, iron locking gate, made by the local blacksmith. The additional space ensured that future generations of Jardeens, Chevins, and Horrys could be buried there.

In 1646, an English merchant ship docked in La Rochelle. Paul Jardeen remembered that it was the same ship which Michel and Elisabeth Marye Légere had sailed on when escaping La Rochelle, just before the siege began in 1628.

Meeting with the ship captain, Paul Jardeen asked, "Were you the captain of the ship when it left La Rochelle in 1628? If so, do you recall Michel and Elisabeth Marye Légere?"

Answering without hesitation, the captain replied, "Oui, I was indeed the captain at the time, and yes, I remember the Légere couple well."

"Is there some reason that you remember them after nearly fifteen years?" Paul asked.

"I remember them because they were a nice couple and they were very cordial to me," the captain told him. "I remember them because they told me that because of their religious beliefs and Michel's political record, their lives would be in danger. No doubt they would certainly have been among the first people arrested and executed, or imprisoned by the French forces on the order of Cardinal Richelieu, the king's chief minister."

"When and where did they leave your ship?" Paul asked.

"I sailed from La Rochelle directly to London with my cargo of exports from several Mediterranean ports of call and those picked up here in La Rochelle. On the voyage from here to England, we discussed many times what options they might have in London. I gave them the names of some important people there whom I was sure would help them to relocate. Because of the French agents working for Cardinal Richelieu who had infiltrated London and other cities in England, I advised them to immediately change their names, and not to identify being from La Rochelle or discuss their religious beliefs with anyone."

"How much did they pay you to transport them to London, and why did they select London?"

"They did offer to pay me, but because of their reason for fleeing France, I declined to accept any payment from them. As far as to 'why London,' it was the biggest city in England and easy to disappear into the mass of people, remaining unfound."

"Wouldn't their native French tongues give them away?"

"No, I don't think so. Remember, the English have always supported the Reformed Church and its people in its battles against the French government. If threatened, the English would hide and protect them."

"Have you seen the Légeres since they departed your ship?"

"Oui, I saw them several times afterward. They were happy and said that they did not intend to return to France, not even for their daughter or granddaughter. It would be too risky. To even try to contact them would be dangerous, because of prying eyes."

"When did you last see them?"

"You may or may not know that there was an outbreak of smallpox in London in 1630. Because they were refugees, they felt safer living in a lower-income section of the city and living by the standards of the people around them. Their neighborhood was heavily hit by the smallpox. To end their story, late in the summer of 1630, they both contracted the disease and died rather soon thereafter."

After meeting with the ship captain, Paul felt unsure of what he had been told, but there was no way to confirm or deny the information that had been given to him. In his mind, it was a moot point. The only person who might find this information relevant was their granddaughter, Elisabeth Marye, and she never brought up the subject. He thought it best not to create a possible distraction in her life, or the lives of Jean-Baptiste and their children or grandchildren. Right or wrong, he made the decision to keep the information secret, and as heartfelt as it might be, it would probably die with him. However, if asked by one of the family, it would be impossible not to tell what he knew.

Chapter 47
Post-Restoration

After the siege of La Rochelle, Catholic clergy all across France rejoiced, for they thought that at last the Reformed movement was merely a passing nuisance that had infected the one true Church. Even though most people of the Catholic faith disliked Cardinal Richelieu, they admired him for having a strong hand in his attempt to put an end to the alleged heretics who had been brainwashed into the Reformed faith. Although the king personally had low regard for his chief minister, it was easier for him that it was Richelieu who did the deed, rather than he himself having to declare war on the Huguenots.

The king had bigger problems with which he had to deal, and the cardinal had other issues to resolve. Besides, the Edict of Nantes remained in effect. Neither man fully realized the resolute determination of the Protestants in France.

Cardinal Richelieu died December 4, 1642. Before he died, Richelieu mentored Cardinal Jules Mazarin, an Italian, to succeed him as the chief minister to the king of France. Mazarin served from the time of Richelieu's death until his own death on March 9, 1661. Mazarin had attended a Jesuit university but refused to join the Jesuit order. Because of his education, he became a diplomat and a politician. At the end of the Thirty Years' War,[42] Cardinal Mazarin was the de facto ruler of France. He was largely responsible for the development of Westphalian concepts and principles that would come to guide Europe's foreign policies and world order.

After the siege of La Rochelle, neither Richelieu nor Mazarin gave much attention to the soaring influence of the Huguenots in French business dealings, the armed forces, or the arts. Louis XIII, until his death in 1643, seemed to adopt a laissez-faire attitude toward the Huguenots; Richelieu and Mazarin were too busy accruing further power for themselves.

The successor to Louis XIII was his son Louis XIV,[40] the "Sun King." This reference to him was related to the fact that France was now at its peak in world affairs. Much of the credit for France's rise in power among the many nations of the world should be given to Cardinal Mazarin.

As a young man, Louis XIII had enjoyed many hunting trips in the woods surrounding the small village of Versailles, just seventeen kilometers from Paris. In 1624, he ordered construction of a small hunting lodge at Versailles. Four years later, Louis bought the seigneury of Versailles from the owner and started enlargements to his lodge. At the age of fourteen, Louis XIII had married Anne of Austria, daughter of King Philip of Spain. Anne did not bear children until she birthed Louis XIV in 1638, twenty-three years after her marriage to Louis XIII. There may be doubt as to the paternal parenting, because of the age of Louis XIII and his failure to father a child for so many years. Also, Anne had many lovers outside of her marriage, including Cardinal Mazarin. This child was Louis XIV, the heir to the throne.

When Louis XIV was just four and a half years old, his father, King Louis XIII, died in 1643. His mother, Anne, became the regent acting for him. Cardinal Mazarin became his chief tutor and educator. As an accomplished politician, Mazarin largely controlled the government and influenced the political views of his young protégé. For the Huguenots, the political and religious ramifications of France were not good. In 1661, upon the death of Cardinal Mazarin, Louis assumed the throne of France and took on the duties of the chief minister. This ended the rule of cardinal ministers. Henceforth, the rule of France promised to be that of an absolute monarch.

After the death of his father, Louis XIV spent much time at Versailles in his father's beloved lodge. For him, it was an escape from the dark and dangerous city of Paris.

After the death of Cardinal Mazarin, the Sun King began a renovation and expansion of Versailles, with plans to establish it as the royal court. In 1678, he began to establish it as the center of monarchy in the hope of gaining more control of the government from the nobles of France, many of whom were Huguenots, and to assure his safety from the criminal element of Paris. He required nobles of a certain ruling status to spend part of each year at Versailles. This step was taken to avoid accruing their own regional power at the expense of his rule as monarch. He believed that religious tolerance was a threat to his political rule of the country. Thus, by the early 1680s, his efforts to establish religious uniformity throughout France generated much public hostility. In October 1685, being a devout Catholic and under tremendous pressure from his second wife, Madame de Maintenon, he revoked the Edict of Nantes. The revocation was ordered at the Palace of Fontainebleau, a hunting encampment south of Paris.

Madame de Maintenon was a devout Catholic who favored persecution of the Protestants and acted under the very strong influence of her Jesuit confessor, François de la Chaise.

The eight most significant articles of the revocation,[41] stipulated in summary, were:

1. All temples of worship of the Reformed Church situated in France, or any territory controlled by France, shall be demolished without delay.

2. Forbade persons of the Reformed faith to meet any longer in any place or private home for the purpose of worship.

3. Forbade noblemen to hold or permit to be held in their houses or fiefdom any Reformed worship; such violations would be punished with imprisonment and confiscation of property.

4. Provided for all ministers of the Reformed Church to either become converts to the Catholic faith or to leave the kingdom, or any land or territory controlled by France, within fourteen days of the issuance of the revocation. Not to preach or exhort Reformed principles and creeds to anyone, the punishment being executed by beheading on the galleys. Forbade instruction in any public or private school in any regard to the creed and beliefs of the Reformed faith.

5. Children born to persons of the Reformed faith should henceforth be baptized by the parish priests, under penalty of a fine of five hundred livres, and for the children to be sent to the churches for that purpose and that the children henceforth be brought up in the one true religion: Catholic, Apostolic, and Roman Religion. Local magistrates were enjoined to enforce compliance with this article.

6. In consideration of persons of the Reformed faith who may have emigrated before the revocation from France or any of the lands or territories, to return, without prejudice, within four months to

their homes or possessions from which they emigrated; those who might choose not to return were subject to having their home and possessions confiscated.

7. Prohibited all members of the Reformed faith, together with wives and children, henceforth from leaving the kingdom of France or its other lands and territories, or removing their goods and effects from the kingdom, or other French-controlled land or territories under penalty of beheading of the men upon the galley, and imprisonment of such subject women.

8. Liberty be granted to members of the Reformed faith until such time as God may enlighten them to remain in our cities and towns therein to continue commerce and enjoy their possessions without bias or prejudice, provided they do not engage in the exercise of said religion, or meet under pretext of prayer or religious services. Penalty for such acts would be imprisonment or confiscation.

Almost immediately after the edict was issued, Catholic mobs throughout France turned out on the streets, attacking and murdering persons known to be Huguenots. Although not totally exempt from such riots, the amity between the Jardeens with the Catholic hierarchy and the charitable benevolence shown to the poor, without regard to religion, prevented bloodshed in La Rochelle like that which happened in most of the rest of France.

By 1661, Jean-Michel, the young son of Elisabeth Marye Horry, had served in the French army in Flanders and was discharged from the service. Before being discharged from the army, Jean met and married a beautiful young French aristocrat named Madeline du Frene. By the end of that year, they were living in Paris, where Madeline was becoming a noted writer of history. She was also an art historian working as a senior curator at the Louvre, the royal palace, and residence in Paris for the king. In September 1662, Madeline gave birth to a baby boy, whom she and Jean-Michel named Daniel, after his uncle, Jean-Daniel, and his grandfather, the Reverend Jacque Daniel Horry. Daniel was raised in the Reformed Church of Paris, where his father was active as an elder. His mother was Catholic, but in name only. Although she paid a monthly tithe to the Catholic Church, she only attended periodically. And although she had sympathy for the Huguenot beliefs, because of her career she did not renounce her Catholic faith.

In 1675, having just turned thirteen, Daniel was admitted to the French Naval Maritime Academy in Le Havre, France, on the coast of the English Channel. Although Daniel was a rebellious youth and a good, yet not superb, student, he was admitted to the academy on the outstanding naval record of his great-great-great-grandfather, Admiral Phillippe Jardeen; the reputation of his great-great-grandfather, Antoine Jardeen, the famous boatbuilder in La Rochelle; and his great-grandfather, Tomas, the skilled designer of boats and ships. The historic nobility of the Horry family in the province of Angoulême and aristocracy of his mother's family in Paris did not hurt.

In 1681, Daniel graduated from the naval academy after six years and he began active duty as a midshipman in the French Navy. In 1682, after only one year of training aboard ship instead of the standard three years, he took and passed the examination for the rank of sublieutenant. Because of his family connections, Daniel was now able to wear an insignia of the royal flag with gold fleurs-de-lis and the royal arms on his uniform. The display of this insignia indicated special royal favor with the crowned monarch. He was assigned to the naval ship *Saint Phillippe*, built in 1663 and named for Daniel's ancestor, Admiral Phillippe Jardeen, as the first mate to the captain. Most of the time that he served aboard was in the island chain of the French West Indies. The seven islands comprising the island chain were Guadeloupe, Martinique, the collectives of Saint Barthélemy and Saint Martin, and the dependencies of Les Saintes, Marie-Galante, and La Désirade. In early 1685, Daniel was promoted to full lieutenant and reassigned to the naval base in La Rochelle as the chief aide to the base commander, Admiral Richârd Montaine. The relationship between these two men was very relaxed. The commander fully trusted Daniel. In fact, all the incoming information from the admiralty, or from the royal court in Paris, was received on a routine basis by Daniel and disseminated to the commander and to other officers with a need to know.

One critical piece of information which passed Daniel's desk in early October 1685 was a message from the admiralty that on October 31, King Louis XIV would announce the Revocation of the Edict of Nantes. Punishment for those who violated the restrictions to be imposed in the revocation order would be severe. It was at this point he knew that his life would depend on his permanently leaving France for exile in another country. He also knew that his father, Jean-Michel, was now an elder in the Reformed Church of Paris, and that his beliefs were too strong to forsake the Huguenot faith and pledge allegiance to the Catholic Church. No doubt his mother would be safe, for she had never totally forsaken Catholic creeds and participation in the Catholic Church.

Daniel began to plan his escape. Meeting the captain of a naval ship from the Netherlands which was visiting the naval base, Daniel asked if they could soon get together at a tavern in La Rochelle. When they were beginning to feel the effects of, perhaps, too many glasses of beer, Daniel led the conversation to religion and found out that Protestantism was the national religion in the Netherlands. Also, the captain himself was a Huguenot.

After further conversation, Daniel mentioned the certainty of the revocation. He said, "I must leave France. Would you be willing to transport me to the Netherlands?"

The captain answered in French, "Oui." He went on to explain, "I will be sailing from La Rochelle at dawn on the morning of October 29. In the evening of October 28, I will host a departure party onboard for the officers and crew. I would invite you, but the commander and senior officers from the base will be present. I will make sure that they get very drunk and will keep them late. They will surely sleep very late the next morning. That will help ensure you're not being seen by other officers. Will it be possible for you to come to the ship at Pier 8, say, at 4:00 a.m.? I will greet you on the pier and hide you away until we sail and are out to sea. Just make sure that no one sees you. Although at that time of the morning, I doubt that anyone will. Wear your uniform, though, just in case you are seen. And if anyone stops and asks questions, tell them that a messenger on one of the ships came to your room and woke you up, telling you that there is an administrative problem with the pending departure of his ship and the captain has sent for you. Oh, I will swap your uniform for a Dutch naval uniform when you are onboard and provide you with papers to legally enter the Netherlands."

"Okay, I will meet you at the designated time."

Just to be sure that the captain was not too drunk to remember, Daniel made a point of seeing him again in the meantime for drinks and brought up the matter of his escape. "I just want to make sure that everything is still okay," he asked the captain in an offhanded way.

"Of course, I am looking forward to meeting you at the ship at four o'clock the morning of the twenty-ninth."

"Very good," Daniel assured him. "I will be there on time."

The next few days were troubling for Daniel. He knew that he was doing the right thing, but he was very worried and anxious about being caught. During the day on October 28, he complained to the commander about feeling ill and asked, "May I be excused from the office early today, so I can rest?"

"Of course. Do you need medical attention?" the commander asked.

"No, sir," Daniel replied. "Maybe a night's rest will do me good."

"Hey, listen to me," the commander told him. "I am going to a party tonight on the Dutch ship. I am sorry you don't feel well, or I would take you along. I will be out late and will probably not come in until late tomorrow, or maybe not at all. Why don't you just be on the safe side and take tomorrow off and rest? I will see you when you are well."

"Thank you, sir," Daniel said as he saluted. *Perfect!* he thought to himself.

Chapter 48
Freedom for One, but Not for the Other

The night of October 28, Daniel got no sleep. In fact, he didn't even go to bed for fear that he might not wake up on time. Normally, he would have one of the sailors on duty in the officers' hall to awake him at a specific time, but that would not be a wise decision this time. So he stayed awake, with just a small candle burning. But it did not give off much light. Since he was allegedly sick, a strong light in his room might arouse unwanted curiosity. However, he did not dress in his uniform, just in case someone might knock on his door. Thinking of a few personal things most valuable to him, he gathered them up and put them in a bag. Then he just sat in his underwear and waited, daring not to lie down, or to allow himself to fall asleep sitting up in a chair. He dared not consume any alcohol. There would be time enough to have a few drinks on the ship. Putting on his uniform would be the last thing he would do. Around three o'clock in the morning, he began to dress. Shortly before four o'clock, he gathered up his bag and walked out the door for what he hoped would be forever; he was throwing away a promising naval career, but that did not matter. This was a step away from a tyrannical government to, hopefully, a future in which he aimed for personal and religious freedom. The stories told about his great-grandparents, Tomas and Margarite, were enough to make him shake with anger whenever he thought about them, and that was often.

He left the building by a side door, so as not to be seen by the on-duty guard in the lobby. Fortunately, it was very dark outside. The moon and most of the stars were hidden by overhanging clouds. It was fairly cold, and the wind was beginning to pick up. It was such a sullen night that it was very unlikely he would meet anyone on the way. The route to the pier was one that he knew by heart. It was just a short walk. As he approached, he saw that the ship had already pushed away from the pier and was anchored in the channel, with the bow facing downstream. When he got to where the ship had been docked, the captain and two seamen were waiting with a small boat ready to row him out to the ship. When they were about halfway to the ship, the captain told him, "Get down and lie out of sight in the bottom of the boat. Do it quietly. Just slip off your seat and down in the boat. A *sentinelle* is watching us from the pier!"

They kept rowing as if they did not see him. They rowed around the aft end of the ship to the gangplank on the starboard side. Being on the opposite side of the ship from the pier, the sentinelle was not able to see, even if the moon had been visible to light up the sky, how many people got off the boat.

The captain told Daniel, "He does not suspect anything. He is just a watchman making his regular rounds. While we were waiting for you, he came out on the pier. I talked to him and told him that I was waiting for one of my crewmen to return from a night of liberty on shore, and that he would be the last person returning to the ship. I assured him the ship would be sailing soon afterward. I doubt that anyone has missed you from your room. And if you were seen by the sentinelle, he probably figured you to be my late-arriving crew member."

The Dutch naval ship which Daniel was about to board that early morning was the *Vrijheid*. Despite its age, it was outfitted with the newest technology of the time. It was of modest size, built for speed, and moderately armed: a perfect ship for intercepting other vessels at sea and, if required, for holding its own in battle.

Once aboard, the captain immediately took Daniel to his quarters and gave him a Dutch naval officer's uniform, with instructions to change into it in the event they had any trouble exiting La Rochelle and, if by chance they were interrogated by the French, to pretend not to understand what they were asking. Also, he must continue to wear the uniform at sea until they cleared the English Channel and were into the Zuiderzee, nearing Amsterdam. Not only would this give him the respect of the crew, it would be an added precaution just in case they were stopped and boarded by a French naval ship.

Just before six o'clock, the captain gave the order to hoist anchor, and the ship was underway. The order was given to proceed through the inner harbor at a slow speed and to navigate close to the middle of the channel in deeper water, so as to not endanger any piers or docks jutting out into the channel on the starboard side, or any pieces of sunken ships. Once they passed the point where Cardinal Richelieu had built the rampart before and during the siege of the city, the *Vrijheid* adjusted the sails for increased speed. When the ship reached the outer point of the channel, the captain ordered a starboard course, which would allow for passage between the easterly tip of Île de Ré and the westerly coast of France. Once the ship cleared the tip of the island, an order was given to steer a north-northwesterly course up to and beyond Brest. The captain was experienced in the course taken, and was careful to miss Belle-Île and the island of Ushant, which is the most westerly point of France. After passing the Quélern Peninsula, the ship took a starboard turn into the English Channel. After changing position to an easterly direction, the captain followed the northern coasts of France and Belgium into the North Sea. At Helder, the ship made a starboard turn from the North Sea into the Zuiderzee and set a southern course to Amsterdam. The trip from La Rochelle was approximately seven hundred nautical miles and took three days at a speed of ten to fifteen knots, powered along by a strong current and a good tailwind.

As the ship approached Amsterdam, Daniel changed back into his French uniform, as custom and immigration agents would come onboard once the ship was docked, and before any of the crew were allowed to depart.

As hoped, the weather, under bright-blue skies and fluffy white clouds, gave them enough wind and currents that they arrived late afternoon on October 31. News of the revocation would not reach Amsterdam for several days, maybe a week or more.

The captain told Daniel to change into his French uniform. No one could depart the ship until custom and immigration agents came aboard. This was normal after a naval ship arrived from a tour of foreign ports. In this case, the Dutch ship had stops in Marseilles, Majorca, Barcelona, and Lisbon.

Before those agents came aboard, the captain coached Daniel. "Wearing your French uniform, tell the immigration agents that you are asking for asylum in the Netherlands due to religious persecution in France. Show him your paper of commission in the French Navy. He will know the meaning of the golden fleurs-de-lis on your uniform. Tell them that just today, the French king revoked the Edict of

Nantes, and that because of your religious preference in France, you are subject to being imprisoned or executed if returned there."

Meanwhile, in Paris, the formed dragonnade force, comprised of selected military soldiers, received instructions to begin arresting Huguenots. The most explicit order from the king was to "immediately arrest all clergy and officials of the Reformed Church, seize church records, and lock the doors of the Protestant churches."

All magistrates in Paris were given orders by the king "to have each of the church officials brought before the court, interrogated on their role in the church, given the chance to sign an affidavit affirming their conversion to the beliefs and creeds of the Catholic Church, and to actively support and participate in its religious activities." Those who refused to sign were to be imprisoned. After fourteen days of imprisonment, if they had not signed a statement of conversion, a date was set for either exile to slavery in a far-off land, or execution by beheading at the galley or by firing squad.

In Paris, the capital city of France, roundup of Reformed Church officials could begin immediately. Roundup in other sections of France would be delayed until the king's order was fully disseminated by couriers.

The next day, dragoons descended on the First Reformed Church of Paris and arrested the minister. Obtaining records of the officials and members of the church, raids began on homes in Paris seeking out these persons. The second day after the revocation and issuance of the king's arrest order, two dragoons knocked on the door of Daniel's parents. Jean-Michel Horry, being an elder of the Reformed Church, and his wife, Madame du Frene, despite her protest of being a practicing Catholic, were both led away in restraints and taken to the Parisian jail. Their hearing before a magistrate was not until three days after their arrest. Jean-Michel refused when presented with the opportunity to renounce his Reformed beliefs and convert to the Catholic faith. He was given a second and a third chance, and each time responded, "I refuse to renounce the Reformed Church and will not revert to Catholicism."

The judge ordered that he be returned to his jail cell, and after fourteen days be brought back before him. He was told, "At that time, if you still refuse the offer to renounce the Reformed faith and revert to Catholicism, you may be given a death sentence. Do you understand?"

"Your Honor, I understand," he told the magistrate. "But you should go ahead and sentence me to death right now, for my answer then will still be NO."

Without giving him a chance to say goodbye to his wife, the magistrate ordered Jean-Michel Horry back to his cell.

The next prisoner to be interrogated was Madame du Frene. He asked her, without speaking her name or giving acknowledgment to her apparent nobility, "Are you a member of the First Reformed Church of Paris, or any other Reformed church in the Kingdom of France?"

"Non, Your Honor," she answered. "I was raised as a devout Catholic and continue to this very day to be a practicing Catholic."

"Have you ever secretly met in someone's home or business to worship as a Huguenot?"

"Non, Your Honor, as I have told you, I am a devout Catholic."

"Have you ever read the Protestant Bible, or have you read books about the Huguenot faith and creeds?"

"Non, Your Honor, I attest for the third time that I am a devout Catholic."

"If you are a devout Catholic, why did you marry Monsieur Horry?" the magistrate asked her.

"Your Honor, I married Monsieur Horry because he was an officer in the French Army. In 1672, he was sent to Flanders to fight for his country in the Franco-Dutch War. He suffered serious wounds in the Battle of Seneffe on August 11, 1674. He was shot in the left arm, which had to be amputated when it became infected from blood poisoning and gangrene. For his injury he was awarded France's highest medal for bravery on the battlefield and saving the lives of the troops who served under him. He is a war hero.

"I married him because I loved him. I married him because of his morals. I married him because of his integrity and because of his sense of social justice. He and I have a mutual interest in literature and the arts. At the time we married, he was a young soldier. By the time that he was sent to the front lines in Flanders, he had risen in rank to that of a senior officer. We have shared memories of many wonderful and beautiful places. Most importantly, I married him because I loved him deeply, and I still—"

The magistrate interrupted and continued to interrogate her. "And what interest do you have in the arts and literature?"

"Your Honor," she replied, "I am a noted historical novelist and a published author of poetry. I studied art appreciation at the Sorbonne, and in Florence, Italy. I am now the chief curator of art at the royal Palace of the Louvre."

"Are you telling me that you work for King Louis XIV of France?"

"Your Honor, I do. I see him every day that he spends at the royal Palace of the Louvre. I accompany His Majesty whenever he wishes to view the art of the palace. I decide on which art to purchase for the palace, where it is to be hung, and when it is to be taken down and put into storage. I am also the curator of the jewels and other collections at the palace."

"Why is that so?" he asked.

"Your Honor, it is at the king's invitation that I can interpret each piece of art and each piece of every other collection in the palace for him."

Without further interrogation, the magistrate, calling her by name and indicating her mark of entitlement, asked her, "Madame du Frene, do you attest under oath that the statements you have made here today before me and this court are true and accurate?"

"Your Honor, I do attest that my statements are true and accurate."

"Your statements will be so reflected in the record of these proceedings," the magistrate told her. "You are free to go now, without penalty or punishment. You are urged to continue to practice your Catholic faith and creeds."

"Will I be allowed to visit my husband?"

"No, visitation with him is forbidden for fourteen days," he replied. "The possibility of visitation rights will be reviewed at that time. You may choose to attend the hearing at that time."

Meanwhile, back in Amsterdam, customs and immigration took information from Daniel and were reviewing it. Based on his naval papers, they acknowledged him as a French citizen. Unbeknownst to him, as the captain had said that they would, they did recognize the insignia on his uniform indicating probable nobility or aristocracy. Recognizing his request for religious asylum, he was granted status as a religious refugee, but not as a citizen.

However, he was cleared to remain in the Netherlands for as long as he wished, but he could never return to France. Also, his record was stamped for a security classification so that his presence in the Netherlands was never to be publicly revealed. Then, the agents offered him a commission in the Dutch navy.

Daniel told them, "I am not prepared right now to make that decision. How long do I have to decide?"

"There is no rush," he was told. "You contact us whenever you decide."

With that, Daniel thanked the ship captain, agreed to stay in touch, and at last, with peace in his heart, walked off the ship and disappeared into the dark unknowns of the city, where no one would know his name or his history.

Chapter 49
Sentencing of Jean-Michel Horry

Fourteen days after Jean-Michel Horry first appeared before the magistrate and was imprisoned, he had to reappear to tell whether he still refused to reconvert to the Catholic faith. All persons of the Reformed Church were commanded to do this, as prescribed by King Louis XIV in the Revocation of the Edict of Nantes. Madame du Frene attended the hearing. When Jean-Michel was brought into the hearing room, she was astonished at how much weight he had lost in the past two weeks. He appeared very gaunt, as if he had had no food at all and could hardly walk without assistance. It was obvious that he was being tortured. She guessed that he was not eating, for he probably would rather die than be tortured and waste away in prison.

"May I please speak in private with my husband?" she asked the magistrate.

Remembering her nobility and connections with the king, he told her, "The king's instructions are specific as to my duties as a magistrate in interviewing and sentencing Huguenots, but the revocation does not specify or offer guidance on a woman having a private conversation with her husband. Yes, the guard will take you to a private room, and you may spend a half hour with your husband. The guard will wait outside the door."

In the room, Jean told his wife that he had been brutally tortured every day since they last met. "At this point, the torture doesn't even seem to hurt any longer. I am beaten several times a day while the guard constantly demands that I rejoin the Catholic Church. My answer is always non—and I am always beaten again. My back bleeds from the cuts that the lash leaves when I am beaten. I am told that, unless I rejoin the Catholic Church, I will be sent as a slave to a prison galleon in the Mediterranean to work as a crewman to help row the ship. Yes, I wish to die here, right now, rather than face that future."

Back in front of the magistrate, Jean was told, "You have had fourteen days to consider whether you will rejoin the Catholic Church and pledge your allegiance to the Church's creeds and beliefs. How do you respond?"

Without hesitating, Jean quietly whispered, "Your Honor, I was once a Catholic, but left the Church because of the wrongs which Martin Luther wrote about and nailed to the front door of a cathedral in Wittenberg, Germany. It is because of the ills of the Church specified in his Ninety-Five Theses that I renounced my Catholic beliefs and traditions. In my Reformed faith, I have found peace with my own personal God and His son, our Lord Jesus Christ. I cannot and will not renounce my Reformed faith for the sake of the king. You are free to do to me whatever you wish, including a sentence of death, if that is your wish."

The magistrate was stunned. No one had ever stated to him in such clarity and conciseness their religious beliefs and willingness to die for their faith. "Please, sit down while I consider your case," he told Jean-Michel and Madame du Frene.

The magistrate reread the Edict of Nantes and the penalties outlined. He considered Jean-Michel's service to his country, his fighting in Flanders, and the loss of his arm. He considered his nobility, the nobility of the wife, her closeness to the king himself, their achievements in life, and lastly, he pictured himself in place as the prisoner, standing before Jean-Michel the magistrate. *What sentence would Jean-Michel hand down to me?* But then realism entered his thinking: *If I set this man free and the king found out that I had not properly dealt with the case, what would be my fate?*

Having made a decision, he ordered, "Jean-Michel Horry, I sentence you to three years in prison for your refusal to reembrace the Catholic faith. Your sentence will be suspended after you have served your sentence. During this time, your wife will be allowed to visit you in prison as often as she chooses. Additionally, you may be allowed to visit your wife in your home three days a month. During these days of leave, you may not leave the city of Paris. Failure to return to prison on the scheduled date and time each month will result in these freedoms being taken from you. Do you understand?"

Jean answered, "Oui, Your Honor. I understand, and I do appreciate your leniency."

Four months and twelve days later, Jean-Michel Horry died in prison. His body was buried in the cemetery of the Reformed Church of Paris. Madame du Frene never remarried, never mentioned her husband's plight to the king, and with great sorrow, she never again saw her son Daniel, nor her second son, Elias, who escaped to England via the Netherlands.

And so ends the story.

On November 7, 1787, 102 years after the Revocation of the Edict of Nantes, religious and civil freedom was restored to all Frenchmen with the issuance of the Edict of Tolerance!

Appendix A

Ninety-Five Theses of Martin Luther (1521)
This documentation of Martin Luther's Ninety-Five Theses was published in the public domain by the Concordia Theological Seminary with permission for reprinting.

The Wittenberg Project

Luther, Martin. "A Disputation of Doctor Martin Luther on the Power and Efficacy of Indulgences." In *Works of Martin Luther,* edited and translated by Adolph Spaeth, L. D. Reed, Henry Eyster Jacobs, et al., Vol. 1, 29–38. Philadelphia, PA: A. J. Holman Company, 1915.

Out of love for the truth and the desire to bring it to light, the following propositions will be discussed at Wittenberg, under the presidency of the Reverend Father Martin Luther, Master of Arts and of Sacred Theology, and Lecturer in Ordinary on the same at that place. Wherefore he requests that those who are unable to be present and debate orally with us, may do so by letter.

In the Name our Lord Jesus Christ. Amen.

1. Our Lord and Master Jesus Christ, when He said *Poenitentiam agite,* willed that the whole life of believers should be repentance.

2. This word cannot be understood to mean sacramental penance, i.e., confession and satisfaction, which is administered by the priests.

3. Yet it means not inward repentance only; nay, there is no inward repentance which does not outwardly work divers mortifications of the flesh.

4. The penalty [of sin], therefore, continues so long as hatred of self continues; for this is the true inward repentance, and continues until our entrance into the kingdom of heaven.

5. The pope does not intend to remit, and cannot remit any penalties other than those which he has imposed either by his own authority or by that of the Canons.

6. The pope cannot remit any guilt, except by declaring that it has been remitted by God and by assenting to God's remission; though, to be sure, he may grant remission in cases reserved to his judgment. If his right to grant remission in such cases were despised, the guilt would remain entirely unforgiven.

7. God remits guilt to no one whom He does not, at the same time, humble in all things and bring into subjection to His vicar, the priest.

8. The penitential canons are imposed only on the living, and, according to them, nothing should be imposed on the dying.

9. Therefore the Holy Spirit in the pope is kind to us, because in his decrees he always makes exception of the article of death and of necessity.

10. Ignorant and wicked are the doings of those priests who, in the case of the dying, reserve canonical penances for purgatory.

11. This changing of the canonical penalty to the penalty of purgatory is quite evidently one of the tares that were sown while the bishops slept.

12. In former times the canonical penalties were imposed not after, but before absolution, as tests of true contrition.

13. The dying are freed by death from all penalties; they are already dead to canonical rules, and have a right to be released from them.

14. The imperfect health [of soul], that is to say, the imperfect love, of the dying brings with it, of necessity, great fear; and the smaller the love, the greater is the fear.

15. This fear and horror is sufficient of itself alone (to say nothing of other things) to constitute the penalty of purgatory, since it is very near to the horror of despair.

16. Hell, purgatory, and heaven seem to differ as do despair, almost-despair, and the assurance of safety.

17. With souls in purgatory it seems necessary that horror should grow less and love increase.

18. It seems unproved, either by reason or Scripture, that they are outside the state of merit, that is to say, of increasing love.

19. Again, it seems unproved that they, or at least that all of them, are certain or assured of their own blessedness, though we may be quite certain of it.

20. Therefore by "full remission of all penalties" the pope means not actually "of all," but only of those imposed by himself.

21. Therefore those preachers of indulgences are in error, who say that by the pope's indulgences a man is freed from every penalty, and saved;

22. Whereas he remits to souls in purgatory no penalty which, according to the canons, they would have had to pay in this life.

23. If it is at all possible to grant to any one the remission of all penalties whatsoever, it is certain that this remission can be granted only to the most perfect, that is, to the very fewest.

24. It must needs be, therefore, that the greater part of the people are deceived by that indiscriminate and highsounding promise of release from penalty.

25. The power which the pope has, in a general way, over purgatory, is just like the power which any bishop or curate has, in a special way, within his own diocese or parish.

26. The pope does well when he grants remission to souls [in purgatory], not by the power of the keys (which he does not possess), but by way of intercession.

27. They preach man who say that so soon as the penny jingles into the money-box, the soul flies out [of purgatory].

28. It is certain that when the penny jingles into the money-box, gain and avarice can be increased, but the result of the intercession of the Church is in the power of God alone.

29. Who knows whether all the souls in purgatory wish to be bought out of it, as in the legend of Sts. Severinus and Paschal.

30. No one is sure that his own contrition is sincere; much less that he has attained full remission.

31. Rare as is the man that is truly penitent, so rare is also the man who truly buys indulgences, i.e., such men are most rare.

32. They will be condemned eternally, together with their teachers, who believe themselves sure of their salvation because they have letters of pardon.

33. Men must be on their guard against those who say that the pope's pardons are that inestimable gift of God by which man is reconciled to Him;

34. For these "graces of pardon" concern only the penalties of sacramental satisfaction, and these are appointed by man.

35. They preach no Christian doctrine who teach that contrition is not necessary in those who intend to buy souls out of purgatory or to buy confessionalia.

36. Every truly repentant Christian has a right to full remission of penalty and guilt, even without letters of pardon.

37. Every true Christian, whether living or dead, has part in all the blessings of Christ and the Church; and this is granted him by God, even without letters of pardon.

38. Nevertheless, the remission and participation [in the blessings of the Church] which are granted by the pope are in no way to be despised, for they

are, as I have said, the declaration of divine remission.

39. It is most difficult, even for the very keenest theologians, at one and the same time to commend to the people the abundance of pardons and [the need of] true contrition.

40. True contrition seeks and loves penalties, but liberal pardons only relax penalties and cause them to be hated, or at least, furnish an occasion [for hating them].

41. Apostolic pardons are to be preached with caution, lest the people may falsely think them preferable to other good works of love.

42. Christians are to be taught that the pope does not intend the buying of pardons to be compared in any way to works of mercy.

43. Christians are to be taught that he who gives to the poor or lends to the needy does a better work than buying pardons;

44. Because love grows by works of love, and man becomes better; but by pardons man does not grow better, only more free from penalty.

45. Christians are to be taught that he who sees a man in need, and passes him by, and gives [his money] for pardons, purchases not the indulgences of the pope, but the indignation of God.

46. Christians are to be taught that unless they have more than they need, they are bound to keep back what is necessary for their own families, and by no means to squander it on pardons.

47. Christians are to be taught that the buying of pardons is a matter of free will, and not of commandment.

48. Christians are to be taught that the pope, in granting pardons, needs, and therefore desires, their devout prayer for him more than the money they bring.

49. Christians are to be taught that the pope's pardons are useful, if they do not put their trust in them; but altogether harmful, if through them they lose their fear of God.

50. Christians are to be taught that if the pope knew the exactions of the pardon-preachers, he would rather that St. Peter's church should go to ashes, than that it should be built up with the skin, flesh and bones of his sheep.

51. Christians are to be taught that it would be the pope's wish, as it is his duty, to give of his own money to very many of those from whom certain hawkers of pardons cajole money, even though the church of St. Peter might have to be sold.

52. The assurance of salvation by letters of pardon is vain, even though the commissary, nay, even though the pope himself, were to stake his soul upon it.

53. They are enemies of Christ and of the pope, who bid the Word of God be altogether silent in some Churches, in order that pardons may be preached in others.

54. Injury is done the Word of God when, in the same sermon, an equal or a longer time is spent on pardons than on this Word.

55. It must be the intention of the pope that if pardons, which are a very small thing, are celebrated with one bell, with single processions and ceremonies, then the Gospel, which is the very greatest thing, should be preached with a hundred bells, a hundred processions, a hundred ceremonies.

56. The "treasures of the Church," out of which the pope grants indulgences, are not sufficiently named or known among the people of Christ.

57. That they are not temporal treasures is certainly evident, for many of the vendors do not pour out such treasures so easily, but only gather them.

58. Nor are they the merits of Christ and the Saints, for even without the pope, these always work grace for the inner man, and the cross, death, and hell for the outward man.

59. St. Lawrence said that the treasures of the Church were the Church's poor, but he spoke according to the usage of the word in his own time.

60. Without rashness we say that the keys of the Church, given by Christ's merit, are that treasure;

61. For it is clear that for the remission of penalties and of reserved cases, the power of the pope is of itself sufficient.

62. The true treasure of the Church is the Most Holy Gospel of the glory and the grace of God.

63. But this treasure is naturally most odious, for it makes the first to be last.

64. On the other hand, the treasure of indulgences is naturally most acceptable, for it makes the last to be first.

65. Therefore the treasures of the Gospel are nets with which they formerly were wont to fish for men of riches.

66. The treasures of the indulgences are nets with which they now fish for the riches of men.

67. The indulgences which the preachers cry as the "greatest graces" are known to be truly such, in so far as they promote gain.

68. Yet they are in truth the very smallest graces compared with the grace of God and the piety of the Cross.

69. Bishops and curates are bound to admit the commissaries of apostolic pardons, with all reverence.

70. But still more are they bound to strain all their eyes and attend with all their ears, lest these men preach their own dreams instead of the commission of the pope.

71. He who speaks against the truth of apostolic pardons, let him be anathema and accursed!

72. But he who guards against the lust and license of the pardon-preachers, let him be blessed!

73. The pope justly thunders against those who, by any art, contrive the injury of the traffic in pardons.

74. But much more does he intend to thunder against those who use the pretext of pardons to contrive the injury of holy love and truth.

75. To think the papal pardons so great that they could absolve a man even if he had committed an impossible sin and violated the Mother of God—this is madness.

76. We say, on the contrary, that the papal pardons are not able to remove the very least of venial sins, so far as its guilt is concerned.

77. It is said that even St. Peter, if he were now Pope, could not bestow greater graces; this is blasphemy against St. Peter and against the pope.

78. We say, on the contrary, that even the present pope, and any pope at all, has greater graces at his disposal; to wit, the Gospel, powers, gifts of healing, etc., as it is written in I. Corinthians xii.

79. To say that the cross, emblazoned with the papal arms, which is set up [by the preachers of indulgences], is of equal worth with the Cross of Christ, is blasphemy.

80. The bishops, curates and theologians who allow such talk to be spread among the people, will have an account to render.

81. This unbridled preaching of pardons makes it no easy matter, even for learned men, to rescue the reverence due to the pope from slander, or even from the shrewd questionings of the laity.

82. To wit:—"Why does not the pope empty purgatory, for the sake of holy love and of the dire need of the souls that are there, if he redeems an infinite number of souls for the sake of miserable money with which to build a Church? The former reasons would be most just; the latter is most trivial."

83. Again:—"Why are mortuary and anniversary masses for the dead continued, and why does he not return or permit the withdrawal of the endowments founded on their behalf, since it is wrong to pray for the redeemed?"

84. Again: — "What is this new piety of God and the pope, that for money they allow a man who is impious and their enemy to buy out of purgatory the pious soul of a friend of God, and do not rather, because of that pious and beloved soul's own need, free it for pure love's sake?"

85. Again: — "Why are the penitential canons long since in actual fact and through disuse abrogated and dead, now satisfied by the granting of indulgences, as though they were still alive and in force?"

86. Again: — "Why does not the pope, whose wealth is today greater than the riches of the richest, build just this one church of St. Peter with his own money, rather than with the money of poor believers?"

87. Again: — "What is it that the pope remits, and what participation does he grant to those who, by perfect contrition, have a right to full remission and participation?"

88. Again: — "What greater blessing could come to the Church than if the pope were to do a hundred times a day what he now does once, and bestow on every believer these remissions and participations?"

89. "Since the pope, by his pardons, seeks the salvation of souls rather than money, why does he suspend the indulgences and pardons granted heretofore, since these have equal efficacy?"

90. To repress these arguments and scruples of the laity by force alone, and not to resolve them by giving reasons, is to expose the Church and the

pope to the ridicule of their enemies, and to make Christians unhappy.

91. If, therefore, pardons were preached according to the spirit and mind of the pope, all these doubts would be readily resolved; nay, they would not exist.

92. Away, then, with all those prophets who say to the people of Christ, "Peace, peace," and there is no peace!

93. Blessed be all those prophets who say to the people of Christ, "Cross, cross," and there is no cross!

94. Christians are to be exhorted that they be diligent in following Christ, their Head, through penalties, deaths, and hell;

95. And thus be confident of entering into heaven rather through many tribulations, than through the assurance of peace.

This text was converted to ASCII text for Project Wittenberg by Allen Mulvey, and is in the public domain. You may freely distribute, copy, or print this text. Please direct any comments or suggestions to:

Rev. Robert E. Smith
Walther Library
Concordia Theological Seminary

Appendix B

Henri IV's Edict of Nantes Grants Limited Toleration to the Huguenots (1598)[43]

Among the infinite benefits which it has pleased God to heap upon us, the most signal and precious is his granting us the strength and ability to withstand the fearful disorders and troubles which prevailed on our advent in this kingdom. The realm was so torn by innumerable factions and sects that the most legitimate of all the parties was fewest in numbers. God has given us strength to stand out against this storm; we have finally surmounted the waves and made our port of safety, — peace for our state. For which his be the glory all in all, and ours a free recognition of his grace in making use of our instrumentality in the good work. . . . We implore and await from the Divine Goodness the same protection and favor which he has ever granted to this kingdom from the beginning . . .

We have, by this perpetual and irrevocable edict, established and proclaimed and do establish and proclaim:

The recollection of everything done by one party or the other between March, 1585, and our accession to the crown, and during all the preceding period of troubles, remain obliterated and forgotten, as if no such things had ever happened.

We ordain that the Catholic Apostolic and Roman religion shall be restored and reestablished in all places and localities of this our kingdom and countries subject to our sway, where the exercise of the same has been interrupted, in order that it may be peaceably and freely exercised, without any trouble or hindrance; forbidding very expressly all persons, of whatsoever estate, quality, or condition, from troubling, molesting, or disturbing ecclesiastics in the celebration of divine service, in the enjoyment or collection of tithes, fruits, or revenues of their benefices, and all other rights and dues belonging to them; and that all those who during the troubles have taken possession of churches, houses, goods or revenues, belonging to the said ecclesiastics, shall surrender to them entire possession and peaceable enjoyment of such rights, liberties, and sureties as they had before they were deprived of them.

And in order to leave no occasion for troubles or differences between our subjects, we have permitted, and herewith permit, those of the said religion called Reformed to live and abide in all the cities and places of this our kingdom and countries of our sway, without being annoyed, molested, or compelled to do anything in the matter of religion contrary to their consciences, . . . upon conditions that they comport themselves in other respects according to that which is contained in this our present edict.

It is permitted to all lords, gentlemen, and other persons making profession of the said religion called Reformed, holding the right of high justice [or a certain feudal tenure], to exercise the said religion in their houses.

We also permit those of the said religion to make and continue the exercise of the same in all villages and places of our dominion where it was established by them and publicly enjoyed several and divers times in the year 1597, up to the end of the month of August, notwithstanding all decrees and judgments to the contrary.

We very expressly forbid to all those of the said religion its exercise, either in respect to ministry, regulation, discipline, or the public instruction of children, or otherwise, in this our kingdom and lands of our dominion, otherwise than in the places permitted and granted by the present edict.

It is forbidden as well to perform any function of the said religion on our court or retinue, or in our lands and territories beyond the mountains, or in our city of Paris, or within five leagues of the said city.

We also forbid all our subjects, of whatever quality and condition, from carrying off by force or persuasion, against the will of their parents, the children of the said religion, in order to cause them to be baptized or confirmed in the Catholic Apostolic and Roman Church; and the same is forbidden to those of the said religion called Reformed, upon penalty of being punished with special severity.

Books concerning the said religion called Reformed may not be printed and publicly sold, except in cities and places where the public exercise of the said religion is permitted.

We ordain that there shall be no difference or distinction made in respect to the said religion, in receiving pupils to be instructed in universities, colleges, and schools; or in receiving the sick and poor into hospitals, retreats and public charities.

Those of the said religion called Reformed shall be obliged to respect the laws of the Catholic Apostolic and Roman Church, recognized in this our kingdom, for the consummation of marriages contracted, or to be contracted, as regards to the degrees of consanguinity and kinship.

Appendix C

Revocation of the Edict of Nantes[44]

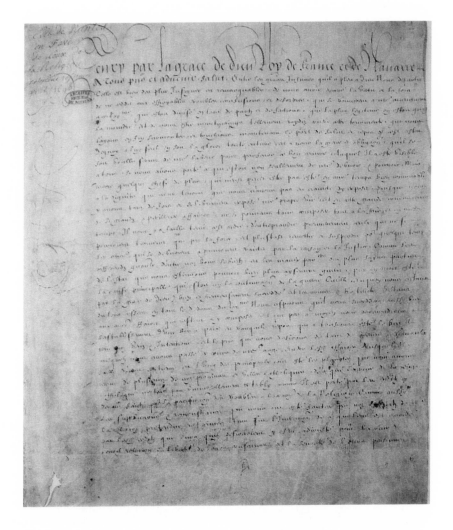

Image of the Edict of Nantes[45]

Louis, by the grace of God king of France and Navarre, to all present and to come, Greeting:

King Henri the Great, our grandfather of glorious memory, being desirous that the peace which he had procured for his subjects after the grievous losses they had sustained in the course of domestic and foreign wars, should not be troubled on account of the Reformed Protestant Religion (R.P.R.), as had happened in the reigns of the kings, his predecessors, by his edict, granted at Nantes in the month of April 1598 regulated the procedure to be adopted with regard to those of the said religion, and the places in which they might meet for public worship, established extraordinary judges to administer justice to them, and, in fine, provided in particular articles for whatever could be thought necessary for maintaining the tranquillity of his kingdom and for diminishing mutual aversion between the members of the two religions, so as to put himself in a better position to labor, as he had resolved to do, for the reunion to the Church of those who had so lightly withdrawn from it.

As the intention of the king, our grandfather, was frustrated by his sudden death, and as the execution of the said edict was interrupted during the minority of the late king, our most honored lord and father of glorious memory, by new encroachments on the part of the adherents of the said R.P.R., which gave occasion for their being deprived of divers advantages accorded to them by the said edict; nevertheless the king, our late lord and father, in the exercise of his usual clemency, granted them yet another edict at Nimes, in July 1629 by means of which, tranquillity being established anew, the said late king, animated by the same spirit and the same zeal for religion as the king, our said grandfather, had resolved to take advantage of this repose to attempt to put his said pious design into execution. But foreign wars having supervened soon after, so that the kingdom was seldom tranquil from 1635 to the truce concluded in 1684 with the powers of Europe, nothing more could be done for the advantage of religion beyond diminishing the number of places for the public exercise of the R.P.R., interdicting such places as were found established to the prejudice of the dispositions made by the edicts, and suppressing of the bi-partisan courts, these having been appointed provisionally only.

God having at last permitted that our people should enjoy perfect peace, we, no longer absorbed in protecting them from our enemies, are able to profit by this truce (which we have ourselves facilitated), and devote our whole attention to the means of accomplishing the designs of our said grandfather and father, which we have consistently kept before us since our succession to the crown.

And now we perceive, with thankful acknowledgment of God's aid, that our endeavors have attained their proposed end, inasmuch as the better and the greater part of our subjects of the said R.P.R. have embraced the Catholic faith. And since by this fact the execution of the Edict of Nantes and of all that has ever been ordained in favor of the said R.P.R. has been rendered nugatory, we have determined that we can do nothing better, in order wholly to obliterate the memory of the troubles, the confusion, and the evils which the progress of this false religion has caused in this kingdom, and which furnished occasion for the said edict and for so many previous and subsequent edicts and declarations, than entirely to revoke the said Edict of Nantes, with the special articles granted as a sequel to it, as well as all that has since been done in favor of the said religion.

Be it known that for these causes and others us hereunto moving, and of our certain knowledge, full power, and royal authority, we have, by this present perpetual and irrevocable edict, suppressed and revoked, and do suppress and revoke, the edict of our said grandfather, given at Nantes in April, 1598, in its whole extent, together with the particular articles agreed upon in the month of May following, and the letters patent issued upon the same date; and also the edict given at Nimes in July, 1629; we declare them null and void, together with all concessions, of whatever nature they may be, made by them as well as by other edicts, declarations, and orders, in favor of the said persons of the R.P.R., the which shall remain in like manner as if they had never been granted; and in consequence we desire, and it is our pleasure, that all the temples of those of the said R.P.R. situate in our kingdom, countries, territories, and the lordships under our crown, shall be demolished without delay.

We forbid our subjects of the R.P.R. to meet any more for the exercise of the said religion in any place or private house, under any pretext whatever . . .

We likewise forbid all noblemen, of what condition soever, to hold such religious exercises in their houses or fiefs, under penalty to be inflicted upon all our said subjects who shall engage in the said exercises, of imprisonment and confiscation.

We enjoin all ministers of the said R.P.R., who do not choose to become converts and to embrace the Catholic, apostolic, and Roman religion, to leave our kingdom and the territories subject to us within a fortnight of the publication of our present edict, without leave to reside therein beyond that period, or, during the said fortnight, to engage in any preaching, exhortation, or any other function, on pain of being sent to the galleys . . .

We forbid private schools for the instruction of children of the said R.P.R., and in general all things whatever which can be regarded as a concession of any kind in favor of the said religion.

As for children who may be born of persons of the said R.P.R., we desire that from henceforth they be baptized by the parish priests. We enjoin parents to send them to the churches for that purpose, under penalty of five hundred livres fine, to be increased as circumstances may demand; and thereafter the children shall be brought up in the Catholic, apostolic, and Roman religion, which we expressly enjoin the local magistrates to see done.

And in the exercise of our clemency towards our subjects of the said R.P.R. who have emigrated from our kingdom, lands, and territories subject to us, previous to the publication of our present edict, it is our will and pleasure that in case of their returning within the period of four months from the day of the said publication, they may, and it shall be lawful for them to, again take possession of their property, and to enjoy the same as if they had all along remained there: on the contrary, the property abandoned by those who, during the specified period of four months, shall not have returned into our kingdom, lands, and territories subject to us, shall remain and be confiscated in consequence of our declaration of the 20th of August last.

We repeat our most express prohibition to all our subjects of the said R.P.R., together with their wives and children, against leaving our kingdom, lands, and territories subject to us, or transporting their goods and effects therefrom under penalty, as respects the men, of being sent to the galleys, and as respects the women, of imprisonment and confiscation.

It is our will and intention that the declarations rendered against the relapsed shall be executed according to their form and tenor.

As for the rest, liberty is granted to the said persons of the R.P.R., pending the time when it shall please God to enlighten them as well as others, to remain in the cities and places of our kingdom, lands, and territories subject to us, and there to continue their commerce, and to enjoy their possessions, without being subjected to molestation or hindrance on account of the said R.P.R., on condition of not engaging in the exercise of the said religion, or of meeting under pretext of prayers or religious services, of whatever nature these may be, under the penalties above mentioned of imprisonment and confiscation. This do we give in charge to our trusty and well-beloved counselors, etc.

Given at Fontainebleau in the month of October, in the year of grace 1685, and of our reign the forty-third.

Notes

1a. Carlton J. H. Hayes, *Modern Europe to 1870* (New York, NY: MacMillan Company, 1958), 147.

1b. Hayes, 147.

2a. Hayes, 139.

2b. Hayes, 140.

3. Hayes, 147.

4. Hayes, 94.

5. Hayes, 148.

6. Hayes, 149.

7. Hayes, 178–80.

8. Hayes, 254–58.

9. Memorial plaque, French Huguenot Church, Charleston, SC.

10. Genealogy research conducted by author.

11. Hayes, 11.

12. Hayes, 11–12.

13. "Hagia Sophia," *Encyclopedia Britannica*, accessed December 8, 2017, https://www.britannica.com/topic/Hagia-Sophia.

14. Hayes, 777.

15. Hayes, 140–41.

16. Hayes, 140.

17. Hayes, 147–53.

18. Judith Chandler Pugh Meyer, *Reformation in La Rochelle: Tradition and Change in Early Modern Europe, 1500–1568* (Geneva, Switzerland: Librairie Droz, 1996), 19.

19. "Reformation," *Encyclopedia Britannica*, accessed December 8, 2017, https://www.britannica.com/event/Reformation.

20. Hayes, 178–222.

21. Hayes, 178, 222.

22. Hayes, 178, 222.

23. Hayes, 247.

24. "Treaty of Montpellier," Wikimedia Foundation, last modified April 9, 2017, 18:38, https://en.wikipedia.org/wiki/Treaty_of_Montpellier.

25. "Treaty of Montpellier," Wikimedia Foundation, last modified April 9, 2017, 18:38, https://en.wikipedia.org/wiki/Treaty_of_Montpellier.

26. Hayes, 269.

27a. "Farthingale," *Encyclopedia Britannica*, accessed December 8, 2017, https://www.britannica.com/topic/farthingale.

27b. "Half-Scale Patterns of Representative Period Silhouettes," Seeing Silhouettes, February 12. 2011, http://seeingsilhouettes.umwblogs.org/representative-period-silhouettes/.

28. "Order of a Catholic Wedding Mass," Catholic Wedding Help, accessed December 8, 2017, http://catholicweddinghelp.com/topics/order-wedding-with-mass.htm.

29. "Consummation," Wikimedia Foundation, last modified November 28, 2017, 19:40, https://en.wikipedia.org/wiki/Consummation.

30. "Pierre de Ronsard," *Encyclopedia Britannica*, accessed December 8, 2017, https://www.britannica.com/biography/Pierre-de-Ronsard.

31. French Protestant Church of Charleston, *The Liturgy, or Forms of Divine Service, of the French Protestant Church* (New York, NY: Anson D. F. Randolph & Company, 1853).

32. Hayes, 220, 223.

33. Hayes, 223.

34. Hayes, 223.

35. Hayes, 223.

36. Hayes, 223.

37. Hayes, 223.

38. Hayes, 243–45.

39. Hayes, 246–52.

40. Hayes, 255–70.

41. Hayes, 269.

42. Hayes, 225–42.

43. Jean Dumont, "Extracts from the Edict of Nantes," in *Readings in European History,* edited by James Harvey Robinson, Vol. 2, 183-85 (Boston, MA: Ginn & Company, 1906).

44. François-André Isambert, "Revocation of the Edict of Nantes," in *Readings in European History,* edited by James Harvey Robinson, Vol. 2, 287–91 (Boston, MA: Ginn & Company, 1906).

45. The Edict of Nantes was originally written by King Henry IV. It is reprinted from Grands Documents de l'Histoire de France, Archives Nationales, hosted by Wikimedia Commons as of June 11, 2018. This work is in the public domain.

Bibliography

Agnew, David C. A. *Protestant Exiles from France in the Reign of Louis XIV.* London, UK: Reeves & Turner, 1874.

Clark, Jack Alden. *Huguenot Warrior: The Life and Times of Henri de Rohan, 1579–1638.* New York, NY: Springer Publishing Company, 1967.

Erlanger, Philippe. *The King's Minion: Richelieu, Louis XIII, and the Affair of Cinq-Mars.* New York, NY: Prentice Hall, 1972.

Fedden, Katherine. *Manor Life in Old France: From the Journal of Sire De Gouberville for the Years 1549–1562.* New York, NY: AMS Press, 1967.

French Protestant Church of Charleston. *The Liturgy, or Forms of Divine Service, of the French Protestant Church of Charleston, SC.* New York, NY: Anson D. F. Randolph & Company, 1853.

Gray, Janet Glenn. *The French Huguenots: Anatomy of Courage.* Grand Rapids, MI: Baker Book House, 1981.

Hayes, Carlton J. H. *Modern Europe to 1870.* New York, NY: MacMillan Company, 1958.

Hirsch, Arthur H. *The Huguenots of Colonial South Carolina.* Columbia, SC: University of South Carolina Press, 1999.

Holt, Mack P. *The French Wars of Religion, 1562–1629.* Cambridge, UK: Cambridge University Press, 2005.

Kirkpatrick, Katherine. *Escape Across the Wide Sea.* New York, NY: Holiday House, 2004.

Taylor, Richard. *How to Read a Church: A Guide to Symbols and Images in Churches and Cathedrals.* Mahwah, NJ: Hidden Spring Press, 2003.

Frank Harrelson

Uncommon Travel Germany. "A Martin Luther
Biography." Accessed December 8, 2017.
https://www.uncommon-travel-
germany.com/martin-luther-biography.html.
Van Ruymbeke, Bertrand. *From New Babylon to Eden: The
Huguenots and Their Migration to Colonial South
Carolina.* Columbia, SC: University of South
Carolina Press, 2006.
Van Ruymbeke, Bertrand and Randy J. Sparks. *Memory and
Identity: The Huguenots in France and the Atlantic
Diaspora.* Columbia, SC: University of South
Carolina Press, 2003.

About the Author

Frank Harrelson is a descendant of Jean Horry (a distant great-grandfather[10th] and his wife, Madame du Frene) and Daniel Horry[9th] (son of Jean Horry and Madame du Frene). Daniel arrived in Charles Towne in the English colony of Carolina in 1692 on the privateer ship *Loyall Jamaica*. Soon after arriving in Charles Towne he married Elisabeth Fanton Garnier, a French woman of nobility from Île de Ré who had arrived with her parents on a different ship. It is unknown if they knew each other before their arrival in America. They had three daughters.

The oldest daughter was Elisabeth Marye Horry. Her first husband was Edward Lewis, who died soon after their marriage. Her second marriage was to Joseph Prince. Both Lewis and Prince were ship captains. The author is a descendant of the marriage of Elisabeth Marye Horry to Joseph Prince.

Mr. Harrelson is a member of the Huguenot Society of South Carolina, the First Families of South Carolina, the Sons of the American Revolution, and is an associate member of the French Church in Charleston. He is also a member of the Sons of the Revolution through his Prince genealogy line.

He graduated from Auburn University with a degree in mathematics, served as a commissioned officer in the US Navy, and subsequently received a master's degree from Clemson University in analytical management science.

He has been married for over fifty years to Sandra Smith of Arlington, Virginia. She is a graduate of the Randolph-Macon Woman's College with a BA in history, and received a master of arts degree from Emory University. They have three daughters. Frank and Sandra presently live in Auburn, Alabama, where they share a home with their middle daughter.